Rave Revie
Austii

Blood and Bone - "... is an action-packed, sensitively written thriller. Hannibal Jones is a hero whom anyone would want on their side. Mr. Camacho creates so many twists and turns that the reader can only hang on until the exciting crescendo. The action spans continents; the characters are chameleons; and the plot is a real corkscrew. A great read from a talented story craftsman!!"

Midwest Book Review

Collateral Damage - "... Austin Camacho brings back his harder-than-hard troubleshooter, Hannibal Jones, in a teeth-rattling tale of murder and treachery. It's conventional wisdom that the second novel by young writers rarely lives up to the promise of their first book. Camacho turns this old adage upside down with a powerhouse writing performance."

Warren Murphy, Two-time Edgar Award winner and creator of The Destroyer adventure series

The Troubleshooter - "... Like the others in this series, this very enjoyable novel features tight writing, plenty of action, and intriguing characters. Hannibal is fast becoming an old friend that this reader regularly looks forward to every time a new novel is released. This author and his three mystery novels to date are well worth the read and worthy of a place on your bookshelf."

Kevin Tipple, Reviewer: Readers Room

The Payback Assignment - "... is violent and thrilling ... The novel is fast-paced with a significant amount of action, and the characters are well- developed. The author wraps up the tale with a minimum of fuss and leaves the possibility for future adventures for both Morgan and Felicity. Fans of action-oriented suspense will enjoy The Payback Assignment."

Angela Etheridge, Reviewer: The Romance Connection

DAMAGED GOODS

BY

AUSTIN S. CAMACHO

Copyright © 2005 by Austin S. Camacho

Cover design by Cathi A. Wong

Published by:

Intrigue Publishing

Intrigue Publishing
7707 Shadowcreek Terrace
Springfield, VA 22153 USA

Printed in the United States of America
Published December 2005

DAMAGED GOODS

Too hot for spring,
But summer's yet to peak.
By counting, it's half over.
But sixty-one days later,
the heat smells like
Eternity.

by Cybele Pomeroy

-1-

FRIDAY

"Do you believe in fate?" Tonya shouted over the thumping dance music. Anita nodded, staring through closely packed dancers at the man in the black suit and Oakley sunglasses. He seemed isolated in the crowd, not talking to anyone, but somehow aware of everyone. Sometimes, Anita did believe in fate. And something about this man told her he could be a big part of her future.

"Not that one." Tonya shook her friend's shoulder and pointed. "Over here, my sister. That's for me." Anita recognized the focus of Tonya's attention. After all, who wouldn't recognize Hugo "Huge" Wilson? He was one of the most successful hip-hop producers around. He kept studios down in Virginia Beach, but Anita knew why he came up to Washington to party. There was still a lot of musical talent left untapped here, and Huge was a star maker, the person who could turn a man with good rhymes or a woman with a decent voice into the next Jay-Z or Toni Braxton.

The Zei was three-levels of flash and pumping energy powered by two disc jockeys, quick cut videos and a light show in constant frantic movement. It was also the somehow sweet scent of frantic dancers sweating out expensive colognes. And overwhelming everything was the music, so thick it actually filled the space and made Anita's throat

1

vibrate when she sipped her cognac. What Tonya called electric was for Anita sensory overload. From the edge of the fifteen hundred square foot dance floor Anita could look up at the two higher levels. The third level of Zei, which Tonya called The Prive, was a private area of the club reserved for members and their guests. Huge was making his way toward The Prive, not hurrying, distributing high fives and soul handshakes along the way.

Despite the whirlpool of activity surrounding Huge as he moved through the crowd, Anita's eyes were drawn back to the man who first arrested her attention. Although the music shifted from house to hip hop to R & B dance and the bass was so insistent that it forced her heart to fall into its rhythm, this man remained a point of calm in the midst of the sensual storm. His was the only head not bobbing, as if he was immune to the siren call of the music. He looked very alert, and he seemed to keep track of Huge's movements without ever looking at him. He was looking for something else.

Unlike Huge, this man made no fashion statement at all. He wore a plain black suit and shoes. He was black, but even lighter than Huge. Here were two men of average height and weight, but one commanded the attention of the entire room, while the other was almost invisible. Despite that, or maybe because of it, the seated man held her attention. She felt that she and the stranger were alike in being out of phase with the world around them.

Anita was there mostly because she had become tired of fighting it. Tonya was a good friend who was determined to save Anita from herself. She had to admit that since Rod left her social life had withered and died for lack of interest. She had come out solely to appease her friend, but now she wondered if this was where she was meant to be tonight.

The stranger stood from his low chair with cat-like grace. Until then, Anita hadn't noticed that black gloves covered his hands. He tightened them as he slid through the crowd toward Huge Wilson. Only then did she become aware of two others moving toward Huge. Wilson's smile never wavered, but his path began to bend.

"Oh my God," Tonya said, leaping to her feet and smoothing her little black dress. "He's heading our way. I told you he was here for me, girl."

Anita kept her seat, uncomfortable as the room's spotlight shifted toward them. It did look as if Huge would walk right into Tonya who was literally panting in anticipation of the moment. The two brothers following him were both very big, like the men you see power lifting in the Olympics, and they glittered. One had a mouthful of gold that flashed when his lips parted, echoing the blonde frosting across the top of his black hair, and his suit jacket shoulders were dusted with glitter. The other man, in a wife beater and jeans, was completely bald. His head glistened in the house's flashing lights. They looked to her like trouble headed her way.

As Huge approached, the music seemed to swell in Anita's head. A follow spot was tracing his movement, light glinting off his gold Rolex and the oversized platinum cross hanging from his neck. As his smile turned toward Tonya, the light moved to envelop her as well. Anita shifted to her side, sliding into Huge's shadow. Inches from her face, his arm rose slowly through that darkness toward the light. He was from another world, a world she didn't know. As his hand moved Tonya's face, it seemed that world would touch hers.

Tonya's eyes sparkled and her tongue touched her upper lip. She looked as if she might pass out at the coming touch. But Huge's hand stopped a whisper away from Tonya's cheek. Another hand had fallen on Huge's shoulder. The big man with the mouthful of gold pulled hard, spinning Huge around.

"Yo, nigga," the big man shouted. "You won't answer my calls, but you'll come up in here and dis me in my own town?"

Huge held empty palms forward and maintained his smile. "No disrespect meant, Frost. We're both busy producers, yo."

"Yeah," Frost said, pushing his face almost into Huge's. "I'm busy busting new talent on the scene, and you're busy stealing it from me."

3

Anita was nearly within reach of the men, close enough to smell their dueling colognes. She noticed Frost's name was cut into his hair on the side facing her. And she saw Huge's eyes flash upward for a second. More than Frost, Huge was aware that he was still in the spotlight.

"Come on, brother, you know it ain't like that. If you'd have signed Big Walter to a decent contract he'd still be with you."

Frost bared his gold teeth the way Anita had seen caged dogs snarl. "I'll show you how we make a contract stick around here." His right hand, on the side away from the spotlight, darted into his pocket. The knife was still opening as his hand came out again. Frost's arm swung out to his right. The four-inch blade swept within inches of Anita's face on its way toward Huge. She didn't even have time scream.

Then the knife froze in space, right in front of her nose. The blade vibrated a little but a black-gloved hand holding Frost's wrist prevented any forward movement.

"That's not the way you want to get into the headlines." The man in black spoke with a relaxed calm that seemed inappropriate to the situation. Then he twisted his arm and somehow Frost ended up on his back. The man in black said, "Excuse me," as he stepped in front of Anita. Then he twisted Frost's wrist and caught the knife in his other hand.

"Who the hell?" Frost asked.

"Hannibal Jones," the man in black said, closing the knife and dropping it into his pocket. "Mr. Wilson had the impression you might be bitter about some recent business. He asked me to help him avoid any trouble." His voice was soft and low, yet somehow Anita could hear him clearly above the noise of the crowded club.

A small circle had opened up around Frost, who stood slowly and brushed himself off. "You're his backup? Please. Hey Hard Dog. Come take care of this."

Frost's bald partner swaggered into the lighted circle. The music continued to thump and the lights continued to flash, but the circle of unoccupied floor expanded a bit more. Hannibal stepped around the edge, maintaining eye contact with the bigger man but holding his fists low. Anita was struck by how round Hard Dog's shoulders were, like two brass knobs mounted on either side of his neck.

"Not the time or place," Hannibal said. "Can't we talk about this?"

In response, Hard Dog swung a right cross toward Hannibal's face. It missed, as did two more fast punches.

"Okay then," Hannibal said. "Let's dance."

Hannibal was bouncing on his toes now, like a prizefighter. His head never held still. Hard Dog punched the air near Hannibal's head three more times while Hannibal circled him, always somehow just out of reach. Then the light was in Anita's eyes and she realized it would be in Hard Dog's face as well.

Because she had to squint, Anita almost missed what happened next. Hannibal's arms were pumping. Hard Dog's head snapped back several times. Hannibal looked almost bored during this display. Anita glanced around and noticed that he was the center of attention now, and that the crowd noise had hushed to a murmur, leaving only the music pushing the action.

Hannibal paused, as if to see what effect his punches were having.

"Enough?"

Anita wasn't sure Hard Dog even knew where he was by then, but he still tried one more time, with a loping right that Hannibal easily sidestepped.

"Guess not," Hannibal said. Then, in what seemed a very businesslike manner, he snapped three side kicks up into Hard Dog's midsection. A final thumping right from Hannibal ended it. Hard Dog was unconscious long before his body collapsed onto the tiles.

After one more brief beat of silence the white noise of human conversation resumed, and Anita felt as if she was waking from a trance. Husky men were gathered around Huge engaged in heated conversation. Club bouncers, she presumed. Tonya had dropped into a chair, still staring wistfully at Huge. And Frost, no longer the center of attention, had also found a nearby chair. His attention was focused on Hannibal.

"This don't end here," Frost said through clenched teeth.

"You want me," Hannibal responded, "You bring your chrome grill on over any time. I'm easy to find." He drew a business card from an inside jacket pocket and flipped it in Frost's general direction. The card fluttered through the air to land on Hard Dog's chest.

Huge wrapped an arm around Hannibal's shoulders. "Hey, you all right, dog," Huge said in a high but clear voice. "Putting you on the payroll was a smart move for sure."

"You said you had some trouble coming from that dude," Hannibal said. "As I told you, trouble is my business. But I think yours is over for now." Hannibal smiled, but it seemed clear to Anita that he was uncomfortable with Huge's casual contact. His smile was convincing, but forced. This was not his reaction to a friend, she thought, but to a client. He was helping Huge with a problem for pay.

"Brother, anything you ever need, you just call on Huge. You know what I'm saying? And I'll have to send you a stack of our latest CD's," Huge said, disengaging and moving back into the party.

"Don't sweat it," Hannibal said. He lowered his voice to add, "I don't listen to that crap."

Then the two men, the star and the man who defended him, wandered off in opposite directions. The music continued, and the open space on the dance floor completely closed except that people carefully avoided tripping over the muscular form spread-eagled on the gleaming tiles.

Anita still felt disconnected, out of phase with her surroundings. As she drifted slowly through the crowd toward Hard Dog she was remembering Tonya's words.

"Do you believe in fate?"

She was jostled hard just as she reached her destination and almost fell over him. There Hard Dog lay, like a man who had simply fallen asleep in the midst of the chaos. His deep chest rose and fell and her eyes followed the small card floating up and down with it. Simple block lettering on it said, "Hannibal Jones" and under that, "Troubleshooter." There was an address and a phone number, and nothing else. If Frost had taken the business card she would have known she was wrong. The fact that he chose to leave it behind told her that perhaps fate had put her in this place at this time for a reason.

Ignored by those around her, she knelt to pick up the card.

-2-

WEDNESDAY

Hannibal hated the numbers. Investigative work was merely drudgery. The physical stuff, the fighting that came with bodyguard duty, that was kind of exciting. Helping people find answers to difficult problems, that part of his job was almost fun. But bookkeeping, record keeping, bill paying and the dreaded taxes made him cringe. Still, it had to be done and this was the morning for him to do it.

The computer in his office told Hannibal that he had finally reached the place he wanted to be. He pushed a button, and electronically transferred a chunk of his most recent fee into his short-term savings account. He was liking the number in that account. It was just a handful of dollars from his target.

Across the room, at the visitor's small table, Sarge sipped his coffee and asked, "So this Huge Wilson fellow, he treat you right?"

"Yeah. As a matter of fact he kicked in a nice bonus. He knew that other producer, Frost, was looking for a confrontation. He's also smart enough to know that that sort of thing is bad for business."

"Yeah, I was wondering about that," Sarge said. "These boys all think they're gangsters. I know that guy travels with his own posse most of the time. They couldn't handle this Frost?"

Hannibal took a big swallow of his own coffee, setting his cup in a shaft of morning sunlight beaming in his front windows. "Sure, if he wanted a mini-gang war on his hands. By ditching them, he tempted Frost into making a move. He knew I could handle the physical stuff, and sort of distance it from him and his crew. But man, I was following that guy for weeks, and he does party hearty."

Sarge was a stocky black man whose hair had receded halfway back on his head, but whose easygoing manner belied his age. He was also a cornerstone of Hannibal's life. Aside from being Hannibal's upstairs neighbor in the building that housed his apartment and his office, Sarge was also the man Hannibal regarded as his best friend. That put him in the position to ask questions no one else could get away with.

"So, at six hundred dollars a day that was a pretty nice payoff. You got enough yet to pop the question?"

Hannibal pushed back from the desk, glaring at Sarge, but grinning as well. "Like it's any of your business, but, yeah, I'm pretty close to where I want to be."

"Like it matters to her," Sarge shook his head, dismissing the idea.

"Maybe not," Hannibal said, "but it matters to me. A brother better have good and plenty of his own before he proposes to a successful lawyer, man. I don't want anybody to think she's going to be supporting me. But yeah, I think I'm about ready to slip this on her hand."

From his desk drawer Hannibal pulled a small gray jewelry box. He flipped it open to reveal a full carat of his future dreams. In shopping for this one piece, Hannibal had learned more about jewelry than he had ever wanted to know. He smiled softly at the clear, colorless ideal-cut diamond, sparkling brightly in its six-prong platinum setting. His mind only touched momentarily on the cost, focused more on what this tiny token represented to him, all the good and potential risk of a lifelong commitment.

"Well, it's about time, I say."

"Yeah? I notice there's no ring on your finger, chump," Hannibal said.

"True that," Sarge said, nodding and staring out the window. "Brother, you just don't know how lucky you are to have a lady like that."

The silence that followed was a bit awkward, but it didn't last long before another of Hannibal's upstairs neighbors pushed through the door. Reynaldo Santiago was short and bulky, and his hair was gathered on the sides and back of his head. After his wife passed away he didn't bring much from his native Cuba except his daughter, his slight accent, and his love for cigars, one of which was already clenched between his teeth.

"Just thought I'd check in before work, fellows. So, what's going on?"

"Just trying to plan out a rosy romantic future for young blood here," Sarge said. "He's still dragging his feet, though."

Ray planted his palms on Hannibal's desk, leaning in close. "What is your problem, Paco? When you going to make an honest woman out of my little girl? She's not going to be there forever, you know. She sees those three-piece-suiters every day at the office, and I sure as hell don't want to end up with one of them for a son-in-law."

Hannibal chuckled and leaned back to avoid the smoke. "Hey, no fair ganging up on me, you two. And Ray, you know you've got to do things just the right way when you're dealing with your daughter. A fellow steps to that woman, you know he got to come correct. As a matter of fact, I was just then trying to think up the right romantic setting to propose to Cindy when you walked in. What do you think about..."?

A tap at the door stopped Hannibal mid-sentence. Then the door swung open and a young black man walked confidently into the room to stop in front of Hannibal's desk. He stood right beside Ray, but seemed not to notice him or Sarge at all.

"You, I presume are Mr. Hannibal Jones?"

The newcomer's precise pronunciation was not the only reason he arrested Hannibal's attention. His hair was cut military-short. He was medium height and build, but his ramrod posture made him look taller. His bearing seemed at odds with his black pants and vest, and the white shirt with French cuffs.

"I am," Hannibal said after a moment. "How can I help you, Mister...?"

"Call me Henry, sir," the newcomer said. "I'm here for Mr. Benjamin Blair. He would like for you to come out to his home this morning to discuss an assignment. He believes you can be of help to him regarding a situation with which he is dealing."

"This morning?" Hannibal asked. "Must be important. Are you Blair's personal assistant?"

"I am his butler, sir."

Sarge barely stifled a chuckle. "Butler. Now there's an occupation you don't hear much about these days."

"Really?" Ray said with a small smile. "I'm a chauffeur, but I don't know any butlers myself. You lay out his clothes and stuff?"

"That would be a valet," Henry replied without humor. His eyes never wavered from Hannibal. "I am in charge of Mr. Blair's household. Mr. Blair is prepared to pay your normal daily fee for a consultation with you this morning. Will ten o'clock be convenient for you?"

Hannibal couldn't tell if Ray was more amused by this arrogant dude or insulted by his attitude. He turned to Hannibal and said, "I got a limousine service to run, Paco. I'll leave you with Jeeves here."

As Ray headed for the door, Hannibal shuffled things on his desk. He knew his schedule was blank for the next week, but he opened his daybook and flipped the page before responding. "Actually, I'd just as soon get out there and meet him right now. Give me the address."

"No need, sir. If we are to leave now, you can simply follow me."

Sarge leaned back in his chair, still fighting an inner laugh. "Another job for the world famous troubleshooter? I thought you were taking a few days off."

"That was the plan," Hannibal said, standing and pulling on his suit coat. "But when a guy like Benjamin Blair has trouble, it's usually serious."

"Ben Blair? Should I know that name?"

"Probably not," Hannibal said. "He's one of the guys who started an Internet company during the boom, but made it stick. Tactical Datamation I think is the name of the outfit."

"If I may sir," Henry said, acknowledging Sarge for the first time. "Unless the stock market has shifted radically in the last twenty-four hours, Mr. Blair is one of the three wealthiest men in the Washington D.C. area."

* * * * *

When Hannibal stepped out the front door of the row house he called home in Southeast Washington D.C. he was dressed for business. For him that meant a black suit and tie, thin black gloves and Oakley wraparound sunglasses. His woman called him a throwback, an anachronism, and on less charitable days, desperately out of style. But his style was his own and he saw no reason to change.

He glanced back over his shoulder at the brick building that held his apartment and his office. When he first saw this place it was a crack house occupied by winos, drug addicts and prostitutes. He enlisted the aid of a small band of homeless men to clean it out and, in the process, found a place in a neighborhood that turned out to be a home worth fighting for. Four of those previously homeless men moved into the other apartments, including Ray Santiago and his good friend Sarge.

Henry climbed into a small Honda and Hannibal prepared to follow. His white Volvo 850 GLT glinted in the sunlight. He had her detailed the day before and was quite pleased with the result. Once belted into her white leather seat he fired the engine up and sat for just a second to listen to her growl and then purr as the engine settled into a smooth idle. Lately he'd been thinking about trading her in, but The White Tornado was perhaps his second best friend. He never called her that in front of anybody, of course. The name just came to him one day when he was pushing down I-95 at close to one hundred miles an hour, blowing every other vehicle on the road out of his way. He loved the car, and it was hard for him to consider letting her adopt another driver.

Hannibal eased through the narrow streets of his neighborhood, keeping Henry's car in sight but still stopping for kids dribbling basketballs or riding skateboards and rollerblades in the Summer streets. People here made do with whatever entertainment did not require money. He'd work his way over to I-66 toward Dulles Airport and within twenty minutes he knew he'd be in a very different neighborhood, where it was all about spending money. With the air conditioner blowing and the smooth jazz of 105.9 FM on the radio, he punched a speed dial button on his car phone. It was time to set the stage.

"Santiago," she said. To Hannibal, her voice was a melody that fit right in with Pat Metheny's tune on the radio.

"Good morning, Cindy. You're in the office way too soon. But then, I'm already on my way to a meeting for a new case. How's it starting out?"

"Hey, baby!" He could hear Cindy drop a stack of books on her desk. "How sweet of you to call so early. Yes I'm in the groove here already today. Got an important meeting myself in a few minutes. I've been given my first Internet business work. One of our clients is opening a new business offering, and I've been handling it. My first one from beginning to end, and all the leading indicators say it's going to be big."

"Not sure what that means, but I guess congratulations," Hannibal said, smiling as if she could see him. "You can explain it all to me tonight at dinner. You're not working late tonight on this important new deal, are you? We are meeting for dinner, right?"

"Oh, thank God you reminded me," Cindy said. "Of course we are. And it's wonderful to have you on a Tuesday night. I don't often get you away from your weekly volunteer work at the homeless shelter. But it's probably best for me to meet you, rather than you coming to pick me up. I might be at the office just a little bit late. Where are we going?"

"I was thinking something really nice tonight. What do you say to dinner on Nina's Dandy?"

He could tell by the sound that she was holding the phone to her ear with her shoulder, but despite the shuffling papers in the background, he knew that question got her full attention. "Hannibal, that sounds fantastic. I'd love it, but on one condition."

"And that is?"

"That you don't wear black for once. Okay?"

* * * * *

Henry pulled up to the curb and Hannibal parked his Volvo next to the Lexus in Ben Blair's driveway. The intensity of the late May sunshine gave the world a sharpness and brightness that seemed beyond reality, even through Hannibal's Oakley's. He paused on the blacktop for a moment to acclimate himself to his present environment. After all, there are town houses and there are town houses. This one was wider than most, and had a two car garage, but was still only three stories tall. Not the grandest he'd seen, but certainly comfortable. It was an end unit on an immaculate, well-manicured cul-de-sac that was designed to imitate a friendly suburban neighborhood, and largely succeeding. Flowers surrounded several of the mailboxes, and basketball hoops stood guard over many of the driveways, including this one. Then Henry called down the stairs from the front door.

"Mr. Jones. Please come in. I'll ask you to have a seat, and Mr. Blair will be with you in a moment."

A three-story townhouse with a formal butler. This spoke volumes to Hannibal.

Inside, everything he saw fit his initial judgment. Too many paintings covered the walls. Globes, sculptures and expensive toys were everywhere. The decor was chrome and wood with functional furniture. This was new money still learning how to behave at this level.

The butler deposited Hannibal in the large eat-in kitchen, handed him a cup of coffee, and disappeared. Hannibal had perhaps two minutes to enjoy the soft jazz piping through the room from some invisible source before a New England spiced voice called his name.

"Hannibal Jones. The troubleshooter. You got to love the way that sounds."

Hannibal stood to shake hands. "Well, not quite as nice as Ben Blair, boy billionaire."

Blair responded with an easy grin. That and the hair apparently plopped onto his head like a pile of straw did give him a boyish look. In fact, he was still on the good side of forty, which made him fairly young for a business success. In Dockers and a golf shirt, he seemed unusually comfortable in his own skin. At the same time he was a bundle of nervous energy, one of those people who have trouble sitting still for long. His trim physique implied that he burned off a good deal of that energy playing sports. He headed for the refrigerator while he spoke to Hannibal.

"I'm really glad you were able to get over here to see me, Mr. Jones. I'm faced with a puzzle that I don't have time to solve, you know? Although I do like puzzles. Consider this: some months have 30 days and some have 31. How many months have 28 days?"

Hannibal smiled. "Well, if you want to be technical about it, all of them."

Blair nodded toward Hannibal as if some suspicion had been confirmed. "Anyway, a friend of mine has been taken advantage of and I want to get the situation fixed. Juice?"

"Um, sure," Hannibal said. Blair placed two tall glasses of orange juice on the table and settled into a chair facing Hannibal. He dropped a cell phone on the table also, next to one that was already there. Hannibal wondered if they were designated business and pleasure, or maybe friend and foe.

"Here's the deal," Blair said, leaning in toward Hannibal. "A friend of mine was robbed of something very valuable to them by someone they trusted. This item could make a world of difference to my friend's life, you know? I need to find the thief and get the item returned. Do you like puzzles, Mr. Jones?"

"You called me about someone else's problem?"

"Well, I can afford your fee, Mr. Jones," Blair said. "My friend can't, you know?

But they saw you in the Zei Club last weekend and told me you were the man who could help them."

"I see. Is she particularly close to you?"

Blair had to be a canny businessman, but Hannibal figured he must be an awful poker player. "Did I say she?"

"No," Hannibal said. "You said they. If it was a man you'd have said 'he' easily enough. I just want to know how personal this is for you."

The lady involved is my cleaning lady, if you must know. No romantic connection or anything like that. But I like and respect her very much, and I want her to have what's hers, you know? And it is a puzzle."

"Is the missing item of great value financially?"

"I'm not really sure," Blair said, standing. "I know it was a gift from her father, and I know he wasn't wealthy. Besides, I don't want you to think this is a money thing to me. Piece of fruit?" Blair was poking in the refrigerator again. It was as orderly as a supermarket cooler. Hannibal noticed that the kitchen held no smell at all, not even of breakfast, and thought the cleaning woman must be quite special indeed.

"I know you're not all about the money," he said to Blair's back. "That Lexus in your driveway has to be six years old."

"You're pretty observant," Blair said, tossing an orange to Hannibal. "You must like puzzles too. I think you're the right guy for this treasure hunt."

"And just what is the treasure?" Hannibal asked, accepting the paper towel Blair offered him.

Blair regained his seat and set to peeling his orange over his own paper towel. "Don't really know. Ms. Cooper told me her father left her a treasure map to what he promised would be a pot of gold. I'm pretty sure he wasn't being literal, but what ever it is, the thief probably has it now. Find the thief, you find the treasure."

Blair was popping orange sections into his mouth while his eyes wandered out the window. Hannibal, slowly peeling his own orange, felt he was also slowly peeling away the layers of his host's mystery. He wondered if this guy suffered from attention deficit disorder or hyperactivity.

"Yes, well to do that I'll have to talk to the lady who's been robbed. I have to know if there's enough to go on for me to even take the case."

"Naturally," Blair said, standing. "Wait here. I'll have Franklin bring her in."

"She's here?" Hannibal asked, also getting to his feet. But Blair was already bouncing out of the room. Hannibal stood confused for just a moment. Then the butler entered from the living room. The woman following him stopped behind a chair.

"Miss Anita Cooper," the butler announced just before he withdrew.

-3-

As silences go, this one was pretty awkward. Anita Cooper was a small woman, certainly less then a hundred pounds and no more than an inch over five feet tall. She was blessed with shiny black skin and the small nose, full lips, high cheekbones and erect carriage Hannibal associated with pictures of ancient Egyptian princesses.

"Mister Blair said you wanted to talk to me?"

"I understood that you needed some help," Hannibal said, finally biting into his orange. It was so sweet he could almost forget the acid it carried.

"I've got some trouble, and your card says you're a troubleshooter," she said, looking up to make eye contact.

"And how do you come to have my card?"

Anita's feet shuffled, and her eyes went down again. "I saw you at the Zei Friday night. I picked your card up off that guy you knocked out."

Hannibal couldn't suppress his smile at that. This girl was more than she showed on the surface. She wore her kinky hair in a short but natural style. Her makeup was so subtle it could be overlooked. And her fingernails were perfectly done, which he knew could not be easy to maintain when one cleaned houses for a living. all of a sudden, he wanted to know her story.

"Why don't we sit down, and you can tell me what the trouble is."

Anita nodded, and smoothed the back of the simple sundress hanging from her shoulders as she sat. She seemed to be waiting for something. Hannibal guessed it might be instructions, or simply permission to speak.

"So, your father left you a treasure of some type?"

"That's what he said." Anita hesitated, as if wrestling with difficult memories. Hannibal rotated his hand as if to say, "Go on."

"Daddy was a research chemist over at Isermann -Börner up in Rockville," Anita said. "Worked there for years, before my mother left even. I stayed with Daddy through high school. He was so proud when I started at MIT. But, you don't want to hear all that."

"Actually, I do," Hannibal said, folding his hands in front of himself on the table. "Whatever you need to tell me that leads up to why I'm here."

Anita licked her lips, took a deep breath and pressed on. "I guess the start was the day Daddy called home from work. I was home for the summer after my freshman year. He was so excited, but all he really said was that he had had a really good day, and that we should celebrate. He sounded so happy. So, while he was on his way home I went out and got a bottle of champagne and a couple of lobsters and all the fixings."

Anita's eyes focused out the window and dampened. Hannibal was prepared to wait, but after a full minute of silence he began to worry that she might not be able to pull herself back if she was gone too long in the past. He asked, "Are you all right?" in a gentle tone.

Anita shook herself. "Sorry. I'm sorry. I could use some... would you like some more coffee?"

Without waiting for a reply, Anita picked up Hannibal's almost-empty cup. She crossed the wide kitchen and started fussing with a complex looking espresso machine. She kept her back to him while she worked.

"I'll make cappuccino," she said. "You'll love it. Anyway, um, see, Daddy was home when I got back. He didn't look happy any more. He said that there had been an accident. He hit a man who was on the side of the road up on 270 on his way in. He shouldn't have left the scene, you know, but he had to make it home first."

The machine made its screaming hissing noise loud enough that if Anita had sobbed, Hannibal might have missed it. She wiped her face once or twice while she worked with cups and heated the milk, but when she returned to the table her face was dry. She even mustered a small smile as she sat down, hands wrapped around her cup.

"Daddy and I had our special dinner anyway," she said. "As it turned out, it was our farewell dinner. Then he called the police and told them what happened. They came and took him away, but he promised me that he had left something in the house that would make us rich when he came back."

"He didn't say what? Or where?"

"He said it was safer if I didn't know," she replied after a sip from her cup. "The long and the short of it was, he was tried and convicted. Not of murder, but the other thing, you know..."

"Manslaughter," Hannibal filled in. "Probably involuntary under the circumstances. And this is very good. Thank you."

"You're welcome," she said, seeming to draw energy from the small compliment. "Anyway, Daddy had never been in trouble before. So he was supposed to do three to five years, right down there in Greenville."

"Cold Springs Correctional," Hannibal said. "Two and a half, three hours south of here. But not a bad place, as such places go. Minimum security."

"They figured if he behaved he'd be out in two years. But in the meantime, there was no money. I left school and got a job with a house cleaning company, but I knew it wouldn't be that long."

The espresso was hot and strong and flavored with just enough cinnamon. Hannibal guessed it was brewed from medium roast Arabica beans. He let it play across his tongue as he listened. "And is your dad still away?"

"Daddy," Anita clenched her eyes together for just a moment. "Daddy died in prison last year. They said it was a heart attack. Sudden. Unexpected."

In that instant, Hannibal's coffee became as bitter as ashes. No, he realized, it was this young woman's life that had turned to ashes in a matter of months.

"I'm so sorry. What did you do? Was there insurance?"

"He had it at work," Anita said, "but it lapsed while he was away. He had left some savings, but with keeping the house going and the, you know."

Hannibal nodded. "The final arrangements. I understand. So you kept working. And I assume you looked for the gift that your father left behind."

"I never found anything that looked valuable in the house," Anita replied. Her fists were clenched tight as she spoke. "Of course, I didn't know what I was looking for. Jewelry? Stocks? An account number? No idea. Anyway, after enough time passed I began to even wonder if there was a hidden treasure. Maybe he just told me that to keep my courage up while he was in prison. But I kept on with life, you know, cleaning and saving up to get back to college. And then Rod came."

"Rod is the boyfriend?" Hannibal asked.

Anita's lips pressed tightly together. "Could you please take off your glasses, Mr. Jones?"

Hannibal slid his Oakley's off his face. Anita stared for only a moment. Maybe it didn't seem as odd to her as it had to some others.

"Are they blue?"

"Sometimes," Hannibal said. "Technically I guess you'd say hazel."

"Men don't have hazel eyes. For sure Black men don't. You are unusual."

"I don't mean to be," Hannibal said. "Now, Rod? The boyfriend?"

Anita locked eyes with Hannibal as if preparing for some reaction. "Rod was my lover, Mr. Jones. He showed up at the house about a month after daddy passed. He said he had known my father in prison, and daddy would have wanted him to take care of me. He had no place to go. I was lonely.

So, I let him stay with me."

Hannibal knew she was steeled against disapproval, but it was not his place to judge her. For him, these were just facts in a case. Every case eventually grew out of people doing wrong and if he tried to sort the good people from the bad he'd never have a client. He sipped his coffee. It had grown cold, but bringing the cup to his lips gave his hands something to do.

"I take it your father told you about this fellow?"

"He had mentioned him," Anita said. "And he showed up at the right time. None of my father's other friends from work or anywhere ever bothered to check on me after the funeral. All my friends were up at school. I was alone, starting to drift, wandering aimlessly. Do you understand that, Mr. Jones? I needed someone to guide me, to help me get through it all. Rod was a strong man, and he just captivated me."

Hannibal hated him already. Of course, Hannibal had a prejudice against guys named Rod. Or Dick. Or Peter for that matter. What were they trying to prove? "So you were comfortable with this guy?"

"I fell in love with him, Mr. Jones," Anita said, fixing him with a defiant stare. "I needed him, and I felt like he needed me. And he asked about Daddy all the time. He spent a lot of time in Daddy's study, almost as if he was trying to make it his own."

"No doubt," Hannibal said. "And at what point did he become uncomfortable there?" Anita looked down. Hannibal's words had been dry. He knew all of this must be embarrassing to share with a stranger.

"It came as a total surprise, Mr. Jones. Six months ago, I came home from work and he was gone. And Daddy's study was a mess. Books tossed here and there, papers just strewn about. I realized while I was cleaning up that he must have been searching for something. Daddy's notebooks were very orderly and organized and I made sure they were all in place before I was done. At first I thought nothing was missing. Then I noticed that a whole box of spare computer discs was gone. I had never thought that Daddy's hidden treasure might be information, Mr. Jones. I think Rod took something out of the computer."

Hannibal had gotten there ahead of her, but this wasn't a real answer. Were they talking about directions to hidden money, the account number of a secret bank account, or a stock brokerage account? It could just as easily be information about a coworker to be used for blackmail. The possibilities were endless, and everything he thought of was intangible. Lost diamonds could be recovered, but stolen information was probably worthless after being used by the thief.

"Right. So he disappeared six months ago, and you haven't seen him since."

"Oh, no," Anita said, leaning forward with her palms on the table. "I saw him last week."

Hannibal also leaned forward, startled the way we so often are when the ending of a story isn't what we expect. "Where?"

Anita's hands locked in an odd way, palms facing with the fingers of one hand curled to hook into the fingers of the other. "I had just finished cleaning Mrs. LaPage's house. I was getting into my car when he pulled up in front of hers. God, it made my heart hurt to see him. I was so flustered I almost caused an accident pulling away. My mind was just spinning. I didn't know what to do. That's why Tonya dragged me out to the club that night. And that's when I saw you."

"Timing is everything," Hannibal said with a smile.

"I think maybe it was fate," Anita said with total seriousness. "You were sent to help me."

Hannibal squirmed under the weight of such a divine responsibility. "I'm not sure I have the solution to this particular problem, Miss Cooper. Why don't you sit tight for a minute and I'll go talk to Mr. Blair again, to see what we might be able to work out."

Anita looked frightened when Hannibal stood. Frightened of being alone, he wondered? In any case, she sat obediently while he wandered into the living room. Hannibal pushed his sunglasses back into place before he stepped into the living room. He stopped at the end of a plush sofa, on which Blair sat watching the tape of a baseball game on his sixty-one inch plasma television screen. The Red Sox were pitching to the Yankees. Blair's feet tapped, and he twitched to the point that he almost vibrated in his seat. Was he a bundle of nervous energy, or did his brain just run at such a frenetic pace that it fired out energy his body had to bleed off. When he looked up, it was as if he was coming out of a trance.

"So, taking the case?"

"Let's get through the basics first," Hannibal said. "Can we talk for a minute?"

Blair didn't hesitate to mute the game and turn his attention to Hannibal. "How can I help?"

"From what Miss Cooper told me, this is too simple. Have you spoken to this Rod? Made him an offer for whatever it is he took?"

Blair shook his head. "I had my people call Marquita LaPage, you know? He's left town again."

Hannibal watched Jeeter swing hard at a pitch that was low and inside. "How far did the police get?"

"Police?" Blair made a noise of contempt. "This isn't a case for the police, if only for personal reasons. I don't want the man arrested, I just want you to find him and get back whatever he took from Anita's house. Besides, police probably wouldn't even believe a crime had been committed, right? I mean, no valuables gone, at least nothing the victim can describe, and no forced entry. No crime from their point of view. This is a case for you, my friend. You know, we're in the same line of work you and I. What do you know about data mining?"

"Not much," Hannibal said. "I guess it's all about extracting the information somebody needs from large databases."

Blair lit up like a school kid. "That's it exactly. That's how I made my fortune, you know, and I think it's what you do too. We're both in the information business, Mr. Jones. The only real difference is that my databases are in computers, and yours are usually in people's heads. That's the only way to find a person who doesn't want to be found in this world. We all leave a trail, after all, it's just lost among all the other material. It's all out there, you just have to dig up the right bits of data."

"Yes, well, buried treasure that might be missing isn't usually the kind of thing I do," Hannibal said. "Ms. Cooper doesn't appear to really be in any kind of trouble. And I did have a little vacation planned. Not to mention, there doesn't seem to be much to go on."

"Please, just do me one favor," Blair said. He picked up a thin envelope from his glass topped end table and handed it to Hannibal. "This is a check for one day's work and a retainer for a week of your time. Please just go to Anita's place and look around a bit. Get your feet wet with the case. If you decide it's not for you, just tear up the second check and move on. I promise I won't bug you again. Okay?"

Hannibal thought that little kid grin must work for Blair nine times out of ten, and he couldn't resist returning it. "Okay, you've got a deal. Let me mull this one over, and I'll let you know in the morning if I'll take the case or not."

Blair stood and extended his hand. "I had you checked out pretty thoroughly, Mr. Jones. If Anita told you her whole story I know you'll pursue this."

* * * * *

Anita Cooper insisted on making lunch for them after Hannibal drove her the five blocks to her home. Her townhouse was a bit more modest than Blair's but the much greater difference showed in the contents. Expensive furniture doesn't really look so special until you have something to compare it with. Hannibal thought her father had bought a home just a little beyond his reach. To compensate, he had ordered the cheapest carpet, the least expensive blinds and the most basic kitchen appliances. They had furnished it along the same lines.

Hannibal toured the house while Anita did kitchen things.

Being a bachelor, he was amused at how neat she kept the place relative to his own apartment. Beyond that, nothing upstairs seemed remarkable to him except perhaps the after-shave lotion in Anita's medicine cabinet. The second bedroom was preserved as if someone lived there, but dust motes floated in the strong shaft of sunlight beaming in through the window. He suspected the room was merely a shrine to her lost father.

On the main level he walked into the odor of tuna fish oil and mayonnaise as he passed Anita. She seemed focused very hard on making the world's best tuna salad sandwiches and soup from a can. The living room held the usual items, although her nineteen-inch television looked puny after standing in front of Blair's home theater screen.

Another flight of stairs led Hannibal to a family room, and finally, a small office. This room showed signs of recent use. Papers were neatly arrayed on the desk. Perhaps Anita used the computer every day to send e-mails and such. Bookshelves lined the room, and one set of them held a row of numbered green notebooks. That didn't mean much to Hannibal until he noticed the floppy discs.

A transparent case on Hannibal's desk holds two rows of poorly labeled discs. Three similar cases stood on Anita's desk. Perhaps a total of one hundred eighty discs, all grouped by color and separated by dividers. The woman was absolutely anal-retentive. Or maybe her father had been. Looking more closely, he could see that the discs were labeled and numbered with great care. Well, she did say her father was a researcher. Maybe he worked at home.

Again, Hannibal's attention returned to the green hardcover notebooks. Each was numbered in sequence with a label pasted to the spine. He pulled down the first one and opened it. The pages were lined but much of the content was drawings and diagrams and writings that he recognized as chemical symbols. Each triangle or pentagram with letters at the corners represented a chemical compound but like the accompanying paragraphs it was all gibberish to him. Curious, Hannibal reached for the last volume, number thirty-eight. It was blank. As were thirty-seven and thirty-six. She must have prepared them in advance. But number thirty-four was full to the last page. The book in-between was absent.

"It's ready," Anita called.

Hannibal bounded up the stairs to find Anita facing him with her back to the stove, pointing toward the table at the front of the house where a glass of lemonade already stood. He smiled a thank-you and moved to a chair while stuffing his glasses and gloves into inside jacket pockets. Green plants lining the windowsill beside him were a silent testament to one more thing he could not do, keep plants alive in his home.

Anita served lunch, in a truer sense than Hannibal was accustomed to. She carried his soup bowl on its plate to the table, and then brought another plate with two sandwiches. The sandwiches were cut in half diagonally and turned so the crusts touched and the filling side faced out. She carried the plates with both hands, and placed them on the table with her face down, almost as if she were bowing to him. Then she returned to the stove, and lifted her own sandwich from its plate, as if she intended to eat standing at the counter by the sink. For Hannibal, that was too much.

"Please, come join me," he said, keeping his tone light. "We need to talk a bit while we eat, so I can get some facts straight."

Anita quickly carried her plate to the table and sat at the other end. In the eerie quiet she chewed slowly, her eyes mostly focused down on her food. Hannibal tasted his own sandwich, leaned back and smiled. It was on rye bread with onions and celery and maybe a hint of mustard as well.

"Hey, that's really good," he said.

When she smiled back at him her nose wrinkled adorably and her shoulders rose a bit. "Thank you," she said, barely loud enough to be heard.

"I'm impressed at how well you keep the house," Hannibal said, sipping his lemonade. "And I noticed everything is very organized. Did your father keep it this way?"

"Daddy was never as organized as he could have been. I

actually kept his things straight for him. It was good to have someone to take care of. We took care of each other."

Hannibal nodded, and sipped his chicken soup. "So, you organized all his work notes and such?"

"Oh yes. It was one way I helped Daddy out."

"So, you couldn't have missed the fact that his most recent notebook is gone," Hannibal said. "Didn't it occur to you that whatever your father meant for you to have might be hidden in them?"

Anita looked down again. "It was just his notes. What could be so valuable in one of those books?"

What indeed? Hannibal could think of a dozen possibilities. Incriminating photographs could lie between the pages. Dirt on a company executive could be written between the formulas, or even trade secrets Anita's father could have sold to another firm. These were the kinds of intangible items that people often paid a great deal of money for. They were also the kinds that lose value quickly once too many people are aware of them. The kind of treasure that is all too often unrecoverable. You can't repossess a person's knowledge.

"Well, one way or another, it sounds as if you won't get whatever it is back unless I can make some sort of settlement with Rod. That means I won't be able to help you unless I can find him, and it sounds as if this guy knows how to keep a low profile. He could be several states away by now."

Anita was looking at the floor again, her fingers laced together in front of her, biting her lower lip. Sitting behind her half eaten sandwich, she looked even smaller than she really was. "Please Mr. Jones. Please try. Whatever my father left me, it's my only legacy from him."

Hannibal pushed his food aside. "I don't even know if I can help you. I need more to go on. So tell me a little about this Rod fellow. Where did he work? What did he do?"

"Rod was very handy," Anita said. "He helped a lot around the house, and sometimes he did odd jobs for neighbors and such."

"I see." Hannibal was starting to form a picture of their relationship, and it was not a pretty one. "He stayed here?"

"He had no place to go."

"Did he give you money?" Hannibal asked, knowing the answer but needing to hear it.

Anita, to her credit, stuck to the truth. "Once in a while he bought groceries and such. But he was real good at fixing things around here. And he helped me, you know, get focused. He helped me with having a purpose in life."

Her designated purpose appeared to be to take care of this man who appeared out of nowhere to take advantage of her and, most likely, to steal the only thing of value left to her. Hannibal was starting to really dislike this guy. "What's his full name, and what does he look like."

Anita squared her shoulders as if reporting to a drill sergeant. "Roderick Mantooth is his full name. He's a little shorter than you but bigger, broader. His hair is black, like his eyes, and he's..." Here she looked out the window, avoiding Hannibal's gaze. "He's white."

That fact seemed a lot more significant to Anita than it was to Hannibal.

"Rod Mantooth? Could that be his real name? Oh, well. You said you saw him at another woman's house. Was he driving?"

"Oh yes, Rod was driving."

Good. "Did you get the license plates?"

"No. I'm sorry, the car was too far away."

Her shyness, bordering on subservience, was beginning to annoy him. "Well, that would have made it a lot easier to find the guy. Do you think you'd recognize the car again?"

"Oh, of course." Anita's smile seemed almost to reflect pride. "You couldn't miss it with those big fins on the back. It's a specially customized car, fire engine red with white interior. Rod calls it a Corvorado."

"A what?"

"The front end is from a 1967 Chevrolet Corvette. From the doors back, it's a 1959 Cadillac Eldorado. You couldn't miss that."

-4-

Hannibal was afraid he might miss the boat.

The entrance gate to the pier was on the water's edge to Hannibal's left as he faced the Potomac River, playing with the ring box in his left front pocket. The Nina's Dandy floated there, her windows reflecting the last few rays of the orange sun at Hannibal's back. He squinted for a while, and then turned away from that reflection, his eyes not shielded by sunglasses for a change. Across the river, tall oaks and maples blazed golden in that reddened glow, and waves like silver sequins lapped at the shore. Everything was dressed up for the occasion.

Unlike his idyllic backdrop, Hannibal felt unnatural in his costume. His double-breasted Italian suit was pure silk, in a color he wasn't sure he could name. Creme, perhaps, or off tan with sort of a gold tone. Anyway, he knew Cindy liked it. His navy blue shirt came with a matching pocket square, so he wore both. He did like the tie, kind of a silvery charcoal with a subtle darker diagonal stripe.

Hannibal flashed back an hour or so, to the moments before he left home. He was standing erect, trying to hold still while Sarge worked to tie Hannibal's tie in an impressive Windsor knot, so much classier than the usual four-in-hand Hannibal whipped into his work ties every day. Sarge appeared to be enjoying Hannibal's plight, perhaps sharing the experience in some vicarious way. Hannibal knew Sarge's life had become a lonely one, for no reason Hannibal could identify. Why were so many good people alone? In any case, Hannibal took joy in his own amazing luck in having a wonderful woman after too many years of short lived relationships followed by long spaces of alone time. He was determined to make this one stick.

Several guests had already boarded the Nina's Dandy, the floating restaurant he had chosen for the special moment. Hannibal wondered if Cindy would arrive in time for them to eat. Then again, he wondered if he would be able to eat. The acid leaping inside his stomach seemed to be voting no.

Only a few blocks separated Cindy's townhouse from the pier in Old Town, Alexandria, but Hannibal was not surprised to see her pull up in a taxi. He suspected that this was not about inconveniencing him to pick her up, or even about not wanting to walk any farther than necessary in heels nearly three inches high, but really about making an entrance. And as far as he was concerned, it was well worth it.

Cindy Santiago's black evening outfit didn't make her look tall and trim, that's just the way her body was made. Her carefully trimmed deep brown hair, usually worn loose, was swept back this evening, just skimming her shoulders. Her face glowed the way children do in Christmas photographs, and her makeup was so perfect you had to look close to know it was there. High cheekbones and tawny skin betrayed her Latin heritage. Dark brown eyes were a little too big, and her smile a little too broad, but to Hannibal they fit together perfectly. Her black silk blouse bore an elegant drape that only served to showcase her abundant décolletage. It flowed down into black velvet pants that accented her high, narrow waist. Her silver chain belt was the perfect accent, and her heels were high enough to make the most of her legs.

"Well, say something, man," Cindy said.

"What could I say that wouldn't get me arrested? You're a vision."

Cindy stepped forward to drop a quick kiss on his lips. "Yeah, well I'm a hungry vision and if we don't get moving dinner's going to float away."

* * * * *

Aside from a gentle rocking, being seating at a table on Nina's Dandy differed little from taking a seat in any upscale restaurant. A band of glass panels surrounded the vessel so that every seat offered an unobstructed view of the river and its thickly wooded coastline. Hannibal watched the oaks and maples slide past, with the occasional dogwood flashing its white or pink flowers that he thought outshone the more famous cherry blossoms. He bit into a piece of sharp, port-wine seasoned cheddar on an unfamiliar cracker and wondered why Cindy chose this particular evening to be so much more verbal than usual.

"Oh, Hannibal this is perfect," she said as the fresh fruit arrived. "I don't know how you always know what I'll want. This is a perfect celebration, maybe just a smidge early, for the Melville's account."

At least she was so excited about work right now that she didn't seem to notice Hannibal's nervousness. "Is that the business with the IPO?"

Cindy giggled at Hannibal's ignorance. It seemed to him that she often did. "DPO, silly. IPO's are a very different kind of offering. Say, isn't that The Awakening? I love that piece."

The sculpture Cindy referred to was of a silver-skinned bearded giant, half-buried in the Maryland shoreline. One arm reached skyward while the other had barely broken through the ground. His open mouth was large enough for a small child to climb into. He seems to be struggling for freedom as Nina's Dandy floats past, much as Hannibal was struggling with words at that moment.

"He seems frozen in time," Hannibal said. "And no man wants to be held static in time, you know. Time passes and life changes are called for, don't you think? It's amazing how much can happen in a few short months."

"You are so right," Cindy said, pushing plates and glasses to make room for the spinach salad. "Melville's has already raised nearly nine million dollars, and their stock is rising instead of falling. This is a good thing, since they gave me a bunch of stock options at the start of this enterprise."

A shadow passed over the table as the majestic vessel floated beneath the Fourteenth Street Bridge. Hannibal shoved a forkful of green into his mouth and wondered why anyone would think to put mandarin oranges into a green salad. The sweet citrus taste didn't seem to fit.

"Is that amount unusual for an IPO," he asked. "I mean a DPO. What the hell's the difference, anyway?"

"Well, a direct public offering is just what the name says. The company can sell stock directly to the public, without a lot of the hateful registration and reporting requirements that IPOs go through. DPOs range in offerings from up to a million, all the way up to twenty five million, depending on the type of offering made. They all have different requirements and restrictions. This particular group is going for twenty-five million dollars, and there's a bonus if we hit the total. There are only a few days left but I think it could happen."

"They must have made quite a commitment to this business," Hannibal said. Then he moistened his dry mouth with a little wine before speaking again. "Sometimes, commitment is a difficult thing. There can be risks, but when you really want something, you have to take action." His hand eased toward his left trouser pocket.

"That's the beauty of this approach for them," Cindy said, moving her hands in a very animated fashion, her face glowing with the excitement Hannibal had seen on the faces of hunters getting close to a deer. "DPOs are designed so small businesses can raise capital in a relatively easy and low cost way. Venture capital and private investors aren't always accessible to them. Then they face the scary task of trying to raise debt financing. DPOs let them raise equity financing instead, and at the same time they give investors a chance to get in early. Hey, here come our entrees. Hannibal, you are so sweet to think of this."

The soft, jazz flavored background music seemed to swell as Hannibal's prime rib arrived. Cindy had chosen the shrimp stuffed with breaded crab. He loved the way her silver necklace glinted in the fading sunlight as she bent to her food with obvious delight. Watching her perfect white teeth tear at the jumbo shrimp, he reflected again on the phenomenon of a woman who could make eating a meal an act of sensuous abandon.

Conversation stilled as they dined, and words seemed unnecessary toward the end of the meal. At some unspoken signal they reached for each other and held hands while they watched evening turn into night around them. They enjoyed the show as Downtown Washington lit up. Their view of the Lincoln Memorial was stunning, but not as moving as the perfect picture that shaped up in front of them as the Washington Monument and the lighted Capitol Dome slid into position to present a postcard come to life. The reflecting pool, stretched out between them and the monuments, appeared to have been placed there in anticipation that these two lovers would some day sit in this exact spot in the middle of the Potomac to see it.

The Kennedy Center and the oddly curved Watergate Hotel complex moved past before the canned music was replaced by live tinkling from the piano at the center of the deck and the sharp but sweet aroma of cinnamon-heavy apple pie drew Hannibal's senses back into the ship.

"I hope that pie is as good as this cheesecake," Cindy said. Her dark eyes told him that she had drunk just enough wine with dinner to loosen her up a notch. Maybe he would try one more time. He emptied his glass, and took Cindy's other hand.

"Cindy, I talked to a girl today who wants my help with a problem, but I think she found it difficult to talk to me. You know, sometimes it's hard for people to discuss what's really important with someone face to face. You know what I mean?"

"Oh, yeah baby, it's the same in my business," she said. "That's what makes the Internet so great. Like for this case I'm working right now. See, unlike an IPO certain DPOs let companies actively advertise and promote the sale of their stock. The SEC even allows the electronic transfer of the company's prospectus to an investor. That way, the company execs don't have to be salesmen and talk to people, you know? Hey, name that tune!"

"What?" Hannibal had to think a minute. She had switched gears twice, and landed on a very old jazz tune coming from the piano.

"Isn't that *Deep Purple*?"

"Yeah, that's it. I want to dance. Don't you want to dance?" They rose together without their hands parting. As they arrived at their spot a few feet from the other two dancing couples, Cindy asked, "So what about that case? Are you going to take it?"

Hannibal clamped his eyes shut and stifled a sigh, accepting that this evening would simply not go in the direction he expected it to. Their night had become her night, and he would simply have to devise another opportunity to pop the question.

"Well, it looks like I'll have time for a case in the next few days. I guess I'll take it after all."

-5-

THURSDAY

For Hannibal it was the start of a typical workday, if there was such a thing. There was a limit to the kinds of trouble people got into, so there were only so many ways for Hannibal to earn his living. Some days, he provided physical protection for someone. Like his last case, that was mostly waiting for something to happen. Some days he delivered messages his client could not deliver themselves, usually backing the message up with violence. That kind of trouble most often ended quickly. Hannibal's time in the secret service had prepared him well for those assignments.

The rest of his workdays were what he called legwork days. That meant doing the drudgework he hated, pursuing leads to find something or someone. His days with the New York police department had prepared him for those days.

After a good long run to clear his head and a frozen waffle breakfast, he brewed a fresh pot of coffee and worked the telephone for a couple of hours. He didn't tell Anita, but she had actually given him a pretty good lead on Rod. The car he drove was a very special customization. Whoever did that work would remember it. And people who do that kind of thing know each other. One call to an auto customizer led to another, on a telephone trail that seemed to move farther and farther west, until he got the comment he was waiting for.

"Mister, only one man on the east coast could have pulled off a chop job like that one."

Hannibal stepped out of his building just before eleven o'clock, pushing his sunglasses into place. A shout from up the block got his attention as he reached for his car door handle. Monte Washington was marching toward him. As always, Hannibal stifled his reaction to middle school fashion. Hannibal was sure Monte's jeans were below his narrow butt, and he wondered what kept them from falling off.

"Dude! I been wanting to talk to you," Monte said. His hair was in tight cornrow braids these days, and his chocolate complexion darkened by the summer sun. "You gotta tell me what it was like, hanging with Huge Wilson. Did you meet Missy and Timberland? And I know he got all the fly honeys, but did he share?"

"I was working, Monte. I wasn't focused on the honeys," Hannibal said. Was Timberland a person? Hannibal thought it was a brand of boots. "And I've been wanting to talk to you too, after the last time I spoke with your grandmother." Monte was the first person in the neighborhood to speak to Hannibal when he first arrived. Much of his drive to keep drug dealers out of the area stemmed from his concern for this one young man and the grandmother who was raising him. For Hannibal, Monte symbolized the promise of the future.

"What's Grandma been telling you now?" Monte asked, sliding his portable CD player's headphones on.

"She told me about your final report card this year," Hannibal said. "I'm not happy. We had a deal."

"It wasn't all that bad, bro."

"You can do better," Hannibal said. "And I wonder if you've been reading this summer like you said you would."

"You want me to waste my time with my head in a book?" Monte asked with a grin. "Maybe we need to hook up a new deal."

Hannibal turned to lean back against his car. He had the feeling he had stepped into a well concealed bear trap. "What do you have in mind, you little hustler?"

"I know you didn't realize what a great opportunity you just passed up," Monte said, padding around in what Hannibal thought were Timberlands. "But since you made the connection, well, you could introduce me to Huge."

"I could." Hannibal looked around his block, smelling the eternal heat of the city and feeling the summer slipping away like Monte's chances at success. Did he realize that he was in a race, and that some of his peers were already running? "But that's a tall order. I think a meeting like that, under positive circumstances, would be worth, let's say a book every two weeks, through the summer, and maybe the same deal after school starts."

"What?" Monte back-pedaled. "You don't want me to have no life at all?"

"Well, if it's not worth it to you," Hannibal turned and pulled the handle of his car door.

"Okay, okay, but for that deal, I got to have five minutes alone with the brother, so I can get him to listen to some of my rhyming," Monte said. "I could be his next big thing, you know?"

"Sure, Monte. Now listen, I got work to do. And you better get to the library and find something good because I'll hook you up with Huge before the end of next week."

* * * * *

Before his conversation with Monte faded from his mind, Hannibal was cruising down I-295, watching for the exit to the Beltway that would point him toward Maryland. The nearest mechanic who would admit to being able to perform the kind of automotive surgery needed to create Rod's car lived across the Potomac in the Southern Maryland county of St. Mary's. It was the same man who had been identified by his peers during Hannibal's telephone investigation.

Hannibal still marveled at how abruptly his urban environment faded to a rural setting. The city feeling dropped away within twenty minutes of driving, when he turned onto Maryland's Route 5 and headed south toward Mechanicsville. He spent a lot of time alone with the Tornado, and he knew just where on the RPM scale she would settle into a smooth and steady cruise. This was the speed at which his Volvo was happiest, and once he hit it he liked to settle back and enjoy the scenery moving past him. At these times he enjoyed his favorite guilty pleasure, the classic rock music that always made him feel so good. None of his friends could really appreciate the Lynrd Skynrd album thumping in his CD player right then, but he was sure the people who lived on either side of the road he was cruising down would love it.

His head was still bobbing when he turned off the highway, and again onto an even smaller road. He slowed to a crawl to drive over the ruts and potholes, eventually moving onto a road barely wide enough to accommodate two cars passing. Willows lined the road, leaning far enough over to occasionally brush the Tornado's white roof. Just as he was beginning to doubt the accuracy of his directions, Hannibal saw four single-story buildings. One looked as if it might hold an office, while the others were clearly garages and work areas.

The pit bull snarling at him at the end of a short chain marked this as rural white territory. Sarge called these people SMIBs, an unflattering acronym for Southern Maryland In-Breds. Of course, Hannibal had been in Black-owned junkyards with a very similar look except that for some reason, the brothers always had rottweillers or Doberman pinschers chained to their gates.

Hannibal sat for a moment, parked in front of a row of vintage cars, and partial cars. He allowed himself those few seconds to decide on the best approach to get the information he needed. Despite the barking dog, no one came outside to meet him, so in his own time he opened his door and stepped out. The car's air-conditioned atmosphere puffed out with him and evaporated, allowing the heat of the day to wrap around him like a soft blanket. The humidity fogged his Oakley's for a second. The smell of oil or transmission fluid was tainted with the odor that rises when someone who chews tobacco has spit in the same place too many times. He looked down to see dust rise from the hard packed dirt surface and settle on his previously glistening shoes. On an impulse, he pulled his gloves off, dropped them on the seat, shut the door and headed inside.

Ten steps later Hannibal opened the door of the first cinder block building. He knew right away why no one had stepped out. A loud compressor was keeping that room ice cold. He saw everything he expected to see there: a parts manual open on a wooden counter, vinyl chairs on the customer side, a Coke machine in the corner, barely clad models on the calendar on the opposite wall, and a hard-skinned, smiling white man standing behind the counter.

"Morning," the man said. "What can I do you for today? You looking for a car, or you want some work done on that 850 GLT outside?"

Hannibal held his hand out for a shake, and got it. "I'm Hannibal Jones, and I'm betting you're Clarence Nash." Nash was in his early fifties, with silver hair and a beard that had simply grown as far as it wanted to and stopped. He wore overalls, but his hands were clean and his shake was firm. Hannibal's research told him that this man was a mechanic, an artist and a salesman. He figured he could probably get away with a direct approach with the man, if he sprinkled it with a bit of flattery.

Nash took Hannibal in with one broad glance, and there seemed to be a great deal of activity going on behind his face. "I'm Nash, but folks here about generally call me Van. And I'm thinking maybe you ain't here about no car. Hardly anybody comes here in a suit, and you ain't no Marylander anyhow. You ain't with the IRS, is you?"

"No kind of law, although I do have some experience in that area," Hannibal said. "I'm private now, just trying to help a client find an old friend. I don't have too many leads, but I think this guy was a customer of yours."

Nash stared idly out the window toward the sound of a power sander being used in one of the garages out back. "Well, son, I've had a lot of customers in the last couple of years, and I don't keep real good records here."

Hannibal leaned an elbow on the counter while he slid his hand into his pocket. "I understand sir. This is rather an odd request. But you must keep some sort of records and I have been authorized to pay you for your time checking them. Of course if my information is right, you'll remember this fellow. I'm told you're the only man alive who could have built his car. Corvette in front, Cadillac in back. Sound familiar?"

While he talked, Hannibal watched Nash's face move from suspicion to irritation to offense and finally to what looked like disgust. For a moment he feared he had miscalculated the best way to approach this man.

"Oh, that asshole," Nash said, his eyes rolling skyward. "Well, if your client really is a friend of his, you ought to get a better class of client. But I'm betting the real reason you're trying to find him is because he welshed on a bet or screwed your client's old lady. Right?"

"Well, something like that," Hannibal said. "He stole something from a lady and I'm trying to recover it."

"Yeah, that figures," Nash said, turning to rummage through a stack of thick binders. "Always talked about women like they was trash. I'll never forget that guy. One of them pretty-boy weightlifters with squinty little eyes and hands like a gorilla's paws. And the job, Jesus what a job."

"You mean the car?"

Nash returned to the counter and slammed a big binder down on it to accent his words. "Damn straight. You know how the sixty-eight 'Vette had that crease on the side of the front quarter panel and the doors?"

"I have to admit I don't know much about old cars."

"Well, they had a crease along them, horizontally, see?" Nash talked while he flipped through blue, perforated pages. "Ran down the side. So when I cut the body in half..."

"You cut the car in half?"

41

"Such a beauty too," Nash said, shaking his head. "But, yeah, he only wanted the front part, before the doors. Just back to the windshield. Then I had to reform the fiberglass on the sides, to make it match up when I mounted it on the El Dorado. That meant cutting the front off that beautiful nineteen fifty-nine Caddy. It's what he wanted, and he paid big money for it too, but believe me, driving that thing must be a bitch."

"My client said he called it a Corvorado," Hannibal said. "Why would a guy want to do that?"

"Why?" Nash looked up, surprised. "Boy, you're talking about driving the biggest, flashiest thing on the road. The 'Vette's all nose, and that El Dorado was all ass, so you end up with this long, racy, high powered bitch that can haul ass while it's hauling you and a half dozen of your best friends. And with the fiberglass nose making her tail heavy, I bet you she's a hell of a street racer. And he could take care of her."

"Meaning?"

Nash looked up again, surprised. "Meaning that he knew the machine. Think he must have been quite a shade tree mechanic, something you city boys wouldn't know nothing about. Hell of a driver too. I rode with him on her shakedown drive. Ah, here he is. Rod Mantooth."

"You sound a little like you admired him," Hannibal said, staring down at the receipt in Nash's book.

"No sir, he was a genuine son of a bitch," Nash said, looking as if he was about to spit. "Had a hateful word for anybody you could name, and thought he was God's gift to the world. Never seen a man swagger like that, except on TV on the wrestling shows. And the way he talked about the ladies. Damn."

Hannibal smiled a bit. It was getting easier and easier to hate this Mantooth guy. "Sounds like I want to watch my back when I find him. But I guess he made an impression on you. Can you give me a description?"

Nash's lower lip pushed forward, and his eyes went up and to his left as he searched his brain. "Five-ten, maybe, but he had to be pushing two hundred pounds and solid as an old oak. Black hair, and black eyes that were, I don't know, kind of cold, you know? Kind of dark skin, too. Not like you, I mean like spics or Italians get. Real hairy arms too. And kind of a craggy face, although I bet women go for him."

Hannibal assembled a picture in his mind, much as a police sketch artist might. He would consult it later if he thought he had the man in his sights. "I'm picturing loud, short sleeve shirts, jeans and cowboy boots."

Nash snapped back. "How'd you know that? Well, it's just the kind of stuff he always had on. He's sure not from around here. He might have been a wannabe surfer dude but from that accent I'd bet he's an Alabama boy. You know, the kind that barely get through fifth grade and learn about loving from their sister."

Hannibal nodded that he got the idea, all the while marveling at the way some rednecks can put other rednecks down. At least he had Nash on his side. He pointed at the receipt again. "So, do you have a copy of his check? I might be able to trace him through his bank."

"Don't really know much about this business, do you?" Nash asked, scratching himself in a way that made Hannibal uncomfortable. "Don't see many checks in this business. But most of my customers don't pay in crisp, brand new hundred dollar bills."

Hannibal's face revealed nothing, but that news hit him like an unexpected punch. Lots of money probably meant that Mantooth had already sold whatever information he found at Anita's home. But maybe, if Hannibal found him soon enough, he could at least recoup some of the money he had received for it.

"Okay, you clearly didn't trust this guy. I'm betting you made him give you an address."

Nash grinned, flashing tobacco-stained teeth. "Sure did. He was living good, too. Had him a room at the Hilton in Washington. He didn't belong in no decent hotel but, I guess in one way them hotel boys is just like me. They take care of you as long as your money's green. Maybe he's even still

43

there. I sure hope you catch up with that son of a bitch. And I hope when you do, you kick his ass."

* * * * *

The second he had the Volvo started, Hannibal cranked the air conditioning up to maximum. Pulling out of Nash's yard his uppermost thought was how much dust he had stirred up and how much of it had settled onto The Tornado's hood. He would have to run through a car wash before the day was out.

By the time he reached Route 5 his mind had returned to his case. He turned the fan down to its lowest setting and pushed buttons on his car phone. The robotic voice of an operator informed him that there were ten Hilton Hotels in the Capital area, but he was only interested in the four technically in Washington. With the Maryland countryside flowing past in an endless wave of green, he called the first hotel.

Hannibal's years as a policeman in New York had taught him how to act like a cop, but one of the less obvious things he had learned in the Secret Service was how to sound like a cop. There is a tone, a pace, an approach to asking questions that people recognize as official. Using the right amount of authority, Hannibal was able to get three hotels to confirm that they had not had a guest named Rod, Roderick or Roger Mantooth in the appropriate timeframe. The fourth Hilton explained that they could not divulge that kind of information over the telephone. Hannibal thanked them and drove on, now knowing where Rod had stayed.

The final phone call ended just as Hannibal was merging onto the Beltway, turning his CD player back up, and noticing the gray Ford in his rearview mirror. Traffic on I-495 was light at this time of the morning, but moving quickly. He wouldn't be on that road five minutes at this pace, so he stayed in the right lane. ZZ Top's raucous white-boy blues slammed out of his four-speaker system, informing him that "Jesus Just Left Chicago." Mouthing the words along with the music, he focused on the vehicle three cars back in his mirror.

The flat gray Ford Fairmont was as close to nondescript as a car could be. Boxy but not too big or small, it would be the perfect tail car, if someone wanted to follow someone else. Nothing distinguished it from the mass of Detroit molded metal on the road that morning. Nothing except familiarity. Hannibal was almost sure he'd seen this car behind him just before he reached Route 5, half an hour ago. Of course, it might not be the same car. Even if it was, there was nothing so strange about another driver taking the best route from the Eastern Shore to the District. Still...

A Land Cruiser was slowly sliding past Hannibal on his left. To Hannibal, nobody needed a vehicle that size unless they were entering a demolition derby. A Voyager trailed it by a little more than a car length, its driver's attention divided by four children bouncing in the seats behind her. Hadn't they heard about seat belts in that household? Well, maybe he would give them a reminder.

A slow smile spread across Hannibal's face and he was singing along with the music under his breath. As he and the band reached the chorus, "Beer drinkers, yeah, hell raisers," Hannibal released his accelerator to let his Volvo drift back so that the four wheel drive Cruiser was completely past him.

"Let's do it, Tornado," he muttered between lyrics. Watching his mirrors closely, he slapped the shifter down into second gear and made a sharp slide to his left. Chauffeur Mom slammed her brakes and Hannibal moved through the space and directly into the third lane. The woman was yelling at her charges, who had flown all about the inside of the van. Hannibal could spare only a sliver of attention to the kids buckling up, because he was watching the Ford, which also jogged hard left. It paused in the middle lane for a moment before moving over to the third and settling in three cars behind Hannibal.

"Well, I guess that settles that," Hannibal said. But already his exit was coming up - exit 2B, leading to that little stretch of I-295 that would take him to Maine Avenue downtown. Pressing the accelerator to the floor, Hannibal felt his engine move comfortably into overdrive as he pulled the steering wheel to dive in front of the Land Cruiser. Again he slid across two lanes of traffic to dart onto the exit ramp, and then downshifted as his car leaned into the sharp right curve. His tires made a small squeal of protest, but only for a second. When he slotted into traffic between two other skillful and determined drivers, there was no gray Fairmont in his rearview mirror. And from there, no one could guess where in Washington he may be headed. Hilton hotels were not among Hannibal's usual haunts.

* * * * *

When Hannibal stepped out of the elevator in Cindy's building he saw that the sign on the door had finally been changed. "Niesewand and Baylor" had lost its senior partner shortly after Gabriel Niesewand went to prison for his involvement in a conspiracy to defraud a wealthy client, and the murder he committed trying to keep that conspiracy a secret. Hannibal had something to do with that conviction. Now the sign read "Baylor, Truman and Ray."

"And Tinker to Evers to Chance," Hannibal thought, reminded of the famous triple play. However, moving those other two partners onto the firm's masthead did put Cindy a step or two closer to full partnership some day soon. Her star was rising very quickly indeed.

Like any major law firm, this one had its gatekeepers, but they all knew Hannibal and hardly raised their heads as he entered the office. When he did get someone's attention, he just pointed at Cindy's door and smiled.

"No one this morning," the receptionist said, meaning that Cindy had no appointments. Nodding thanks, Hannibal pushed Cindy's door open and stepped quietly inside.

Not a corner office yet, he reflected, but still quite an impressive space for a young associate. Her desk was covered with papers, books, and small sheets containing her hastily scribbled notes. Tastefully decorated he thought, with a lovely, subtle fragrance from the bowl of floating violets on a side table.

Cindy herself was nowhere to be seen, so he dropped into the visitor's chair closest to her desk. While he waited he picked up one of the firm's brochures, curious to see what else had changed since Niesewand's departure. He saw now that the firm specialized in "Emerging Business, Technology and E-Commerce (EBTEC)." Must everything have an acronym, he wondered? "At Baylor, Truman and Ray we recognize that fast-moving businesses have special needs. We have assembled a multidisciplinary team of attorneys to serve those needs — including attorneys with backgrounds in the intellectual property, securities, corporate, real estate, land use, telecommunications, environmental, labor and litigation practice areas..."

Hannibal wasn't sure how you could use the word "specialize" with a collection of areas like that, but there was pride attached to the fact that his woman, Cindy Santiago, represented the "securities" part of that list for emerging businesses. What would his brochure say, if he had one? "Hannibal Jones recognizes that life is hard and unfair. He specializes in helping people who are in trouble and need help to get out of it." Not so impressive, he thought, but it did sound more like real work.

Cindy rushed into her office in a navy blue suit and heels. She froze when she saw Hannibal, delight dancing in her dark eyes. Her arms were filled with large bound volumes of legal precedent, and she clutched a pencil between her teeth. One long strand of hair had worked loose and hung down to tickle the tip of her pert Latin nose.

"Now here's a lovely surprise," she said, once she had dropped the books on her desk and pulled the pencil free of her mouth. Hannibal stood and they shared a brief but warm embraced, ending the hug with a quick kiss. "Just in the neighborhood?"

"Actually, my current case brought me nearby, and I thought you might like to run out for a late lunch. Or have you eaten, already?"

"Oh heavens no. In fact, I really can't get away today. Do you want me to order something in? We can eat right here while I get some of this research done."

Not exactly what Hannibal had in mind, but he said, "Sure, that sounds great. If I can use your computer for a minute."

"Help yourself," Cindy said, rolling her chair a little out from her desk. Hannibal pushed the visitor chair over beside her and tapped the keys while she spoke into her intercom. The two quickly became immersed in their own tasks and sat in a comfortable silence until a young lady who may have been hired for her cuteness laid food on Cindy's desk and withdrew without a word. Cindy put her notebook down and corralled her soup and salad. Hannibal leaned back and began unwrapping his hot pastrami on rye.

"Well, this is kind of cozy," Cindy said. "So tell me how this new case is starting out. Missing person, right?"

"Well, sort of," Hannibal said after his first bite. The meat was hot and fresh, with a generous slathering of sharp, stone-ground mustard. Perfect. He sipped from his lemonade to clear his mouth. "The guy apparently stole something from a young girl he was staying with. I found out he had a suite at the Capital Hilton over on 16th Street right after he left the girl."

"What did he steal?" Cindy asked. "That's one of the most expensive places in the City. Certainly the most expensive of the Hiltons."

"Well that's just it," Hannibal said, tracking mustard down his thumb with his tongue. "We don't know what he stole, but it does sound like he's already sold it, doesn't it? Anyway, he was only at the Hilton for a week. I think he found a new mark pretty quickly."

"Okay, so you got a forwarding address, right?"

"You could be a detective," Hannibal said. "Actually, he left both a previous and a forwarding address, one in Denver, the other in Miami. But as I just confirmed with on-line mapping services, neither address actually exists."

"Okay, so he's somebody who's used to keeping a low profile. Where do you go from here?"

"From here I go back to the victim for more background info. But enough about my day. How's that DPO going?"

"Spectacular," Cindy said, pushing her fork around to gather the last of the dressing from her salad bowl. "I was just putting together a presentation for some new potential investors."

"I thought this was a great investment. Do you have to sell it?"

Cindy shook her head, still smiling. "My poor investment-ignorant Hannibal. One of the biggest problems with DPOs is the lack of a secondary market to trade these securities in. I mean, unlike shares of say, TRW or IBM that change hands by the millions every day on the New York Stock Exchange, the stock of DPO companies is kind of illiquid."

"Meaning it's hard to sell," Hannibal said.

"Well, yeah. There are sales restrictions, and they're not on an exchange so, yeah, we have to sell them." She stood, smoothed her skirt, and leaned over for another kiss. "You know, lunch was nice, but I owe you a real, home cooked meal. I'm thinking pollo con quimbobó y platanos with some black beans and rice."

"Okay, pollo is chicken, right?" Hannibal stared into her eyes with both hands on her waist, gently tugging, trying to drop her onto his lap. "That does sound good. Tonight around eight? That would give me time to straighten up."

Her eyes broke from his as conflict flashed across her face. "I've got a lot to do here, baby. Not sure how I can swing it tonight."

"Yes, I know, you're ever so busy. But tell me this: when will be a better time? When will you not be busy?"

At the gentle urging of Hannibal's hands on her waist, Cindy lowered herself onto his knees, wrapping an arm around his shoulders and brushing his nose with her own.

"Yeah, I guess you're right. Okay. Dinner tonight, at your place. My man comes first."

"That's what I like to hear," Hannibal said in a very soft voice, "and maybe I'll have a little surprise for you then. Of course, if something comes up..."

"No, I absolutely promise." Cindy's mouth pouted and she batted her seductive eyelashes. "I would never want to disappoint my honey. If I don't come through..."

"If you don't then you get a spanking," Hannibal said, wagging a finger at her.

"Oh?" Cindy said, turning her face to look at him out of the corner of her eyes. "Do YOU promise?"

* * * * *

It was close to three o'clock when Hannibal again parked in front of Anita's home. He noticed that her lawn was turning brown, partially from being cut too short. Sometimes a person can pay too much attention to some jobs and do more harm than good. He imagined this girl polishing the finish off furniture too, or destroying clothes by washing them too often.

Anita opened the door before he could ring the bell. "It's good to see you again," she said. "Have you solved it all so quickly? Found Rod and brought back whatever he took away?"

"Not quite." Hannibal stepped into her sterile front room. "Thank you for meeting me here. I'm glad your schedule is so flexible."

"Oh, I have a full day's work but I always start early and finish early," Anita said with evident pride. "So please, have a seat and tell me what you've learned. Coffee?"

Hannibal continued to stand at the counter separating the kitchen from the living room. "Sure, coffee's fine. I wanted to tell you where we are with the investigation. First of all, your friend Rod will not be easy to find. He's covering his tracks pretty well, using false addresses and so forth. So I've decided to approach this from two different directions. First, I'm afraid I'll need to question this LaPage woman. You said you saw Rod coming out of her house."

He watched Anita nod as she fussed about the kitchen. She was dumping out the coffee she had brewed for herself, making him a fresh pot. "Mr. Blair might not like that.

They're neighbors and I think they belong to some of the same associations and such."

"I'll check with him," Hannibal said. "The other best chance is to figure out what your father left here that anyone would want to steal. He must have told Rod about his treasure. People get lonely in prison, and sometimes that makes them talkative. Maybe he really did expect the man to come here and protect you. In any case, I think it must have been something he took away from work, maybe insider trading information or pharmaceutical trade secrets."

"I don't think Daddy would do anything like that," Anita said as she poured freshly filtered water into the back of her coffee maker.

"Even so, I think I need to talk to some of the people he worked with."

Anita paused for a moment in the middle of measuring scoops of coffee. "I'm afraid I don't know any of the people Daddy worked with."

"I see. Well, I might find some leads in his office, if I can poke around in there a little more."

"Of course," Anita said. "Whatever might help. Say, I've got some corn muffins here. Why don't you go ahead to the study and when everything's ready I'll bring a tray down to you."

Walking down the carpeted steps to the office, Hannibal was shaking his head, silently admitting that Anita's subservient attitude was starting to irritate him. But then, if the girl had shown a bit more backbone, this Rod would never have been able to take advantage of her as he did. Hannibal always thought all women raised by men would be more like Cindy, who spent her formative years with just her father. Perhaps Anita was looking for a replacement for her lost father when Rod appeared on the scene. If so, he must have enjoyed being taken care of and catered to in a way Hannibal never would.

While one part of his mind toyed with that personality puzzle, the rest of it explored the office, searching for some evidence that Anita's father had connections with anyone else at Isermann -Börner. Nothing on the desk or any of its cubbyholes yielded a clue. He leafed quickly through the books on the dust-free shelves. It didn't take long to ascertain that Mr. Cooper never made personal references.

Letters? Memos? Hannibal turned his attention to the gray metal filing cabinet in the corner. He yanked at the handle. Locked. Well, that was a good sign. Maybe there was something inside worth hiding. Not wanting to wait for Anita, Hannibal drew a small plastic kit from an inside jacket pocket. The case was about the size of a credit card and no thicker than a computer floppy disc. From it he drew two slender bits of spring steel. He slid the metal slivers into the filing cabinet's lock and five seconds later, pulled the top drawer open.

The file folders were all neatly labeled, and most of the labels meant nothing to Hannibal. Chemical compounds, he guessed, or abbreviations for them, except for the folder at the very back whose label read, "rules." Curiosity drew his hand toward it, then past it. In the dark in the back of the drawer a sparkle had caught his eye. It was the glint of metal on what appeared to be a leather strap.

Hannibal pulled the unexpected object from the drawer. A dog's collar, he thought, but for a good sized animal. It was a simple black leather strap about fourteen or fifteen inches long, with a square silver buckle. Odd that the collar would be locked in a file cabinet, he thought, and stranger still that he had seen no evidence of a dog or even a cat in the house. He had seen no food, water bowl, pet toys, or any of the usual telltale signs.

The collar made him curious, but didn't seem relevant to his investigation. Idly, he pulled the "rules" folder out with his free hand, dropped it on top of the filing cabinet, and flipped it open. It appeared to contain only five or six sheets of paper, with several lines handwritten in a very fine and precise script, with gold ink. Not a man's hand, more likely Anita's. The hair on the back of Hannibal's neck rose to attention as he scanned the first few numbered lines.

#1. I worship my Master.

#2. I worship my Master's body.

#3. I will serve, obey and please my Master.

The numbers went up to ninety, but that was enough for him. Hannibal flipped the folder closed and just managed to get it back where he found it when he heard a gasp behind him, followed by another sound, like a partial sob. He turned to see Anita, her mouth open and her face flushed bright crimson. Her eyes darted left and right, as if she would run off if not for the tray she was holding. The tray held a coffee pot, cup, sugar and creamer set, and a plate of muffins. After a moment of paralysis, she appeared to buckle at the knees. Hannibal moved to help her, but she carefully placed the tray onto a chair and knelt in front of it, facing down at the tray as if the empty cup was endlessly fascinating. Hannibal suddenly felt like an intruder. He also felt very slow, having not realized at first that the object in his hand was a symbol of shame for the woman he was trying to help.

"This is yours," he said slowly, before realizing how pointless that comment was.

Anita squeezed her knees with her hands, and nodded her head.

Hannibal was treading into unfamiliar waters, but some things seemed to string together. "Rod?"

Her head moved up and down again, and he saw a tear drop to her skirt.

"Please," he said aloud, "please stand up." In his mind he was screaming, "For God's sake, get off your knees."

Anita rose and turned to face him with unexpected grace. She seemed to be staring at his navel, but for the firs time Hannibal wondered if her downcast gaze was the result of shame or training. He let the silence hang, quite sure that she knew the questions that needed answers. When at last she spoke it was in a voice so well controlled that it surprised him.

"When Rod got here my life had no direction, no purpose. I had dedicated much of my life to my father, and he to me. When he died I had nothing. No one. Life just happened to me. It was all spinning out of control. Rod, he explained my purpose, gave me a role in life. Mostly he was good to me. Gave me direction and trained me."

"Trained you?" Hannibal's stomach twisted tight, like a knotted dishrag. "To do what, to be his servant, his slave?"

Silent tears began to slide down Anita's face. "I needed guidance. He showed me how to behave and what to do."

The water on Hannibal's skin wasn't tears, but sweat, sending a chill up his spine. "Did he," no easy way to ask, he decided. "Did he beat you?"

"He didn't want to," she said. "Only when I made him do it. Only when I was bad. Or if I wasn't learning."

Hannibal suddenly remembered the collar in his hand, black leather that matched his glove. He dropped it on the filing cabinet. "Learning what, I wonder," he said, mostly to himself.

Anita's tears flowed more freely and she gave a soft sob before answering this time. "He made me do things. Things I never did before. But it made him happy for me to do these things and I needed to learn the joy of making him happy."

She sounded as if she was giving a memorized speech. Hannibal's hands trembled with rage and he clenched his fists to stop them. She stood still, as if waiting for something. His reaction? Condemnation? Her next order?

Hannibal reached slowly forward, to place his hands lightly on her shoulders. "Look at me." No reaction. He raised his left hand to whip his glasses off. She flinched when his hand moved. He pointed to his own eyes. "Look at me."

Anita raised her face slowly, as if fighting against some invisible hand pressing down on her head. When she made eye contact, Hannibal thought he could see all the way down into her fractured soul. He clenched his teeth, but it did not stop his breath from hissing through them.

"Listen to me. I know this man did things that damaged your spirit, maybe some things you're very ashamed of. But none of this is your fault. You hear me? This man turned you, twisted you in ways you couldn't possibly defend against. But believe me, I will find him, and I will make sure he pays you back for everything he took from you. I swear to you he will pay."

Anita broke down completely, crying aloud, her face twisted into that mask that looks so much like laughing if you could turn off the sound. Sobs rocked her body and she leaned close enough for her tears to dampen Hannibal's shirt.

"Please," she gasped out, in rhythm with her crying, "Please, sir. Please don't hurt him."

-6-

The little town of Vienna, Virginia sits about a dozen miles due west of Washington, D.C., a straight shot down I-66. By that time in the afternoon there was quite a bit of traffic flowing in both directions. Ben Blair's office was there, on the 12th floor of a glass tower. Hannibal was grateful he was headed there from Anita's home, a pleasant ten minute drive due south. Just enough time for him to appreciate Blair's commute, and have an idea why he chose to live in a townhouse in Tysons Corner instead of the mansions he could afford that gathered around Washington like Hollywood Indians surrounding the fort, an hour or more away. Not quite enough time for him to recover from Anita's final words before he left her, or to manhandle his rage at Rod Mantooth into a manageable form. His jaws ached from clenching them against his own anger.

The parking lot was free, at least for the first two hours, and Hannibal had no plans to be there that long. He found the air conditioning a little overdone in the lobby. It made the marble columns and tile flooring seem even more impersonal. Two other people waited for the elevator, but neither spoke during that wait, or during the elevator ride.

When at last he entered the Tactical Datamation offices, Hannibal faced a mature receptionist who sat as a calm veneer in front of a beehive of activity. Her dyed auburn hair was well lacquered in place, and her smile was equally frozen. To her left and right, people clattered at computer keyboards or wheeled their chairs around to confer with coworkers. He could see that they worked in a bullpen atmosphere, without the usual cubicle walls separating the workers. When anyone stood, they walked quickly, as if the person they wanted to speak with might get away. Or, more likely, they moved in fear that their latest inspired idea might escape them before they could share it. A week in this place would drive Hannibal to try to leap through one of the sealed windows. Maybe that was why buildings like this one never had windows you could open.

"How may I help you, sir?" the receptionist asked, with that air of power one gets when one stands guard at the gates of the rich and famous.

"Hannibal Jones to see Ben Blair."

The Gatekeeper seemed to scroll Blair's schedule behind her eyes. "I'm afraid no one sees Mr. Blair without an appointment. Can I write you in for tomorrow morning?"

"He'll see me," Hannibal said with a calm smile. "We have personal business."

"I'm sorry," she replied, matching his calm demeanor. "Mr. Blair sees no one without an appointment."

"Just tell him I'm here."

"Sir," she added just an ounce of weight to her voice, "Mr. Blair's schedule is extremely tight."

This could become tedious. Hannibal placed his gloved palms on the oak reception desk. "Neither of us has time for this, so we will proceed in one of two ways. In the next ten seconds, one of us is going to walk into Mr. Blair's office and ask if he will see me right now. Which do you prefer?"

Hannibal kept his eyes on The Gatekeeper's but his other senses told him that the buzz of activity to his left and right had stopped. Perhaps they had never seen this woman challenged and waited to see if she would scream or call the security guard or pull a revolver out of her desk. In the end, nine seconds later, she stood and walked with perfect posture down the hall behind her. Normal activity did not return until Hannibal could hear her heels clicking back toward him. When she returned her smile had not moved an inch.

"Please follow me, Mr. Jones," she said with a small nod. She escorted Hannibal down the hall, which took two turns before ending at a closed office door. When she turned to wave him inside, her smile was as cordial as when he first saw her.

Blair's office was laid out in three areas. To Hannibal's right a sofa and love seat in soft beige formed a conversation area. On his left, a round table and five steel chairs seemed to constitute a business area. The control center was dead ahead.

The desk was no deeper than an arm's length, with a stack of four shelves on each end. Wings on each side formed a "U" shape, and each wing held a keyboard and flat screen. Papers were stacked neatly on each of the shelves and across the desk. In the midst of this power cockpit, Blair looked up at Hannibal with one eyebrow raised in curiosity.

"I'm impressed Jones. Nobody gets past Margaret, you know?"

"You just have to know how to ask," Hannibal said.

"So do we have progress?" Blair asked, then as an afterthought, "Oh, have a seat."

Blair waved toward the loveseat, but Hannibal stepped toward the round table. "I had a question, but first I wanted to clear my next step in the investigation."

Blair nodded, and then refocused on his right hand computer. Hannibal stood still while Blair finished whatever he was in the middle of. He appeared uaware of how rude most people would find his actions. Less than two minutes later he stood and walked toward the table. He pulled a chair out, spun it, and sat straddling the seat.

"Okay, what can I do to help you find our man?"

Hannibal stood behind a chair, his hands on the corners of the back. "Well, the obvious things didn't get me anywhere. Our boy Rod is clearly working at not being traced. The most obvious and best lead has got to be your neighbor, Ms. LaPage. But Anita told me you were members of the same clubs and such. Wanted to make sure I wouldn't be causing any trouble if I questioned her."

Blair lowered his eyelids to half-mast and pushed out his lips. His thinking pose, Hannibal assumed. "No, I don't think you're likely to cause any repercussions. She probably thinks I'm crass and crude already, so what harm can you do to my rep, you know?" At Hannibal's quizzical expression, Blair added, "Marquita LaPage is old money, Mr. Jones. I'm a tech driven upstart. We go to the same clubs and eat in the same restaurants, but we live in different worlds. If you think you can get anything out of her that will lead us to this Rod and Anita's valuables, go for it."

"Good. I'll be interviewing her when I leave here."

"Fine," Blair said, his eyes straying briefly to his computers. "Now, you had questions?"

"Just a couple," Hannibal said.

"Me first," Blair said. "What five letter word become shorter when you add two letters to it?"

What?"

"Nevermind. Just a puzzle. You're the man who likes puzzles. Anyway, what did you want to ask me?"

Hannibal watched Blair's eyes as he spoke. "First, who knows I'm pursuing this investigation?"

"You, me and Anita," Blair said without hesitation. Then he added, "Henry of course. That's it."

Hannibal leaned forward a bit and tilted his head a little to one side. "One last question, Mr. Blair. Are you having me followed?"

"Excuse me?"

"I think someone's tracking me. If I'm right, this person is very good."

"Why would I have you followed?" Blair asked.

"Good question."

Blair ran his fingers through the straw thatch on his head and stood. He walked around the room, becoming animated again. "You know, Mr. Jones, I think I said before that you and I are in the same business. But it's more than mere data mining. We both deal in trust, you know?"

"Trust?" Hannibal leaned back. "I thought it was information."

Blair wandered like a moth in a roomful of candles. "Information? People are already being bombarded with information. It's all there at their fingertips these days. They just don't know what to do with it. One piece of software I'm working on right now retains, analyzes and orders people's financial records. It will detect warning signs and alert you when there's a credit card with a lower interest rate you could qualify for, or when you can get a cheaper mortgage or car loan. Things everyone wants, you know? But for it to work, you've got to trust me to have your credit history and financial records."

"I don't ask clients for credit histories."

Blair swooped in toward the table at a pace that made Hannibal shrank back. "No, but for you to help them, they have to trust you with their darkest secrets, things they'd tell no one else. That's because more often than not, trouble comes from keeping secrets. Am I right?"

Hannibal thought about Anita's leather collar and nodded.

Blair seized his small victory with both hands. "Yes. The whole point of the services we offer is trust. The trust of the client is the number one business asset of our age. And I wouldn't have hired you if I didn't trust you to do what you need to do to get the job done. Besides, six years as a cop in New York City, half that time as a city detective, then almost eight years in the secret service. Who could be more trustworthy?"

"How?"

"I told you I checked you out, didn't I? Anyway, the bottom line is, if I thought I needed to have you followed I'd have just hired somebody else, you know?"

Hannibal nodded again as he stood. "Yes, I guess I do know. Sorry, but I had to ask."

"I understand," Blair said. His voice had calmed back down and he sounded like the little boy again, instead of the fanatic he was just seconds before. "So, is Marquita LaPage your next stop?"

"Right. She should be able to give me a lead as to Mantooth's path after he left the area."

"Well I hope she's home," Blair said. "I heard the place was up for sale."

At the door Hannibal paused and turned. "Shorter," he said.

"Excuse me?"

"The five letter word that becomes shorter when you add two letters to it," Hannibal said. "The word is short."

* * * * *

The sun was sliding down the left side of the sky when Hannibal pulled into Marquita LaPage's driveway, throwing a series of long black shadows across the landscape. He was barely two miles from Blair's townhouse, yet the difference was startling. While Blair's home looked smaller than it was from the outside, Hannibal was now surrounded by detached houses making a big outward showing of their size. Marquita LaPage's colonial crouched behind six wide white columns whose shadows pooled to his right, to become one thick slash of darkness reaching to the neighbor's yard.

Hannibal parked behind the silver Lexus and stepped out onto the asphalt. The sprawling, three-level structure stood proudly on its corner, yet the signs of neglect jumped out at Hannibal as he headed for the door. The lawn had not been mown or edged in quite a while, giving it a disheveled appearance relative to the yards on either side, which appeared to suffer from compulsive neatness. The mailbox flap was ajar, unable to hold back the crowd of neglected envelopes. And the rows of violets along the path to the three steps were gasping for water.

The doorbell gave a merry chime, but nearly thirty seconds of silence followed. Hannibal was reaching for the button again when the door swung inward. His first reaction to the vision before him was that he might have awakened a ghost.

The woman half hidden by the door wore dull platinum blonde hair that accented her apparently bloodless skin. The exposed arm was rail thin, and he could see her ribs through her silk dressing gown. Her makeup was smudged, as if it had

61

been applied yesterday or maybe the day before but never washed off. Somewhere underneath the lipstick and mascara lay a pert nose, high cheekbones and full, pouting lips. If not for the bags under her eyes and her haggard expression she might have been beautiful. As it was, this pale specter gave him a chill. Judging from her bulging eyes and trembling lower lip, he scared her even more.

"Ms. LaPage?" Hannibal asked. The woman nodded. "My name is Hannibal Jones. May I come in for a moment?" Her light brown eyes looked around him as if she hoped someone was standing behind him. "I just want to speak with you for a moment." She tried a tentative smile and Hannibal returned it.

"What's this about?" she asked, with an accent Hannibal didn't recognize.

"It's about a man you know. Rod Mantooth."

On hearing the name, Marquita stiffened and a series of emotions moved across her face too quickly for Hannibal to identify them individually. Surprise was certainly among them, and fear and something like resignation. Then she forced a bigger smile and tilted her head in a welcoming bow.

"Of course. Please come in, Mr. Jones."

Marquita led him through a broad living room into a plush sitting room. White carpets appeared to cover the floors of the house everywhere Hannibal could see. The furniture was a soft cowhide and hand-rubbed maple. But dusting had been left too long undone, and the carpet had not been vacuumed in a while. The air conditioner labored more noisily than it should, as if it had not been serviced in months.

Marquita never spoke another word as she waved Hannibal onto a sofa in the sitting room and busied herself at the bar across the room. The sofa smelled of spilled bourbon, probably the same stuff Marquita was filling two tumblers with.

"You needn't pour for me, ma'am," Hannibal said. Marquita gave him a quizzical look, pushed the second glass aside, and tipped her head back to swallow half the contents of the first. Then she walked very slowly to stand in front of Hannibal, bowed low and smiled as seductively as she could.

She was not quite steady on her feet, but she tried hard to sway her hips anyway.

"So, Hannibal eh? That's rather an unusual name," she said in what sounded almost like a French lilt to him, or like the Haitians he knew. "So what would you like, Hannibal? Maybe a little dance first? I dance well, they tell me. Or do you have a favorite game? Or perhaps you'd just like to go right to it?" Her arm rose with surprising grace toward the stairs.

Hannibal rose to his feet, his palms faced toward his hostess. "Look, I don't think you understand."

Marquita took two steps backward, her eyes darting from side to side, confusion or nervousness making her lick her lips. "Wait. What did I do? You can't... I mean you have to at least tell me what I did wrong."

Hannibal's mouth became very dry and his stomach lurched. Marquita's behavior was bringing back an ugly recent memory. "Oh my God. Did he do it to you too? Look, just sit down a minute."

His voice must have been more menacing than he had intended, because Marquita dropped to her knees in apparent terror. Her back was straight, her legs spread wide, and he could see she wore nothing under her nightgown. Her head was raised, but her eyes would not look high enough to see his face. This must be a practiced pose, he thought. But he had to be sure.

"You know the rules, don't you? Even after number three."

Instantly she replied, "I trust my master. Above all else, my only desire is to please my master. I am always in complete submission to my master."

He waved a hand, and Marquita stopped talking. She sat there on the floor, her feet on either side of her hips, looking almost straight ahead, as if waiting for instructions. As gently as he could, Hannibal grasped her upper arms and very slowly lifted her to her feet. Here skin was cold and clammy.

"Ms. LaPage. I know what you must think, but I'm not here as a friend of Rod Mantooth's."

Marquita's eyes spent a few seconds trying to focus before she asked, "Master didn't send you?"

"No, ma'am. I just wanted to ask you a few questions about him."

"Then, you're not like the others? He didn't send you?"

"Others?" Hannibal asked. "Other men have come to see you?"

"Oh no." Marquita's face twisted into a strained expression that looked to Hannibal more ghastly than the faces he had seen on men who suffered violent deaths. "Oh my God no. You're not one of them? And I just..." She was babbling, her face bright red with what he guessed must be shame. At least he knew that was what he would be feeling.

"Relax," Hannibal said. "I'm not here to hurt you. You're safe now."

"Safe?' Marquita said in a far away voice. "Look what I've become. How did I ever come to this? How can I be safe now, after what I've become?"

Hannibal thought she was about to break away from him, just before she passed out in his arms.

-7-

Standing and watching. Hannibal hated it. He hated the feeling of frustration and helplessness. He hated not being able to take action. Standing and watching was a role for someone else. But at that moment, it was all he could do.

Dr. Quincy Roberts stepped away from Marquita's bed, watching her chest rise and fall with deep, slow breaths. He eased out of the room past Hannibal who stood in the doorway and softly closed the door after Roberts passed.

"Thank you again for coming," Hannibal said, following Roberts to the living room.

"I'm not sure why I did." Roberts was old enough to be Hannibal's father, but even through his thick glasses one could still see a youthful gleam in his eye. In fact, his thick gray beard would have given him a Santa Clause look if his cheeks weren't so pale. He wore a golf shirt and casual slacks with Docksiders. Hannibal wondered if he had called the man from his boat or the golf course.

"You came because you knew I was desperate," Hannibal said, lowering himself to the sofa, "and because you knew you were needed."

Roberts fished a pipe out of one pocket and a lighter out of another. "And perhaps because you saved one of my patients from being wrongly convicted of murder not long ago. I gave her a mild sedative to help her rest for a while. But that woman needs an internist as much as a psychiatrist. She's in bad shape."

Hannibal threw up his hands. "She was hysterical, man. When she passed out I figured the cause was more emotional than physical. Believe me, she's been assaulted mentally and emotionally. But that's not what you meant by her being in bad shape, was it? What kind of physical problems are we talking about?"

Roberts got his pipe lit and sucked on it hard a couple of times before speaking. "Well, for one thing she's a little dehydrated. I suspect that's from using alcohol in place of water. And I think she's malnourished too."

"There are lots of women that thin around here, doc." Hannibal relaxed for the first time in an hour. It could have been the cherry scent of Roberts' tobacco or Roberts' own calming manner, but whatever the cause, his shoulders lowered and his breathing deepened. "And those problems sound pretty easy to fix. You just check her into a hospital for a day or two..."

"I can't do that," Roberts said. "And what did you mean, assaulted mentally? It looked to me like she was alone here."

"She was when I arrived," Hannibal said. "But she's terrified of something, or someone."

"A typical client of yours, if I remember."

Hannibal sighed aloud. "She's not my client, but I think she's been abused by the same man who practically enslaved a client of mine. I'm looking for this guy, and she might be my best lead when she wakes up. She's hysterical, and you said she's in rough shape physically. That part's probably all self-induced, right? So why can't you admit her someplace safe?"

Roberts chuckled, pushing puffs of smoke out between his teeth. "She's not my patient, my friend. She's an adult and there's no evidence that she's in any immediate danger to herself or others. I can help her if she decides to check herself into a facility when she wakes up."

"That's not likely. She's ashamed of what she's done with this man, or for this man. I don't think she'll want to go anywhere. But I sure don't think she should be here alone, not after this."

"I agree she would benefit from some looking after," Roberts said. "Without actually speaking with her, I'd say there's evidence that she really doesn't care enough to take care of herself right now."

Hannibal stood, hands in pockets. "So, we seem to have ourselves a situation here."

Roberts rose as well, nodding. "No, my friend. I believe you have yourself a situation. You are not responsible for this woman in any way. But I sense that you don't see it that way."

"I found her like this," Hannibal said, waving to take in the whole house. "How can I leave her like this? How can you?"

Roberts was already moving toward the door, as if he was afraid he might get stuck in the house. "Here is what I will do. Give me a call tomorrow and let me know what the situation is. If she is willing, I will stop back out and check up on her, see if she wants my help. And by the way, you'll receive a bill for this house call."

"Of course." Hannibal followed Roberts to the door, and shook his hand as he opened it. "I really do appreciate your responding to my panicked call. And I guarantee you won't get stuck for a bill. My client has deep pockets, and I consider this part of the expenses on my case. He'll see that this was necessary for me to follow the trail."

"Good luck with your new charge," Roberts said. "Me, I may just get home to the Mrs. in time for dinner. I'll check on Ms. LaPage in the morning and see if perhaps she does want to be checked into a facility for better rest."

As the door swung closed, Hannibal muttered, "Dinner" and pulled out his cell phone. After listening to his own answering machine message, he called Cindy's house and listened to hers. Next, he called her office, still not sure exactly what he was going to tell her. He knew he couldn't just leave Marquita's house, but the reasons seemed too complex to put in order.

This time the phone only rang three times. When the connection was made it had the hollow echo of a speakerphone, and he wondered if he would even need an explanation.

"Hey honey," Cindy said. "I'm almost out of here, honest. Just wrapping up some stuff and I know I'll be a little late but I'll get there."

Well, at least she recognized his number on her phone's caller I.D. screen. Relief and irritation played tug-of-war in Hannibal's mind. Maybe that's why his voice came out flat and neutral.

"Listen, sweetheart, maybe it's just as well you're still at the office. The case has already produced some odd twists, and, well, this would be a bad time to leave."

"I understand, baby. That's the way it goes with two busy professionals, eh? Well, let's just make it tomorrow, okay?"

Just like that. No questions, not even an expression of disappointment. He could be a hundred miles away with another woman for all she knew. In fact, he was with another woman. It was irritating.

"Yeah, okay, tomorrow," Hannibal said.

"Okay, hon, let's both get back to work. Love you."

Like that, she was gone. Hannibal dropped his phone in a jacket pocket. Whether he liked it or not, at least he understood her dedication. Why, on the other hand, was he still at Marquita's house? She was not a client, nor had she even asked for help. As Roberts had said, she was an adult who was responsible for herself. Why couldn't he just walk away and return to his own life?

He turned a slow circle, taking in the undusted furniture, mail piled on a small table and the kitchen cluttered with several days worth of dishes. The dished had clearly been left where they were used, many still holding bits of food. She may be responsible for herself, but he could see that she couldn't take care of herself right now.

Shaking his head at himself, Hannibal pulled off his gloves and went to the kitchen. The floor was sticky in spots, but he ignored it and started stacking dishes in the sink. One job at a time, he told himself. Scraping food off plates and putting them in the dishwasher, Hannibal wondered if his motivations were just selfish. He had to face it. He didn't know Marquita LaPage at all, certainly not enough to care about her. But he knew staying there made him feel better, and that leaving would make him feel like crap. He also knew that he wouldn't think much of a man who could casually walk away from a sick, abused woman.

He turned as a new noise captured his attention. The sound started low, but built up in seconds. It would have been a scream if it weren't interrupted so often by a panting breath. Hannibal wondered what would happen if Marquita hyperventilated.

He raced to the bedroom but hesitated at the door. When he opened it, the odor pushed him back for a moment. He recoiled from the distinctive smell of unwashed clothes, spilled liquor and something more. Something sour. As he approached the bed he saw the source. Marquita lay face up on a king size bed, eyes on him, her lips barely an inch from a pool of fresh vomit. The shame he had seen in her eyes before was more evident now.

Hannibal walked around to the other side of the bed, placed his hand on her stomach and pulled her toward him, away from the mess. When she turned, she rolled easily into his arms. He sat on the edge of the bed, cradling her like a frightened child.

"Take it easy," he said. "You're not alone and you're not going to be. In fact, I think we're going to make you well."

Her skin was clammy, her eyes wild, her voice raspy as she weakly tried to pull away. "Stop it. Stop being so nice to me. Treat me like I deserve. Ain't you never seen a Cajun whore before?"

Only then did Hannibal register the golden tint beneath the paleness of her skin. It seemed irrelevant at the moment, except perhaps to pinpoint a pattern of behavior for Mr. Rod Mantooth. If Hannibal was right about that, it was just one more reason to hate this man he'd never met.

In the time it took him to form that thought, Hannibal realized that Marquita was asleep. Her head rested on his left forearm and her breasts heaved against his thigh. He knew she might awaken at any moment, and would need watching all night. He also knew he needed to find this Mantooth fast, and that meant being alert tomorrow. While Marquita settled into a soft snore, he pulled out his cell phone and pushed buttons. When he made the connection he could hear the sounds of people working at partying. The club was hopping for a Wednesday night. Under the circumstances, he dispensed with most of the pleasantries.

"Sarge, this is Hannibal."

"I recognized the voice, man. I'm working you know. What's up?"

"Listen, can you get someone to cover for you for the rest of the night?"

"Are you kidding?" Sarge asked. "Man, I just got here."

"I know, but I need your help, brother. Got a job here that's liable to take all night, but it calls for a man who can be tough and who knows how to go easy too."

"You mean right now?" Sarge growled into the phone.

"It's pretty important. Besides, how much can they need a bouncer on a Wednesday night?"

When they met, Sarge was homeless, hanging at the shelter where Hannibal volunteered. Sarge had stood with him, fought with him against junkies, winos, and in he end, the drug dealer whose living depended on a crack house. Today Sarge had both a home and a steady job, but Hannibal knew the risks they faced together bonded them in a way that made Sarge's answer absolutely predictable.

"Where you at?"

After sharing Marquita's address, Hannibal considered the present challenge of cleaning her up. He decided it had to be a multi-step process. First, he lowered her head to the relatively clean pillow. He pulled the down comforter from her bed and folded it twice lengthwise on the floor. Next, he lifted her from the bed, startled at how light she was, and lowered her sleeping form onto the comforter. Then he pulled the sheets from the bed. In the fully finished basement he found both a laundry area and a linen closet. After shoving the soiled sheets into the washer he went back upstairs, made the bed and transferred his charge to the fresh, crisp sheets. Her faint moan implied that even in her sleep she appreciated the difference.

The next step was to clean out the available poisons. Starting with a sweep of the bedroom and progressing to a full circuit of the house, Hannibal picked up a veritable saloon's worth of bottles, most of which had been opened but only one or two already empty. The woman was partial to serious whiskey - Jack Daniels, Yukon Jack, Jim Beam, Chivas Regal, and Courvoisier. He found a trash bag under the kitchen sink and filled it with the bottles.

As he opened the medicine cabinet in the master bathroom, Hannibal wondered if his actions would meet Dr. Roberts' definition of compulsive behavior. Here he was, scanning a total stranger's shelves for drugs that might offer themselves to abuse. He supposed she could sue him for emptying prescription bottles into her toilet. Had she asked for a guardian angel? The truth was that he had shoved himself into her life without invitation, or even permission. His internal monologue halted when his fingers wrapped around an unmarked vial. It contained white pills, marked "Roche" on one side with a small number "2" under the word.

The doorbell jerked his head around.

"Sarge," he said, pocketing the bottle as he jogged down the stairs. A grim face greeted him when he opened the door. Sarge stood in a black, sleeveless tee shirt and jeans, a baseball bat in his right fist.

"All right, what's the problem here?"

Movement spotted over Sarge's shoulder froze Hannibal's answer in his throat. Was someone actually crouching behind the car parked across the street? Hannibal pulled Sarge inside while his left hand eased toward the holster under is right arm. The world became very still, except for the stuttering crackle of crickets. He slipped his sunglasses from his face, staring hard at the BMW across the street. After a full minute of staring his eyes ached, but he saw no signs of life. Irritated with himself, he drew Sarge inside and closed the door.

"Man, something's sure got you jumpy," Sarge said. "What

the hell is going on?"

"I'm sorry," Hannibal said, heading for the kitchen. "I thought I saw something. Been thinking I was being followed, but not really sure."

Hannibal pulled a glass out of a cabinet and rinsed it several times before filling it with water. It carried the sharp taste of chlorine and fluoride and all the other things they add to city water to kill germs and discourage human consumption. While he drank, Sarge looked around the kitchen, and then glanced into the living room.

"Maid's day off?"

"Maid's month off I think," Hannibal said after his drink. "The woman who lives here, she's in bad shape. She needs looking after, and I needed somebody who'd stay here all night and baby-sit. Somebody I could trust to stay alert, and could also trust to not do anything to harm her."

Sarge nodded his comprehension. "Bad shape? In what way?"

To answer, Hannibal waved Sarge to follow him. They mounted the spiraling staircase in silence, as if they were walking through a library, or a morgue. At the bedroom, Hannibal eased the door open. A narrow shaft of light fell across Marquita's bed. Now that she was finally resting, her features appeared delicate, frail, the way Hannibal imagined Snow White when he was a child.

"She's been abused, buddy," Hannibal whispered. "Physically. Emotionally. Sexually if I understand the story. The man responsible is the man I've got to find to help my client. Can you watch over her for the night?"

"God, she looks so helpless. Fragile, like a doll, you know?"

As if she sensed that she was being talked about, Marquita's eyes fluttered open for a moment. Hannibal watched Sarge's rough face soften as he stared into Marquita's fawn colored eyes. He seemed to make a connection there. Perhaps it was the empathy of a man, homeless not long ago, who could see this woman as downtrodden despite her apparent financial status. While they watched, the ghost of a smile touched the edge of Marquita's lips and she slipped back into sleep.

"Don't you worry," Sarge said. "I'll take care of her."

-8-

FRIDAY

Hannibal's tee shirt was soaked by the time he was approaching the end of his morning run. He felt a little stitch in his left side, but nowhere near enough to slow him down. It was a good day. He had started on time, and would finish a little early. He took a perverse pride in his own anal retentive nature, suspecting that certain people he waved to five mornings every week used him to determine whether or not they were on time for work.

It was getting harder to keep his breathing quiet, but he tried anyway, relishing the morning sounds and not wanting to blot them out of his own ears. Anacostia was one of the roughest of urban inner city areas, yet it still offered an early morning symphony for those awake to hear it. Even there, birds chirped and whistled and sang at the edge of dawn. However, the main theme there was carried by groaning garbage trucks, and the taxicab horn section. The overhead whine of jet engines replaced the woodwinds, and all the sounds melded together in a way neither nature nor an orchestra could imitate.

As he reached his own block Hannibal slowed to a walk. The view to his home was a path of brick buildings, cracked sidewalks and broken bottles. This area of the nation's capital was rundown and generally impoverished, yet it tried hard to cling to its dignity. Hannibal loved his neighborhood because it was a real neighborhood. He knew his neighbors, and his neighbors knew him.

As rough as it was, it was a neighborhood in transition, within a city in transition. Ahead lay a few blocks of abandoned or condemned buildings, many still inhabited. But a few block to his left stood a series of new, high-priced town houses. If he ran in the other direction, crossed the Anacostia Bridge and went a few blocks up Potomac Avenue he would bump into the congressional office buildings that flank the Capitol, less than two miles away. In Washington, it was an easy walk from the halls of power to the abandoned halls of slum apartments.

Having almost regained his breath, Hannibal leaned on the sandstone banister and mounted the steps up to the stoop at number 2313. Hannibal remembered the first time he walked up those steps. The building was a crack house then, and the owner had paid him to flush the squatters out. He looked down at the dark stain on the stoop left there by his own blood after his first attempt to do his job. He had returned with a small team of men gathered from the homeless shelter where he volunteered. Sarge and the others had helped him take the building back. Ray, a former client, had helped too. Afterward, he had decided to stay there, and the others did too. They had fought for the building and found a home.

Closing the outer door behind him, Hannibal glanced to the right out of habit to read his own name on his office door. Then he walked left around the central stairway. He unlocked and opened the fourth of five doors down the side of the hall. Once inside he took a deep breath. It was refreshingly cool inside, since the owner had replaced the ancient boiler with a modern furnace and installed central air conditioning.

The flat wasn't luxurious, but it was just enough for Hannibal. Big, sliding double doors stood in for walls between the rooms. With all of them open he could see through his two extra rooms to his bedroom at the front of the building. To his right, past the bathroom door, his small but functional kitchen waited. For just a moment he debated with himself whether breakfast or a shower should come first, but the shower won out.

* * * * *

After arranging to meet with Anita in the afternoon, Hannibal drove to Marquita's house. Pulling into the driveway around ten o'clock he was met with a few surprises. First, the sprinklers were running. Then he noticed that the lawn had been mowed. Curiosity drove him to open the mailbox. It was empty. Even greater curiosity spurred Hannibal to the door. Five seconds after he pushed the doorbell, Sarge pulled the door open.

"Hey, Hannibal. Good to see you man. The doc's already here, doing an exam on her."

Hannibal followed Sarge into a house that was transformed. The carpet had been vacuumed, maybe shampooed. The mail was stacked neatly on an end table. Swiping a black-gloved finger across the entertainment center proved it had been dusted.

"So I guess you kept busy through the night," Hannibal said.

"Well, they taught me in the Marines to keep my quarters ship shape," Sarge said. "The galley gave me the most trouble. I don't know how the woman could stand to get food in that place. Anyway, I figured she'd find it easier to get back to normal if she wasn't living in a crap hole."

Hannibal lowered himself onto the edge of the sofa, almost afraid to ruin the house's showroom appearance. "You did quite a job. Did you get any sleep at all?"

"I caught a few winks off and on up in the bedroom."

Hannibal cocked an eyebrow. "Her bedroom?"

Sarge shook his head with a grin. "It ain't what you're thinking. Markie woke up screaming in the night. The night terrors, you know, like I've seen alcoholics get."

"Markie?"

"That's what her friends call her," Sarge said, dropping into the recliner. As he spoke, his fingertips slowly rubbed his left palm. "We got to talking a bit. She was too scared to stay in there by herself so I sat with her a while. She dozed off and on, and so did I. You were right, buddy. She sure as hell didn't need to be out here by herself last night."

Hannibal nodded. "And she dug her nails pretty deeply into your hand, I see. You're a good man, Sarge."

"She's a good woman," Sarge said. "Hannibal, how could a man break a woman down like that?"

Before Hannibal could answer he heard his named called from upstairs. He and Sarge stood immediately and jogged up the stairs to Marquita's bedroom. The door was ajar, but Hannibal pushed slowly on his way in. Marquita was under the comforter, just as he had left her, but nothing else was the same. Both the disorder and the smell he had faced the first time he entered the room were gone. Roberts perched on the edge of the bed, speaking to her in hushed tones. Marquita had regained a little color and Hannibal could see a hint of African heritage, although her background was overwhelmingly French, judging by her features. She looked more centered than she had the night before, but her knit brow told Hannibal that it was still hard for her to focus.

"Now, will you be all right in here alone, while I go outside to talk to Mr. Jones?" Roberts asked. "He's a friend."

"I know," Marquita said, smiling for a second in Hannibal's direction. "He's the man who was here when I collapsed. He was very sweet to me when he could have taken advantage."

"Yes, but we need to speak out in the hall for a moment."

"I'll be fine, doctor, if Archibald can sit with me for a little while."

Hannibal's face jerked toward Sarge. "Archibald?"

Sarge raised a finger in front of Hannibal's face, his course voice bristling. "You don't never need to call me that, hear?"

"Hey," Hannibal raised his palms toward Sarge. "I'm the last guy who'd make fun of anybody's name, man."

Still, he was chuckling as he backed out of the room. Roberts followed him into the next room and pushed the door closed behind himself. Hannibal waved Roberts into the vanity chair while he stood rather than sitting on the bed.

"So how's she doing, Doc? Is she checking herself into a nice rest home?"

Oh, I don't think so," Roberts said. "She's still in rather bad shape, but she's pretty resilient, and if she keeps drinking lots of water to flush the alcohol out of her system I think she'll be okay." He looked up at Hannibal, the weight of his knowledge dragging his face down. "Someone used this girl badly, in ways I don't see too often. Too many men, too many ways, and there are signs that when the men couldn't do it to her themselves they used other things. And there are strap marks. She was really lucky."

Hannibal shook his head. "Doesn't sound too lucky to me."

"I mean lucky you came along when you did," Roberts said. "She's hideously undernourished and dehydrated. If she had stayed in this house one more day, not eating and self-medicating with alcohol to dull her pain, who knows what would have happened to her. It was a fortunate turn of fate that brought you to her door before she was too weak or too drunk to answer the bell."

"Yeah, timing is everything," Hannibal said, thrusting his hands into his pockets. His hand hit a small bottle there. He pulled it out and, on an impulse, handed it to Roberts.

"Say, Doc, I found these in Marquita's medicine cabinet. Something dangerous? If she was trying to commit suicide, maybe she should be under observation."

Roberts shook a couple of the round pills into his hand and flipped one over to see the markings. His bushy white eyebrows rose.

"No, people don't try to hurt themselves with flunitazepam. They leave it to someone else"

"Fluni-what?"

Roberts looked up and Hannibal with new weariness on his face. "Do you know the more common name Rohypnol?"

"Is that the same as roofies?" Hannibal asked. "The so-called date rape drug?"

"That's it," Roberts said, dropping the pills back into their bottle. "It does have sedative or hypnotic effects. Rohypnol really can incapacitate a girl; prevent her from resisting sexual assault, for instance. One of these is as powerful as ten Valium and can keep a person compliant for eight hours or more. I have to believe someone was using these to keep Ms. LaPage in a compliant frame of mind."

"That's sick," Hannibal said. "To sneak drugs into a girl's food or drink to take advantage of her?" He paced from one corner of the room to another. The sun coming in the window was annoying him.

"You found these in her medicine cabinet?" Roberts asked. Hannibal nodded. "Well then, I hardly think they were sneaking them into her."

Hannibal stopped, mid-pace, and turned to stare at Roberts. "You mean you think she knew? Yeah, of course, she must have. Well, it makes sense I guess, if you want to be controlled. But that's crazy. Why would anyone accept being drugged like that?"

"Ah, Hannibal," Roberts said. "This sort of naiveté ill becomes you. People will allow you to do anything once you've gained their trust. Whoever was here, whoever did these things to Ms. LaPage, He would appear to be a master at gaining women's trust."

Trust, Hannibal thought. Blair called it the number one business asset of our age. And maybe it was the number one asset of the sexual predator as well.

"What do we do now, Doc?"

"Well, she'll need some looking after," Roberts said, standing, "but I don't think there's a medical solution for her problems. When she's regained her strength I would recommend psychiatric counseling. If she's interested, I'd be happy to have her as a patient."

* * * * *

The bedroom door was open just an inch or two, and Hannibal stood in front of it for a moment before pushing it wider. Sarge sat on the far side of the bed beside Marquita who was propped up on a collection of pillows and wrapped in a soft yellow silk robe. A shaft of light from the window cast a warm glow around her. Despite obvious exhaustion, she seemed animated as she chatted in low tones with Sarge. Color was already returning to her face. Her hair was shiny and now that it was brushed out it turned out to be longer than Hannibal had realized. It was hard to believe she looked this good, considering what Dr. Roberts had said about her health. Could one night's sleep make that big a difference?

As he pushed the door open, Sarge and Marquita turned toward him. She presented the smile of a practiced southern hostess but her hand clutched Sarge's a little tighter.

"It is good to see you again, Mr. Jones. Is the doctor gone?"

"Yes ma'am. He says you're doing much better. I have to say you sure look a lot better than you did just last night. Do you think you're up to talking to me for a while?"

"She's pretty worn out, Hannibal," Sarge said. "What do you need with her, anyway?"

Had Sarge been a canine, that question would have been a low warning growl. Hannibal hadn't expected this protective stance, but it was clear from Sarge's body language that he was standing guard over the girl. Hannibal smiled and pulled the chair from the vanity to sit close to the bed. "I have a client who had dealings with the man who hurt Marquita. I've been hired to find him, and she might be able to help me do that."

"You know, buddy, I don't know if this is stuff she needs to be talking about right now." Sarge had puffed his chest out and squared his shoulders as he spoke. Hannibal was sure it was an unconscious response, the subtle signals he had learned to send in order to get his way as a bouncer without having to get physical with drunks. There was no percentage in conflict with Sarge. Hannibal kept his focus on Marquita LaPage.

"Ma'am, I know this other girl's problems aren't your concern, but I'm going to ask you to think about your life since Rod Mantooth left here. From what I saw, you've been punishing yourself and here's why I think you've been doing that. I think you've been waiting for him to come back. And I think you hate yourself for wanting him to return. You're doing everything he told you to do, hoping he'll walk back in that door, but you know damn well that's not what you ought to want."

As Hannibal spoke, Marquita's soft brown eyes widened and her breath became fast but shallow gasps. When she finally looked down, she appeared on the verge of tears. Long blonde tresses dropped over her lowered face like sheer curtains closing on a window that was too easy to see through.

"Stop it, man," Sarge said, squeezing her hand. "Can't you see what this is doing to her? Besides, that's all bullsh..." Sarge's eyes cut toward her for a second, "that's all bull, man. The last thing in the world Marquita wants is for that bastard to come back here."

"Uh-huh." Hannibal nodded his skepticism, his lips drawn in against his teeth. "Right. So. Where's the collar, Ms. LaPage?"

Marquita shook her head with such violence that her hair sashaying in front of her like a dancer's skirt. Then she slowly looked up through the sheer wall of hair.

He asked again. This time it was just above a whisper. "Where's your collar, Ms. LaPage?"

For a frozen moment, the only movement in the room was the rising of tiny dust motes in the shaft of light falling on the bed. Those bits of matter were so small that they needed only the heat of the sun to put them into mindless flight. For humans, weighed down by guilt and pain and self-loathing, movement can be considerably harder. Eventually, Marquita moved her head to the side, indicating the small table beside the bed on Hannibal's side. A small sniffle came from behind her hair, and three drops of her soul rode gravity down to thump into the comforter.

Hannibal's hand moved very slowly to the table, and quietly slid the drawer open. From inside he lifted her hated prize. It was gray suede with a silver buckle and tiny rhinestone studs along its length.

"What the hell?" Sarge said, his face contorted the way it would be if he drank sour milk. "You didn't actually wear that thing, did you?"

Marquita's head moved slowly up and down. Hannibal tossed the collar on the bed.

"You kept it close at hand. Symbolic of his ownership right? Evidence that you belong to him. But he abandoned you didn't he? Cast you aside. Was a part of you hoping he'd appear at the door and require you to wear that collar again? No, more important question. Aren't you tired of loving and hating this man, this life? Would you like to stop wondering if he'll come back here?"

When Marquita spoke, her voice was small and distant. "I am so worthless. When he was here, I existed to serve, and I was, God forgive me, I was happy in his service. I did things I never believed I could do, but it gave him pleasure and somehow that became my only goal. I can't explain. I hated him, hated myself for needing to please him." When no one responded, she looked up, using one hand to part the curtain of her hair. "How can I ever be free of this man?"

"You'll be free of him if I break his neck," Sarge said.

Hannibal didn't want to go there. "Mantooth has done bad things to other women, Ms. LaPage. He's also a thief. If I find him, I'll make sure he can't come back here. That will take the decision out of your hands."

"Hannibal can find anybody," Sarge added.

Marquita stared at the collar in front of her. She raised her hand, then made a frustrated fist and lowered it, as if she was afraid to touch the thin leather strip. "What can I do to help?"

"Atta girl," Sarge said with a smile. "The only way to get a monkey off your back is to shake it yourself." He captured her hand again and she held his up, shaking it, as if drawing strength from him. Hannibal figured Sarge for the best tower of strength he knew. She would need it, for what he was about to ask.

"Ms. LaPage," he began.

"Please call me Marquita. You may have saved my life, and that makes us too close to be so formal."

"Ms. LaPage, I need to know more about how this man works. I need to know how he met you, and how he insinuated himself into your life."

Marquita's face collapsed in on itself, as if her very muscles were at war with each other. Then she nodded her head once, quickly, as if agreeing to something. Then, to Hannibal's surprise, her eyes came up, clear and bright. When she finally spoke, it all came rushing out.

"How we met? He was a simple handyman when we met. When I moved up here, after daddy passed, I didn't know anyone. But the investments were here, you see, the real estate holdings and so on. I bought this house, but it's really too much for just me. Rod helped with the yard work, and did all that landscaping with the flowers out front. He also extended the deck."

"Jesus, babe, why'd you get such a big house anyway?" Sarge asked.

Marquita's smile returned for a moment, and her eyes sparkled as she looked at Sarge. "Ah, mon chere, I had to have space for big parties, didn't I?" Her accent, well hidden at first, began to assert itself.

"Did Mantooth attend your parties?"

"Oh, mon Deux, non! He was not of the station. But we spoke, day to day. He told me he lived nearby and did a lot of work for local residents."

Hannibal knew exactly where he was living at the time, or more accurately, whom he was living on. "And you liked him?"

"Not particularly at the time. We flirted a little. I guess I was flattered by his attention at first, but it soon became annoying. In fact I fired him."

"He do something to you?" Sarge asked. His anger was still evident in his voice and his breathing, which had become deeper.

"One day, when I returned from the grocer, he was here working on the yard. He helped me bring the packages in.

Then, when I thanked him he said he wanted a more personal thank you. He became very aggressive, and tried to kiss me, to hold me, but I pushed him away. I told him to get out, and that was the last I saw of him for a while."

"Why would you ever see him again?" Sarge asked through clenched teeth.

Marquita held his big hand in both of hers. "Because I am a stupid, worthless woman, mon chere, that's why." Then to Hannibal, she said, "I saw him in Atlantic City. This was weeks later. He was dressed in very expensive clothes this time. I had only seen him in work clothes. And he had a new car, a huge red convertible, like a Cadillac but not really."

Hannibal saw the confusion on Sarge's face and said, "It's a custom job, half Caddy, half Stingray. I've got a line on the car. So you saw him in a casino?"

"Yes. He recognized me, and walked right up, so forceful and full of himself. He was with another woman, but he just told her to go away. Then he looked me in the eye and told me I was going to be his. He had money now, and more coming, and I would belong to him."

"What did you say?" Sarge asked.

"Well naturally I..." Marquita stopped herself, her hands falling to the bed between her covered legs. "Well the truth is, I found it rather exciting. This rough, tough man declaring that he would have me. But I walked away from him. That was on a Friday night. And the very next day, here he was at my door with flowers and tickets to a show, doing it the right way. I don't know why I went with him. There was something about him that made it hard to say no."

"Yes, I keep hearing that," Hannibal said. He didn't mean to be unkind, and he regretted the remark as soon as he made it. "How long did you date?"

Marquita became quiet for a moment. The rising sun shifted its beam of light lower in the room, taking the spotlight off Marquita. Without that glow she now looked more like an ordinary, vulnerable woman. But now the light was on her hand, locked in Sarge's at the edge of the bed.

"There was no dating. Not really. We came here that same night. I didn't intend to invite him in but he came in anyway. We drank. We kind of... well, he spent the night, you know. Then he..."

"You don't have to do this," Sarge said.

"He was just here, and he never left. He just took my life over. At first, I admit it; it felt good in a way to have someone take over. To have no responsibilities except just to do what he thought was best. Then he introduced me to the lifestyle."

"The lifestyle?" Hannibal repeated, implying that he needed more of an explanation.

"He taught me how to be a submissive. And as long as I was good, did what I was told, he was so good to me and I was so happy and..."

The tears were back, but in an eerie way her breathing remained quiet. One sob shook her body. Sarge looked from Hannibal to Marquita, mouth partially open. He looked scared, an expression Hannibal had never seen on that dark, round face. He appeared to be waiting for Hannibal to do something, but Hannibal could not imagine what that could be.

"Marquita, I know this is difficult for you," Hannibal said. "But knowing any of Mantooth's contacts would be very helpful. You mentioned other men who came here?"

"Jesus, Hannibal, you don't need to go into all that," Sarge said. "And she don't need to dredge it all up again. Just go find this bastard."

"It doesn't matter," Marquita said, sending a dark laugh through her tears. "I'm sure it's no secret. He brought his friends in here and treated them. Made me treat them. And I treated them good, I'll tell you. They all had me. Every way you can imagine. Ways I never imagined before. Then after he left, he still sent them. Said if I was obedient he'd be back for me. So you see I'm just a whore, a common whore."

Marquita was about to collapse, but Sarge gathered her in one of his big arms. "You are no such thing, Markie, this guy just knows how to manipulate people. Hannibal, you just get out there and find this guy so I can kill him. You hear me? Now, where'd the doc put those pills he left you, baby?"

While Sarge tried to calm his charge with one hand and searched the end table for medicine with the other, Hannibal stood.

"Yeah. Listen, I'll check in a bit later. I'm going to get with the client and see if I can get any kind of lead on this guy. Listen, I'm sorry Marquita. I didn't mean..." Words seemed pointless, so he stopped dropping them. Sarge was right. Hannibal needed to find this man before he broke one more spirit.

* * * * *

Anita opened the door to Hannibal the way she might greet an auditor from the Internal Revenue Service. Hannibal remained pleasant, because he understood. He was now a symbol of her problems, branded with the smell of her garbage, which he was poking through out of necessity. He was a walking reminder of all the things she had done, the things almost no one else even knew about. He was used to it. People hired him to go through their garbage, even when they themselves couldn't stand the smell.

After declining her offer of coffee, Hannibal returned to the office downstairs. Anita followed, her eyes focused on him with a new intensity. He resisted an urge to tear through books and papers. Instead, he turned to Anita with a small, soft smile.

"Now, Ms. Cooper, You know I'll be discreet with everything I learn, right?"

Sensing an incoming request, she smiled, lowered her lids and gave a shallow nod. "What else do you need to know?"

"I'm convinced the prize Rod took is something your father brought from work," Hannibal said. "I've got to find out what your father was working on. To do that, I'll need to speak to people who knew your father at work."

"But I don't know any of father's coworkers."

"I know," Hannibal replied. "I need to find them, and that means I need to see correspondence. Where did he keep his letters, Anita?"

Anita lowered her head and slowly paced to one side of the room, as if searching for a memory on the floor. Then she turned, seeming to scan the bookshelves for input.

"I don't think father ever wrote letters," she said. "He had few distant friends, and he saw the people at the lab every day. I don't think he ever communicated with them from home. Unless..."

Her voice trailed off as her head turned to her right. Hannibal's eyes followed hers to the desk, and the keyboard that rested on it.

"Of course. E-mail." Hannibal started toward the chair, and just as quickly backed off. "No. You. Sit down, Anita. You know the passwords and stuff."

Anita dropped her slender frame on to the seat, her fingers poised over the keys.

"How many e-mail accounts did your father have?" Hannibal asked, standing close behind her, hands on knees.

"Only one, I'm sure."

"Well, open it up," Hannibal said.

Anita stared straight ahead at the screen. "You want me to open my father's private e-mail?"

"What, don't you know the password?"

"I do."

"Then open it."

His words prompted Anita's fingers to immediate response. She was a puppet, and it was altogether too easy to pick up her strings. Hannibal resolved to make requests of this woman, rather than demands, from then on.

As the Microsoft Outlook window blossomed onto the screen it looked at first as if Anita's father had never deleted a message. The list of received e-mails filled several pages. In some cases that would mean an exhaustive search to narrow down good targets for questioning. In this case it would not be that difficult. As Anita scanned down the list Hannibal saw that at least eighty percent of the messages were from her.

Hannibal realized that he knew next to nothing about Anita's father. The fact that he had kept every e-mail his daughter sent him from college suddenly cast him in a very different light from the overindulgent and obsessive biology nerd Hannibal had imagined up to that moment.

A tiny stifled sob returned Hannibal's focus to the woman before him. Anita had opened the last e-mail on the list and was reading her final electronic communication with her beloved father. Her head shuddered, and he sensed that he would lose her completely if he didn't force her to move on.

"All right, Anita, I need you to close that."

"Daddy loved me so much."

"Yes he did," Hannibal said. "Now, I need you to get back to the list please and put those messages in order by the date, most recent on top."

Scanning down the list, Hannibal saw only three or four other names that recurred on a regular basis. "Let's take these three. Hathaway, Gaye and Trumble. Open each e-mail you see from them. Let's see what we can find out."

Hannibal scanned the notes as quickly as he could. He wasn't looking for details, just to get a feel for the relationship. All three were apparently past coworkers, and after seeing a couple of notes from each of them it was clear that Trumble would be the first contacted.

"Why can't they all be like you, Mr. Trumble," he asked the computer monitor, "with a nice e-mail tag line with their phone number and address? It won't be so easy to find the other two."

"I don't understand," Anita said. "Can't you just push reply and e-mail them?"

"It's a nice thought," Hannibal said, "but people don't generally share information about their friends with strangers through e-mail. Still, it might not be real important if Trumble stayed in touch with all his old buddies the way your father did."

* * * * *

"I was over optimistic," Hannibal said while shaking small dots of steak sauce onto his porterhouse. "The phone call was pleasant, but it was a dead end."

"I'm sorry." Cindy brushed an errant strand of hair back and shared a broad smile that deepened her dimples. "Haven't been able to get my brain away from work. What were you saying?"

Hannibal had hoped that a good steak would get her mind off her job. Bobby Van's and one or two other places were contenders, but for his money Morton's served the best aged, top-prime porterhouse steak in the city. Or, more accurately, for their money. Cindy always insisted they go Dutch at places like this.

"Just that this lead to Anita Cooper's father didn't pan out. This Ron Trumble character." Hannibal took a deep, relaxing breath. It wasn't the expensive appointments that drew him to a restaurant like this, or the attentive service. Hannibal loved being wrapped in the red meat smell of a good steak place. The smell hinted at so much: freshly cracked peppercorns, sautéed onions, mushrooms, and the scent that arises when flames meet a well marbled cut of beef.

"Oh, yes," Cindy said, sliding her knife through her steak. "This is the girl who likes it rough."

"I don't know if that's really true. But this guy she was with sure did a number on her."

Cindy waited to speak until she finished chewing. She was beautiful in her navy blue power suit and Hannibal briefly wondered how many she owned. She wore her hair up that day, but by six o'clock a few locks always shook themselves loose from captivity. When she looked up, she seemed surprised to find him hanging on her words.

"You make her sound like a victim, and maybe she is. But trust me, my gallant knight, there are plenty of women out there just waiting for a man to come along and hand them just what you described this Rod character did. There's a market for muy macho hombres with plenty of machismo."

That doesn't justify it, he thought. Aloud he said. "Weak women."

"Maybe just different tastes." She pointed at him with her fork. "You are so limited in your view of humanity. And judgmental."

The juices filling his mouth as his teeth pushed through the black crust surrounding rare meat numbed Hannibal to what could be an insult.

"Well, no man could ever do that to you, right?"

"Oh, hell no," Cindy said, adding her lilting laugh. "Some man came at me with all that master shit, I'd have to stab him in his sleep." She put her fork down beside her plate, placing her fingers together in front of her face. "But then again..."

"Then again what?"

"Well, you know, as play," she said, her eyes wandering out the window behind Hannibal, reflecting the night-lights on Independence Avenue. "I mean, don't you ever think about, you know."

"Not sure I do know, babe."

Cindy dug into her baked potato. "Well, like, being tied to the bedposts with silk scarves. That kind of thing sometimes does sound a little exciting."

"Right, and I'm sure you're just waiting for a man to tie you down and beat you."

"Well, hold up a minute," Cindy said, warming to her subject. "Think about it. There's a world of difference between a beating and a spanking, isn't there?"

"Okay, change of subject." When her eyebrows rose he said, "I am not comfortable talking about that stuff with you. I know we'll both be working tomorrow, but where would you like to go tonight?"

Cindy's eyes went down to her plate. "Sorry sugar, I can't go out partying tonight."

He slid his hand across the tablecloth to take hers. "Worn out, hon? I know it's been a long day. Why don't we just pick up a nice bottle of wine and go back to my place?"

"No, you don't understand, baby. I've spent so much time on the DPO that my other cases have gone by the boards. I need to get back to the office for a few more hours."

"Excuse me?"

Cindy's shoulders dropped. "I am so tired. But at that firm, anybody who's not putting in ninety hours every week just isn't going to move up. And then you have stuff like this cocktail party we're all expected to be at tomorrow night. It just gets to be too much. Damn it. They think they own you. They think four hundred grand per entitles them to your whole life. And you know what? They're right. They own me."

Hannibal shook slightly, as if an unexpected glass of ice water had been thrown into his face. Was it a slip, or a jab? He had never put an actual number next to Cindy's income in his mind. That casual comment seemed to force a shift in his world. She wasn't his girl anymore. He was hers. He was the helper, the junior partner in their relationship. At that moment he remembered the ring he still carried in his pocket every day, waiting for the right moment to make his claim on her future. The ring felt far heavier now. Maybe he should wait for her to propose to him.

Right behind that thought her later words pushed through. They own me, she said. The firm came first. The money not only made her the natural alpha in their relationship, it made her firm her first priority. They took precedence. He was hers, and she was theirs.

"Fuck that."

Cindy's head snapped back, her eyes wide. He realized he was squeezing her hand harder than he had intended. And the couple at the next table looked over at him, and then quickly looked away. He had been a bit louder than he had intended too.

"Hannibal? What's wrong?"

"You tell me. Is Baylor, Truman and Ray more important than me? Than us?"

"Of course not," she said. "That's not what I meant." But he noted the second of hesitation before her statement.

"All right then, let's go," Hannibal said. "We haven't had enough alone time lately."

* * * * *

The drive back to Anacostia was much quieter than usual, at least in terms of conversation. Hannibal turned the stereo up louder than he generally did when she was aboard and played music he had never played before with Cindy in the car. He didn't know if Cindy had ever heard of Def Leppard, and didn't really care. She sat in silence against the passenger door while he drummed on the steering wheel and sang along to "Pour Some Sugar on Me."

He parked in his unofficial designated space in front of his building and walked around to help Cindy out of the car. She squeezed his hand as he walked her up the outside steps, unlocked the hall door, and marched down the hall to his own apartment door. He was just turning the knob when she finally spoke.

"It really bothers you, doesn't it?"

"The crazy hours you work?" Hannibal asked, guiding her through the living room toward the kitchen. He needed to pop that bottle of wine. She spoke again before he could reach the light switch.

"My income. I never knew. I never thought."

Hannibal turned and pressed his face very close to hers in the darkness, aware that his breathing had gotten heavy. "This is not about money."

Cindy found his light eyes in the darkness. Her respiration rate was up as well, he noticed, her breasts rising to brush against his chest. "Really. Just what is this about? The precious male ego?"

"Don't push me, Cindy."

She pushed.

He pushed back.

-9-

SATURDAY

Hannibal drove the white Volvo very slowly through Marquita's neighborhood, dodging kids who were chasing basketballs they'd thrown through driveway hoops. It was a quiet area on a Saturday morning, looking too much like a television sitcom neighborhood for his tastes. Cindy was again slumped against her door, but this time she wore a soft smile and her eyes closed. Hannibal's fingers drummed lightly on the wheel, keeping time to a George Duke tune called "Love Has No Rhyme, No Reason." He knew the truth of that.

"Listen, thanks again for agreeing to talk to Marquita," Hannibal said. "I know you've got your own giant load of work, but she can't really focus and she's got financial matters that have to be straightened out."

"I'm happy to help, Hannibal, you know that."

She looked so serene with the sun adding an extra glow to her smooth, golden complexion. He hated to say anything, but he couldn't just let it lie. He had to go there.

"Listen, about what happened last night, I wanted to..."

Cindy snapped up as if pulled by a string, thrusting a finger at his face. "Don't you dare apologize for last night. It was you, and it was real." More softly she added, "And, it was fun."

"I just don't want you to think I'm one of those guys who..."

Cindy turned toward him, resting a hand on his thigh. "Baby, please. You are the kindest, gentlest, most considerate lover on this earth. But every once in a while, a girl wants her man to just bend her over the kitchen table and give it to her like he really means it."

"Jesus, Cindy!"

"Why, I believe you're blushing, my gallant prude," Cindy said, flicking his nose with a fingertip. "Seriously, it's good sometimes to know that I turn you on so much that you just really need it."

They rode in silence for a long minute. Hannibal finally broke the quiet, thinking aloud.

"I just don't understand how a woman can let herself be treated the way Anita and Marquita were."

Staring out her window, Cindy said, "Do some research. It would really help you understand this case better."

"What do you suggest? Should I look in the library under sicko?"

"Try the internet, darling," Cindy said. "There's a whole subculture hanging out in chat rooms, doing in cyber space what they'd be afraid to do in public. Spend some time in a BDSM room. It will really open your eyes."

"A beady what?"

"BDSM," she said more slowly. "It stands for bondage, domination, submission and masochism. I think. Actually, I think the D might be for discipline, and the S could stand for sadism. Anyway, the acronym is what you'll hear most. Either way, lurking in those chat rooms might give you some insight into these girls, and this guy you're after. And who knows. You might even get turned on." She gave him that impish grin she used whenever she teased him.

Hannibal turned the wheel a bit more sharply than necessary, shaking Cindy to the other side of the car as he pulled into Marquita's driveway.

He was halfway to the door when he turned to see Cindy trailing the nails of her left hand along the Tornado's hood.

She looked up and Hannibal wondered if she could tell that he could feel her nails on his spine.

"You know, it's time for you to get a new car," she said with a sweet smile. "Something different." He knew she said it just to annoy him.

Inside, Sarge greeted Hannibal with a handshake and Cindy with a brief hug. Then he steered them into the sitting room. The drapes were pulled back, allowing sunlight to fill the room. The house smelled clean now, not the antiseptic Lysol odor of the process but the freshness that results. The quiet was no long oppressive, and when it was broken Hannibal greeted another change.

"Good morning, Hannibal," Marquita said, smiling. She was sitting on her sofa in a terrycloth robe and fuzzy slippers, one foot curled beneath her. Her skin, maybe a half tone lighter than Cindy's, shone like just-polished Brazilian Agate. She had washed and brushed her blonde hair into a gentle wave, revealing a half-inch of light brown roots at her scalp.

"Marquita, you look so much better," Hannibal said. "Whatever that old doctor's doing, it's working."

"Thank you," Marquita said with a soft smile, "but really it's all what my dear Archie is doing. I'm still not myself, but getting there. Now, who is your friend?"

Hannibal took Cindy's hand and walked her over to Marquita. "Marquita LaPage, this is Cindy Santiago. Cindy is my," a pause while he stumbled over the right label, "my lady. She's also a lawyer and a very smart woman."

Cindy took Marquita's hand. "I'd like to help if it's okay with you. I know sometimes when people have troubles, their finances don't get the attention they should."

Marquita's eyes turned away in embarrassment, but came quickly back to Cindy's. "I'm having a hard time keeping my mind on things these days, and even the tiniest decision seems to be too much for me. In truth, my affairs are a mess right now."

"Well I specialize in straightening out those messes."

"You have a kind face," Marquita said. "For a lawyer, I mean." Cindy grinned. "Oh no," Marquita rushed to say, covering her mouth. "I didn't mean it that way. Oh, mon Deux."

"It's okay." Cindy shook with inner laughter. "I know exactly what you meant, and I take it as a compliment."

"But you are so kind to offer to help me," Marquita said. "Just like Hannibal. I am a stranger to you. Why? Hannibal, why are you being so helpful?"

A short silence hung in the room, and Sarge rushed into it. "He's chasing the guy."

"Rod?" A visible shiver scampered like a rat down her spine.

"I'm trying to help another of his victims, remember?" Hannibal said. "This other woman, Anita, he moved in on her just like he did you."

Marquita looked into the carpet. "Dommage. I know what he does to us women. Did he take much of her money too?"

"Actually, he took something much more important to her. I'm not certain but I think it's medical information of some sort that her father left her. Maybe something she could patent. Could be worth a fortune."

He was largely talking to himself, still putting it all together, so he was startled when Marquita held her arm out, hand fluttering up and down like a schoolgirl anxious to answer the teacher's question. "Like a formula?"

"Well, maybe."

"Then I may have seen this prize."

* * * * *

The air out on the deck was still and dry. The sun sliced into them like an x-ray and Hannibal worried if Marquita's pallid skin might burn in minutes. But this was where she wanted to be, so he pulled off his gloves, folded his jacket over the back of his chair, and sipped his iced tea while she stared into the woods beyond her property, and stared into the past. Hannibal, Sarge and Cindy waited in their Adirondack chairs while Marquita traveled back to a worse time.

"Rod had rented a beach house up at Ocean City. He took me there a couple of times. Never alone, you understand. This particular time there were two other men there and three other girls. There were a lot of rooms, and couples would wander off in different combinations from time to time. Rod seemed to like being the ringmaster in that sort of circus. The men they would always try to think of something they hadn't made you do before. Like they were testing how far they could make us go."

Hannibal could see the setting in Marquita's face, as if she really was back in that beach house, reduced to property by the animals in Rod Mantooth's circus. He felt Cindy squeezing his hand hard, but kept his eyes on Marquita.

"The other girls. Was one of them a sister? Did you hear the name Anita?"

"No," Marquita said. "Always white girls. I was always the darkest, like the spice added to the recipe. Except for one time. There was this one, Mariah I think her name was. Polynesian, maybe, or Asian in some way. She was real trouble. Always anxious to go off with the men, wanting to push them as far as they pushed us. And too curious. That's why I remember."

"What did she do?" Sarge asked. He sat very close to Marquita, leaning in. From time to time his big hand would move toward hers, but he would hesitate as if he feared she might break if he touched her.

"There was this room. No one was allowed in there. He said he kept his money and his important papers in there. But she didn't listen. So this one time I was in the kitchen getting more beer. I drank a lot that weekend, didn't I? Anyway, I heard Rod shouting and I ran to see what it was about. The girl, she had gone into his special room. There was a computer, and I guess she liked computers or something. Anyway she was standing with one of the round discs, like a CD in her hand."

"A CD-Rom," Hannibal muttered to himself.

"Yes. It was this little golden disc. And he asked her what she was doing, or something like that, and she sort of shrugged her shoulders. He shouted that the disc could be worth ten times what she was worth. And then. Then he slapped her. God, it lifted her right off the floor and that disc spun across the room and slid almost to my feet. I looked down and there was a white label and it said "formulas." Or maybe it was "formulae," you know, with an e.'"

Hannibal took another long sip from his tea. It was very sweet and so cold it hurt his teeth. "What happened to the girl?"

Marquita looked up. "You don't really understand how it works, do you? He ordered her to her knees and she knelt. He ordered her to put her face on the cold hardwood floor. She screamed that she was sorry and begged him to forgive her. She was already crying when he pulled off his belt. I didn't stay around to watch."

Marquita probably didn't even notice that she was crying too, but Sarge did. Silent tears left tracks down her fast-drying cheeks, and she seems oblivious to the others. Sarge used a finger to wipe the water from one side of her face. Hannibal stood slowly, eased down the steps to the patio, and began to wander into the yard. When he felt the pressure easing around his chest, he noticed that he was followed.

"It's hard for you to hear, isn't it?" Cindy asked, just as they reached the tree line of the narrow wooded area separating them from the next yard.

"Last night," Hannibal said.

"Not even!" Cindy said, turning him to face her.

"I seen it when I was little," Hannibal said. "Soldiers who thought their foreign born wives were just kids or slaves or something. And now this guy. I just don't want to be him."

"You could never be him."

"Last night," Hannibal repeated.

Cindy's laugh was one sharp snort. "Well hell, if you're going to be extreme about this, then it's your whole race."

Hannibal's eyes widened. "You mean blacks?"

"I mean men. Every man is him in some small way. It's just a matter of degree."

Hannibal stepped forward onto last year's dry leaves beneath the verdant canopy. "Maybe. I know I've seen Sarge mean. But now I see him gentle as a lamb with Marquita. How do you figure them coming together, huh? Kind of like a fairy tale. The bouncer and the princess."

"Maybe they're just destined to be together," Cindy said, following her man into the thin shade. "Don't you believe in fate?"

"You mean like kismet? Destiny? What will be will be?" Hannibal thought for a moment. "I believe if I step into empty space I'm destined to fall. I think it's pretty much up to me whether or not I take that step."

"Really? Well, master of your own fate, what's your next step to finding this Rod character?"

Hannibal turned away, hands on hips, head shaking. "I've got to find out if Anita lost a disc with something valuable on it. Was her dad stealing formulas from Isermann –Börner? And I've got to find those guys he worked with. Such pretentious names. Brendon Hathaway. Elliot Gaye."

"Elliot Gaye, the combinatorial chemist?"

"What?" Hannibal spun to stare at Cindy, her face mottled by the splotchy shadows of leaves above them.

"Well, you mentioned Isermann –Börner a minute ago. Gaye works for them."

"A client?"

"Not really, but an influential social contact. He'll be at that fundraiser tonight. It's one of those things that, if you're in certain industries, you don't dare miss it."

"You're going to be there," Hannibal said.

"Yep, and if you're real nice to me, you could be too." Hannibal smiled for a second, but then the smile sort of slid off his face. "Hey," Cindy said, "I know it's not your kind of thing, but…"

"It's not that. It's just that, you know, it's too easy."

"What's that mean?"

"You know me. I don't believe in coincidences."

"Yeah I know," Cindy said, her eyes sparkling. "Doesn't stop them from happening though, does it?"

-10-

With much reluctance, Hannibal handed the White Tornado's keys to a boy displaying too much acne and attitude, and headed into the hotel. The Omni Shoreham was a huge, imposing structure, hogging eleven lovingly landscaped acres of Rock Creek Park in Northwest Washington. Since the 1930's the Omni has hosted countless celebrities, several presidents and other world leaders. It was no place Hannibal was ever likely to spend a night, but it was a regular choice for these events people referred to as galas. Tonight's gala, a Gourmet Gala to be precise, would benefit St. Jude's Children's Research Hospital. Hannibal was certain a lot of people were there out of a pure love of children. The fact that every noted pharmaceutical company was represented he attributed to enlightened self-interest on the part of researchers who were showing both support and deference to what they hoped would be a major customer.

Cindy naturally wore a well-fitted black gown with a single string of pearls and a different pair of black heels high enough to show her legs at their best. They had compromised on Hannibal's appearance without much debate. Cindy had agreed to his wearing a simple black suit, although she did give him a Structure tie with a nice subtle design. Hannibal had agreed to go without his usual protective camouflage. No gloves and, more significantly, no sunglasses. It was a concession because he didn't like to show strangers his eyes.

He also didn't like to think about what his eyes probably told people about him.

"What did you call this guy? Some kind of chemist?"

"Combinatorial," Cindy said, handing her wrap to a coat check girl. "Combinatorial chemistry is an integral part of drug discovery, dear. Speeds up research and development, so useful compounds get developed more quickly and less expensively. Gaye was one of the combinatorial chemists who contributed to the completion of sequencing human genes."

Hannibal rolled his eyes. "Check out the big brain on Cindy tonight."

She held her arm out for him to take. "I memorized that bit when I was working a very small IPO for one of Isermann – Börner's baby competitors."

They sped through the lobby, their heels clicking across the marble as they passed between arched columns and beneath huge cut-glass chandeliers. The hotel was labyrinthine, boasting a couple of dozen ballrooms and meeting rooms, but Cindy steered them without confident certainty toward the gala's reception. The instant they transitioned to the carpet of the ballroom a blonde Amazon spotted them. She was about four-fifths legs, and her black strapless gown was designed to make that conclusion unavoidable. Her lips were a little too full for a white girl and covered with a lipstick that made Hannibal think of candy apples. She stalked toward them wearing a broad smile, her eyes scanning Hannibal like the light beam of a Xerox machine. Was she memorizing him for later examination?

"Cindy," the woman said, putting an arm around Cindy's waist and kissing the air beside her right cheek. "I am so glad you decided to come. Now the real fun can begin."

"Hi Glory. Hannibal, this is Gloria Deitz. International law. One of my best girlfriends at the firm. Glory, hon, I'd like you to meet Hannibal Jones."

"Oh my God, Cindy, I can't believe you've been keeping this gorgeous man under wraps all this time," Glory said, gushing like a schoolgirl as they moved toward the bar. "And you never said about his eyes. What a simply luscious shade of blue. Or wait, now they're looking green. Yummy."

Hannibal had counted to ten in his head three separate times before parting his artificial smile to ask "Would you ladies like a drink?"

"Oh, be a dear and get me an appletini," Cindy said. Her eyes promised him a reward for this evening, and his eyes accepted.

"Vodka rocks," Glory said. As Hannibal turned to the bar he heard her chattering on to Cindy. "You are so lucky. Now, what do you call him?"

"Hannibal?"

"Well yes, but I've never heard you call him anything else. He must have a nickname or something."

"No, just Hannibal," Cindy said.

"Wow. Doesn't it make you think of that cannibal character in the movies?"

Hannibal collected the girls' drinks from a smiling bartender and quickly handed them off. He tried to pretend that he and Cindy were the only people there, hoping her girlfriend would take the hint.

"Cindy, do you see any signs of that guy I wanted to meet this evening?"

"I haven't seen Elliot yet, hon. But I do see the right crowd of pharmacists and techies." She nodded to Gloria and gave her a sly wink. "Glory, we're going to wander over in this direction and shake a few hands."

"I got ya," the blonde replied in conspiratorial tones. "Gotta network, gotta work the room. That's what makes you the best, Cindy. I'll catch you on the bounce back."

Hannibal felt out of place walking around empty handed, so on their way across the polished marble floor he stopped at one of the many bar setups for a drink. Only women carried wine at these events, so he asked for an acceptable substitute.

"Scotch, rocks" he said to a large Black bartender. The man seemed to lean forward, as if his response was for their ears alone.

"Single malt or double, sir?" Hm. Regular or high test? Was the bartender trying to embarrass him, or school him?

"Oh, um, single malt?"

"Yes sir," the bartender was pleased. "Laphroaig okay?"

"Oh, sure. Of course."

"Very good sir," The bartender poured with practiced ease and handed over the glass in such a way that Hannibal had to lean in to get it.

"Good stuff," the waiter said. "Next time, ask for it by name."

"Thanks, brother."

Walking through the throng of political and business movers and shakers, Hannibal wondered how there could be any poverty in Washington. Charity balls were more popular than Wizards games, and the price of admission was obscene. But the little circle of men they sidled up to now seemed less well off than some they passed. These were rented tuxedos and Mall store shoes like he himself wore. He didn't doubt their importance, but it seemed clear that these cocktail sippers actually worked for a living. Cindy seemed to consider the little circle before breaking in, singling out a particular balding, round-faced man and signaling with her chin that he was their quarry. Then she hovered innocently, waiting to catch the fellow's eye. When he turned to her, she turned on the charm.

"Cindy Santiago," the man said, raising his Manhattan toward her. "What a pleasure to see you this evening. Gentlemen, this is the young lady who helped me straighten out that awful patent office mess last year."

The other men all seemed to know what a mess that was, and murmured their approval toward her. Then Cindy said, "Good to see you Elliot. I'd like you to meet Hannibal Jones, the fellow I told you about who solves other sorts of problems."

Elliot's mouth opened with his smile now, and he beamed at Hannibal the way he might at a professional athlete or perhaps a rock star. "Yes, the troubleshooter I've heard about. Well, what a life that must be. A good deal more exciting

103

than branching nucleotides I'm quite sure." The others all seemed to agree, and Elliot wasted no time in introduced Hannibal around the little circle.

"So you're a real life P.I., eh?" a particularly thin fellow holding a pink drink said. "Sort of like Sam Spade. Get it?" Even without the emphasis on the last name, Hannibal managed to get it. He just didn't manage to smile. Instead he sipped his Scotch, an act that improved his mood right away. It was smooth and far smokier than any he had tried before. He smiled at the skinny guy, which seemed to surprise everyone.

"You're gracious, considering what a putz Franklin is being," Elliot said. He had the small, delicate hands Hannibal associated with scientists for some reason.

"Hey, it's not like it's the first time I've heard that," Hannibal said. "And actually, the job's not much like it looks in those movies."

"From what I've heard, a private eye is just a professional tough guy," another drinker threw in. "More like Shaft, right?"

Hannibal thought he was turning to Cindy, but she had wandered off and left him to deal with these gawkers alone. Not wanting to respond to the last remark, he looked up at Elliot, who seemed to sense his discomfort.

"No no. I'll bet he's more like Ellery Queen. You know, a thinking man's detective."

The last thing Hannibal wanted to discuss at a charity gala was his profession. While he was trying to think up a new subject to introduce, Franklin spoke up again.

"Well, what do you think, Jones? Which archetype detective are you?"

Hannibal closed his eyes and tipped his head back, emptying his glass before speaking. "Actually, I think I'm more like the illegitimate child of Spenser and Hawk. That is, if it was possible for them to, you know, do that kind of thing." Then he pointed his head toward the nearest bartender. "As it happens, Elliot, I could use your help with a case I'm working on. Let's refresh our drinks."

They headed toward the bar but through further head signals Hannibal guided Elliot Gaye to the door and out into the hallway. Gaye took a deep breath as soon as the door hissed closed behind them.

"Sorry about the attack of the geek patrol. Every one of those fellows is a genius, but their social skills are somewhat lacking. I understand why you'd want to get away."

Hannibal raised an eyebrow. "That's kind of harsh. I mean, I hated it, but they're just curious kids, and I know I've made fun of their kind often enough."

"Humph. I've got to admit you're not what I expected at all," Gaye said.

"And that wasn't a dodge back there," Hannibal said. "I really do need your help on a case."

"Really?" Gaye began to wander down the hall, and Hannibal stayed at his side. Despite himself, he seemed to Hannibal to be one of the kids, in awe of real life. "How can I help?"

"Well, I'm involved in an investigation involving the death of Vernon Cooper. Do you remember him?"

"Vernon was in prison when he passed, right?" Gaye asked. Then he lowered his voice to a conspiratorial whisper. "Did he die under suspicious circumstances?"

Hannibal closed his eyes to keep them from rolling. "I think he may have been involved in something that turned out to be over his head. Did you ever hear of a valuable, er, treasure he had hidden for his daughter?"

"A treasure?" Gaye stopped and looked around the hallway while one set of pudgy fingers stroked his highest chin. "Remember when I told you every one of those guys back there is a genius? I meant that. But Vernon, he was above all of us. I know he was working on something special, but he kept his counsel, and people in our business, we tend to stay in our own lane."

"Of course," Hannibal said. "But is it possible some others might not have been as circumspect as you? What about this Hathaway character?"

Gaye looked down, as if trying to find his shoes. He bared his lower teeth, sinking his top chin into the rolls beneath it. Hannibal surmised that this was his "make a tough decision" face.

"Hathaway. He was a cowboy. Too wild for the pharmaceutical arts, if you ask me. Left the company rather suddenly. I think he may have stolen proprietary information, some of the results of some research he was working on." Then he looked at Hannibal, as if a new idea had struck him. "This is just rumor, you understand. I haven't seen any evidence of wrong doing or anything."

"Relax, Elliot. May I call you Elliot?"

Gaye beamed. "Certainly, um, Hannibal."

"In my profession, you never reveal your sources. So, just between you and me, is it possible that Cooper and Hathaway might have been mixed up in something together?"

"Oh, I don't think so," Gaye said. "Cooper was a straight arrow from all I saw. But you might want to interrogate Hathaway. Could be a lead."

Hannibal turned, and bit his lips to keep from laughing. When it passed he said, "I might want to ask him a few questions. Know where he took off to"

"Well sure. Hathaway's living large, and the new startup company he jumped to wants everybody to know they got him."

* * * * *

The reception was even more crowded when Hannibal returned, but Cindy found him in seconds. His attendance at this event had served its purpose in his mind. It had been a good dance, so he wasn't particularly unhappy when Cindy presented him with the piper's bill. He performed escort duty well through the reception, a silent auction, a truly tasty dinner, and even during the musical performance by a has-been country crossover band. He graciously allowed several nerds to dance with Cindy, including Elliot Gaye who seemed to be built for country dancing.

It was just shy of eleven o'clock when Hannibal began the cross-town drive down Connecticut Avenue toward his own neighborhood. Traffic was blessedly light as they rolled past the ostentatious buildings of embassy row, and for once Hannibal didn't mind stopping for a light at every corner. He relaxed into his seat and pulled his tie down an inch from his throat.

"I owe you an apology, sweetheart," he said. "That wasn't half bad, and it's nice to just spend some time out on the town with my girl."

"What's funny is, we were both working," Cindy replied. "I had to make connections for the firm, and you had to question Elliot. Just shows you can have fun, even when you're on the job."

"Yep, and it was pretty fruitful for me. As it turns out I should be able to talk to this Hathaway guy tomorrow."

"So he didn't go far?" Cindy asked.

"Nope. Elliot said his new company is in Grayson County, but hey, it's still in Virginia so how far away can it be?"

Cindy patted his free hand and smiled. "That's my Hannibal. Often wrong, but never in doubt. And by the way, sugar, what did they call you in school?"

"Mostly my name," Hannibal said as they passed the Washington Zoo entrance. "I was just Jones to a lot of the teachers."

"You mean you really didn't have a nickname?"

"Like what? Hanny?"

"I don't know. Most people with unusual names pick up a nick name."

Hannibal stared up into the traffic light's red orb for a moment, letting the past catch up to him while he waited for the light to change. "My parents were oddly proud of my name," he said. "Of course, they didn't know about Thomas Harris' cannibalistic character when I was born. They just knew about the general from North Africa who nearly held off the Roman legions using elephants in his army, a couple of hundred years before Jesus was born. They named me after him because they wanted me to have something to shoot for, I guess."

Hannibal's telephone rang, cutting off further conversation. He checked his watch, muttered, "What the hell?" under his breath and poked a button on the dash.

"Jones? Where the hell you been? Don't you check your messages?"

"Blair?" Hannibal asked, slowing for another traffic light. "Listen, I was at a formal dinner and a silent auction, so I turned the phone off. Do you know what time it is?"

"Of course. But while you were out partying, Anita hasn't had so nice an evening. She's in the hospital. She's been beaten pretty badly."

-11-

SUNDAY

To Hannibal, Inova was a chain store just like Rite-Aid or Seven-Eleven. There seemed to be one on every corner in Northern Virginia and the fact that they were hospitals didn't make him any more confident in them than he was of the service in the Olive Garden. Chains generally give you consistency, but rarely special service.

When Hannibal called Inova Fairfax a minute after Blair disconnected, he learned that Anita was resting comfortably in a private room that must have been provided at Blair's insistence. He didn't want to disturb her, and there was little he could do at a hospital at midnight anyway, so he left her to the doctors' care.

After a restless night he entered the hospital corridors at eight o'clock and rushed to Anita's room. He half expected to find Blair at her bedside, but instead it appeared that he had sent his second. Henry stood at the foot of the bed, dressed exactly as he was when he entered Hannibal's office days before. With his hands clasped behind his back he reminded Hannibal of the black jockey figures he had seen on rich people's lawns in racing towns like Saratoga. He wondered if black butlers were as rare as live black jockeys.

"So happy to see you here," Henry said in a tone that could have been condescending, or maybe it was subservient.

Hannibal didn't trust his perceptions on that score, so he merely nodded toward Henry and moved to the side of the bed. The rhythmic beeping of Anita's monitors failed to reassure him. She smelled of iodine and alcohol, and her appearance started a twisting ache in his center. Both her eyes were blackened, her lower lip split and her nose swollen into a new, inappropriate shape.

"I am so sorry," Hannibal said. "I had no reason to think you were in any present danger."

"Not your fault," Anita mumbled through swollen lips. "This has nothing to do with you or the case you're on."

"What utter nonsense," Henry said in the same proper speech pattern. Despite his irritation, Hannibal shared his skepticism.

"Anita, you're a brave girl, and stronger than I knew, but you can't do this by yourself. You have to tell me who did this to you."

Anita clenched her eyes tight and pushed her lip out like a stubborn child. "I don't know who hit me. I didn't see. He just came up behind me when I left the market last night. I shouldn't have been out so late."

"This is really too much," Henry said. "Miss Cooper you really must tell us."

Hannibal clenched his teeth and waved a hand toward the door. "Henry, could I speak with you for a moment?"

Hannibal led Henry around a corner to a small, unoccupied waiting room. He closed the door and turned off the television. Henry stood in front of him, erect as always, as if awaiting instructions. For an instant he reminded Hannibal of his worst moments with Anita. But Henry's eyes never wavered when Hannibal spoke to him. Instead he met Hannibal's gaze in a direct and perhaps defiant way. That at least betrayed an unexpected inner strength. Still, Hannibal had to be firm with him and lay down the rules of this game.

"Look, pal, what you were doing in there, that's not helping her any. Anita needs to be handled pretty gently right now."

"Yes sir," Henry said. "And may I inquire as to your intended actions, now that you realize that she is at physical risk?"

Hannibal shook his head. "My intended actions? Well, basically, I intend to find this Rod Mantooth and kick the living shit out of him. Then I'll get back whatever he took from Anita. And then maybe I'll just kick his ass again. That sound like a plan to you?" Hannibal pulled his phone out of his jacket. "Think I can get your boss at his office this early?"

"He is at the health club right now," Henry said. "Perhaps I can help?"

"Not likely," Hannibal said. "I've met another of Rod Mantooth's victims and if he sent somebody after Anita I'm afraid the other girl might be in danger too. I want to lay on some protection for both of them, so I need to get authorized to spend the money."

"Oh, well then it's not a problem," Henry said. "Mr. Blair has authorized me to tell you to use whatever resources you need in order to bring this matter to a successful close. I have his checkbook if you need ready cash."

Hannibal considered Henry's words. This certainly simplified the situation. "Alright then," he said, pacing and thinking aloud. "I can put Isaac on Anita, leave Sarge on Marquita, and get Ray on the road following the custom car angle while I follow the Hathaway connection."

Hannibal looked up to find Henry smiling, more with his eyes than with his mouth.

"What?"

"You are, in fact, the colorful character Mr. Blair said you were," Henry said.

"Me?" Hannibal said. "I'm not colorful, brother, I'm just for real. You're the dude that's colorful. Look at you. Whatever possessed you to become somebody's servant?"

Henry lowered his eyelids and spoke with a little more force. "Mister Blair needs me. I keep his world spinning while his head is in the stratosphere. And you're one to talk about anyone's vocation. A man who spends his life mucking about in other people's misery."

"Mucking about?" Hannibal repeated, imitating Henry's enunciation. "Man, you've spent too much time with those Brits. But I'll tell you, sometimes poking through other people's garbage is important. Sometimes it's the only way to solve their problems."

"Indeed." Their eyes locked, and Hannibal realized that somehow he had made Henry's point for him.

* * * * *

An online map service told Hannibal that he could drive three hundred and forty miles southwest and still be in Virginia. And since that was where he could find Brendon Hathaway, Hannibal filled his gas tank and drove onto I-66 west, pointed toward Grayson County.

While most of his mind focused on driving and scanning for police cars, a part of him was still reeling from his web surfing the night before. He had taken Cindy up on her suggestion and visited a few Internet chat rooms. It took him a while to find what he was looking for, but armed with the abbreviation she had given him he soon found himself lurking in a place where he thought the role play would have made Anita feel right at home not long ago. His actual first name was accepted well as a screen nickname. He quickly learned that those who didn't capitalize their names, mostly women, were treated like children in some chat rooms, and like outright slaves in others. When they typed their conversations, He was struck by the odd convention of capitalizing even pronouns attached to the Dominant people, and the use of lower case by submissives, even to the pronoun "I." He saw that somehow they could change the color of their type, and lines in one color represented actions rather than speech. In some rooms, the actions were pornographic. In others, rapes and other violent acts were carried out. Sitting at his computer, in contact with the others only through a screen, he still left feeling the need for a shower.

Sunday morning traffic locked Hannibal into a slowly rolling grid at the start of his drive. He didn't mind, because his car was his office for the day. While he watched the bumper of the Escalade moving in front of him in fits and starts he made his first call.

"Isaac, what's on your schedule today?"

"Well, I'm working security for a concert tonight," Isaac said. "Of course, if you need me for something I can cancel."

"I don't want to get you in trouble now that you've got a full time job, buddy."

Isaac's smile came through the telephone speaker as clearly as if Hannibal could see him. "Now Hannibal, if it wasn't for you Anna wouldn't even be talking to me. You need me, you got me."

When the Redskins dropped him from their rolls, Isaac Ingersoll became an abusive husband. Hannibal helped Isaac's wife and son to leave him before he did any permanent damage. Then, after getting to know him, Hannibal helped Isaac to get counseling and to being the process of reconciliation with his family. For that, Isaac would always be grateful.

"Isaac, there's a lady lying in Fairfax Inova Hospital recovering from a serious beating. Serious, as in black eyes, cracked ribs and a broken nose. She's healing, and her nose has been reset well enough that no one will ever know. I don't want any more harm to come to her."

There was a short pause. "And if the guy who did all this shows up?" Isaac asked.

"Then you can have him."

Like a reformed smoker or drug addict, Isaac Ingersoll had developed strong feelings about people who clung to his former vice. He was also six feet four inches tall and weighed something over three hundred twenty pounds. He was fully capable of teaching any man who battered women what it was like to be on the receiving end of a good beating. Hannibal was certain that Anita would be safe as long as Isaac was at her hospital door.

Traffic was just thinning when Hannibal called Sarge.

"How is Marquita doing, buddy?"

"It's amazing, Hannibal," Sarge replied. "She's so much stronger than she was yesterday. I think she's ready to go out to the market this morning."

"Glad to hear it, Sarge. Just make sure you go with her."

"You know I'd stick with her every minute if I could," Sarge said.

Hannibal rolled over the crest of another hill. Modest farms greeted him, and miles of pasture formed a patchwork quilt from his vantage point on the winding roads. "Well, starting today I want you to do just that, on the payroll," Hannibal said. "Don't want to take a chance that whoever visited Anita might want to visit Marquita."

Sarge's voice dropped an octave. "It would be a mistake for anybody to come out here and try to hurt Markie."

Hannibal knew that Ray would be sleeping in, so he waited until he reached I-81 before that call. He was already feeling his ears pop when he turned toward Roanoke, climbing into the mountains. The road's twists became sharper and more severe, with the shoulder disappearing from time to time. The depth of the forest on all sides and on the mountains ahead of him imparted a calm he was sure no drug could match. The mist that settled on the mountain highway cooled the air. Hannibal lowered his window a bit so that he could taste that mist and inhale the sweet clean scent of the mountains. While he was lulled by the countryside he called Ray and explained where he was in his latest case.

"It sounds like you want to catch this Rod character pretty bad, Paco," Ray said. "Not sure how I can help."

"Then you're not thinking Ray," Hannibal said, pushing the White Tornado into a curve fast enough to leave rubber behind on the road. "I'm pretty sure our boy's back in the area. I doubt he's stupid enough to go back to Vienna, but you've got a fleet of limousines on the road all the time, running all over the capital area, Northern Virginia and half of Maryland. All I ask is that you tell your drivers to keep an eye out for a candy apple red car that looks like a Stingray married a Caddy and they had a baby."

"Sure thing Hannibal," Ray said. "But speaking of getting married and all, have you popped the question to Cindy yet?"

Hannibal yanked the wheel, pulling his car back from drifting into the oncoming lane. He crested a rise and for a second it looked as if the entire world was laid out in front of him. Highland meadows and valleys, laced with streams and creeks, stretched out for miles ahead of him. The term "God's country" appeared in his mind unbidden.

"Not yet, Ray. The right time hasn't come up."

"I'm not getting any younger, pepe," Ray said.

Hannibal tapped his brakes as the road dived into a two-lane valley.

"I want those grandkids while I can still walk them to the park," Ray said.

"Ray, some things you just can't rush."

"You can call me Papa."

"Like hell," Hannibal said, although the thought made him grin.

* * * * *

Five hours after he left the hospital, Hannibal pulled to a stop under a hanging red light in Independence, in the heart of Grayson County. The highlands of the Blue Ridge Mountains looked much like New England to him. The little village had been carved out of the lush greenery of high alpine meadows and the tranquility made the twenty-five mile per hour speed limit a blessing, not something to curse about as he did so often closer to home.

After getting Hathaway's address from directory assistance, Hannibal had printed out directions from a mapping web site to guide him there. As he slid through the intersection of Routes 58 and 21 he picked up the sheet to make sure he was going the right way. He hardly saw a soul on his way, and he wondered if the entire population of Independence might still be in church.

It took only seconds to leave the town behind and return to streets lined by rail fences. Another ten minutes passed before

Hannibal pulled up in front of Hathaway's home. From there, no other houses were in sight. It seemed like a lot of house for a single man, despite the fact that its earth brown color and soft yellow trim allowed it to almost blend into the surrounding scenery. Three dormers stood out of the slanted roof above the porch that wrapped three sides of the structure. The garage behind the house was a perfect match and Hannibal could see there was a room above the garage that would serve as a studio if the owner were of an artistic bent. To a man looking for a peaceful and safe place to live, this would seem like paradise.

Hannibal listened to his feet crunching on the gravel path, then to the squeak of old wood as he mounted the stairs to the porch. Wreaths hung on each of the four front windows, and the windows of the dormers as well. Patriotic bunting hung over the front rails of the porch on both sides. Festive for the end of spring, he thought. Hannibal pressed the doorbell and stood back so that he could be viewed through the glass. After thirty seconds or so a latch turned and the door opened half way.

"Good afternoon," Hannibal said, flashing what he hoped was a disarming smile. "Brendon Hathaway?"

Hathaway looked into Hannibal's sunglasses for a moment, and then scanned down, his body beginning to shake in a silent chuckle. "You one of them men in black? Looking for aliens?"

Hannibal thought that might not be too far wrong. Hathaway was average height but very long waisted with legs too short for his body. He stood with his thumbs hooked in his belt loops and elbows out to his sides, as if he needed them for balance. His equine face held upper teeth almost twice as big as they should have been, and the long mane flowing out the back of his straw Stetson only made him look more horse-like.

"Actually, sir, I was hoping to get a few minutes of your time. I'm doing a background investigation on a Vernon Cooper. I understand that you worked with him?"

"Oh, yeah, in my last job," Hathaway said, nodding. "Golden Pharmaceuticals made me an offer when they built out here, and I had to get away from that city life. Come on in. We can talk on the patio. You want a beer?"

Hathaway was already walking away. Hannibal followed. When he closed the door behind himself he noticed the electronic security system. Even way out here, he thought.

The flagstone patio held two umbrella-topped tables and a gas grill that Hannibal at first mistook for a kitchen gas stove. Hathaway pulled a pair of mugs from under the grill, went to a short stainless steel refrigerator and started pumping.

"You keep beer on tap out here?"

"Well, we were partying out here last night, and we'll be back here tonight," Hathaway said, pouring foam from the top of the two mugs before setting them on a table. "The boys out this way sure love to party. There. Now we can talk like civilized people."

"Yes," Hannibal said. "Nothing's more civilized than having a draft in your own yard. You certainly have hit the jackpot, Mr. Hathaway."

"Buddy, please. Everybody calls me Buddy. And yes, life is pretty damned good right now. I was able to bring something special to the table at the new company. I imagine old Vernon did the same. How's he doing?"

Hannibal took a moment to enjoy the reddish caste and slightly burnt roast aroma of his brew before tipping it to his lips. The frosted mug chilled his lips just before the smooth, malty liquid flowed between them. He didn't know that Bass ale was even available in a keg.

"I'm afraid he never achieved your level of comfort," Hannibal said. "I'm sorry to tell you that Vernon Cooper is dead."

Hathaway's mug stopped halfway to his mouth. It hung there for a few seconds while Hathaway seemed to consider this news. His lower lip moved forward just a bit and he nodded as if in salute to a fallen comrade. Then he raised his glass and drank down nearly half of its contents.

"That's really a shame," Hathaway said at last. "The man was a brilliant pharmaceutical chemist. If not for him... well. You never know, do you? Anyway, at least his little girl must be doing well with his legacy. What was her name?"

"Anita," Hannibal said, leaning forward. "But no, she's not doing all that well."

"Well, she should be. Why didn't she make use of what he left her?"

Hannibal could hear a slight wheeze in Hathaway's chest. Perhaps he was asthmatic. "That is precisely why I'm here. Ms. Cooper knows that her father left her something of value, but he never told her what that legacy was. Now, we fear that someone has stolen or destroyed it."

"Now that," Hathaway said, waving his beer at Hannibal, "that would be a crying shame."

"Indeed. That's why I have to know what her inheritance was. I can't find it for her if I don't know what I'm looking for."

Hathaway sat back in silence, his mouth forming a hard vertical line. Hannibal stayed quiet, knowing that further pressure would not help. He imagined he could smell the beer from the night before on the table and the patio stones. Hathaway's mouth dropped open but he considered his response for a few more seconds before actually speaking.

"Sorry, Jones, but I can't tell you that."

"Excuse me?"

"That's somebody else's business and not mine to tell," Hathaway said. "I can't help you."

Hannibal took his time rising to his feet. "I don't think you understand. This is for his daughter. If it's anybody's business it's hers. The guy who stole from her took advantage, and took things that probably can never be recovered. The one thing I can do is get back what her father wanted her to have. And you're saying you won't help?"

"I'm saying this is my town and I intend to keep it that way. And I'm saying it's time for you to leave."

* * * * *

Independence lacked even a single hotel, and Hannibal was quite pleased about that. He had booked one of the four rooms in the Davis-Bourne Inn, a Queen Anne Victorian mansion that was earning its living as a bed and breakfast. After changing his clothes he had enjoyed a fine lunch on the wraparound porch watching a young couple sharing lustful stares on the porch swing. Then he moved to a rocker and pulled out his cell phone. He was admiring the landscaped grounds and colorful gardens when he heard a familiar voice at the other end.

"Virgil? It's Hannibal. Can I get you to help me out for a day's pay? Great. No, this actually might call for a little finesse. Yeah, and bring Quaker with you. No, finesse isn't really his style, is it? Well, that's why I called you first."

* * * * *

Brendon "Buddy" Hathaway sometimes thought that the best thing about his new life was that he could play his country music as loud as he wanted it without anybody whining. His outdoor speakers really rocked the house, but now that his last couple of guests were getting into their pickups he would go inside and turn the music down.

It had been quite a bash, with what might have been a record crowd of good old boys. He was pretty sure there were a couple of fellows there that night that he had never seen before. Not that it mattered. He had plenty of beer and the ribs had come off the grill just about perfect. Of course, that was five hours ago, but there were plenty of chips, nuts and pork rinds to keep anybody from going hungry.

Hathaway felt a chill as he stepped inside. He understood why. The side door had been standing open for hours, making the air conditioner run full tilt. He pulled the door closed and headed for the stairs. He had enough beer in him to guarantee a good night's sleep. He was just reaching for the banister when he realized what was missing. The door hadn't made the little beep noise that indicated the alarm was on. He needed to go set it at the box by the front door.

As he turned his bleary eyes toward the door he realized that he wasn't alone. The skinny guy in front of him had wild brown hair over an angular face, sitting on top of a pencil neck. Hathaway thought he looked a lot like the star of the old Max Headroom television show.

"Who the hell are you?" Hathaway asked. "I didn't say anybody could stay over tonight."

The stranger shrugged. "Sucks, don't it?"

Then someone pulled a cloth bag over Hathaway's head and cinched its edges tight around his neck. Hathaway swung his arms wildly for a few seconds, but lack of oxygen combined with the impact of hours of heavy drinking turned his efforts to fight into meaningless thrashing in the dark. He felt a deeper darkness descending on him, and wondered if he was to die without ever knowing why.

* * * * *

Hathaway's eyes fluttered open grudgingly, as if they blamed him for the pain bursting behind them. His hair was hanging in front of them, and he was staring through it at the wooden box he was standing on. He tried to raise his head without success. His arms were tied behind him, and he could not lower them. They must be tied to the ceiling, he reasoned.

"Hey, sleeping beauty's awake." That was the voice of the intruder Hathaway had seen just before he was attacked.

"Good," a deep, flat voice said. "Let's get what we came for and get the hell out of here."

"What do you want with me?" Hathaway asked. Twisting his head he managed to get a brief look at the second man. He was very big and very black, with puffy arms and hands. The whites of his eyes had a brownish tint. Hathaway had seen that look on homeless men in Washington; men he assumed were drug addicts. This could be bad.

"You think he'll talk if we just slap him around a bit?" the white intruder asked.

"Talk?" Hathaway asked. "Talk about what? Who the hell are you?" At that, the white man walked closer. The room was very dark, lit by only a couple of candles in a distant corner.

"You can call me Quaker," the first man said. "It ain't my official name, but it'll do. There's a fellow at Isermann – Börner wants to know exactly what you and Cooper stole from them. Something about proprietary information?"

Hathaway let his head drop. Did they think they could beat his secret out of him? Let them try, he thought.

"Look at him," the Black man said. His words slid out like the voice of Eeyore in the Winnie the Pooh cartoons. "He's kept his secret long enough now he won't open up to anybody for anything. Besides do we really need to know?"

Quaker paused and thought a moment. "Well, I guess all we really need to know is that it's not something he'll blab around, Virgil."

"That's easy enough." Virgil said. "We just stick him in a hole and cover it up."

The room felt very close right then. It was hot, and the humidity made it so much harder for Hathaway to breathe, especially with his arms cinched upward as they were.

"Well, that might be easier," Quaker said, "but it's not all the boss asked for."

"So what?" Virgil asked, in a louder tone. "You want to waste a couple of hours down here, punching and kicking this idiot? I say we ice him, we hide him, we leave. Neater that way."

One of the candles went out, making the dim visions ever harder to see. Hathaway could smell the smoke from the extinguished wick. He was finding it hard to think, but the conversation he was hearing seemed clear on one point.

"Hey, are you guys arguing about killing me?"

"Shut up," the bigger man said.

"Look," Quaker said in a tired voice. "I know it's work but if we get the information we can leave him alive. That way, nobody's looking for us real hard."

"He's making sense," Hathaway said, feeling his stomach lurch. Trying to stay on his feet was making him queasy, but if he relaxed his legs it threw his arms into agony.

"Didn't I tell you to shut up?" Virgil said. Then, to Quaker, "See what I mean. He's a hard case. We could be here all day getting him to tell us what they stole. If he's dead, the story ends right here."

"I don't know man," Quaker said. "Maybe you're right." He pulled a knife from his pocket. The blade flicked out at the touch of a button.

"Wait a minute, fellows," Hathaway muttered. "It ain't a secret worth killing for. Not that big a deal, really."

Virgil grabbed Hathaway's hair, lifted his face up, and then let it drop. "He's drunk. He won't even feel a good beating and he'll probably pass out. Then he won't be able to tell us jack."

Hathaway's mouth was getting very dry, and his eyes ached from trying to look up at the two arguing faces. Throughout their conversation the two thugs never looked at Hathaway. In fact, they acted as if he wasn't even there. Yet this was all about him, and he wasn't about to let some darkie talk this pencil neck into killing him just to make their lives easier.

"Look, we can work this out if I just tell you what I took, right?"

"Who the fuck cares?" Virgil snapped. "See, he'll say anything to try to save his own ass. Now he's going to hand us some crap about taking money from the till or something."

"No, really," Hathaway said, shaking his head. "If I tell you, then you won't have to kill me, right?"

"He'll lie," Virgil said, walking away. "And then he'll run straight to the cops if we let him go."

"Maybe not," Quaker said, turning his back to Hathaway. "What if we just got the dope on Cooper? Then he'd have no reason to run scared to the cops and we could just go home."

"Yeah, that's right," Hathaway said. "I'd have no reason to tell anybody about you. Please." It was getting hard to breathe, and he felt like he was going to throw up any minute.

Virgil turned on Quaker, holding a knife that looked to Hathaway like a machete. The man was clearly near the end of his tether, teeth flashing in a hateful grimace. "Look, we don't need this cracker, and he probably don't even know what Cooper took."

"Addiction!" Hathaway had shouted the word and begun sobbing. The other two men finally turned to look at him. "Cooper cracked it. He was a genius in brain chemistry. I never got past pain medications."

Virgil wheeled and in the near-darkness Hathaway saw the blade in his hand rise over his head. Quaker put a hand on Virgil's chest.

"No, man. I ain't gonna let you kill him if he don't need to die. You don't need to die, do you boy?"

-12-

Monday

Hannibal decided to take breakfast on the front porch, enjoying a sunrise that made every shape and color sharper than a cinemascope panorama. The natural beauty of the area was both stunning and humbling, the way visiting the pyramids of Gaza or meeting Halle Berry in person would be. He was glad for the opportunity, even if he did have a pragmatic reason for dining al fresco.

Just as Hannibal was crunching up the last strip of bacon he spotted Hathaway stalking toward the porch steps. His watch told him it was not quite seven-thirty. Good. Hathaway would have to get to work soon. Their talk would be short, and since it was taking place in such a public place, it would not be too loud or violent.

Hathaway walked straight to Hannibal's table and dropped into the chair facing him. Rage crushed his lips together and his brows were so tight his eyes were barely visible. He still smelled of hangover, carrying a little of that odd mixture of liquor and vomit. So, he had changed his shirt but not taken time to shower. Hannibal finished his juice, and decided to break the silence himself.

"Coffee, Mr. Hathaway?"

"You think you're damned smart, don't you boy?"

"Excuse me?" Hannibal signaled the waitress and pointed to his cup.

"I'm sober now," Hathaway said. "I know you sent those two monkeys last night to interrogate me. Quaker, and Virgil."

Hannibal suppressed a smile. "Pretty goofy names."

"Obviously code names. But I know you sent them to torture me for information."

The waitress cast a worried glance at Hathaway as she placed coffee in front of him and refilled Hannibal's cup. Hannibal gave her a reassuring wink but waited until she had gone before he responded to his visitor.

"It sounds as if you had more to say to these two visitors than you had to tell me. Did they hurt you? You don't look too bad. I mean, no scars or bruises are showing."

Hathaway sipped from his cup, then lowered his voice and leaned toward Hannibal. "What's this about? Blackmail? Is that your game?"

"Don't get insulting," Hannibal said in a stern tone. "I told you I needed to know what Vernon Cooper's treasure was so I could help his daughter recover it."

"You want to talk about insulting?" Cooper snapped. He started to stand, but then his eyes moved around the big porch, noticing the concern in people's eyes. He sat back down, and Hannibal was pleased to see the slightest hint of a smile at the corner of his mouth.

"Insulting was waking up with my hands still tied behind my back, looking around and realizing that I had been in my own garage loft all the time. Them boys had me pretty damned scared."

Hannibal watched a pickup truck stop at the intersection to let two others get past. Monday morning rush hour, Grayson County style, he thought. "Sounds like it wouldn't have worked if you weren't already drunk and tired. But, since you are clearly assuming that I already know what you told them, how about just filling in a couple of open spaces. Like, why keep Cooper's secret so dearly? Did he help you with your own special discovery?"

"Well, yeah, okay, Vernon put a lot of work into the new migraine medication and gave me the formula free and clear in exchange for me keeping mum on his addiction formula." Hathaway was calmer now. Blackmail must have been his real concern. He would be a ruined man if evidence surfaced that his new medication was developed at Isermann –Börner on their time. They could sue, and a court might take proprietary interest of the formula away from Golden Pharmaceuticals.

"You took that discovery to Golden, and they made you a star," Hannibal said. "But was Cooper's own discovery important enough to steal for? To kill for?"

"Are you kidding?" Hathaway's voice dropped to a whisper now, and his eyes became wild. "Maybe you don't get it. Cooper understood brain chemistry better than anybody I ever even heard of. This was the real deal, man, a genuine cure for addiction. Think about it. Freedom from cigarettes, cocaine, even heroine, in seventy-two hours. You think guys will pay big for Viagra? This could be the pharmaceutical find of the century. That's why he hid the formula. He planned to sit on it for a couple of years until he had no obligations to Isermann. If it wasn't for that accident, you know, but still his daughter was going to be set for life based on that one discovery."

Hannibal's mind took flight before Hathaway finished. Could Cooper's formula really mean the end of junkies on the street? Freedom from the grip that crack had on his city and its people? Maybe even an end to alcoholism? How much would a pharmaceutical company pay to control the prescription medication of a lifetime?

"Well then," he said, rising from his seat, "I guess I'd better be about the business of finding this magic formula, eh?"

"And I'd better get to work," Hathaway said as he moved toward the steps. "Hey, I sure wish you luck. And you know what? Forget about them boys last night. They gave me a good scare, but they could have been a lot rougher and I guess you needed to know what I knew."

"I'm sure they'll appreciate your understanding, Mr. Hathaway."

"Buddy," he called from the sidewalk. At least you know where to start your search. Who else but a pharmaceutical company would want Cooper's secret?"

"Who else indeed?" Hannibal wondered aloud. Could there be an underground market for this stuff, maybe to sell bundled with illegal drugs? Or, might someone want to hold this chemical, keep it off the market, to sell to wealthy cocaine users for an exorbitant price?

A pensive Hannibal moved toward the door to check out and settle his bill but some buried instinct caused him to turn around. There was a nondescript man across the street near Hannibal's car. He wore running clothes and stood with hands on knees, but Hannibal had the feeling this jogger had been staring at him. As soon as Hannibal spotted him, the runner moved down the street at a fair runner's pace. Probably just his own paranoia, Hannibal thought.

Except that the man hadn't had a drop of sweat on him.

* * * * *

Cindy met Hannibal in the hall outside Anita's hospital room. His pulse always gained a few beats per minute when he saw his woman and reacted to her smile, her hair, and her impressive shape. But lately he was more aware of her accessories. Her blue, man-tailored business suit was from Ann Taylor's. The matching heels were Jimmy Chou. Her small clutch purse was a Louis Vuitton if his memory served him. She had always looked like a million dollars. Now he wondered how many thousands she was wearing.

"Thanks for pulling away from the office," he said, taking her into his arms for a quick peck on the lips. "I know you're busy, babe."

"I can still claim a lunch hour, and I'm always glad to meet you, lover. Besides, things are running themselves pretty well. The offering is taking off at a surprising pace. We've got some good buzz on the street."

"Great," Hannibal said with a smile. Her scent only amplified the warmth her smile granted him. She was wild flowers and vanilla and maybe some sweet wood and something else. Was this the Estee Lauder Intuition he gave her for Christmas?

"You okay?" Cindy asked.

"Just breathing you in, babe," Hannibal said. "Did you have time to work with Marquita on her finances?"

Cindy slipped an arm through Hannibal's and started toward Anita's room. "Hey, when my man puts me on a mission, I take action. The first thing we did was list her property on the market. She doesn't need that much house, and it's a lot to take care of anyway. She also has quite a bit of rental property scattered around the area, some heavily mortgages but some almost free and clear. A few letters to creditors will keep them off her back until we can raise some cash and streamline her debt picture. Now we just need to get her packed up and in a nice new place in time for the sale of this place."

"Sale? Kind of optimistic aren't you?"

"You don't know the market in that area, lover," Cindy said, flashing her triumphant smile. "We've already got two offers, both higher than the asking price."

The tinny intercom calling for an anesthesiologist reminded Hannibal why they were there. As he steered Cindy into Anita's room he whispered, "Remember, you're the good cop."

The room was quiet except for the intrusive beeping of electronic monitoring equipment. Isaac towered at the foot of the bed with his thick arms crossed, his pale Nordic eyes already focused on the door. His face lit with a smile as he recognized the newcomers. On the far side of the bed, Henry stood in what Hannibal feared were the only clothes he owned, just staring down at Anita's sleeping face as if he thought he could heal her through force of will alone. Hannibal gestured toward Henry, but spoke to Isaac.

"He been here the whole time?"

"Well, he takes breaks for food and sleep, but, yeah," Isaac said. "Devoted." Isaac knew about devotion the way a recovering alcoholic knows about sobriety. A reformed spouse abuser, he responded to classes and therapy by becoming a fanatical family man. Hannibal didn't think it worked that way very often, but when it did it was an encouraging triumph of the spirit.

"Isaac, would you please take Henry out for a cup of coffee or something?" Hannibal said. Henry's head jerked up and he moved to Hannibal's side with a quiet grace that had to be the result of long training.

"I'm charged with monitoring her progress," he said, his words very quiet and yet very hard.

"I need to speak to her without interference," Hannibal said. "You were right before. I may have to be stern to get the information I need and I can't have her looking to someone else for support. Don't worry. Ms. Santiago will look out for her interests."

Henry glanced in Anita's direction, muttered, "Five minutes," and left the room. Isaac followed, and Hannibal turned his attention to the patient.

Anita had no mouth or nose tubes, but fluids were still dripping into her arms. The bruise on her right cheek had turned a pale orange, which did not match the purplish crescents under her eyes. Someone had straightened her nose, a process that Hannibal knew from experience was painful. A red line and a tiny bit of thread showed that her lower lip had taken a stitch or two.

Hannibal took Henry's post on Anita's right and nudged her arm. Her eyes opened and a warm smile was stillborn as she realized that a substitute had taken Henry's place. Her eyes darted from Hannibal to Cindy on the other side of the bed and back again. Her brow creased with worry.

"Mr. Jones, what are you doing here, and who is your friend?"

"This is Cindy Santiago," Hannibal said. "She's an attorney, here to make sure I don't violate your legal rights in any way. She is also connected to your case in another way

129

I'll explain later. As for me, I'm here to find out who hurt you. In order for me to continue, you will have to be open and honest with me."

Anita's jaw set. "I told you, I don't know who hit me. Why won't you believe me?"

"He could come back," Hannibal said. He detected blood on Anita's breath. Had her assailant loosened a tooth?

"It's not your job to protect me. You should be out finding my father's legacy, whatever it is."

Before Hannibal could explain, Cindy leaned forward to take Anita's hand. "Ms. Cooper, I want you to know that I've spent some time in the last couple of days with another woman who might be classified as a victim of this man, Rod Mantooth. He left her emotionally crippled and on the verge of suicide by drinking herself to death. Forget about Hannibal's quest or whatever connection you might be able to regain with your father by receiving your mystery inheritance. I need to know where this man is, and if you know, you owe it to every woman alive to tell me."

The beeping accelerated and seemed to become louder in the otherwise silent hospital room. Anita stared hard into Cindy's eyes and squeezed her hand until their fingers were white. Her eyes crinkled, fighting to contain tears and begging the other woman for understanding.

"I don't want revenge," she said. "I just want my money."

"You contacted him somehow?" Hannibal asked.

"I saw him," Anita said. She seemed to overcome the tears, but words poured out instead. "I saw him. I was coming out of the Giant and there was that car, sitting in the parking lot. I dropped my groceries and waited for him. When he came to the car he looked right through me, as if he didn't recognize me. I told him I knew he had taken something from the house."

"You confronted him?"

"He must have sold whatever he took, I figured, so I demanded a share of what he got. I told him he owed me at least that much."

Hannibal doubted the conversation went quite that way, but the result was pretty clear. "He laughed in your face, right? I mean, he sure didn't see you as any kind of threat. So why would he be so rough?"

"He said I was stale. Used. He needed fresh..." Anita's entire face clenched and the tears finally flowed down the sides of her face.

Cindy completed her sentence. "He needs fresh meat. That bastard."

"I was so angry, and ashamed." Anita sobbed now, not trying to hide it or hold back. "I wanted to hurt him, but I couldn't. So I took my keys and I made a scratch. Right on the door of his precious car."

Good for you, Hannibal thought.

"That was very brave," Cindy said. "Very brave and stupid. Look what he did to you. But Anita, why didn't you tell the police who it was?"

"They'd put him in jail," Anita said. "If he's in jail, I'll never get any of my money."

Hannibal knew she had other, deeper reasons for not sending Rod to jail. Hannibal couldn't guess how it might affect her if she was the reason for Rod getting arrested.

"Okay, you just stay here and rest up and heal," Hannibal said. "I'll find this guy and when I do I'll make sure you're made whole. I swear it." Hannibal knew that commitment could have two meanings, and he meant it both ways.

* * * * *

Only Cindy's presence enabled Hannibal to contain his frustration as he slogged through the stagnant midday traffic. Fairfax Inova was in fact in Falls Church, Virginia, positioned so that Washington was accessible without having to leave the highway. But even after the Monday lunch hour, driving the beltway was like swimming through maple syrup. After a couple of miles on I-495 he turned onto I-66, which moved even more slowly. His tension was compounded by the fact that he had surrendered the stereo to Cindy, who flipped the radio to the smooth jazz station. In this kind of traffic, with the air conditioner blowing full blast, he desperately wanted to rock out.

Eventually he reached the Constitution Avenue exit, dropped Cindy at her building, switched to an AC/DC CD and got back on Constitution for what he knew would be a leisurely roll east. Driving slowly through the city didn't bother him the way slow motion on the highway did. After all his years in residence, Hannibal still enjoyed the eclectic architecture that downtown D.C. offered. Nodding his head to "Highway to Hell," he smiled at the city's internal conflict, symbolized by the contrast of the ostentatious Smithsonian buildings on his left and the park-like stillness of the Capital Mall on his right. Tourists rushed about on his left, trying to see how much they could see in one day. On his right, locals meandered across the thin grass on their bikes or on foot.

Then he maneuvered onto I-395, which moved a little faster and dropped him onto I-295, which flowed faster still. That carried him down past the Navy Yard and across the river into his own neighborhood, Anacostia.

Hannibal stepped out into the humidity, surprised to see Marquita's silver Lexus a few spaces ahead of his own. In the hallway he was even more surprised to hear movement in his office. The door was ajar. Hannibal rested his hand on the Sig Sauer hanging under his right arm and stepped toward the door, careful not to make a sound. The opening was just wide enough for one eye to see through, but the view prompted a soft smile. Marquita stood leaning back against Hannibal's desk. Sarge had an arm around her waist and was pressing forward slowly for a kiss. It was the kind of moment that makes a man feel like a voyeur, but also makes it hard to turn away.

Then Sarge's free hand tenderly touched Marquita's thigh, and Hannibal saw her flinch. Sarge froze, the moment shattered. Hannibal felt Marquita's pain, but he knew that Sarge carried his own scars. He was a survivor, a man who had come through firefights in Vietnam, fistfights in Mississippi, the spiral into homelessness and the long climb back to self-respect. Hannibal wasn't sure he could take another blow to the heart. He was strong, but Marquita was damaged goods, and trying to hold her together could break him apart.

Hannibal took two silent steps backward, then almost stomped forward and pushed the door open. Sarge snapped erect and pulled back from Marquita, who grew a quick, nervous smile.

"Didn't expect to find you guys here," Hannibal said, pulling his jacket off and hanging it on the tall coat rack beside the door without looking directly at his guests. "Hang on a sec. Be right back."

Hannibal walked through the next three rooms of the converted flat to the kitchen at the back and pulled a bottle of filtered water from the small refrigerator. Sarge and Marquita were more composed when he returned with it to the office. Hannibal gave Sarge a questioning look.

"I wanted to get Markie away from that house for a while." Sarge said. "Then, when we got here I decided to show her your office, you know, give her the tour."

Hannibal went to the coffee pot on the small table beside his desk and poured the water into the reservoir.

"I think that was a good idea. I was going to call you, but since you're here I can update you in person."

"Did you find out something from Anita?" Sarge asked. Hannibal poured Hawaiian Kona beans into the other side of the coffee maker, hit a button, and spoke over the whirring sound of the beans being ground.

"My client, Anita Cooper, was beaten pretty badly Saturday night."

After a brief pause to inhale the aroma of fresh-ground beans, he sat behind his desk and continued.

"This morning she admitted to me that Mantooth did it." Marquita sucked in a breath and her fawn colored eyes stretched wide open. "Yes," Hannibal continued, "He's back in the area."

Marquita's shock and fear pushed her into a different world from Sarge's immediate rage.

"We gotta find this son of a bitch."

"No," Hannibal said, keeping his voice calm. "I gotta find him. You need to stay on your assignment. Keep Marquita safe until this is over."

Marquita clung to Sarge, placing a hand on his chest as if wanting to literally cling to his heart. Mantooth had a lot to pay for, but bringing these two together could turn out to be an unintended consequence of his evil. Good could come of it, but they needed time. Hannibal pulled a credit card out of his wallet.

"I want you to take Marquita out of town. Someplace with lots of people, but peaceful. An amusement park, or the beach or somewhere. Here, it's a legitimate expense for the case. Get her to someplace nice while I'm on the hunt."

* * * * *

Once Sarge was packed and on the road, Hannibal filled a mug with coffee and sipped on his feet. He found himself pacing his office with no leads, no clues and no next step. He had done some skip tracing work before, but Mantooth was being more elusive than anyone Hannibal had pursued before. He seemed to live on cash alone, no credit card or checks. He used an alias for hotels and, it appeared, any other services he used. Still, people have pasts and people make mistakes. With no better course available, Hannibal hopped back into the White Tornado and headed for the courthouse to check for public records. Again, the midday traffic on I-295 was onerous. He could always amuse himself for a few minutes reading the license plates around him. He was certain that the Washington area had the highest per capita rate of vanity plates in the country. Decoding them was always amusing, at least for a while. When that grew boring he decided to have a consultation with a doctor.

"You must have me on speed dial," Quincy Roberts said after a secretary passed Hannibal's call to him. "What kind of trouble are you bringing me now?"

"Not trouble, Doc, just a couple of questions," Hannibal said as 2COOL 4U slid past him on his right. He looked at the driver. She wasn't.

"I'm free for about fifteen minutes," Roberts said. "But I'll bill you anyway. What can I do for you?"

"First, tell me why a guy would steal the formula for a new painkiller. What with aspirin, acetaminophen, ibuprofen, codeine and a dozen others already there, what's the big deal?" Now a guy in a suit was rolling past in H8 2 W8. Why was the right lane moving so much more quickly?

"You could just as easily have asked, why was ibuprofen of any value after acetaminophen was found," Roberts said. "To oversimplify, every one of the drugs you named works differently. If a new one came along that lasted longer, or worked better for arthritis pain or migraine headaches, it could be worth a fortune. And since development cost is so great, stealing the formula saves a company a great deal. But these pharmaceutical companies have very good security."

"Yeah," Hannibal said, "but you can't really defend against a guy working on an undocumented project, right?" At least this much of Hathaway's story held up. It wouldn't be hard to fake notes, show failure when there was success, or simply work on one thing while appearing to work on another, especially if you had a coworker covering for you.

"Okay, now a more theoretical question. What would you say if someone told you they had developed a cure for drug addiction?"

"I would say that they are either lying or several years ahead of medical science," Roberts said. "It's theoretically possible, at least for the chemical dependency, not the psychological slice."

"So it could be done? And it would have commercial value?"

"Its value today could hardly be measured," Roberts said. "To free people of drug addiction with a simple pill or shot instead of years of therapy? It's like a pharmaceutical holy grail. And yes, it's possible in theory. One could develop a vaccine I suppose, that would create antibodies that could destroy the drug before it could affect you. Or it might just prevent the drug from passing through the blood-brain barrier. You'd be full of the addictive material, but you wouldn't get the high, and that would make breaking the addiction cycle much easier. Squashing the brain's addiction response would be much harder, but still possible I guess. Hannibal, should I take it that this is more than a theoretical conversation? What you're talking about could be the pivotal pharmaceutical advance of our age."

Hannibal was listening, but also watching for his exit. As it came near he signaled right, which prompted the driver beside him to speed up to fill the gap Hannibal was about to drive into.

"You dick!"

"I beg your pardon?" Roberts said.

"Sorry, Doc. Thanks a lot for the background info. I think what you're talking about is what someone stole from one of my clients, and now I have some ideas about how the thief might want to sell the formula. Hey, I need to focus on driving right now."

"Keep me posted on this new theoretical discovery," Robert said. "I have some patients who could be saved by just such a miracle drug."

* * * * *

The balance of the day consisted of the kind of grunt work most private detectives pay their bills with. Hannibal searched court files, property records and motor vehicle records for any sign of a recent address for Rod, Roderick or Roger Mantooth. He accessed Mantooth's prison records for past addresses, and ran each one down to its predictable dead end. Mantooth had listed no next of kin or emergency contact numbers. Credit bureau records proved equally useless. Military records appeared nonexistent. The few numbers that matched his name in national telephone directories proved to belong to solid citizens who could not be the man Hannibal sought.

When he finally returned home Hannibal's frustration burned in his stomach like bad Mexican food. This time, as he entered his building he looked to the left, toward his own apartment. But, feeling that his work day shouldn't be over, he turned right and went to his office. He had just turned the doorknob when Ray entered the building behind him.

"Hey, how's it hanging Paco?" Ray called. "You found the bad guy yet?"

Hannibal shook his head as he flung the door open. "This one's being a bitch, and I'm afraid I'm running out of time. Any sign of the Corvorado?"

"Oh, that half Cadillac thing? Nada. None of the driver's has spotted it. And from your description, it would be pretty hard to miss."

Hannibal nodded, but said nothing more as Ray climbed the stairs to his own apartment. There was plenty for them to talk about, but Ray looked tired at the end of a long workday, and Hannibal had to admit he was focused on Mantooth, an abusive thief who had gone to ground very effectively.

Inside, Hannibal poured the remains of the morning's pot down the sink and pulled out a French press to brew one more perfect cup. Ray had a point. That car would be almost impossible to miss if it was on the streets anywhere in the area. That raised an ugly thought. Had Mantooth moved on? Despite his apparent arrogance he may have realized that beating Anita would raise his profile enough to catch someone's attention.

At his desk, Hannibal stared into the transparent cylinder as if all the answers he needed were swirling inside with the coffee as he pushed the plunger down. But as shadows lengthened in the room, his computer monitor drew his attention. After filling his mug, he tapped a key and thought about the community he had so recently poked his virtual nose into.

In search of more insight, Hannibal returned to one of the chat rooms he had visited Saturday night. He hoped that a stranger might tell him what neither Anita nor Marquita could: how a woman could get caught up in this game of dominance.

As soon as he logged into the chat room he was greeted by several identical messages, "Hello Hannibal Sir." He selected one of the speakers, nicknamed charmer, and after a few fumbles managed to open a private window.

"Hello. Can we talk for a minute?" Hannibal typed. Even through the computer it felt more like hitting on a girl in a bar than like the start of an interview.

"Yes Sir," charmer responded. "How may i serve You?"

Hannibal was tempted to tell her to drop the "Sir," but decided that if she did, it might make her less likely to respond. "I'm new here and just trying to learn," he said. "Would you be willing to tell me how you got involved in such violent role-play?"

A short pause. "Violent? Not sure i understand, Sir."

"Are you new as well?" Hannibal asked. "Don't you know what these guys do to their girls?" This time the pause was much longer.

"You aren't familiar with the lifestyle at all, are You Sir?"

"I admit I'm not," Hannibal typed. "Just trying to learn." The next typed line was the first of many surprises for him.

"This is not merely online play for me, Sir. i am submissive in R/L." This, he had figured out, was the abbreviation for "real life." For some reason, his mouth felt drier and he gulped coffee before typing again.

"You are a masochist then?" Reading his words he wondered if he had just insulted her. To her credit, charmer surprised him again with a calm response.

"BDSM is not about violence, Sir. It's something sexy and trusting you do with someone you care about. i trust Master completely and take joy in pleasing Him. In return, He protects and nurtures me."

"And it's okay for this person you care about to beat you?" Hannibal asked.

"If Master punishes me, it is because i have done something wrong and deserve it."

He easily imagined Anita saying those words not long ago. He sipped his coffee, wanting to push the conversation farther.

"And if he decides to lend you out to other men? Do you deserve that too?"

"Master would never do that, Sir." charmer said.

"How can you be so sure?"

"Sir, are you a reporter?" charmer asked.

"No, I promise you I'm not." Hannibal replied. "Please help me understand how you can be so confident he wouldn't give you away."

"Master loves me," charmer said. "And besides, that is one of my limits."

"Limits?" Hannibal asked, pausing to think before typing again. "I don't understand."

"When He took me as His own, Master gave me His rules, which i must obey. At the same time i gave him my limits, which are the things i will not or cannot do. i would not be collared by a man unless we could agree on limits. Nor would a Master take a sub who did not respect His rules."

Hannibal sat back farther from the glow of the screen. He knew that the collar signified ownership, but apparently it did not suspend all rights. Had Anita or Marquita established limits? That seemed unlikely. Perhaps Rod had only shown them one side of this life. And maybe this whole thing wasn't as black and white as Hannibal had assumed.

"Your limits don't include his beating you?"

"As i said, Sir, Master would not punish me unless i deserved to be punished."

"But it's up to him how much of a beating you deserve," Hannibal said. "He could injure you, brutalize you." At this point his thoughts flowed directly into the keyboard, almost like thinking aloud.

"Are You purposely testing me, Sir?" charmer asked. "You can tell Master that I have no fear. He is not a brute. I have never needed to use my safe word, nor do I ever expect to."

Hannibal's eyebrows rose at another new concept. He realized that just observing one evening had not taught him all of the code. "Please explain safe word," he typed. This time he stared hard at the screen, watching the words pop up with even greater interest.

"This is the word Master has given me as proof that he will protect me, even from Himself. If I feel that He may hurt me more than He intends, or order me to do something that will be harmful to me in the long term, then I say my safeword and He will stop what He is doing."

Hannibal wondered if Marquita would have taken other men if she felt she had a choice. Did she have a safeword to defend herself from actions that would destroy her spirit? His mind burned with more questions than before.

"Sir." The word drew him back to the screen. "May i please go now? This conversation is becoming a little uncomfortable."

He was no closer to understanding why a woman would volunteer for degradation this way, but he now knew that there were layers and shades to this "lifestyle" beyond his immediate grasp. That in itself was insight.

"Of course, you can leave whenever you want," Hannibal typed. "I don't own you. And thank you. You have been very helpful." Then, as an afterthought, he added, "Tell your master that I said he should be very proud of you."

"Thank You, Sir." was the final line she posted. Hannibal shut down the Internet connection, gulped more coffee, and sat back in the dark for a long while. He sipped the dark liquid, smiling both at its flavor and a sudden thought about Anita. She may have been just like this charmer at one time, but no longer. As angry as he was about her confronting Mantooth, he was proud of her courage. She had managed to strike one blow for womankind. She didn't scar him, but she hurt his favorite possession.

"Whoa!" The thought hit him so hard he splashed coffee on his desk. He realized that there was a reason no one had seen the car, and it had nothing to do with Mantooth leaving town. Hannibal snatched the phone off the desk, pulled a card out of his jacket pocket and punched in a phone number. He was more anxious than he wanted to admit to himself while the phone rang, and was grinning like a fool when it was answered.

"Clarence Nash," he said, sounding as giddy as a game show host. "Thank God you're still at the shop. This is Hannibal Jones."

"Hannibal? Oh, yeah, I remember now. The guy in the black suit. Hey, funny you should call. You'll never guess who was in here this morning."

"Please tell me that bastard Rod Mantooth brought that custom car back to you."

"You got it," the mechanic said. "Man, he was fixing to bust. Somebody done keyed the driver's door bad. He brought it straight to me, wouldn't let nobody else touch it."

"I knew it!" Hannibal was pacing the office, too excited to sit. "How long will you have it there?"

"Couple days," Nash said. "Had to order the paint. Not much call for this particular mix today. Then there's a couple day's work after I pull the door off."

"Pull the door?" Hannibal asked. "It's a scratch, right? You fill in the paint and buff it out."

Nash's laugh roared out of the phone. "You sure don't know much about cars, son, at least not this kind of car. The whole body's dipped in chrome and airbrushed with twelve coats of paint. Each of those layers has got to dry before the next one goes on. It won't be ready too soon."

"Okay, Clarence," Hannibal was calmer now, and sat on his desk, leaning against the computer to share its comforting warmth. "Can I get you to call me when it's ready so I can meet Mr. Mantooth over there?"

"Don't see why not, as long as you meet him after he's paid me and left," Nash said. "Can't promise I'll remember, but I'll try."

"Uh-huh. Do you suppose a C-note would be a memory aid?"

"A hundred dollars?" Nash said. "Why, that's better for the memory than that ginko Balboa stuff."

Hannibal hung up with a new outlook on life. Now he was certain he would catch up with Rod Mantooth, finally meet him face to face in a few days and learn what he had done, if anything, with Vernon Cooper's miracle drug. He had a lot of good news, but he would brief the clients in the morning. Right then he would call Cindy and see if she could tear herself away from business long enough to join him for a late dinner at that little Thai place she loved so much.

A smaller voice at the back of his mind hoped he wasn't celebrating too soon.

-13-

Tuesday

Morning phone calls brought Hannibal a number of surprises. First he learned that Anita was recuperating at Blair's house. Blair had decided that she shouldn't be alone, and this way Henry could keep an eye on her. Then he learned that Blair had taken the morning off to work from home. That would save Hannibal some driving time, since he had originally intended to meet with both Angela and Blair. Henry met Hannibal at the door of Blair's vertical mansion.

"Good morning sir. Very good to see you again. Please come in."

"I'll make you a deal, Henry," Hannibal said, stepping across the threshold. "If you'll stop calling me sir, I'll stop treating you like some servant who shouldn't stick his nose into Ms. Cooper's business. What do you think?"

Henry pursed his lips, weighing his options for a moment before choosing one. "Very good, Mr. Jones," he said after a pause, but his smile seemed more genuine and Hannibal accepted the small step.

They climbed a long flight of stairs and walked down a hallway under a small cut-glass chandelier toward what Hannibal assumed was a guest room. Henry raised his hand to tap at the door when they heard a scratching noise from the bathroom beyond. The door stood open and Hannibal walked past Henry to look inside. He found Anita kneeling in front of the bathtub, scrubbing it out.

"That can't be good for those ribs," Hannibal said.

Henry was behind him a second later. "Ms. Cooper. Really!"

She turned and stood, straightening her short apron in front of her. "Really yourself, Henry. I can't just lie here all day and let this place fall farther and farther behind."

Hannibal didn't even know how to describe the absurdity of the scene, but his smile seemed to break through their conversation. "Ahh, domestic discord," he said, not realizing the pun until he had said it. "Could you take a little break so I can fill you in on the news?"

"Have you found my father's prize?" Anita's face brightened like a child's on Christmas morning as the men trailed her to her temporary room. To Hannibal's surprise the room held two comfortable chairs in addition to the full size bed and dresser. The scent of jasmine filled the room, and he wondered if that was always the case or if its present occupant had introduced it. Anita bounced onto the bed, not looking at all like a woman who had been beaten badly enough to be hospitalized. Hannibal sat in one chair. Henry chose to stand.

"Tea?" Henry asked the room.

"Oh, please," Anita said.

"And coffee," Henry added, nodding toward Hannibal.

"Uh, sure."

Henry wafted away without a sound, and Anita stared at Hannibal until he realized he shouldn't wait for Henry to return.

"Well, to directly address your question, no, I haven't found what was stolen from you. But I do now know what it was."

"Oh, I've had such childish fantasies," Anita said. "Like it was a treasure map to hidden gold, or a ton of stock in the pharmaceutical company, or even the deed to some island he bought over the years." In her glowing eyes Hannibal could see the innocent youth that Rod Mantooth could not resist dominating.

"In fact, it was nothing so exotic, but perhaps something even more valuable and certainly it was way more important. Your father apparently discovered the formulation for a drug, or maybe a vaccine, that would actually enable a cure for drug addiction."

"You mean like methadone?" Anita asked.

"No, not a substitute, but something that would make an addict not need his drug any more. I've consulted an expert who tells me that the value of such a discovery could be astronomical."

"An actual cure?" Anita asked. "You mean like if you've been using crack every day you could take this stuff and you could kick crack just like that? Why, that would be a Godsend to all of humanity! Henry, did you hear?"

Henry had just placed a tray on the table beside the bed. He handed Anita her cup, then offered a second to Hannibal. "Just that your father is a hero, Ms. Cooper. I expected no less."

"There's more," Hannibal said, sipping his coffee. "I don't know where Mantooth is, but I do know how to find him soon. He'll be returning to the repair shop where he got the crazy car built in a few days. I'll be there to greet him."

Anita's reaction was a curious combination of fear and elation. Her mouth formed the "O" of stunned surprise, but her eyes reflected a reluctance to even consider the possibility that Rod might be captured or hurt.

Standing to the side, Henry stayed silent, standing with a saucer in one hand and the handle of a cup in the other. Hannibal knew that he was fully engaged, but his face was as passive as a tax investigator at an audit. Hannibal considered recommending him to the Treasury Department for secret service work. He was very good at being present but somehow remaining invisible.

Anita's eyes suddenly focused like a laser on Hannibal's glasses, as if to center her mind on one thought and blot out all others. "My father did something no one else was able to do."

"That appears to be the case," Hannibal said. "Everyone I've interviewed has told me that he was a brilliant man."

"He was a genius," Anita said, her smile spreading to envelope her face again. "The best pharmaceutical biochemist in the world. Mr. Blair was right. His discovery will change the world. You will get it back, right?"

"I'm certainly going to do my best," Hannibal said, not sharing her smile. "Meanwhile, I think I need to go brief Mr. Blair himself. After all, he's paying the bills."

* * * * *

Ben Blair's home office was both smaller and simpler than Hannibal expected. The cherry wood desk appeared to take up most of the space, with three tiers of open shelves in place of a traditional hutch. The phrase "organized disorder" came to Hannibal's mind as he stepped in. Papers and computer discs covered the desk and all three shelves, even crowding the flat screen monitor, but Hannibal suspected that Blair knew what each was, and that every sheet of paper was exactly where it belonged. An acoustic guitar standing in the far corner struck him as the one incongruous note.

Hannibal stood quiet while Blair tapped at a keyboard with steady intensity, like a virtuoso charging through the end of a Dvorak sonata. When he reached the finale, he released a big breath and turned his easy, boyish smile on Hannibal. The straw thatch on his head was uncombed and one could hardly guess that seconds ago this man in a faded Planet Hollywood tee shirt and shorts was directing a billion dollar empire through his simple Dell computer.

"So, Mr. Jones, what do we know that we didn't know forty-eight hours ago?"

"Well, as I just told Anita, I've caught a break in the search for Rod Mantooth. He left his car at a shop for repair and I'll be alerted when he returns for it."

Blair waved Hannibal to a chair. Not until he sat did he realize that Blair was burning incense in the room. He wasn't sure, but he thought the scent was called chamomile. Hannibal got a mental picture of Blair, relaxing like a sixties hippie, strumming a tune in his incense fogged room, maybe getting high.

"That's not catching a break," Blair said, crossing his right ankle over his left knee. "That's due diligence. I knew you were the right man for this job."

"Thanks. I think it will do a lot for Anita's self-esteem if this man is made to pay for hurting her."

Blair nodded. "Unfortunately, it might be impossible to prove that he's committed a crime. What about the property he stole? Do you think you'll be able to recover it? Or is there any evidence that he's already sold it?" Blair maintained his usual casual attitude, but the fingers of his left hand drummed a rhythm on the desk and his right foot, shook frantically in space.

"Interesting that you didn't ask if I've learned what he took. But, you've known all along, haven't you? Or at least suspected, right?"

Blair's smile didn't drop, but it hardened. "I'm not sure I get your meaning."

"It never occurred to me that you knew anything about your cleaning woman's father," Hannibal said, "but Anita says you knew enough to tell her that he was a genius. I'm thinking you suspected from the beginning that the only thing he'd hide for her that could be of great value was some new pharmaceutical breakthrough. Then I remembered that among your holdings is an on-line pharmaceutical company."

Blair lowered his foot to the floor and sat forward just a bit. "Whatever Cooper came up with has to be of great value, based on what he told her. Someone is going to make a great deal of money from his discovery. Now it's out there where anybody might capitalize on it. I'm the only one who would make sure Ms Cooper gets her fair share of the wealth a new wonder drug will generate. But I can't do that unless the formula is recovered."

"How very altruistic of you," Hannibal said, standing. "Well, you're my client and I will do all I can to protect your interests. But you should know that Anita has retained an excellent business attorney who will make sure her interests are protected as well."

Blair's smile returned to its former lightness. "Ah, this would be Miss Santiago, right? She's with Baylor, Truman and Ray I believe, one of the finest business firms in Washington. I'm quite sure that we will work quite smoothly with them on this matter, once you've recovered Ms Cooper's prize."

Any response Hannibal might have considered was pushed out of his head by the ring of his cell phone. Blair indicated that he should take the call, so he pulled his phone out and pushed the button. At first all he heard was distant sobbing.

"Hannibal? Sarge. I don't know what to do."

Hannibal didn't think he had ever heard desperation in Sarge's voice before.

"What's going on, man? Where are you? Is that Marquita in the background? Is she all right?"

"I brought her down to Virginia Beach to relax a bit. Now she's freaking out," Sarge said, his voice pumping fear into the telephone. "I've just now calmed her down enough for her to tell me why. She saw him Hannibal. She spotted Rod Mantooth down here."

-14-

Finding a parking space on the narrow streets of Georgetown late in the morning challenged even those who lived and worked in the area. Because Hannibal seldom frequented the northwestern quadrant of The District, the search became a major test of his ingenuity. The row houses in Georgetown didn't seem significantly bigger than the ones in his own neighborhood or anywhere else, nor did they have any more space around or behind them. Yards seemed tiny, and to him a brick front was a brick front. The fact that these places sold for upwards of a million dollars made little sense to him. But he wasn't there looking for a home. After failing to learn anything about Mantooth from public sources, he was looking for a man who might have access to less official but more valuable information.

It had taken Hannibal a few minutes to calm Sarge down. He had insisted that Sarge stay with Marquita and not go looking for Mantooth on the beach where she had spotted him. He had promised that he would join them that night. Then he headed for The District to find an old acquaintance. He was driving against the major flow of traffic on I-66 at this time of day and had no trouble holding a speed in the sixties. While he drove he contacted the one person he knew in Virginia Beach who might be able to help him.

"Huge Wilson, you are one hard man to talk to on the phone."

"Well my posse has to protect me from the nut jobs, the local fans, and especially the would-be rappers and hip-hop singers who'll do anything for an audition," Wilson replied. His voice's purity, reminiscent of Eddie Kendricks' falsetto, always surprised Hannibal.

"Listen, Huge, I can use some help and I think you once said that if I needed anything…"

"Of course," Huge said, and Hannibal could hear him smiling into the phone at the other end. "In my biz, street cred is very necessary, dog. I said if you ever need anything and I meant it. Now what we talking about?"

"As it happens, it's your street credibility that will make you so valuable right now," Hannibal said. "I need to find a guy named Rod Mantooth. He robbed and beat up a sister up here, and I have reliable intel that he's hanging in Virginia Beach right now. He's a white guy, but he's got underworld connections and likes to live large. I figure if he's making contact with the drug dealer crowd your contacts might spot him."

"Beat up a sister?" Huge said. "Shit, if he's on the streets of Virginia Beach my posse will run him down. You want me to take care of this, or just save him for you?"

"Please just locate the fool for me if you can," Hannibal said. "I'll be down there tonight and I'd like a shot at recovering the stolen property."

"You just lay back and leave this one to me," Huge said. "E-mail me a good description of this asshole and a picture if you've got one, and we'll get down to business."

That conversation had ended just in time for Hannibal to switch onto Route 29 and let the Key Bridge carry him over the Potomac. That dropped him within a couple of blocks of his destination, Café Milano. Still, it came as no surprise that after wandering the claustrophobic warren of one-way streets for a few minutes he ended up parking behind the Shops at Georgetown Park. It was too hot for even a short walk. Hannibal pulled off his suit coat and locked his shoulder holster in the Volvo's trunk before proceeding. He covered the necessary three blocks with his jacket draped over his arm.

Hannibal had called ahead, knowing that he was likely to find Anthony Ronzini having an early lunch. Freddy, Ronzini's personal protector, greeted Hannibal at the door. Hannibal knew that square head, thin sandy hair and broken nose. Freddy had the mass of a heavyweight fighter and the light tread one would expect a middleweight to have. Hannibal nodded a greeting and raised his arms for a pat down. They had not met under the best of circumstances.

"No need for that," Freddy said. "You clean?"

"Of course. I won't disrespect Mr. Ronzini at a meal."

Freddy turned to lead Hannibal into the restaurant. On their way to Ronzini's table they passed three or four familiar faces. Café Milano was one of those places that attracted Washington's power elite. Hannibal had his coat back on by the time they reached the patio. Stepping into the glass-fronted area was a quick trip to Europe. Plants and flowers flanked two long rows of tables wearing white tablecloths. The blossoms and leaves looked as if they were catered to as much as the diners. Hannibal guessed the room's capacity at around a hundred, and he was sure that it was ninety percent full that day.

When he reached Ronzini's table, Hannibal looked around slowly, wondering how many of the men nearby were in Ronzini's employ. While not a major force in the local crime scene, Ronzini was a player and was not without influence. His round Italian face turned toward Hannibal and offered a congenial smile.

"Sit, Mr. Jones. Have you had lunch? At least have an espresso with me." Ronzini raised his left hand and a waiter stepped toward them.

Hannibal lowered himself into the seat facing Ronzini, who sat behind a huge salad filled with things Hannibal wasn't sure he could name. He saw eggplant, peppers, tomatoes and the fake lettuce Cindy called arugula. The other stuff hardly looked like food, although some of it might be cheese of some sort.

"Thank you, Mr. Ronzini," Hannibal said, more for Freddy's benefit than his host's. "I wasn't expecting so warm a welcome."

Ronzini stabbed the salad, raising the sour cheese odor. "Hey, you've held up your end of the deal. I wasn't so sure."

"I never doubted you," Hannibal replied. "We had an understanding. I had less faith in your son, but there haven't been any problems." Ronzini's son had been running a crack house until Hannibal was hired to chase the bad element out of that building. Hannibal declared the building and the neighbors on its block, to be under his personal protection. Ronzini had been drawn into the conflict and overstepped his son to end it by making an agreement with Hannibal. He would keep his son's drug business out of Hannibal's neighborhood, and Hannibal would take no further action against the young drug dealer. The agreement created a relationship between the two men based on honor and mutual respect. And after fighting for the building Hannibal decided to make it both his home and his place of business.

"And what brings you to see me now?" Ronzini asked between bites of his antipasto. "I'm thinking this isn't a social call."

Hannibal bit back his pride and forced a less arrogant expression onto his face. "Actually, I'm here to ask for a favor," Hannibal said.

"Of course you are."

"I have no idea how I might repay you for this favor."

"We will not speak of such things," Ronzini said. "I know what you will and will not do. At some time I may need a favor and you will do the right thing." Then, to the waiter, "Please bring my friend here a cup of espresso, no lemon I think." Then his eyes returned to Hannibal. They were the eyes of a fox, incisive, dissecting Hannibal as he spoke.

"I'm looking for a man," Hannibal said, choosing his words with care. "This man has beaten and abused women. He also stole something important from one of these women. I need to get it back. I may also want this man to pay for his treatment of these women. Unfortunately, I haven't been able to find out anything about this man through the normal avenues."

"And you think I should know something of this man?"

"This man has a criminal history and I believe he may have connections, important connections you might know about." Hannibal said. Two nearby diners' eyes flicked toward him, and Hannibal knew they were Ronzini's men. "The more I know about my quarry, the easier it will be to locate and deal with him. And before I take this man down, I'd like to know what kind of enemies I might be making. This man's name is Rod Mantooth."

Ronzini continued through his antipasto. No hint of recognition showed on his face. Just before he finished his food, the waiter reappeared with espresso for Hannibal and pasta for Ronzini. Freddy, at the next table, didn't seem to eat. Hannibal's face showed his surprise at Ronzini's food.

"You should have ordered." Ronzini said.

"Not hungry. Just never seen ravioli in a cream sauce like that."

"When it's round we call it *cappellacci*," Ronzini said, spreading a clean napkin across his lap to protect what had to be a two thousand dollar wool suit. "These are filled with spinach and ricotta. A wonderful flavor. And I know this man, Mantooth. At least, I know of him. He's from the old neighborhood, Bensonhurst."

"Really? I had the impression he was a low life," Hannibal sipped his espresso. It was very hot, and maybe the strongest he had tasted. He smiled and took another sip before putting his cup down.

"Yeah, ten years ago he was busting into banks. Five or six years ago he got busted, but I think he's on the streets again."

"Can you tell me who he's working for, or with?" Hannibal asked.

Ronzini chewed a pocket of pasta, shaking his head slowly, either at how good the food was or at how silly Hannibal's question was. "What you really want to know is, who is this guy and what kind of friends does he make. Do you know where this man is?"

"I've tracked him to Virginia Beach," Hannibal said. "I intend to confront him there. Our meeting could get messy."

Ronzini laughed out loud. "Really? Well, wait twenty-four hours and let me check into Mantooth. It shouldn't be hard to find out what you want to know."

"Thank you, Mr. Ronzini." Hannibal said, swallowing the last of his espresso. "Now, if you'll excuse me, I need to get on this bastard's trail. I'll wait until tomorrow and call you."

"No," Ronzini said, in a stern voice that made Hannibal stop half way to standing up. "You won't contact me again. I'll call you when I have information for you."

* * * * *

The smell of fine Italian cuisine had accentuated the one lie Hannibal had told Ronzini. His stomach was growling for food. As soon as he reached his car he headed for the nearest Wendy's drive through. The drive home was a lot more pleasant with a burger on his lap and a container of French fries in his door's map pocket. By the time he pulled into his parking space lunch was a memory and Hannibal's mind was focused on packing for a long drive south. His thoughts shifted only when Monte met him on the sidewalk.

"What's up, Hannibal. Still working a hot case?"

"As a matter of fact, I still am," Hannibal said, "and I have to take off for Virginia Beach this afternoon."

"Hey, you gonna be catching up with Huge?" Monte asked, following Hannibal up the stairs.

Hannibal stopped just inside the door, sensing a variety of elements dropping into place. "Actually, Monte, I will be checking in with him. How'd you like to meet him?"

Monte took in a giant breath, and word rushed out of him like water over a cascade. "Are you for real? You think I could meet him, in person, like shake his hand and actually talk to him? Man I'd give anything for a chance like that."

"Maybe," Hannibal said, unlocking his apartment door. "What's it worth to you?"

"Huh?"

"I'm ready to make you a deal."

Monte backed off as Hannibal entered his place, perhaps sensing that he was about to step into a trap. "What kind of a deal."

"A book every two weeks."

"What?" Monte said, his voice rising higher.

"Like I said, you read a book every two weeks for the rest of the summer, you bring me a nicely written report of said book, and I'll see if your grandmother will let me take you with me to spend some time at Huge's studio."

Monte stomped in a small circle in the hall, and Hannibal wondered what kept his pants from falling down. They were already several inches below his waist. "That's the deal," Hannibal said. "Take it or leave it. I have to get packed right now. It's a three and a half hour drive and I'd like to be there before sundown."

* * * * *

Marquita greeted Hannibal at the door with a strong hug. Although caught by surprise, Hannibal returned the embrace before guiding her to the sofa.

"Hey, little bro," Sarge said to Monte while pouring four sodas. "Didn't expect you to be coming along."

"It was a last minute decision," Hannibal said. "I filled him in on the bare bones of the case on the way down."

"Well, Hannibal, I'm damned glad to see you, brother," Sarge said. "Markie has been a wreck since this morning, but I knew you getting here would make her feel better."

Sarge had splurged on a comfortable condo within sight of the ocean in the city's resort area. The great room was set up for entertaining. The kitchenette had everything they could need for meals, the table would seat six, and the living room area held a television, stereo, a comfortable wicker love seat and two chairs. Fresh flowers dotted the whole space and, even at six o'clock, sunlight flooded the room through the sliding glass doors. The balcony beyond them offered a wide view of the Atlantic, but watching the waves was not Hannibal's priority.

"I'm sure Marquita feels quite safe with you around, Sarge," Hannibal said, settling into one of the wicker chairs.

"Sarge will never leave my side," Marquita said, her feet tucked beneath her on the couch as if she wanted to protect them. "I know he will look after me, but you, Mr. Jones, you can go out and find this man and do something."

"You gonna hunt this guy down and terminate him?" Monte asked with a grin.

"I'm not terminating anybody," Hannibal said with a stern look in Monte's direction. Then he turned to Marquita. The air conditioner was blowing hard and must have been for quite a while. It gave Hannibal a slight chill and made Marquita's nipples press into her lightweight tank top in a way that seemed somehow inappropriate to Hannibal. "Now, Marquita, tell me what you saw."

"I saw him," she all but shouted. "It was Rod, right out there on the beach."

"Alone?" Hannibal asked. "Just walking down the beach in his flip flops?"

Marquita ran fingers through her long platinum hair and curled her lips inward. Sarge sat beside her and stretched out an arm to wrap around her but she shrugged it away. Her thin form shook with ragged breaths and her hands covered her eyes. After a few seconds of silence she was able to look at Hannibal.

"I'm sorry. We were down the beach from here, maybe a mile or so. There is this lovely boardwalk with cute little shops full of useless trinkets and soft ice cream cones."

"We were just walking along," Sarge said. "Not really paying attention to where we were, you know? We turned off from the beach on a whim and wandered a block or two up a lane of houses."

"That's when they went by," Marquita said.

"They?" Hannibal asked, prompting her on.

"It was a red Jeep, or one of those four wheel drive things," Marquita said. "The top was off and it was just open. And there he sat in the front passenger seat. I swear he looked right through me without seeing me. I just screamed."

"You're sure it was him?" Hannibal asked.

Marquita sat forward, her fawn eyes locking onto Hannibal's. "I could never forget that face."

"Sarge, what did you do?" Hannibal glanced at Monte, who sat with eyes wide. He could see that the lady was badly shaken but he had sense enough to stay quiet. Sarge was quiet at first too, but not for the same reason.

"Worthless," Sarge said under his breath. "Never even saw the man. All I knew was, Markie was screaming. By the time I knew why, the car was long gone."

"But you know what this guy looks like, right?" Monte sounded anxious to help. "We can just hit the street and cover the area. Nobody ever notices me so I could follow him and come get you."

"Appreciate the offer, Monte," Hannibal said. "But let's collect a little more data first. Marquita, you said Rod was in the passenger seat. Who was driving?"

Marquita's brows closed together, as if she had never considered the question before. "He wasn't alone," she said as if surprised by the revelation. "There was a younger man driving. Tall, beach boy type, blonde, like a body builder. And the three girls crammed into the back seat. Wait, one of them I had seen before. Yes. It was the witch called Mariah."

"Wearing?"

"Who knows?" Marquita said, waving a hand.

"You do," Hannibal said in a harder voice. "Just recall the scene. Picture it in your mind."

Marquita closed her eyes and despite the cool breeze in the room perspiration broke through the skin on her face. "The boy was bare-chested. Rod wore a Hawaiian shirt. The girls wore bikinis, all three. Solid colors, like three Italian icees. Cherry, lemon and lime."

Hannibal broke into a grin. "Now that's a picture that will be hard to miss. I've also got a couple of other leads to follow up on. But it's getting late and I feel like I spent the whole day in the car. How about I take everyone to dinner?"

Marquita showed a sudden burst of energy, bouncing to her feet and heading for the refrigerator. "Oh, I was going to make my special Jambalaya for Archie. See, I bought everything I need. I'm sure I can make enough for the four of us. Believe me, it will be better than anything you could get at a restaurant."

She ended with a nervous laugh. The men sat quiet. After a moment she turned toward them, one side of her smile gone but the other side still bravely holding up.

"I really just don't want to go outside again so soon," she said. "If we can just stay inside this one evening?"

"Of course," Hannibal said. "It sounds wonderful."

"Sure," Sarge added. "We can rent a movie or something. Make an evening of it. You guys know how to play tonk?"

Monte gave Sarge a sidelong look and raised a tentative eyebrow. "Archie?"

-15-

Wednesday

Hannibal took a deep breath as he stepped out of his motel, for no other reason than that he loved the salty fresh smell of the ocean. He had booked a room in the Best Western Oceanfront. True to the name, his room did have a pleasant oceanfront view, despite the fact that the motel faced the even less impressive Budget Lodge and stood practically in the shadow of an Econolodge. But the view didn't move him, in either direction. It was the smell of the seashore that made him smile.

It was clear that location meant nothing to Monte. He was hopping around like the dancing hamsters on the internet as they stepped out into the flashbulb-bright early morning sunshine. Hannibal wondered if he would be bouncing off the ceiling in the car.

"You know where you're going, right?" Monte asked as they got underway.

"I have the address and the streets are numbered sequentially. I think I can find it."

From 11th to 21st street was not far, but it would take them a while. Traffic wasn't the only reason for their slow progress, although the streets were packed with both cars and foot traffic. Hannibal reflected that, geography aside, Washington D.C. was at heart a northern town, at least from a cultural perspective. The vast variety of restaurants, museums, and theater options hinted at that fact, but the true giveaway was the pace. People in The District had someplace to go and wanted to get there.

Virginia Beach, on the other hand, was a true Southern city. It was the biggest city in the state, but it still behaved and thought like a small town. That made the traffic very similar to driving conditions in Miami. Drivers were too busy looking at the people and shops they passed, and of course watching the ocean when they could spot it between the towering hotels, to be concerned with speed. It was as if there were no local residents, and everyone in town was on vacation.

As he headed up 21st it occurred to Hannibal that every seaside city must have been designed by a New Englander. The style of the buildings never changed. Then he passed Peabody's, which had "the biggest dance floor in Virginia Beach" if their sign was to be believed. This was a bit more modern than the rest of its surroundings, but still had an air of that quaint small town feeling.

A few blocks later he pulled into a small parking lot behind a squat, unassuming building that could have been a residence that was just a little bigger than its neighbors. When they left the car Monte raced to the door, back to Hannibal and back to the door. Hannibal tried to remember what it was like to be a pre-teen boy. His memory failed him.

A tap at the door brought a very large, well-tattooed fellow to the door. He was perhaps twenty years old, with a huge forehead, dreadlocks and a questioning expression on his face.

"Hannibal Jones to see Huge Wilson. He's expecting me."

The doorman's head moved backward on his neck. "You the nigger laid out Hard Dog?" Hannibal nodded. "Dayum!" He offered Hannibal a handshake that jumped into a series of movements, a more complex process than Hannibal could follow. It ended with the doorman pressing a fist forward. That part Hannibal recognized. He punched into the man's fist and they all went inside.

Dim lights, dark carpet and plentiful mirrors promoted the illusion that the building was bigger inside than it was outside. The doorman led them through a narrow hall to a wider control room area. Hannibal recognized the large mixing boards that lined one side of the room and wondered how anyone could master the vast array of switches, knobs and slider pots. The board faced a glass wall, beyond which a solitary Black woman in a jogging suit and headphones stood speaking into a hanging microphone, reading from a sheaf of paper.

Monte saw none of this. He saw only one of the two men behind the board, a slight man with close cut hair and two armfuls of tattoos showing below the sleeves of his vintage tee shirt.

"Huge!" Monte said leaping forward. When the man turned toward him he switched to, "Mister Wilson. Holy shit it's really you! Oh my God."

"Chill out, man," Huge said in his natural falsetto. "We're working on something here. Give me just a minute."

Huge was also wearing headphones and Hannibal realized he was hearing the woman's words while the rest of the room was in silence. They stood watching the silent performance for another two minutes, until Huge raised a hand to signal the woman to stop.

"That was off the hook, Delicia," he said into a microphone. "Now take five while I chat to a couple of visitors for a minute." The woman smiled and left the recording room by a second entrance. Monte's eyes were riveted on her impressive rear end.

"So this is your little friend you wanted me to meet," Huge said to Hannibal. "He's got a good eye for talent. Monte, right?"

"Ohmygodican'tbelieveit."

Huge sat back in his rolling black leather chair. "Hannibal told me you were a hustler. Said you got your name from running a three card monte game and that the day he met you, you took him for a bundle. That true?"

"Well, yeah," Monte said.

"Well you sure don't look like a hustler to me. Why don't you sit here for a bit and let T.L. here give you a quick rundown on what we're doing here today. Delicia is going to be the next Missy Elliot. While you do that, Hannibal and me got some business."

Huge stood, took Hannibal's arm, and led him out of the room. They moved down the darkened hall to a small conference room. There was barely enough space for the simple cherry wood table and the eight chairs around it. As they entered Hannibal was struck by two conflicting sensations: the sight of a half-full coffee pot, and the smell of leftover marijuana smoke. Huge started pouring coffee before he noticed Hannibal's reaction.

"Oh, you don't blow the chronic, do you?"

Hannibal did a quick mental translation. "No, it's not for me. Or Monte."

Huge's head bobbled like a sports figure doll as he handed Hannibal a Styrofoam cup. Huge was physically slight, but there was no denying the energy the man generated, the subtle sense of power, and his total comfort with the power he had.

"You told me your friend had no interest in school, right? Let me talk to him. I ain't a gangster, you know. Never pretended to be, but I'll tell you, the G's don't fuck with me cause I can give them the beats that get asses on the floor, and that lets them clock the dollars."

Hannibal nodded, but didn't sit because Huge was still standing. Huge wasn't a gangster, or a "G" as he and his friends would say, but he commanded respect. On reflection, Hannibal realized that his relationship with Huge was in many ways similar to the one he had with Ronzini.

"So, you haven't asked me about your Rod Mantooth problem," Huge said, starting to walk around the table. "I love that name."

"You'll tell me when you have something."

"This is my city, brother man," Huge said, spinning to point a skinny finger at Hannibal. "You think it's hard to find one funky white dude? Shee-it. But of course, your call last night made it too easy. We got one for you."

"Got one? Who?"

"Lime," Huge said, pulling a note pad from the hip pocket of his baggy shorts. "We got Lime." From the pad he pulled a photo and two pieces of paper, which he dramatically slid across the table's glossy surface. Hannibal scooped them up and examined them one at a time. The photo was a candid shot of a beautiful young woman with a cream complexion that could have made her part Asian, or Hawaiian, or Middle Eastern, or half a dozen other possibilities. Her hair was long, thick and naturally wavy, the color of balsa wood with blonde streaks. Bright green, slightly slanted eyes stared out above a tiny pert nose and full, challenging lips. This was the girl in the lime colored bathing suit. The other papers bore an address and details of the time and location of the sighting.

"One in the morning?" Hannibal asked. "And she wasn't with Mantooth?"

"My man said she was patrolling the beach, still in that bikini. Not sure if she was dropping off or picking up, but it sure looked like a drug run to my partner. That was taken on the boardwalk just before shit started shutting down. He clicked a lot. I kept the rest. Man, I'd put her in a video in a heartbeat. And check it, she don't look like a woman who's been abused, do she?"

Hannibal saw as much strength in her face as in her long striding legs. "Maybe she likes it. Or, maybe she's a partner. Or maybe she likes girls."

"Only one way to know, bro," Huge said. He had come full circle and stood facing Hannibal now. "One thing's for sure, she'll lead you to the man you want to meet. You go check it out, and come back to pick up Monte tonight sometime."

"What do you have in mind for him?"

Huge's grin was so broad it was infectious. "Gonna show him how it all works, dig? Introduce him to some people who wish they'd stayed in school. Some people who had a lot of money go through their hands and got nothing cause they didn't know how to handle it. You just leave this one to me, brother. Now, you going down the beach to meet this bitch? Tell her to introduce you to this player so you can straighten his ass out?"

"Something like that," Hannibal said.

Huge leaned back, scanning Hannibal up and down. "You don't do undercover, do you? I mean, a black suit on the beach in summer is going to stand out a bit. You need to loosen up some if you're going to get within half a mile of this ho."

When did a lazy pronunciation of the word "whore" come to be a synonym for woman, Hannibal wondered. "I'll keep my distance. Besides, if I take my jacket and shirt off I'll stand out even more. I don't have any tattoos."

* * * * *

But back at his car, Hannibal started the engine, cranked the air conditioner to maximum and got back out. He folded his jacket and laid it on the back seat. He laid his tie atop that and opened the top button of his white shirt. Then he rolled his sleeves up to just below his elbows and returned to the driver's seat. For now, that was as incognito as he was prepared to be.

A little known CD by *The Georgia Satellites* pumped his speakers while he drove southward down Atlantic Avenue, almost to Rudee Inlet. He cut right on Fifth Street, almost the end of the resort area beach, and eased a short way down Salem Avenue. Just like Atlantic City, he thought. As soon as you get a few blocks from the Boardwalk it stops being a resort town and starts showing its less impressive side.

Hannibal had always heard that Monopoly was based on Atlantic City, because that was the Boardwalk he knew about. He reconsidered that assumption as he drove past Baltic Avenue and turned up Mediterranean. The modest houses he was passing were surely the least expensive properties on this particular board. He cruised slowly up the narrow street until he spotted the address Huge had written down. He parked between an aging aqua Fairlane and a drab green Chevette.

Walking toward the wooden cottage Hannibal was praying that the drivers of the two cars were careful. If paint from either one got scraped onto his white tornado, he might just have to have the car put down.

The mystery girl lived in a second floor flat she apparently rented from the building's owners. She had a separate entrance at the top of a long flight of white wooden stairs. Hannibal wanted to meet the woman face-to-face. He was building a cover story concerning confusing her address with someone else's on his way up the stairs. It wasn't necessary. His knock drew no response.

The view between the curtains on the inside of the door offered little. A white gas stove, Formica kitchen table and metal tube chairs implied a place that hadn't changed much in decades. Drab wallpaper and chipped linoleum might mean a place that the model-shaped occupant didn't spend much time in, but the dog's water bowl meant regular return visits home.

From the landing he had a good view of what appeared to be a typical, middle class neighborhood, leaning toward the low end. He saw bicycles in driveways, chain link fences were more popular than the white picket variety, and a woman in shorts and a tank top sat in front of the neighborhood grocery store on the other side of the street. Ah, the all-knowing, all seeing neighborhood observer, Hannibal thought. Where would private detectives be without them?

Hannibal smiled his way over to the stringy-haired blonde whose freckled skin had seen too much sun and not enough sunscreen. She raised expectant eyes toward him but offered no greeting.

"Well, hi," Hannibal said. "You look like maybe you can help me."

"Yeah, but why would I want to?" she replied.

"Because you're a nice person," Hannibal said, offering his hand. "My name's Hannibal and you are…?"

She took his hand, amusement lighting her eyes. "Fay. How do you do? You looking for somebody?"

"I was hoping to catch up to this young lady." Hannibal showed her the five-by-seven Huge had given him. "A friend gave me her address. Does she work during the day?"

Fay flashed uneven, tobacco-stained teeth. "Mariah? Naw, she's the wind, like in the old song, you know? Real party girl."

Hannibal nodded, making a show of taking Fay's words seriously. "Party girl, eh? Well, any idea how long she'll be away? Maybe I should come back next week."

"If you was smart you wouldn't come back at all," Fay said, pulling a cigarette out of a pack of Kools. "She's hooked up with some guy she met on the beach. But I happen to know she'll be home in the morning."

Hannibal let his eyebrows rise in wonder. "Really? Now how would you know that?"

"Cause she asked me to feed and walk her dog." Fay lit up and took a deep drag. Hannibal waited. "I told her I'd help her out for one day and no more."

Hannibal pushed his hands into his pockets, pursed his lips and nodded as if lost in thought. "So she met a guy on the beach. Wonder if we're talking real competition here. Fancy car, big money?"

"Oh yeah," Fay said. "A player for sure. He flashed, and she went for the cash."

"Tourist you think?" Hannibal asked, and looked at Fay as if only she could tell. "Not a local fellow?"

"Local boys don't wear those flashy Hawaiian shirts," Fay said, blowing smoke into the sky, "and they don't rent beach houses right on Lake Holly. She told me he's up there someplace."

* * * * *

Lake Holly turned out to really be two small lakes, a few blocks apart from each other in the middle of the city. The water lay just inside Pacific Avenue, which was just inside Atlantic, and stretched from about 16th Street down past 6th. Hannibal knew because he had meandered up and down the

166

streets in the area, getting a feel for the locale. He drove with his window down and his shirt completely unbuttoned. Through his sunglasses he saw that condominiums, apartment buildings and single-family homes co-existed peacefully on the shores of the lakes, two blocks from the boardwalk. No one looked like a year-round resident, although most of them had to be.

He turned off his CD player because several variations of beach music seeped into the car from hidden sources, changing each time he turned a corner. Sometimes it seemed as if everyone he saw was dancing to the prevailing beat. Women wore Capri pants or bathing suits, regardless of their age or size. Men dragged their feet when they walked. The sun baked him through his undershirt. On almost every corner the smell of burgers, tacos and chicken reminded him that he had missed lunch. Then he would cross the intersection and forget again.

One house standing proudly behind a white picket fence drew his attention as he drove very slowly past. It was traditional brick with white painted wood, the glassed-in porch presenting a solid, conservative front. A young man was carrying a pony keg toward the door. Three women stood in his way, laughing as they drifted left and right to clear a path. Their two-piece bathing suits were the color of cherry, lemon, and lime.

And there he sat. There on the front steps of that impressive vacation home in a quiet section of the resort area, within easy walking distance of the beach. It was him. It had to be.

Hannibal didn't turn his head toward the house, but he had a full ten seconds to appraise Rod Mantooth as he rolled past. Hannibal judged him to be about five foot ten, with great broad shoulders and thick, swarthy arms. His short-sleeved shirt hung open. A tangled mass of curly hair burst out from the uncovered space. Thick hairy legs grew from the bottoms of his shorts and ended in broad, spatulate feet.

Stretching his peripheral vision to its limit Hannibal took a mental photograph. The wavy black hair was not quite long enough to touch Rod's shoulders, but it was striking out in all directions atop a large, square head. Olive skin carried a deep tan. Black marbles were sunk into his craggy face where eyes should have been, but the marbles were flat, dull and lifeless.

Women would say this face had character lines, but Hannibal saw no hint of character in the man's careless grin. Charles Bronson's face was creased this way, but Bronson never grinned like that. This was more the old Rod Steiger, or perhaps early Broderick Crawford. Did Broderick ever go by Rod?

And then Hannibal was past the house and he dared not look back for fear of attracting attention. The target had been sighted. Now Hannibal made the subtle shift from being on the hunt to actually stalking his prey. Now the game was changed.

Now the monster had a face.

* * * * *

When Marquita answered the door her eyes pierced Hannibal's dark lenses and somehow she knew. He could feel it. She nodded hello, opened the door wide and walked back inside. Sarge sat behind a tall glass, on a stool at the breakfast nook that separated the kitchen area from the living room. The glass' contents were topped with small green leaves.

"Markie was just showing me how to make a proper mint julep," Sarge said. "Of course you're supposed to have a silver cup. No idea why. So, how'd things go today? I see you relaxed a little bit." Hannibal had buttoned his shirt and pulled his coat back on, but left his tie in the car.

Marquita kept her eyes on her own glass, crushing leaves at the bottom with a spoon, releasing the fresh scent of mint into the air. "You saw him, didn't you?"

"Yes. Him and his whole party family. She's still part of the gang." He slid the photograph across the counter. Marquita's breath caught in her throat.

"Damn you're good," Sarge said with the robust energy of a fisherman who feels the big one hit his line. "So now we're in business right? We waltz over there, rearrange his face a little, find out what he did with whatever he's got, then make sure he's in no condition to do this to any more women."

Marquita grabbed Sarge's forearm and whispered, "No."

"Baby," Sarge began.

"No, Marquita needs you," Hannibal rushed to say. "And your plan wouldn't work anyway, if I read the situation right. It looks to me like this guy's a lifelong player. I think this formula he stole from Anita's house is his one-time big score. No beating is going to make him give it up."

"It'd be fun," Sarge said.

"Hannibal shook his head, but he was smiling. "Yeah, it would, but we can't do this one for fun old friend. I'm going to have to get close to this guy, find out if he still has the prize and if so how he plans to cash in on it. If it's already gone, maybe I can track it down and recover it. Even if I can't I'd need to track down the money he got and get that to Anita as compensation."

"Well, he won't like that idea," Sarge said with a wink.

"No. In that instance, you might get your chance to be persuasive with the boy."

A whirring blender stopped conversation for a moment. After ice cubes became crushed ice Marquita poured the result into her glass. Sarge took a big drink from his own glass, slurping through the crushed ice.

"So, I take it you've got a plan?" he asked.

"Sort of," Hannibal said. "I'll start with the girl in the morning, and see if I can get invited to join the party."

"Will you stay for a while, then?" Marquita said. "I would be happy to cook, and Archie said he would rent a movie for us to watch."

"She still doesn't want to go out," Sarge said in conspiratorial tones, as if Hannibal might not understand.

"We can make it an evening," Hannibal said, "on a couple of conditions. First I have to get across town and recoup a certain little G before he gets adopted by the hip-hop nation. And we'll both be back for dinner and a movie or two, if we can order in. You don't need to always be doing for us."

"Amen to that," Sarge said.

* * * * *

A danceable beat rolled in a continuous loop inside Huge Wilson's studio at a volume Hannibal could barely detect. It seemed to move up through his feet rather than seeping into his ears. The mood was the same cheerful intensity he had left hours before. Sometime during the day Monte had changed entirely, except for the look of joy on his face. The youngster was showing one way hip-hop may have gotten its name. He couldn't hold still, and Huge seemed to be getting a kick out of seeing the boy so happy.

"Hannibal you would not believe it," Monte was saying. "We recorded an entire track, from beginning to end. Man it's like science, only its music. Did you know you have to use a lot of math to lay down the beat? You got to know the number of beats per minute, and the notes, I mean, all music is made up of math."

"You don't say," Hannibal said.

"Seriously. And did you know that Huge went to Old Dominion University?"

"As a matter of fact I did," Hannibal said, with a nod toward Huge. "I do like to know a little about my clients. And it seems you've become a young producer yourself. He's even got you looking the part."

"Couldn't have my man hanging around here looking like he wasn't down with the flow," Huge said. In fact, the changes were small but the look was different. In place of the generic tee shirt he had arrived in, Monte had on a thermal undershirt with the sleeves pushed up. White painter's pants replaced his denim shorts and a new Wizards cap sat on his head, backwards of course. The big difference to Hannibal's eye was a pair of suede boots where K-mart sneakers had been. Red laces reached only to his ankles, leaving the top half of each boot hanging open. Behind his smile, Hannibal thought, "You look like a bum. Is that the style?"

"Hey, what you see ain't all we got when we went out," Monte said, dropping into the far corner, pulling forward a real surprise, a stack of paperbacks. "Look at all these. Huge says if I want to be a serious G, I need to get through these. I think I can get them all read before school starts."

Now Hannibal was impressed. Among the music oriented volumes he saw *The Beat: Go-Go's Fusion of Funk and Hip-Hop*, a book that details the origins of Washington D.C.'s original music form. He also saw *Yes I Can* by Sammy Davis Jr. and *The Autobiography of Malcolm X*, both pretty hefty volumes he had read in his youth.

"You think you can get through all these during the summer?"

Monte brushed invisible dirt off his shoulder. "Man, Huge says I'm a young Black man on the move, and I can do anything. Don't you think I can?"

Hannibal glanced at Huge, feeling that he had misstepped. "Well, of course I do. Huge is right, a man can do anything he puts his mind to. Huge here could be a teacher if he decided that was what he wanted to be."

Huge stood up, his arms wide. "Hey thank you man. I take that as a big compliment. And you know, you could be a rapper."

Monte burst into high-pitched laughter. "Oh, yeah, I'd like to see that shit."

"Language," Hannibal said.

"What you saying, Little G?" Huge said. "The man got faith in you. You ain't got no faith in him?"

"Well, I get that stuff about doing whatever you put your mind to, but this is different. I mean," Monte flipped a thumb toward Hannibal, "I mean look at him."

"Hey, fellows," Hannibal started, but Huge cut him off.

"That's cold, little G. My man here's pure street. I can see he's a soldier. Bet he's got soul he ain't showed yet."

Hannibal shook his head in frustration. "Huge, you don't have to…"

"No way," Monte said. "He couldn't even find the beat. You ever hear that crap he listens to?"

Hannibal had somehow been pushed out of this conversation about him. Trapped between reversing his position on self-determination, disappointing Monte and embarrassing himself, he could only stare with his mouth open when Huge clapped his hands in front of himself, aimed both index fingers at Monte and said, "Double or nothing," in a challenging tone.

"Double what?" Monte asked.

"Hannibal raps, you finish a book every week through the summer, with a report."

Hannibal stared down at Monte's hat, avoiding eye contact, praying that he would not accept the dare. Monte stared back at him, lower jaw jutted out.

"You're on, Huge. Sorry Hannibal, but not everybody can do everything."

* * * * *

Fifteen minutes later, Hannibal was fighting to breathe deeply. He stood alone in the studio. A microphone, smelling of sweat, hung from the ceiling directly in front of him and large headphones pressed into the sides of his head. Half a dozen young men stood on the other side of the glass wall, including Monte who was clearly having the time of his life. He had taken small cash bets from the others about Hannibal's hip-hop debut. Hannibal closed his eyes and tried to remember a single rap song, thinking he could simple imitate someone else. Not one came to mind. There was that Will Smith bit from when he was a teenager. Was it *Parents Just Don't Understand*? It was hopeless. Raised on American Forces Network in Germany, Hannibal was a rock and roll fan, and in terms of music he was stuck in the seventies. Accepting the embarrassment he reached up to slide off his glasses.

"No, no, leave them on." Huge's voice came from the headphones. "Those shades are part of who you are, and we want to capture that."

"Capture what?" Hannibal asked. "Hey, can you hear me?"

"The mike's open, brother. Now face the mike but turn to the side. Don't look over here. Just listen to me."

"Huge, I don't know how to do this," Hannibal said, but he turned to his right. Music came into his head. Not music exactly, just a beat. It seemed awfully fast.

"Take off your shirt," Huge said. As Hannibal pulled his coat off, Huge asked, "Do you listen to any kind of music at all?"

"Sure. All the time."

"Okay, name three or four bands you like," Huge said. "And put your jacket back on. There you go."

Hannibal had never worn a suit coat without a shirt before. It was comfortable. "You don't know the bands I like."

"Don't bet on it, bro," Huge said. "I sample from every body. Just run some names."

Hannibal thought as the beat slowed a bit. "Let's see. Aerosmith. ZZ Top. AC/DC. Whitesnake."

"Judas Priest?" Huge asked. "Foreigner? REO? Journey?"

"Yeah," Hannibal said, a smile stretching his lips. The beat seemed to spread out more, a pre-disco drum line dropped in and the base line strengthened and simplified.

"Now pick out a driving song," Huge said. "Something that gets you over the Beltway." Hannibal's head began to move back and forth a little, and with his eyes closed he mentally thumbed through his CD collection.

"So many good tunes," he said, almost too low to hear.

"One with a sexy undercurrent. Lots of innuendo. Aerosmith is always good. Or…"

All of a sudden, Hannibal was mentally singing along to an AC/DC anthem that seemed to sit quite comfortably on top of the beat.

"Alright, you're in the car," Huge's seductive voice murmured in the headphones. "You're all alone." The beat got louder, stronger. "You're imagining how this song would sound if you just said the words instead of singing them." Hannibal's whole body was moving now, and he was aware of being watched but somehow feeling isolated from the audience, invisible.

173

"Go ahead. I want to hear what's in your head."

The beat was booming in his head, blasting, the words mixing smoothly with it, and Hannibal just wanted to join in. Not wondering how silly he must sound, he faced the ocean of sound and jumped in.

"She was a fast machine, she kept her motor clean,

She was the best damn woman I'd ever seen,

She had me sanctified, telling me no lies.

Cause she was knocking me out with those American thighs.

She took a lover's share,

She had me fighting for air,

She told me to come but I was already there,

Cause the walls was shakin',

The earth was quakin'

My mind was achin'

We weren't faking, cause…"

At that point, Huge's falsetto joined his in the headphones:

"You shook me all night long, shake it baby, shake it baby, shake it baby."

And in the distant background, he could hear Monte say, "Oh my God," in a pained, plaintive voice.

-16-

Thursday

Hannibal winked at Fay as he stepped out of his car. He didn't think she recognized him at first, which would have been no surprise. He had not been sure he recognized himself in the mirror that morning. After winning his bet with Monte, Huge had taken some delight in helping Hannibal get into character for his return to Mariah's place. Under Huge's stylish eye he had learned to tie a do-rag, knotted at the back of his head. When he said he was aiming at "low level hustler," Huge had escorted him to what he described as the low-rent hustler's boutique: the nearest Wal-Mart.

Huge recommended a simple white tank style undershirt and dark cargo pants. The pants needed to be hanging lower than Hannibal was comfortable with. Huge's fashionable compromise was for them to be worn over a pair of swim trunks. He completed the look with a pair of black and white shell toed sneakers. Hannibal was stunned to be able to put the whole "costume" together for about thirty bucks.

"Am I cool now?" Hannibal had asked.

"Too cool," Huge had said, snatching the Oakley's from Hannibal's face. "You said low level hustler, right?" Huge replaced Hannibal's shades with the first pair of black plastic sunglasses he saw on a nearby rack. "Now you got the cheap hustler thing going on."

Hannibal was at least happy about the undershirt choice. It was another hot day, mid-eighties even with the ocean breeze coming in from the East. But he didn't think the weather was what prompted Fay to allow her knees to lazily drift apart while she smiled at him. He figured he must now fit the profile of the men who qualified for her unsubtle flirting. He nodded a quick thank-you for the offer and turned toward Mariah's stairs.

Hannibal's plan was simple. He would introduce himself to Mariah and come up with some excuse for her to introduce him to Mantooth. If he hung around for a while he would either figure out where Mantooth would hide something valuable or learn that he had already cashed in on the Cooper formula. Whether or not Mantooth had already turned the formula into money would determine his next move.

At the top of the stairs he rapped at the small pane in the top of the door. After the third series of knocks he accepted that no one was home. This was an unexpected wrinkle in his day. Had she been and gone? He could certainly get an update from Fay across the street. He really didn't want to play games with her, but he might not have any choice.

Halfway down the stairs Hannibal found himself faced with another visitor about to climb them. He took her in at a glance: pale complexion, platinum blonde hair hanging past shoulder length, big bosom, narrow waist, long legs. She wore spike heels and a short, white denim skirt. In place of a shirt or blouse she wore a yellow bikini top. Lemon yellow, he reflected, and one more article that he would have given no significance a month ago. A braided leather choker encircled her neck.

The girl paused on the fourth step, looking up at him in surprise. Hannibal did not want to be established as the one who didn't belong there, so he spoke first.

"You looking for Mariah?" he asked in stern voice.

"No," she said, spinning a key chain on her finger. "I just came back to pick up some stuff."

Her Nordic blue eyes held questions, but her words and keys had answered his. "You must be the roommate," he said, holding out a hand. "They call me Smoke."

"Really? I'm Sheryl." She offered her fingertips for a barely-there handshake. For an awkward moment they shared the staircase. Then Hannibal stepped aside and waved Sheryl forward. She offered a shallow bow and went to the door. When she unlocked the door Hannibal followed her inside. The apartment smelled like dry dog food. Sheryl looked around, surprised but not resistant. Hannibal crossed his arms and leaned back against the door.

"She's not here," Sheryl said, waving a hand at the rest of the apartment. Her swirl-patterned nails extended her fingers by almost an inch.

"That's all right," Hannibal said with a cold smirk. "You're going to take me to her." Then he locked her eyes in place with his and would not let them go. He stayed in character and tried to project the attitude he had observed during his chat room visits. After a few seconds he could see tiny tremors in her shoulders. Finally she pointed behind herself without moving her eyes from his.

"I, um, have to get some stuff."

"Then get it and let's go," Hannibal said.

Sheryl's eyes shifted left and right. Then she darted into the rear of the apartment. Hannibal heard barking and yipping from the unseen room. A dresser or bureau slid across the floor. Then it moved back into place. The dog whined the way small dogs do when an owner rubs them but they know they'll soon be alone. Then came the hurried click of stiletto heels and Sheryl appeared, carrying a medium sized handbag.

'What's in there?" Hannibal asked.

"Stuff," she said. When he pushed away from the door she added, "It's for Rod."

He opened the door. "I'll follow you."

Halfway down the stairs, Sheryl said, "You might not want to do this."

"What, meet Mariah? You afraid she's not my type?"

At the bottom of the stairs she stopped and turned. "I know Mariah can be wild, and I bet she gave you a serious come on, but..."

"But?"

"Mariah, she's Rod's girl."

"You mean one of his girls," Hannibal said. "I bet you are too."

"No, no really," she grabbed his forearm. "Mariah likes to flirt but she's Rod's girl and things could get real ugly if another guy shows up looking for her. Ugly for her."

Hannibal took Sheryl's wrist to lift her hand from his arm. He held her arm vertically, squeezing and gritting his teeth against the part he had to play. He increased the pressure until she gasped. His voice dropped into a hoarse, grating whisper.

"Listen here, bitch. I will get real ugly unless you get in your car and take me to her. Ugly on your ass. You feel me?"

Sheryl whimpered and gave a series of vigorous nods. Hannibal forced a smile as he released her. She hurried to her car, a white Volkswagen beetle. Hannibal opened the passenger door, waved good-bye to Fay, and settled in next to Sheryl.

Sheryl was a timid driver, which was all right with Hannibal while they traveled through residential areas. Again he rode through the familiar streets and watched the neighborhoods shift. He could pay more attention to his surroundings now that he wasn't driving. Children scampered, streetlights changed and before long, well-tended residences became expensive rental properties. During the drive Hannibal fiddled with her radio until he found a hip-hop station. He couldn't sing along, but Sheryl could watch him bob his head beside her. It would help to establish his character. She didn't talk during their journey. Hannibal wondered if that was due to fear of him or of Rod's reaction when they arrived.

When they reached the two story brick house with the white picket fence Sheryl pulled her Beetle into the driveway. There was off-street parking for three but hers was the only vehicle present. Stepping out of the car, Hannibal noticed how quiet the neighborhood seemed. It felt deserted, but he suspected that experience had taught Mantooth's neighbors that it was best to stay out of sight. By the time Hannibal walked through the gate, Sheryl had been to the door and was on her way back down the walk.

"There's nobody home," she said, shrugging. "No point hanging around here, right? Let's go back to my place and party, huh? I got the stuff in my purse."

Hannibal was sure that "the stuff" was one of the many illegal substances people used to enhance the "party" experience. But he had no interest in sex right then and even less interest in this girl whom he thought of as Lemon. He was wondering how long it would take him to search what looked like a five-bedroom house. Hannibal had not wanted Rod to see his car, in case he wanted to maintain surveillance on the man later, but now he wondered if he should have driven. As it was there was little chance of a quick getaway if one were called for. He was weighing the risk of getting caught rifling Rod's place when a movement down the block caught his attention. He whipped around, scanning the street, but didn't see anyone. Had there been a man back there, peering over the hood of that parked Continental?

Hannibal had lost that feeling of being followed on the long drive down from Washington, but here it was again. Did Huge send backup? No, not his style. Sarge? He could never have tailed Hannibal without being spotted long before now. Was Rod smart enough to post a lookout?

Before Hannibal could even process his own thoughts, a Jeep with an inefficient muffler roared around the corner. The vehicle almost tipped over as the driver, a young white kid with bulbous shoulders, whipped it into the driveway. Mariah hopped out of the back with a bag of groceries. In person, Hannibal could plainly see that she was Hawaiian or from some other Pacific Island. A second girl climbed more carefully out of the topless vehicle. The cherry bathing suit barely covered the important parts of a young black girl with smooth creamy skin and straightened hair. She was thicker than Anita in the thighs and hips, but otherwise the same make and model. The driver, a transplanted surfer-dude from the West Coast, stepped down and waved to Sheryl.

Rod Mantooth walked around from the passenger's side. His obsidian eyes scanned Hannibal up and down like an x-ray machine. He had a killer smile, the kind you see on torturers in World War II movies. Hannibal stood his ground as Rod moved toward him like an ebb tide. In person, the man was a primal force, raw energy, and suddenly Hannibal understood.

Rod stopped within three inches of Hannibal, craning his bull neck to stare into Hannibal's face with a coarse defiance, which his mild words belied.

"I see Sheryl brought company. And what's your name, dude?"

Hannibal stared back, fighting an unexpected urge to back down. Rod must have expected every dog to tuck his tail when they met. If he thought of himself as the alpha male he would suppose the rest of the world saw him that way too. Hannibal knew he had to show his teeth.

"They call me Smoke. Who the hell are you?"

Hannibal could feel the other four holding their breath while Rod took stock of him.

"I'm the dude who owns the house you're standing in front of, dude. This is my crew."

Hannibal nodded and jerked his chin at Mariah. "I come looking for her."

"Oh, you know Mariah?" Rod turned toward her, and she reacted. She appeared to feel something, maybe a jolt of fear. If so, her face said it felt good.

"Not really," Hannibal said. "Spotted her on the boardwalk a couple of nights ago and it looked like she was a good connection for some... product. She belong to you?"

"That's right," Rod said, thrusting a hand toward Hannibal. "Rod Mantooth. You want to talk to Mariah, you talk to me." Hannibal took Rod's fist in his own and endured a fierce, crushing grip. Because he expected it, he managed to keep his hand from being mashed.

"So, I guess you the man," Hannibal said. "That's cool. I don't know nobody down this way, not yet anyway, so I guess I need to know you. Let's go inside and talk a little business."

Rod seemed to still be evaluating Hannibal when Mariah closed in on them. Hannibal noticed that her white, spaghetti strap heels were also quite high. Three-inch heels made good legs look great but Cindy had told him they were bad for the feet. These girls didn't seem to mind. Mariah showed small but perfect teeth and ran her fingertips up Hannibal's chest.

"Let's keep him, daddy," she said over her shoulder to Rod. "I might get bored while you're training the newbie."

Rod smiled with only one side of his mouth. "We'll see if you earn that kind of a reward. Come on inside, dude."

They walked through the porch, which was choked with wicker furniture. Crossing the main threshold Hannibal spotted an alarm box beside the doorsill. A small white fixture hung in the upper left corner of the room. A motion sensor, Hannibal knew. Rod certainly didn't want any uninvited visitors.

The house itself was cool inside but that wasn't the reason that Hannibal felt small bumps rising on his skin. He sensed an odd tone, a mood filling the air as if an electric undercurrent connected everyone in the room. Mariah appeared to float free, not at all like the captive woman Sheryl had implied. The blonde boy rested a hand on the back of Sheryl's neck, guiding her steps and making a clear declaration of ownership. The third girl, the one Hannibal still had labeled Cherry in his mind, stayed in Rod's trail, following at a respectful distance. She didn't seem as comfortable in the heels or in the atmosphere as the others were, but her tentative smile expressed a brave effort to show she had what it takes. Hannibal stopped in the middle of the room, looking at no one in particular.

"Hey, Bucktooth. Any of these other people got names?"

A quick flash of anger rose and just as quickly faded in Rod's eyes. "It's Mantooth, dude. My man here is Derek. He takes care of people who can't remember my name right."

The younger man stepped forward and shook Hannibal's hand. "Derek Steel," he said through an exaggerated smile.

"Derek Steel?" Hannibal repeated. "That your real name, or you work in porn?"

Derek's face darkened in a diluted imitation of Rod's. "Do it say Smoke on your birth certificate, wiseass?"

"All right, don't get excited," Hannibal said, already knowing that at some point he was going to have to kick this boy's ass. "Derek it is. Now what about the ladies?"

"I guess you already know Sheryl," Rod said. The platinum blonde lowered her gaze to smile at Hannibal's shoes. "Mariah, she's the queen bee." To Hannibal's surprise, Mariah also faced him and lowered her eyes. "The new girl is Missy." Again, eyes lowered and her head bowed. Derek chuckled and Rod wore a look of pride. Hannibal's impression was that he was fishing for a compliment.

"You sure got them trained good."

"Ah, a man who knows," Rod said. "Sheryl, get Smoke a beer." Sheryl's head bowed slightly again, and she walked as quickly as she could without running toward the kitchen. Like that, Hannibal was accepted. Rod pressed his fists into his waist and made another proclamation.

"You girls get those groceries put away while I show Smoke around the place."

Rod ushered Hannibal upstairs for a tour. They peeked into three bedrooms with queen size beds and another, Rod's of course, that held a king size bed. Hannibal also noticed the alarms wired to every window. On their way back down a hall they met Sheryl. She was holding a tall mug with both hands. As Hannibal approached her, she presented it to him with a smile and another small bow of her head.

"Thanks," he said, accepting the mug. Then, unsure if thank you was expected under the circumstances, he added, "Good girl." Better to be condescending, he thought. Sheryl's face brightened, and she glanced at Rod as if she had made some point. Rod ignored her and moved Hannibal on through the house.

They returned to the ground floor to see the two smaller bedrooms. One of them held only a single bed. The fifth held no bed at all, having been converted into an office. A computer and every peripheral Hannibal could name were crowded onto a cheap desk, the kind you buy as a kit and have to assemble. The computer's flat screen monitor still bore a small sticker indicating that it had been a free upgrade. Brand new, Hannibal thought. He noted the stack of CD ROMs on the desk, but doubted that the disc Rod stole from Anita would be lying there among the clutter.

"Nice setup," Hannibal said. "How fast is it?" He stepped forward toward the computer desk. Rod's right arm shot forward, barring Hannibal's progress.

"You don't go in there."

"Hey, I just wanted to see…"

"It's seven hundred megahertz," Rod said. "The house came with the high speed cable internet connection. And, you don't go in there."

"Okay. I'm not the kind that gets in somebody else's stash."

"That's good," Rod said with a cold smile. "Bad things happen to that kind."

Hannibal's voice dropped low and he held Rod's eyes. "Yeah, like the shit that happens to guys who threaten me." Then he raised his palms, smiled and stepped back. Challenging Rod was not the way to get into his sick little family. Hannibal would have to surrender the alpha male position but retain enough respect to capture, and maintain a firm grip on, the number two spot.

Turning away he noticed that Mariah had seen their exchange. She diverted her eyes from his but her smile communicated far more than her eyes would have. Then Rod snapped her name and she almost shivered. The warm frisson of fear, Hannibal thought. A chill. A tingle. That same feeling he enjoyed on a good roller coaster as a kid. She got it from Rod, and she seemed to like it.

"Go tell Missy it's time for her to model those new swim suits. Want her to look just right for our little party. We'll be in the living room waiting."

Mariah dared a pout. "You're going to pick her," she said in a voice dripping with disappointment. He raised an eyebrow, and she hurried away.

In the living room Hannibal surveyed the scene for dynamics. A white leather sofa sat beside a black leather recliner. A white easy chair was turned at a ninety-degree angle to the recliner. A small coffee table was in front of the sofa. Sandalwood scented smoke drifted up from a stick of incense burning on the table. The ottoman at the end of the coffee table was accessible from either chair.

Rod plopped into the big recliner. Derek planted himself in the center of the white leather sofa, his arms stretched across its back. He was comfortable in his place as second chair, dominating the part of the room that Rod didn't hold. Too bad for him.

Sheryl entered the room from the far side, nearer Rod than Derek. She paused as Hannibal crossed in front of her, hooking the ottoman with a foot and dragging it closer to Rod's chair. He turned to sit on the ottoman and face Rod. Sheryl started to pass him, moving toward the sofa.

"So tell me big man," Hannibal began, "what's this big party you were telling Mariah about?" As he spoke his left hand darted out, fingers sliding into the back of Sheryl's waistband. Without losing eye contact with Rod, he pulled her down onto his knee. He could only imagine the exchange of expressions between her and Derek. He had to keep his attention on Rod to demonstrate that Derek's reaction, and Sheryl's feeling on the matter, were of no concern to him. Rod's grin told him that he had made the right move.

"You know, I got an instinct for people," Rod said, pushing the chair back and raising the footrest. "I like you. I think you and me, we're from the same school."

While Hannibal tried to keep the acid bile down out of his throat, Mariah stepped back into the room. Hannibal noticed that the other two men had dropped their shoes at the door.

Mariah had changed from her beach flip-flops to white spike heels. She tapped over to Rod, whispered, "She's ready" through a seductive smile, and lowered herself to her knees in one smooth motion. Shifting over onto one hip she rested both hands on the arm of the chair with practiced grace, and centered her chin on the backs of her hands. It was "I Dream of Genie" cute, and Rod rewarded her with a pat on the head. Hannibal had seen it described in writing on a screen, but watching a woman actually move through those motions was entirely different.

"She's exquisite," Hannibal said. "I take it the sister is newer."

Rod actually glowed at the compliment. "Yeah, well, some guys raise retrievers, right? This is harder, but a lot more rewarding. Okay, Missy, you're on."

All eyes followed Missy's entrance. She wore a one-piece suit in the same cherry red as the bikini she had on before. She stepped across the room as if she was on a runway and flipped her long, thick mass of straightened black hair in a childish imitation of a fashion model move. She turned slowly, arching her back a little. Even on the exposed parts of her perfectly rounded behind her complexion was uniform, smooth and even, like Belgian chocolate. Rod nodded and smiled, and waved her away.

"Isn't she the sweetest?" he said when Missy was gone. "Mariah found her. Practically begged to get in with us. I think she knows who can train her right. The party I mentioned before will be her, uh, her initiation. After that, I'm thinking of a long sea voyage. I'm getting sick of this place."

"Really?" Hannibal said. "Wish I could just get in the wind for a while. Had to leave D.C. in kind of a hurry."

Missy returned in another red outfit. This time she wore a satin tank top that didn't quite hang to her navel, and a thong that left her rear completely exposed. After noticing the perfect shape of her legs as they moved, Hannibal's gaze moved up to her eyes. The smile was real, but he could see that Missy wasn't totally comfortable in this bathing suit. He didn't understand why a woman would agree to embarrass herself this way, but it reflected a weakness of spirit that made him ache in a place he couldn't identify.

"So, a big party, eh?" he said, keeping his emotions out of his voice. "Sounds like big fun, especially if this initiation is what I expect it is."

Speaking across Rod's lap, Mariah said, "I'm hoping that Daddy will invite you tomorrow night, Smoke. He'll be occupied for quite a while with the newbie and I'll need someone to," he hung on the sigh that filled her long pause, before she said, "talk to."

Hannibal's urge to answer was interrupted by a gentle hand kneading his shoulder. Sheryl seemed to be expressing an interest in him too.

"That's the one," Rod bellowed, capturing everyone's attention. "That's the outfit for you, Missy. You wear that to the party, and in fact I think you should have it for the big cruise."

Missy smiled and nodded her head in a move that was almost a curtsy. She left the room a bit faster than necessary, as is she was in a hurry to get out of sight. Hannibal wished he could comfort her, tell her that the nightmare she had volunteered for would end soon, but his focus was on Rod's words.

"Cruise? You mean the party's not going to be here?"

Rod emptied his glass and handed it to Mariah. "Sure it is. Day after tomorrow. But I'm planning on a nice, long trip next week. Floating on down to The Keys maybe. I'll just take my crew here on down for some tropical fun."

"Damn, you must have some heavy bread," Hannibal said. He thought, *Damn, you must have already sold the formula.*

Got a nice deal in the works," Rod said, his eyes glazing over as his face adopted a dreamy expression. "Soon as I tie up some loose ends with this deal I'm working on, life's going to be the way it should have been all along."

"All right! Sounds like your star's on the rise," Hannibal said. He thought, *All right! He hasn't completed the deal yet.*

"Smoke, what's coming is going to make everything before look like small time," Rod said, rubbing Mariah's head again. "I been working on this one for a long time. Had to make the right contacts, lay some groundwork, you know. But this is it, the big score, and after that I'll have some serious juice."

"I can see it. At sea, on your own yacht I bet, with just your posse here," Hannibal said, checking the faces in the room. "Classy, but it seems to me things ain't too balanced here. I count three fine ho's, but only you two G's."

"We manage," Derek called from the sofa.

Hannibal leaned in closer, pushing his sunglasses up his nose with an index finger. "Look here, an operator like you might need some serious backup when you roll with the big boys." Halfway through that sentence Hannibal glanced over at Derek and snorted. "You know, somebody who'll get some respect when they talk to people." He felt Sheryl's hand slowly rubbing his back. She had already switched sides.

Hannibal also felt Rod's hard eyes assessing him. Had he overstepped? Holding eye contact with the man, Hannibal handed his glass to Sheryl and said, "I'm empty" in a flat tone. She hopped off his lap and headed for the kitchen. Rod's smile grew in very small increments. His gaze shrank the room to just the two of them.

"I might be able to use somebody who knows how to make a deal."

"I'm as street as they come," Hannibal said, the easiest lie he had ever told. "Been hustling all my life. I know how to deal."

"Can you fight?"

"I get the job done," Hannibal said, grinning.

Rod turned toward Mariah, as if for a hug. "Takes more than muscle, right babe?"

Without warning his beefy arm swung back like a flail toward Hannibal's smile.

-17-

Hannibal's left hand snapped up, catching Rod's wrist a couple of inches before the fist reached his face. Rod's arm hung there in space, vibrating in Hannibal's grip, testing his strength. That backhand blow might have broken Hannibal's jaw if it had reached its target. Rage boiled up from his gut but he kept it locked behind clenched teeth. As much as he wanted to break Rod's grinning face, he knew that a fight at this point would not get him any closer to his real objective, Anita Cooper's stolen legacy. Instead he pushed his face even closer to Rod's, pressing his chest against the arm of the chair, showing his teeth like an angry wolfhound. His free hand rose to his face and he slid his glasses away. His stare focused every ounce of his fury on Rod's empty eyes.

"You do that again, sucker," Hannibal said in a low flat voice, "you'd best be prepared to throw down."

Rod returned his stare, and it was obvious that he was not intimidated. Hannibal noticed how quiet the room had become. No one moved. After a few tense seconds, Rod's arm relaxed and he pulled it away from Hannibal's grip. One eyebrow rose, and a new appraisal seemed to be taking place.

"They green?" Rod asked. It took Hannibal a moment to realize that the conversation had moved to a discussion of his eyes.

"Sometimes. Sometimes blue in the right light."

Rod's flash grin returned. "A nigger with hazel eyes. Well I'll be damned." He swung his hand forward at Hannibal's head, but it was a playful feint this time, and Hannibal blocked it with ease. "You're unique. I like unique. Fits in with my destiny."

Hannibal backed away, swallowing Rod's casual use of the hated word. A cold glass pushed into his hand, indicating that Sheryl was back. "Oh, you got a destiny and shit?"

"Yeah. I'll tell you about it sometime, if you end up sticking around."

"Well, that might be interesting," Hannibal said, standing, "but right now I'm getting a little itchy about where I left my ride." Hannibal gulped down half of the beer. Everyone but Rod stood up, as if to recognize his leaving.

"I'll drop you at your car," Derek said.

"Don't sweat yourself. Blondie here can take me. She knows where I'm parked."

"I wouldn't mind giving you a ride," Mariah said, moving in and cutting Sheryl out of Hannibal's space. She gave him a warm parting hug, one hand sliding into his back pocket to squeeze his behind. He held his smile, but caught the disapproval on Rod's face and the disappointment on Sheryl's. If he wanted to maintain the delicate balance in his relationship to Rod, he needed to be aware of the lines he should not cross.

"Maybe another time," he said, returning the hug before pulling away. "For now, I think Sheryl will take good care of me. Let's roll, Shorty."

* * * * *

Sheryl pulled into a parking space three cars ahead of Hannibal's car and pushed the gearshift into park. Hannibal thanked her for the lift and popped his door, more than ready to return to the normal world.

"Don't you want to come up?" she asked. "For a drink or something?"

"Or something?"

By way of explanation, Sheryl leaned to the side and pressed a kiss onto Hannibal's mouth. Despite its startling degree of passion, the kiss seemed tinged with desperation and loneliness, two things Hannibal didn't expect a woman in her position to feel. But then, maybe being treated like a second-class citizen had its similarities to being alone.

"That's nice babe, but I got things to do."

"Don't you like me?" Sheryl asked, sliding a hand across his chest. "You pulled me away from Derek, so you must want me."

"Don't worry, I'll make sure I get the chance to break you off, but you're going to have to wait. I can drop by tomorrow."

"But I'm ready right now," she said, sliding her fingertips up the inside of his thigh. "And tomorrow we're all going with Rod up to someplace in Maryland to pick up his car. Right now the apartment is empty. And I saw how Mariah was looking at you back at the house."

"So?"

"So I might not get another chance at you," Sheryl said, hiding her eyes for just a moment. "I know she's prettier, but I know how to make you happy. I swear I do."

Her tongue flicked into his ear. He turned his head to avoid it and found himself kissing her again. Hannibal struggled to keep his mind clear. Had Rod instructed her to seduce him, to test him, sexually? If so, it might seem suspicious if he resisted her too well. Or she could be a gift from Rod, stressing his ownership of his girls in the way he did with Marquita. In that case, Sheryl might be punished if she failed to arouse him.

She was panting now and somehow she was able to cling to him after he left her car. They managed to climb the stairs to Sheryl's apartment while entwined like dates after the prom. Sheryl fumbled in her small purse, found the key, and got the door open. No yipping greeted them. He figured the dog was with Fay, that poor woman sitting across the street who must have hated Sheryl right then for bringing home a good time that she herself was interested in.

Once inside, Sheryl backed toward one of the bedrooms, pulling Hannibal along like a dancer whose waltz partner had decided to lead. But he was quite sure that waltzing was not her objective. He followed with awkward movements, not really sure of the steps in this particular dance.

The room, no more than twelve feet square, barely held the twin bed, dresser and vanity table. White walls and thin carpet made the space feel cheap, but the thick purple comforter on the bed told him that Sheryl wanted to brand the space as her own. He wondered if she had the same plan for him.

"I am going to make you feel so good," she said, mumbling into Hannibal's chest while she struggled to pull his shirt up and off him. She nibbled at his exposed chest while one hand slid downward to cup his crotch. Only then did Hannibal realize that his body was not responding to her as she expected. Sheryl whimpered, a sound halfway between pleading and fear.

"What?" she asked, staring up at him. He wasn't sure if she was asking what was wrong, what she had done wrong, or what he wanted her to do next. Her worried eyes and half-open mouth said she was terrified that he might not find her desirable. Some part of him wanted to reassure her. Another part wanted to break away to reassert his loyalty to the woman he loved. Those circuits crossed in a way that caused his mind to conjure an image of Cindy. That image spurred his body to an instant response, and Sheryl felt the reassurance she needed swelling in her hand. Catching his breath, Hannibal pushed her gently away.

"You a wildcat, Shorty," he said, forcing a crooked smile. "No need to rush, baby. Let me get to the bathroom. Then you and me can have some fun."

Sheryl's reluctance showed when she pulled her hands away from Hannibal's body and dropped backward onto the bed. He stepped into the bathroom and closed the door.

This was very much a girl's room. Not that it was overly clean, but the collection of products overwhelmed him. The small counter was covered with bottles and jars in every conceivable shape and color. The edge of the bathtub was equally littered with shampoos, conditioners, and cleansers of every stripe and a bewildering assortment of ways to remove hair from the human body.

While considering his surroundings Hannibal shoved his hands into his back pockets. His right pocket, which he expected to be empty, was not. He pulled out a small slip of paper on which was written a telephone number. The 571 exchange told him it was a cell phone. Only Mariah had been close enough to slip something into his pocket. So, she wanted to risk Rod's anger by having Smoke ring her number. This level of independence struck him as mysterious for a woman who played submissive.

None of which helped him deal with his present situation. Hannibal stared at himself in the mirror. At least he assumed it was his own face. The character staring back at him, wearing a do rag and cheap sunglasses, reminded him that he needed to stay in character to get closer to Rod in order to separate him from the Cooper formula. But the man inside knew that this situation involved more than business. His love for Cindy was the cornerstone of his reality, the most authentic thing in his life. He could not imagine cheapening their relationship by having sex with a woman he just met, especially since he met at least two of her previous lovers on the same day. Actually, they would be concurrent lovers.

On the other hand, his dedication to the case was absolute. And wasn't maintaining his cover for the good of a client a sufficient excuse for anything he might do? Especially if no one ever had to know he had done it?

Disappointed with what the man in the mirror was trying to convince him to do, Hannibal opened the medicine cabinet. Considering all the preparations scattered about the room, curiosity drove him to wonder if there was anything left that could be in the medicine cabinet. It was clogged with contents. Among the band-aids, dental floss and aspirin he spotted something that looked familiar. The small prescription bottle was half full of Rohypnol, the roofies Rod had fed to Marquita to dull her resistance. He remembered Dr. Roberts saying that one of them hit like ten Valium. Now here was a possible solution. If she was passed out or sedated enough, he could do anything and she would never know. This meant that he could do nothing at all, leave her sleeping, and tell her tomorrow that she had been a great time. He closed the medicine cabinet, winked at himself in the mirror, and slipped the little bottle into his pocket. He could pull this off, and in fact, it could be fun.

Reaffixing Smoke's arrogant swagger, Hannibal reentered the small bedroom. His smile never wavered at the sight of Sheryl on her back, topless, with the comforter pulled just high enough to reach her hipbones.

"Damn you look yummy," Sheryl said, her eyes gliding up and down his frame. "Climb in and I'll give you the ride of your life."

"I think that's going to be the other way around," Hannibal replied. "But first, you got anything decent to drink around here?"

Sheryl rolled away from him toward the end table on the other side of the bed. The comforter went with her, revealing her full nakedness. When she turned back one hand gripped the neck of a Jack Daniels bottle. The other balanced two glasses. Hannibal took the glasses first, setting them on the dresser before pouring each half full from the bottle. He was thinking of something else to ask for to prompt Sheryl to turn around again so that he could drop a pill into her glass, when he heard a thump from the front of the apartment.

Derek had pushed the door open with such force that it slammed against the wall. His fists were clenched so hard that his knuckles were white. His chest seemed to expand to twice its size with each deep breath. His eyes flashed more with rage than surprise. The frozen tableau that greeted him was certainly self-evident. Sheryl sat naked on the bed while Hannibal poured whiskey into two glasses. She may have been the offender, but his focus was on Hannibal as if only the two men were in the room.

"What the fuck?" Derek spat the words like venom.

Hannibal deflected the verbal attack, turning to Sheryl. "What the hell's he doing here? He got a key?"

Torn between them, Sheryl stammered. "I didn't lock it.

Derek this isn't..." her voice trailed off, as is she couldn't think of just what this was not.

Hannibal turned back to face the other man. It was Derek's play. He had several options to choose from. His next move would determine how well he came out of this encounter.

"You son of a bitch!" Derek stepped forward, cocking his right fist like an arrow he was about to launch. It was not the smart play, but it was the one Hannibal expected.

"You don't want none of this, boy," Hannibal said in a low tone.

"Like hell." Derek's left hand waved forward, sweeping away an attack Hannibal never launched. The instant before Derek fired his right fist forward Hannibal flipped a glass full of Jack Daniels into his face. Derek howled as much in anger as pain. Hannibal sidestepped Derek's long loping right, planted his feet and snapped his own fist up into Derek's solar plexus. The blonde's mouth hung open for a second and he dropped to his knees.

Hannibal grabbed the boy by his hair and turned his face upward. When he pulled his other fist back to smash downward he heard Sheryl gasp. It was the sound of a woman who didn't want to see someone she cared about get hurt. That made it easy for him to stop. Derek stared up through a haze of fear and Hannibal wondered if this was the way the boy felt when he looked at Rod.

"We was just about to have a little fun, punk, and I didn't see your name on the bitch anywhere," Hannibal said. "I ought to break your face just for ruining the mood, but I think Rod likes you and I kind of like the idea of partying with his crew for a while so I'll let you slide this time. But check it, you get in my way again and I will fuck you up serious." He bent low to shove his face close to Derek's. "You getting this white boy? Or do I have to stick my dick in your eye so you can see where I'm coming from?"

Derek was panting and shaking like a recruit on the first day of basic training. "I get it. Really. I get it."

Derek's head snapped forward when Hannibal released his hair. Hannibal stepped backward, pointing at Sheryl. "This moron just cost you the best ride of your life, bitch. Maybe I'll catch you at the party, although I got my eye on the Island girl." He was out the door and down the stairs before either of the others could gather an appropriate comment. Good. Derek was scared of him, and Sheryl believed he was ready to bed any willing woman. If the set up had been a test of some sort, they would both report back to Rod with exactly what Hannibal wanted him to hear.

Hannibal was already reaching for his car door handle when he realized how close his bumper was to the big black Cadillac Escalade parked in front of him. Plenty of adrenaline was already pumping through his system and if some clown had so much as dusted the white tornado's bumper there would be hell to pay. He stepped forward and looked down. The SUV was backed to within an inch of his car. He looked up, casting a nasty glare at the tinted windows. When the well-dressed drive stepped down to the street Hannibal felt encouraged. He was big enough to hit. He had the black hair and uneven complexion of a Sicilian and his suit and shoes proclaimed his loyalty to his Italian brothers.

"You got a problem?" Hannibal asked. "Move this piece of shit."

As if he hadn't heard Hannibal's words, the driver said, "Get in. Boss wants to talk to you."

"Why don't you put me in the car, dickhead?" Hannibal said, taking a step back to firm his stance. The driver remained still, and the back door popped open. The occupant looked back at Hannibal, scanning him up and down.

"I hardly recognized you, stud. But if you're still on that case, I got something you want." Anthony Ronzini leaned out of the car. "Come take a ride with me, and let me tell you something about your prey."

-18-

"You packing?" the driver asked. His arms were folded in such a way that his right hand could have been resting on the butt of a gun in a shoulder holster.

"And you are?"

"They call me Wheels. You packing?"

"Right ankle," Hannibal said. The driver nodded, and Hannibal bent to raise his pants and slowly pull the Smith and Wesson Model 42 Centennial Airweight revolver from its holster. He took the gun by its two-inch barrel and tossed it to the driver. "I'll need that back."

"Who else would want it?" Wheels asked, pocketing the piece. "Cell phone?" Hannibal tossed his phone too. Wheels sneered at it. "Pager?" Hannibal shook his head. "Blackberry?" Again, Hannibal shook his head. Wheels gave him a dismissive puff of air, pocketed the phone and got back in the driver's seat. Hannibal stepped up into the back seat beside Ronzini.

Hannibal was not comfortable getting into Ronzini's vehicle without backup. He didn't like the look of the driver, or the expression on the face of the bruiser in the shotgun seat, whom he knew as Freddy. They both remembered how Hannibal had taken Ronzini out of a car at gunpoint with Freddy helpless to interfere. He especially didn't like going anywhere with Ronzini without someone else knowing where he would be. But he understood the rules of this game. Now that Ronzini appeared to have come through for him, he knew he would just have to play it out and trust to the old gangster's honor.

"Can I ask where we're going?"

"Sure, sure," Ronzini said in a manner that seemed a bit too gracious. "A friend of mine has a nice little place down at the south end of the beach. We'll talk there."

They rode in silence for twenty minutes or so before turning into a driveway at the edge of the coast. A breeze blew in off the ocean and the air was crisp with salt and that odd electricity that seems to blow in off the Atlantic. The sky was just beginning to darken and Hannibal stood for a moment staring out to infinity where the ocean seemed to merge with the firmament. He thought he saw a dolphin break the surface but he might have been mistaken. If not, then the ocean itself was laughing at him from far away. Cool, damp air whipped around him, energizing him. He was still until Wheel's waved him inside.

In Hannibal's eyes the beach house was a transplanted mansion. He followed Ronzini and Wheels through a vast living room to a formal dining room, aware of Freddie behind him but not turning to look at him. Wheels kept on to the kitchen, but Ronzini turned off at a formal dining room. He settled in to the chair at the head of the table, so Hannibal dropped onto the one at the other end. While Freddie placed an ashtray and cigar at Ronzini's elbow, Hannibal heard an espresso machine making its locomotive sounds in the kitchen. He sat patiently, because to do otherwise would be disrespectful.

Wheels placed huge cups of cappuccino in front of Ronzini and Hannibal. Freddie laid a folder full of loose papers at Ronzini's left. Then both men left the room. This, from Ronzini, was a conspicuous show of respect in return. Respect, and trust.

Hannibal sipped from his cup, smiled as the rich flavor filled his mouth, and then sat up straight. "Okay, so I've met our boy, and he's everything I expected. Now, what else do I need to know?"

"You need to know who this man is," Ronzini said, using a

penknife blade to snip the end of his cigar. "You need to know the path this Roderick Mantooth is on, so you can see how your path intersects it."

Hannibal settled back in the wooden chair, crossing his ankles under the table. "He's on the fast track to hell. He's just a mean, tough street punk. Like you."

Ronzini struck a wooden match and lit his cigar. "Well, same streets anyway. Brooklyn. Dyker Heights. Bensonhurst. But he's really an ambitious tough guy with tunnel vision, who can't see his real part in the big picture. Like you."

"So it all starts in your old neighborhood," Hannibal said. The dense cloud of smoke made him crinkle his nose.

Ronzini didn't seem to notice. He pulled a pair of reading glasses from an inside jacket pocket and opened the folder. "It starts in 1989, the first time cops pinch a sixteen year old named Rodney Johannsen for stealing a car. He pleads guilty to a reduced charge and..." Ronzini raised his eyebrows toward Hannibal.

"His record is wiped clean," Hannibal said in disgust. "This is how the justice systems gets petty thieves off to a good start."

"Right," Ronzini said, puffing his cigar again. "Two years later he gets busted for assault. The guy he beat half to death was an off duty cop. Then he starts getting big ideas. By 1992 he caught my attention by stealing a couple of ATM machines."

"Robbing," Hannibal said, correcting Ronzini by reflex.

"No, stealing. He got a bulldozer and some chains and yanked them right out of the walls."

Hannibal's jaw dropped. "You're kidding. Nobody's that arrogant, not that young."

"Hell, that's just the part the cops know. I know he spent a year up in the Bronx. Friends told me he sold a hundred pounds of weed to some drug dealer, then turned around and stole it back. Hell of a way to raise starter capital. And when he comes back to Brooklyn in '94 he's Roderick Mantooth. He's what, twenty at this point, and we get word he robbed a guy by bashing his head in with a baseball bat."

"Still a punk," Hannibal said in a thoughtful tone, "But you can see he kept on chasing the big score." Hannibal had resented the lecture form of Ronzini's presentation at the start. Now he was starting to see patterns and gain new understanding of the man he had spent the afternoon with. Ronzini shuffled sheets of paper, his glasses sliding low on his nose. Sometimes Hannibal saw him as a gangster, but other times he looked like a businessman. Right then, he looked a bit scholarly. A senior professor, tenured in the crime department, Hannibal thought.

"Now we're up to '94," Ronzini continued, "and our boy Mantooth has a gang together. They're doing the usual petty break-ins, mostly up in the Bronx and out in Staten Island. Then they decide to rob a bank in a mall. They do it Mantooth style, busting in the door with sledgehammers."

"Tell me they caught him."

"Boy lives a charmed life," Ronzini said. "Bank reported a loss of three hundred grand. I figure they padded by about a third. You'd think that was the big score for this jamoke, but his crew stayed in business, stealing cars, shaking people down, doing odd jobs for the local mob. Then a couple months later he's driving the getaway car for more home invasions out on the island. That seems to have stopped after they found someone home. A woman was shot in the head. Not sure if it was him or one of his crew. Anyway, I think the crew fell apart after that."

"Even the bad guys don't want to hang with this wacko," Hannibal said. He and Ronzini lifted their cups at the same time, sipped, and put them down. Something about that made Hannibal uncomfortable.

"Don't know much about 1995. He got busted for beating up a guy, so maybe he was working protection or enforcement for somebody. Anyhow, he pleads guilty to lesser charges again, but now the cops are watching him. Less than six months later he whips up on a club bouncer."

"Isn't it usually the other way around?" Hannibal asked.

"The way I get the story, Mantooth tried to get into a club that was too exclusive for him. The bouncer went after him with a club. Mantooth not only took it from him, but cracked him in the head with it. And this is when he decides he ought to get out of New York." Ronzini shuffles more papers, puffs, and sends another stream of acrid smoke Hannibal's way. "We pick him up in Miami in '96, accused of stealing a Lexus and changing the VIN number. He paid the owner off to get him to drop the charges. And it's apparently about this time he gets deep into this dom-sub stuff." Ronzini looked up. "You know about that stuff?"

"He dominates submissive women," Hannibal said, nodding. "He's pretty good at manipulating women's feelings. Makes me crawly."

"Good," Ronzini said. "It ought to. Our boy apparently meets a woman down there with money, takes over her life and makes her his slave."

"Patient zero," Hannibal said under his breath. "Or victim zero. The trail of broken women starts right there."

"From all reports he did her pretty bad before he emptied her bank account and kicked her to the curb. Then he bought a little club down there and life got good for him. Don't know if you know much about Miami, but at that time down on South Beach things were pretty rough."

"Miami Vice," Hannibal said. "Art deco and big boats."

"Yeah, and biker gangs and drug addicts and derelicts all over. Right about the time he got this club going, it started to get cool for sports stars and rock stars to hang out there. He had three or four girls at this point, and he had them waiting on him and on whoever he told them to service. Real dominant types didn't like what he did to his women, but they just stayed away from him. Then he put the word out that he was connected to the mob. The real crime bosses didn't like that but it seemed harmless and they let it slide. The rumor made him and his place cooler to the rap and rock crowds. They all think they're gangsters. The mob sent a man to make contact, you know, explain the rules to him. Set up a cozy little live-and-let-live deal. He let the dealers do their thing in his place, the right people drank free, girls worked in there without giving Mantooth a cut, and like that."

Hannibal reached for his cup, only then realizing that his jaws were clenched so tightly that it required a conscious effort to open his mouth. The brew was still hot, still strong, but it now had a bitter taste. Ronzini was quiet, as if waiting for Hannibal to digest the information.

"This guy's no businessman," Hannibal said after a moment. "Even with the mob nod, I can't believe he ran a club successfully."

"Didn't last long," Ronzini said. "Less than a year later the club is destroyed in a fire that looks mighty suspicious to me, but the insurance company paid. He dumped the money into a bigger, better place, subsidized by another woman of means, and managed by a girl who knew the bar business but I guess didn't know much about men."

"You'd think hanging with the big guys would have smoothed this clown out," Hannibal said. "If the Madonnas and K.D. Langs didn't change his behavior toward women, somebody like 50 Cent should have shot him. How's he still walking around doing this stuff?"

"Guys like this don't change. Look here," Ronzini said, pulling individual sheets of paper from his folder and flipping them aside. "Accused of beating up an employee because the guy took a break without permission. No charges filed. Smashes a pro football player in the face with a beer bottle in his own VIP lounge. No suit filed, thanks to some nasty threats. Oh, this is nice. Gets in a fight with a professional weight lifter. The guy was the ex-husband of one of Mantooth's subbies. The weight lifter left town right after that. Later claimed that Mantooth flew a bunch of guys down from New York to go after him. Let's see, caught driving a stolen car. "

"Charges dropped," Hannibal said. Ronzini nodded.

"Beat up patrons in the bar."

"Charges dropped," Hannibal said again.

"Arrested for assault and attempted murder after he stabbed paparazzi multiple times for taking his picture."

"My God. Charges dropped again? What the hell sat this guy behind bars?"

Ronzini chuckled. "Well, it wasn't until 2001. Guess he shouldn't have told that undercover FBI agent about the neighbor he wanted to have whacked. Turns out the guy was a witness to a crime one of Mantooth's pals committed. The feds did some digging and turned up enough to threaten charges for murder, robbery and racketeering. That was enough to make him turn in some pals in exchange for a three year vacation in a minimum security cell."

"Which is where he meets Vernon Cooper, and where the story begins for me." Hannibal hated the indiscriminate way luck got handed out in the universe. Career criminals get their share just like heroes do.

"In what way?" Ronzini asked. "What is your business with this man?" Ronzini leaned back and drew hard on his cigar. For the first time it occurred to Hannibal that Ronzini had done all this research without really knowing why Hannibal was chasing Mantooth. He knew this was business, knew it was about recovering stolen property, but little else. Hannibal smiled, nodding in recognition of his obligation. But at this point he was no longer begging for help. They would now speak as equals.

"Okay, Tony, here it is. Mantooth had a cellmate in the joint. The man was a chemist who developed something very special. Mantooth found out where the formula was hidden, and sometime after that this man died suddenly in prison. When he got out, Mantooth stole the records of the formula from his old cell mate's daughter."

"A new pharmaceutical?" Ronzini asked. "I ask this because drug people have expressed an interest."

Hannibal looked at the floor. "Not a drug."

"If not a new narcotic, then what?" Ronzini sat still, exuding calm, but Hannibal felt the pressure of his eyes. It wasn't his secret to share. It wasn't any of Ronzini's business. It wasn't something a career criminal ought to know. But he felt an obligation here. And in some ways, this was a man he could trust. He took a deep breath, and let it out while saying, "Shit" under his breath.

"From all reports, it appears to be the beginnings of a cure for addiction."

Ronzini's mouth dropped open, and a small smile curled his lips. "So. In Hitchcock terms, this is the McGuffin. Drug dealers undoubtedly want to destroy the formula. Drug manufacturers want to own it. Or, even this could be dealt illegally. Imagine being able to use cocaine without worrying about getting hooked."

"I don't care who wants it," Hannibal said. "It belongs to the girl."

"Unless Mantooth sells it to make his big score," Ronzini said, pointing his cigar at Hannibal. "This, we can expect soon. One of the friends he made in Miami is on his way up here with a great deal of cash. He must mean to trade it for this secret formula."

"Then tell me, am I going up against the Cuban mob if I snatch the prize?"

"Think about it," Ronzini said, leaning back with his hands laced over his ample stomach. "What do you know about this man now?"

"I know this guy has been chasing the big score all his life, and never managed to make it stick," Hannibal said, standing and beginning to pace. "His temper gets in his way half the time. He's desperate to land the big fish, and he thinks he's got it on the hook now."

"And one other thing." Ronzini leaned forward, using an index finger to drive his point home. "Consider the reason for the time lapse. Why does he still have the formula to sell?" When Hannibal didn't answer, Ronzini shook his head, looking disappointed. "He offered this prize to the local people, those who run this city, and they turned him down. They turned him down in Washington. They turned him down in Atlanta and Philly."

This brought a smile to Hannibal's face. "He's not a made man. I don't get it, but I guess the real players don't want anything to do with him. How come?"

Ronzini spread his hands wide. "He's messy and he gets his mess on other people. That's why you can do this thing. Even though he's inside, he's an outsider."

"So if I can figure out how to get the formula away from him…"

"He won't stop if you do," Ronzini said, in a very matter of fact tone. "You know you'll have to take him out."

"That ain't me," Hannibal said.

"It would make you some important friends."

"Those friends I don't need," Hannibal said.

"We'll see," Ronzini said, standing. "You're a blunt instrument, my friend. When the time comes, we'll see."

As they headed for the car, Hannibal held his tongue, not offended by the comparison to a blunt instrument, but still bristling at Ronzini referring to him as friend.

-19-

SATURDAY

"You should have seen it, Sarge," Monte said through a mouth full of pastry. "My man was riding that beat old school. Rhyming like Nelly on speed, boy. I never had so much fun losing a bet in my life!"

At the stove, Marquita said, "Now I begin to wonder if there is anything our Mr. Jones can't do."

Hannibal smiled, shook his head, and bit into another of the powdered sensations, even as he listened to more sizzling in a big skillet in front of Marquita. She flipped the little pastries in a couple of inches of oil as they floated to the surface, then fished them out and laid them on paper towels. She called them beignets, and they filled the suite with a sweet scent. They tasted like powdered donuts without holes, only lighter than anything he'd ever gotten from Dunkin Donuts or Krispy Kreme. And the fact that he, Sarge and Monte were sucking them down as quickly as she could pull them out of the pan and powder them meant they were still warm as he chewed and washed them down with hot, fresh coffee.

"Oh, he has his limits, Markie," Sarge said, at the table in his undershirt. "Boy can't dance a lick. Can't cook for squat. And don't get him for a partner in pinochle."

"Thanks for the support, pal," Hannibal said, delivering a

playful punch to Sarge's shoulder. "Like everybody else I just do what I can. Now Marquita here, she can cook."

"There is more I could do," she said, ladling the last of the beignets out of the pan.

"What else?" Hannibal asked with a shrug. "You put up with me calling at a ridiculous hour after I picked up Monte last night, because I forgot to check in and let you know we were okay until I was getting ready for bed myself. You made us this super breakfast. You hung around here an extra day when I know you'd rather be as far from Rod Mantooth as possible. What else could you possibly do?"

"I could testify," she said, and Hannibal felt the chill that raced through her body as those words flew out. "I could go to court and testify. If you could get Anita to talk about Rod beating her, between us I bet we could get him thrown into jail."

Sarge reached her in three long strides and wrapped his beefy arms around her. For a moment she shook within his embrace. "You," Sarge said in a soft voice, close to her ear, "are a very brave woman."

"Yes, that would call for a great deal of courage," Hannibal said. "You and Anita would have to explain your history with Rod to the police. And you would have to make them understand why you did certain things." Hannibal's eyes cut to Monte, who seemed to understand that this was no time to be asking questions. He filled his mouth with a beignet as if to assure his own silence.

"Yeah, baby, then you'd have to face the whole thing again in open court," Sarge said.

"If you got through it all, Rod probably would end up in jail for a few years." Hannibal said. "A strong, direct approach. But we're not going to do it that way. It doesn't fulfill my mission, and I have an idea that will."

Sarge stepped away from Marquita, as if he did not want to spatter her with his anger. "What do you mean, your mission?" What's more important than getting this guy off the street?"

Hannibal counted to ten in his head. Then he asked Sarge a

question that seemed irrelevant. "When you see a guy being loud and abusive with his girl and you're working as a bouncer, what's your first priority? Protect the girl from harm? If it is, I assume you separate them."

Sarge backed off a step. "Well, my job's to maintain order in the house. I generally just tell the jerk to take it somewhere else. But this…"

"Is no different," Hannibal said. "I need to recover that formula. I have to make Anita whole. Besides, nobody wants Rod to be able to come back in three or four years and sell this formula for a fortune and live happily every after. Right?"

"Okay," Sarge said. "Didn't you say Rod's out of town today? Maybe we should go up to his house and toss the joint until we find the formula."

"Naw. Breaking and entering's not one of my strong points, and his alarms looked pretty sophisticated. I'm planning to make him think I've already got it."

"But, how can you make him think that?" Marquita asked.

"That all depends on you," Hannibal said, leaning back. "I'm convinced that the disc you saw Rod get so excited about during your little cruise contained his big break. If you remember it well enough for me to make an accurate copy, and if I set up the situation just right, we might just con the con man."

"You mean that disc that cost Mariah a beating?" Marquita's eyes moved up and left as she searched her memory. "I know it was gold colored, with a white label and numbers on it. 4-9-3 maybe? Not so sure. Then words like base line formulae or something of the sort, in a very small, fine handwriting."

"That's excellent," Hannibal said, watching Marquita light up again, as she did whenever she received the slightest praise. "Now I propose that we all check out and head back up north. I'll go to the source of the disc, since I'm pretty sure Anita wrote all the labels, and get an apparent duplicate made. Then I'll come back down here tomorrow, attend this big party, and find out if I'm slick enough to skin this cat."

* * * * *

For Hannibal, the drive back to Washington was like a day in his office, if his office had been moved to an MTV sound studio. Before they reached the Virginia Beach city limits Monte had shoved a CD into the machine. Huge had given him a collection of discs he had either performed on or produced. Hannibal waited until the end of the first head-splitting rap tune before shutting it off, explaining that he had some work to do.

"Hey man, don't you want to hear your greatest hit?" Monte asked, waving a disc at Hannibal.

"Is that what Huge made when I was in the booth?"

"Yep. This one's mine. He sent one for you too."

"Yeah, well, maybe later when I'm too drunk to be embarrassed," Hannibal said. Now chill while I make a few calls."

First he called Anita to make sure that no unexpected health problems had arisen. Mother Washington was sitting with her, so he learned that she was eating well and feeling better since Mother Washington had called in a hairdresser to get her back to looking normal. She still had bruising around her nose and seemed depressed much of the time. They would be there when he arrived to talk about whatever he could do to get her stolen property back.

He then called Cindy's number, got no answer, and left a message on her machine. On a guess he called her office number. Again no answer. Hoping for information he tried the main number. A receptionist answered, which even on Saturday was not really a surprise. She explained that Ms. Santiago had already been in the office that morning and would be back soon. He asked to be switched back into her voicemail and left a message for her to call him as soon as she was free.

Then he gritted his teeth, focused on the rolling road ahead, and let Monte have his way with the CD player.

* * * * *

By the time he pulled up in front of Anita Cooper's home, Hannibal had a crick in his neck and a persistent headache dancing behind his eyes from driving into the sun. He shut off the engine, deciding to sit for a moment and enjoy the quiet. He had followed Sarge back to their building and dropped Monte off across the street before proceeding to Anita's. Along the way he had tried Cindy's home and cell phone numbers, before leaving another message at her office. Missing her was probably contributing to his headache.

At the door Hannibal tried to keep the pain out of his smile. When Mother Washington opened the door he knew his plan wasn't working.

"Oh, child, are you all right?"

"It's just a headache, ma'am," he said, stepping through the doorway. "Anita?"

"Downstairs waiting for you. Now you be kind, you hear? She's not looking her best."

At the bottom of the stairs Hannibal discovered that Mother Washington had been both right and very wrong. Physically, Anita did not look her best. The pale bruising under her eyes made her look jaundiced, and her right cheek was swollen just enough to make her face appear lopsided. Her nose was also still a little bigger than it should have been, swollen during its healing process. Her lower lip looked as if she had split it, maybe by smiling too much or crying too much. It was healing, but the red line down the middle told him that doctors had removed the stitch too soon.

On the other hand, her eyes were bright and lively, and her posture a tiny bit more erect than before. She was holding her head up. This last beating may have given her strength, he thought, or maybe it freed her from Rod Mantooth for good.

"Why are you looking at me so funny?"

"Sorry," Hannibal said, smiling. "I just didn't expect you to look so good."

Anita flushed crimson at his remark. "You're so full of stuff. But, listen, Mother Washington said something about you having an idea on how to get Daddy's formula back. Did you actually, I mean, have you seen Rod?"

"Yes, we've met now," Hannibal said, avoiding her eyes as he walked toward the computer desk. "And I know he hasn't sold your father's formula yet, but he will soon, unless I can trick him into showing me where he stashed it. What he has is on a gold CD-Rom."

"Oh, one of these," Anita said. She slid a storage case forward on a shelf and blew dust from its top before opening it. The case held two rows of CDs. Light glinted off them, stabbing into Hannibal's eyes, sparking the pain again. He forced himself to look at the labels.

"Marquita remembers seeing one of these in Rod's possession. She says it had a white label that said something like formula."

"Right." Anita flipped through the discs, all of which bore white labels. She moved slowly through the stack, and then turned to Hannibal with a crooked smile that twisted his heart. It had to hurt her to smile.

"One of the formula set is missing. It's number 4-9-3."

"That is exactly what Marquita said. Wow, that writing is so precise. Did you make all the labels yourself?"

"Of course," Anita said. "Daddy's writing was atrocious and we never could figure out how to print the labels so they'd come out even."

Hannibal lowered himself slowly into the desk chair. This was being too easy. "It's the bait I need. Can you make me a duplicate of the missing disc?"

Anita's eyes flashed and he could almost hear her pulse quicken. "Will it help you to get Daddy's real disc back?" When Hannibal nodded, she said, "I will make it exactly like the one he took. We're going to get my legacy back."

Five minutes later Hannibal and Anita went upstairs, drawn by the aroma of chicken and the inviting crackle of oil in a deep pan. When they entered the kitchen Mother Washington spoke without turning.

"Child, could you get my pills from my pocketbook? I left it up in the guest room."

Anita nodded and headed up the stairs. Mother Washington waved Hannibal toward her. He stood beside her, watching the chicken turning golden almost as if she were willing it to do so. She pushed pieces around with a slotted spoon and spoke in a lower tone.

"This man, this Rod Mantooth, you met him?"

"Yes ma'am."

"He a monster," she said as if she'd known him all her life.

"Yes ma'am."

"You take care of him, you hear me? You stop him."

"What would you have me do?" Hannibal asked, looking at Mother Washington's matronly face. "Want me to shoot him? Or just drop him down a well?"

Her eyes shot fire at him, and her breathing grew deep and labored. Hannibal could clearly see that she saw nothing funny in this situation. "That child will never be right. That man hurt her in ways only a woman can be hurt. You just make sure he don't do it no more, you hear? The Lord loves all his children, but sometimes I don't understand it."

* * * * *

Hannibal's street was quiet when he pulled into his traditional parking space, across the street from his building. Not much movement for a Saturday afternoon, not even kids running up and down the street. It was even too hot for troublemakers that day.

Stepping out of the White Tornado he could smell the heat rising from the asphalt. The humidity pasted his clothes to his body, but he paused a moment to listen to an unfamiliar tapping sound. Three doors down, a lone workman was hammering at a windowsill, putting a flower box in place. Wilson had been working on upgrades there for a few weeks. During the week he patrolled the many parks in the District. The park police got little respect but they did get a steady paycheck and on the weekend, pride of ownership pushed him to keep improving his home. Hannibal thought Wilson was a good addition and wondered if he was a sign that the

211

neighborhood was coming back, or just one step in the cycle of gain and loss that had haunted Southeast Washington for the better part of a century.

Inside he wasted no time losing his jacket and tie and rolling up his sleeves. Then he filled the coffee pot basket with the Hawaiian Kona coffee beans that he special ordered from a supplier in Rehoboth Beach, Delaware called The Coffee Mill. He filled the reservoir with filtered water from the refrigerator. He listened to the grinder do its thing and stood by long enough to fill his lungs with the aroma at the start of the brewing process. That done, he grabbed the disc he had gotten from Anita and went upstairs.

His knock at Sarge's door prompted some physical shuffling on the other side, and what Hannibal would swear sounded like clothes being readjusted. He took a step backward, grinning as he imagined Sarge's embarrassment. He didn't have to imagine for long. When Sarge pulled the door open, wearing jeans and an undershirt, Hannibal could see extra color in his mahogany face and his smile was much broader than usual.

"Sorry to interrupt."

"Oh, you didn't interrupt anything," Sarge hastened to say.

"Whatever, man. Want me to come back later?"

"Don't be silly, brother," Sarge said, waving his friend inside. "Want some coffee?"

"Not that sludge you make," Hannibal said, following Sarge into the kitchen. "I got the real stuff brewing downstairs."

Sarge pulled out two large mugs bearing a globe and anchor and, ignoring Hannibal, poured two cups of coffee. "You know, I been thinking about this plan of yours, Hannibal. I think it's got one big hole in it."

"Really?" Hannibal dropped the disc on the table to pick up his cup. "Well I'm always willing to listen, buddy. What did I miss?"

"Your exit strategy's weak," Sarge said, leaning back against the sink and taking a big swallow of coffee. "What if you get busted after you've scored the prize? You could find yourself cornered and outnumbered, know what I mean?"

"I think I do," Hannibal said, suppressing a smile.

"Now what you need," Sarge said, completely serious, "is some backup. I figure if I follow you down there and hang back, outside…"

Hannibal sipped, and fought screwing up his face at the bitter taste. "Damn, that coffee is awful…" When Sarge raised his eyebrows, Hannibal added, "Good. Awful good. But man, I have a sneaking suspicion that all you really want is to get close enough to get your hands on Rod Mantooth. I don't know if I want to put you in that…"

"Mon Dieu!" Marquita, having just stepped into the kitchen, stood with one hand raised to her mouth. Hannibal and Sarge turned toward her, not sure what had caused her reaction until they followed her eyes down to the table.

"It is the disc," she said. "That is the one Rod had on the boat."

Hannibal smiled, scooping up the CD-Rom. "That's what I needed to hear, Marquita. This is the duplicate I had Anita make and it sounds like she got it just about right."

Hannibal's smile faded in the face of Marquita's reaction. The golden disc pulled her eyes like a magnet, and as she stared her lower lip began to quiver. Although it was just a copy, the object in his hand was, for her, a physical object with a direct connection to the depraved and demeaning treatment Rod gave his willing followers. He quickly pushed it behind his back.

"Well, listen, thanks for all your help," he said on his way toward the door. "I'm going to go downstairs and get myself together for tomorrow. And get myself a decent cup of coffee. See you guys."

* * * * *

Hannibal watched his car clock tick over to six pm before he turned the key from ACC to off to save the battery. Some merciful clouds had blown into place and his daylong headache had faded at last. Parked down the block from Cindy's Alexandria townhouse he watched the river darken by slow degrees as the sun dropped behind the city in his rearview mirror. People were slowly filtering into Oronoco Park in anticipation of the cooler temperatures that come with sunset. He sipped hot, strong coffee from his travel cup. His friends at The Coffee Mill had convinced him to try a Costa Rican coffee they imported and it was a winner. These beans had been darker with a fierce aroma. The nutty flavor of the brew blunted his irritation at waiting. After all, a guy should not have to stake out his girlfriend's house.

He had called Cindy a couple more times before deciding that the woman had to go home some time, and he would meet her there. He pulled out his cell phone, planning to try the three numbers one more time. As he did he remembered another call he should be making. Checking the slip of paper in his pocket, he punched in the numbers Mariah had given him. After just two rings, a low husky voice answered.

"This is her? Who's this?'

"Smoke, baby," Hannibal said. "What up with your beautiful self?"

Pause. "Oh, hey, I can probably get that for you. Let me call you back in a minute, okay?"

Hannibal muttered agreement into an already dead phone. He figured he must have called at a bad time. Shrugging, he tried Cindy's cell phone again, and again found it turned off. As soon as he hung up, his phone rang.

"Smoke honey, is that you?" Mariah's voice was more breathy this time, dripping with exaggerated sexiness. There was also a faint echo, as if she had moved to a smaller room. Maybe she had slipped into the bathroom for this conversation. Hannibal pulled on his street voice, like an uncomfortable shirt that was nonetheless right in style.

"Yeah, baby. Just wanted to know what was going on with that party tomorrow. Your boy don't play none of that redneck shit, do he? I'm ready to get crunk."

"Don't worry," she said, panting as if in anticipation. "I'll make sure you get your party on. And Rod will have the dance tracks booming, loud and heavy."

"Good deal," Hannibal said. "Between you and Sheryl this ought to be a hell of a party." He needed to know what kind of story Sheryl and Derek had come up with.

"Yeah, she told me you were all that," Mariah said. "From what she said, I want to make sure I get my turn. And we won't have to worry about her getting in the way."

"What, you beat her down or something?"

"No, silly," Mariah giggled, surprising him by sounding very young for a moment. "You must have turned her out, cause Derek was scared of losing her. He collared her last night. Replaced that braided leather piece of shit choker with a real nice silver band. So now she does what he says, and I know one thing he won't say she can do is you."

Hannibal's mind snapped back to the hidden collars he had found in the last few days and the looks on Anita's and Marquita's faces when confronted with them. Now Mariah sounded quite casual as she dropped this news into his ear. Was that funny? Should he laugh? Should he care? What was the right response? Before Hannibal had time to gather his answer, Mariah rushed into his silence.

"Hey, don't you worry about that. I'm twice as good as Sheryl. I know stuff she never thought about, and do stuff she's afraid of. And I can take a hell of a lot more."

He knew the right answer now. "Like to walk right up to the edge, eh? Well all right then. But dig, I don't want to get in no pissing contest with the big dog. If Rod and me rumble, I'll have to put him down hard."

"Rod will be busy with the newbie," Mariah said, with an edge in her voice. "While he's training her, we can be upstairs. He won't even care."

Right, Hannibal thought. That was why she was hiding in the bathroom. Well, whatever the punishment was for straying off the preserve, she probably enjoyed that too. Aloud he said, "All right, Shorty. I'll slide in around, what, eight o'clock? Then we'll see how well the big dog trained you."

Mariah whispered, "Yes Sir," and her words surprised him as much as the soft tone in which she said them.

By the end of that conversation Hannibal felt tired. The sun had disappeared while they talked, and he leaned back in his seat to consider the next night in more detail. With his eyes closed he could picture Rod's summerhouse and imagine all the players and where they would be.

* * * * *

Hannibal jerked upright at the tapping on his window. Cindy stood on the other side of the glass in a green velvet sweat suit that fit like it was painted on. Her smile implied total ignorance of his frustration at trying to contact her. He pushed a button, rolling the window down.

"How long have you been sitting out here?" Cindy asked. Hannibal's stern expression pushed her face back a few inches. "What are you doing out here?"

"Waiting for you to come home," Hannibal said. "I couldn't imagine where you were."

"Oh honey, I was in the office all day. This IPO is really taking off and if I do this right…"

"I called the office. No answer, no response to my message. No answer at the house, no answer on your cell."

"Oh, babe." Cindy pulled the car door open, shaking her head. "I'm so sorry. I never checked for messages at the office all day. And I thought I told you I don't carry that cell anymore. Why didn't you 'berry me?"

Hannibal powered his window closed and stepped out of the car, stretching. "Bury you?"

"My Blackberry, silly," she said, trying a tentative hug. "That's the only place I check for messages anymore. You could leave a voicemail, or you can text me or drop an e-mail. I know I gave you the number."

Of course she had, but he had never entered it into his cell phone. Standing there under the streetlamp, feeling her arms around him made all his irritation drain off into the ground. Her cologne reminded him how much he had missed her.

"I just wanted to spend some time with you."

"Well, it's not too late," she said. "I've got a pork roast upstairs and I was thinking of making that mojo pork you like."

"With the Papaya Mango Salsa?"

"Well sure, if you'll help me chop up all the stuff." Their embrace tightened and, for a moment, their mutual obsessions with their professions faded into the warm night breeze. He pressed his mouth to her ear, delivered a soft kiss, and whispered.

"I have an idea how to spend the time while the roast cooks."

"Ooooh, stop." But as they moved toward the door with his arm around her, they both knew she meant just the opposite.

-20-

SUNDAY

"Damn, you know how to make a girl work up a sweat."

Hannibal sat up in the bed, elbows propped on raised knees. "Back at you, beautiful. Just wanted you to know I miss you when I'm away."

"Well, I like the way you show it." Cindy rolled toward him onto her left side, resting a hand on his. "And I love your eyes in this light."

Cindy's bedroom was filled with the first light of day, casting a glowing sheen on her golden skin. Her hair, moist from their activity, hung free around her neck and shoulders in the natural curls that he loved and she fought to control most days. Hannibal had nudged her awake before six, and they had made love through the sunrise. Now, as their breathing and heart rates returned to normal, he worked at recording the damp glow of her skin, her animal scent, and the sensuous sound of her afterglow breathing. He held that multi-sense image in his heart, like a hologram, to get him through the times when they were apart.

At moments like this he felt that God had designed her just for him, and that he could never be worthy of this special gift. She deserved the finest wine, gourmet meals, cruises to the islands, and so much more.

"I should have at least brought flowers," he said, his thought leaking out through his mouth.

"Ever the romantic," Cindy said, leaning to kiss his arm. "You could always read me some poetry."

"Ha! You know I don't get poetry. And besides, as much as I'd like to lie here with you for a week, I got to get my ass in gear. I have a very long day ahead of me."

"We all do, baby," she said, pulling open a drawer in her side table. "It's the summer solstice, the longest day of the year. Did you know?"

"Not one of the dates I mark on my calendar."

"Well, lie back and listen," Cindy said, retrieving a small book from the drawer.

Hannibal lay back, lowering his eyes to half-mast. Cindy sat cross-legged on the bed, the sheet pooled around her waist. She held the book the way parishioners do on Sunday when they are about to launch into a hymn. Hannibal listened while his eyes traced the curve of her full breasts and the inverted "V" of her rib cage.

"This is by one of my favorite local poets, Cybele Pomeroy. It's called Summer Solstice." Cindy cleared her throat before reading the lines in slow, solemn tones.

> "Too hot for spring,
> But summer's yet to peak.
> By counting, it's half over.
> But sixty-one days later,
> The heat smells like
> Eternity."

Afterward she lowered the book, establishing eye contact with Hannibal even as she blocked his view of her breasts. He could see by the movements of her eyebrows that she expected some reaction from him. He was sure that the short poem held some deep meaning, but for the life of him he could not imagine what that might be, so he said what he always said when someone read him poetry.

"Pretty."

"Pretty?" Cindy said, dropping the book back into the drawer. "You're hopeless. Didn't you feel the desolation, the sense of resignation in those words? It's never been so hot, and it feels like it might never end. The longest day is a metaphor for, oh, never mind."

"Hey, I think I started this conversation with saying that I don't get poetry."

"You don't want to get poetry," Cindy said, standing, "which is why you'll never get it."

Hannibal swung his feet to the carpet. "Well regardless of how the stars are aligned it's going to be a long day for me, but at the end of it I should be at the end of this case and collecting a fat payoff."

"Yeah, long day for me too," Cindy said. Hannibal thought he saw stars in her eyes as she stared through him. "A long day of anticipation. Tomorrow morning when trading starts I'll know just how successful our offering has been. Tomorrow's the pivotal day. All my work and planning has led up to this. I just don't know how I'm going to get through this day."

Hannibal felt that she was already gone someplace, leaving him behind. He stood and headed for the shower.

"Well, babe, I know how I'll get through it. I've got a party to go to."

* * * * *

The White Tornado slid into a parking space a little more than a block away from Rod's house, facing the bulbous sun hanging low in the sky but still far from surrendering to the night. Hannibal mentally went over his simple plan for the hundredth time before stepping into the street and heading for Rod's house.

He had thought through his straightforward tactics on the long drive back down to Virginia Beach, and again after the short nap he caught on the beach. He had gone through all the motions in his mind, considered what could go wrong and reviewed his exit strategy. He didn't need back up for this, but it was wise to be prepared and to have his head in the game all the way. Mostly though, he thought about the number of people who would be happier if he were to execute the monster known as Rod Mantooth. Of course he wouldn't be a killer to please anyone, but if all went as planned, it might be that someone else would take care of the problem soon.

Loud southern rock alternated with hip-hop sounds blasting from Rod's house. As he mounted the steps to knock on the door, Hannibal could already smell the alcohol. He wondered how well he would fit in tonight. He'd settled for simplicity - tight new jeans and a bright red sleeveless Puma tee shirt that matched his shoes. The shirt was half tucked in because he knew that Huge paid two hundred dollars for the white Helmut Lang belt he was wearing and it seemed sacrilegious to cover it up.

The woman who answered the door had Angelina Jolie's lips and waterfalls of dark brown hair flowing down around her shoulders. Between the twin cascades he could see a bit of studded black leather at her throat. She glanced only briefly at Hannibal's face, and quickly lowered her gaze.

"Good evening Sir," she said. "May I ask your name?"

"They call me Smoke."

The woman nodded and stepped back, pulling the door open. Hannibal stepped inside, ignoring the woman as he assumed he was supposed to do. The room was dark, the air thick and laced with marijuana smoke. The music boomed from the stereo on Hannibal's right, the baseline so insistent that he could feel his heart beat falling into synch with it. He removed his glasses and hung them on the front of his shirt. As his eyes became accustomed to the gloom he saw three men he didn't recognize, all white, and three women following and fetching for them. The girls varied but were all well proportioned and dressed to display their assets in tight, short skirts and open shirts or plunging necklines. Everyone seemed to be dancing and drinking, which, Hannibal supposed, was what made it a party.

When Rod came toward him the others parted like a human Red Sea in his path. A large, hairy hand thrust forward and Hannibal shook it in a fierce grip.

"Dude," Hannibal shouted, "This is off the hook. Thanks for the invite. Now where's the beer?"

Rod let a hearty laugh burst out of him. "There's a keg in the kitchen."

Hannibal slipped off in that direction, while Rod returned to his other guests. A blue bulb burned over the sink, allowing Hannibal to find the beer, and others to reach the table that served as a well stocked bar. A second table was groaning under the weight of shrimp on ice, Swedish meatballs, hot wings, chips and dip. Hannibal filled a glass from the keg and was just tipping it to his lips when he felt fingers squeezing his ass. Mariah pressed her breasts into his back and breathed vodka fumes over his shoulder.

"I been thinking about you, G."

"You been on my mind too, Shorty," Hannibal said, turning. "You want to dance?"

"I want to fuck," she said, staring into his eyes. Hers looked like Alaskan Husky eyes in the blue light. "But we'll have to wait until the initiation starts. I'm on call to Rod until then."

"Okay," Hannibal said, slipping an arm around her waist. "Until then, why don't we go out where the music is and get a groove on?"

With six couples dancing, the front room was just about full. Hannibal knew he wasn't a good dancer, but none of the other guys were either so it hardly mattered. Partners switched often, but Mariah danced more with Hannibal than anyone else. The way she was cutting through the vodka supply, Hannibal was astonished that Mariah could continue to shake it so hard and remain vertical. The new girl, Missy, looked very happy, getting the lion's share of Rod's attention. Derek and Sheryl also looked happy together. She wore her collar with pride, and Hannibal thought that maybe this was what she wanted all along, like a woman who flirts with another man to make her lover jealous enough to propose. In her mind, did the collar equate to an engagement ring?

Then he noticed that the other three women also wore collars or more subtle chokers. Missy's neck was bare, but so was Mariah's to Hannibal's surprise. So she didn't belong to Rod after all.

* * * * *

One of the unknown couples left, then a second. The men shook hands with Rod, thanked him for the invitation and complimented him on the good time. The women actually knelt and bowed their heads. This was an interesting parting ritual that Hannibal thought would certainly not go over well if Cindy were a guest. He had never seen it before, even in the chat rooms, so he figured it must be one of Rod's innovations. Before long Hannibal found himself sitting on the sofa with Rod, their heads bobbing in rhythm to the dance grooves. Mariah and Sheryl moved their bodies in a mesmerizing way in the middle of the room, as if locked in some sort of competition to see who could find the most enticing gestures. Rod pulled out a small pipe, lit it, and inhaled deeply before passing it to Hannibal. Hannibal put the stem to his mouth, but then pulled it away as if he had just remembered something.

"Man I got to tell you," Hannibal said, exaggerating a slur in his voice, "You really know how to par-TAY."

"You ain't seen nothing yet," Rod roared over the pulsing music. His irises were almost as big as his eyeballs. "Wait till you see the Rod man in about a month. I am going to open the biggest, hottest club in Washington. Might even give you a job if you want to go back up there."

Hannibal nodded and handed the pipe off to Derek who was walking past. "I can see you got big plans, man, like you got an ironclad lock on the future. But tell me something. How can you be so sure it's all going to go your way?"

For a second, Rod looked confused. "It just is. You see, I have a destiny. The big score's been waiting out there for me for years. It can't avoid me. It's..."

"Your destiny. I get it."

Rod's reaction to Hannibal's skepticism was interrupted by the third couple saying their good-byes. The music continued to throb, smoke still filled the air and the lights were still dim, yet some subtle change came over the house as Rod closed the door and the only people present were those who were with Rod the day Hannibal met him. Missy continued to dance like a woman in a rap video, but each move took her a little closer to Rod. Sheryl was dancing toward Derek. Mariah pressed closer and closer to Hannibal, but his eyes stayed on Missy. She reminded him of the women cast as African priestesses in old movies. She appeared to be in an ecstatic trance, her eyes glazed over, and her mouth agape. As she came within Rod's reach he threw an arm around her. His hand sank into her hair and he pulled smoothly rather than yanking or tugging. Missy gasped, bending backward before her knees buckled and she sank to the floor.

Mariah's teeth scraped Hannibal's neck and he turned to face her.

"Let's go upstairs, lover," she whispered. "He'll be busy for quite a while."

"I'll go pick us a room," Hannibal replied. "You get us a couple more drinks." With a deep nod Mariah headed for the kitchen. Hannibal climbed the steps just ahead of Derek and Sheryl, not wanting to see her face and not wanting to see what Missy was probably doing to Rod in the living room. Hannibal turned into the first room, farthest from Rod's. Once inside he slipped a tiny plastic bag from his pocket and palmed it. Almost show time, he thought.

Mariah entered the room less than a minute behind Hannibal and closed the door. Her left hand was wrapped around the neck of a half-full vodka bottle. Her right held two glasses. She placed them all on the dresser and turned quickly into Hannibal's arms. Her kiss was hot and deep, her tongue swollen in his mouth. He gripped her shoulders and with slow, steady pressure he pushed her away. As their lips parted, Mariah stretched forward to nip Hannibal's shoulder with her teeth. In response Hannibal squeezed her shoulders until she whimpered in pain.

"You think you got a hook in me?" Hannibal asked with unaccustomed ferocity. "You ain't shit to me, girl. Don't you ever even think about marking me, understand?"

"Yes, Sir," she replied. His stern tone seemed to arouse her even more. She stood staring up into his eyes, panting softly, and he wondered if he caused the same frission of fear she felt from Rod. Looking down into her waiting face he felt, for just a moment, the rush of power that comes from having total control over another human being. It thrilled and sickened him.

"You all sweaty from dancing all night, Shorty. You better get in that bathroom and get yourself real clean if you want to be with me."

"Yes, Sir," Mariah said with no hint of irony or sarcasm.

When Mariah stepped out of the room Hannibal poured two drinks. By squeezing the small plastic bag between two fingers he poured its powdered contents into one of the glasses. He had practiced to be able to do this even with someone watching, in case he needed to. The crushed Rohypnol dissolved in seconds. He was swirling the vodka around in the glass when Mariah returned. He pushed the glass toward her.

"I think you need a taste before we party."

Hannibal sipped from his own glass. Mariah swallowed the contents of hers like it was water.

"Now lose the shoes and get up on the bed," Hannibal ordered. Mariah pulled off her heels and stretched out on the comforter, grinning like a child in line at Disneyworld.

"Not like that," Hannibal said, still standing by the door. "Get your ass up." Despite her confused expression, Mariah leaped to her feet in front of the bed. "I want to see you dance," Hannibal said. "Up on the bed. I think I'd like a nice, slow, striptease."

Mariah's eyes lighted and she gave a docile nod before stretching to the radio on the headboard. Once she managed to find some slow, smoky music, she stepped up on the bed.

"I hope you find me pleasing, Sir. I wouldn't want to disappoint you and get punished for it," she said. Her eyes said just the opposite. But Hannibal noticed that her words were a little slurred and as her hips began to sway her balance was shaky. The liquor? The drugs? Maybe both. In any case, he watched her move through a sultry and seductive dance and spend nearly five minutes teasing with her blouse before finally taking it off. While trying to unhook her bra she stumbled in the comforter and dropped to her knees. Hannibal rushed forward, concerned that she might bang her head on the headboard. Mariah raised an arm to protect her face from an anticipated attack.

"I am so sorry, Sir," Mariah said. "I don't know what happened to me. Didn't drink that much."

"Don't worry about it," Hannibal said, putting an arm behind her for support. "We'll skip the rest of the dance. You look like you're ready to party now."

Mariah shook her head in a vain attempt to clear it. "But I wanted to be clear for this one. You are so hot. This feels…" She looked deep into Hannibal's face and her caramel colored eyes focused with absolute clarity for a second. "This feels like when he gives me…"

Her mouth was trying to form the letter "R" as Hannibal lowered her back onto the bed. She would sleep through the rest of the night while he executed his scheme. Silently wishing her sweet dreams, he threw back the rest of his drink and eased out of the room. Muffled sounds from down the hall told him that the other two couples were fully involved. He slipped down the stairs with more stealth than was necessary. In the living room he unlocked the three locks that secured the front door. Then he went to the telephone and memorized the number on its face. A soft squeal from upstairs caught his attention. He had no way to know which room it had come from, and decided it didn't matter. He moved into the computer room and pushed the door as close to closed as possible without letting the latch click.

It was almost show time. In the darkened room Hannibal loosened his belt and pulled the CD case from inside the front of his pants. While his left hand casually tossed his decoy CD Rom on the floor, his right pulled out his cell phone and pushed a preset number. The phone's glowing face cut into the darkness of the room. It rang only once before his call was answered.

"Hey," Hannibal whispered. "Your turn. You sure you're up to this?"

"I want to," Marquita replied. "I need to do this."

"Okay." Hannibal gave her the number, then stepped into the computer room's closet and slipped out of his shoes. He left them behind and returned to the living room, all the while listening to the clicks and buzzes as Marquita made the connections for a three-way call. On the way he reflected on the courage Anita showed when she damaged Rod's car and freed herself from his emotional grasp. Now he hoped that Marquita would free herself, and her act of defiance could well require an even greater degree of courage.

Crouched beside the front door, Hannibal listened to the phones ring out of synch in the room and on his cell phone. Four. Five. Six. How many times would Rod let it ring? Would he just ignore it? That was one way Hannibal's simple plan could fail.

After eleven rings Rod picked up the phone upstairs and snarled, "What?" Now, Hannibal knew, Marquita had to get his attention right away and hold it.

"This is Marquita LaPage. You remember me?"

There was a pause during which Hannibal could hear a young girl trying to stifle a whimper. Rod said, "Sure I remember you. I stayed at your place and you served me while I made connections. You were a nice bit, but I'm kind of busy right now."

"I need to tell you how I'm going to take it all away from you."

Another pause. Then Rod asked, "How'd you get this number?"

"I know all about you now," Marquita said. "I learned a lot after I met Anita Cooper. She told me what you stole from her." Hannibal could hear the tremble in Marquita's voice, but he was betting Rod could not. He was accustomed to women being intimidated when they spoke to him.

"You silly bitch. Anita doesn't even know what I took."

"That's where you're wrong," Marquita said. "We know. And I wanted to hear your voice when the thief we hired took it away from you and left you with nothing."

"You ain't got the guts for that kind of action," Rod said. But Hannibal could hear a doorknob turning. He reasoned that the phone upstairs must be wireless and Rod was about to check on his treasure. Marquita's call had done the trick. He was just rattled enough.

Hannibal yanked the front door open. The high-pitched alarm drove daggers into his ears as he scrambled toward the computer room. A roar almost as loud came from upstairs. Rod thumped down the narrow flight of stairs shouting unintelligible curses. Before Rod reached the first floor Hannibal was in the computer room closet working to slow his own breathing. He held the closet door open less than half an inch, just enough for one eye to see through. He crouched immobile on his haunches, tracking Rod's movements by sound and trying to ignore the sweat sliding down his forehead. He heard Rod slam the front door shut, and push buttons until the alarm stopped sounding. The door swung open again, and Rod must have stepped outside, trying to see whoever had left. More feet pattered on the stairs. Derek's voice asked, "What's up?" Rod told him to stay there and watch the door.

As Hannibal had predicted, Rod's next move was to storm into the computer room and slam that door as well. When he clicked on the light his eyes zeroed in on the CD-ROM lying on the floor. He stood in gym shorts only, his broad feet splayed below him, blonde hair swirling around his legs.

In the closet, Hannibal drew his aura in as his instructors had taught him to do in the secret service. He was still as a stone and just as silent. If Rod had looked right at him he might not have seen him. In the silence he watched Rod pause for three long seconds. In his mind he was shouting, *Don't think it through, just react.*

A delighted smirk twisted Rod's lip and he said, "Asshole had it and dropped it trying to get out." He scooped up the disc, not looking too closely at it. Instead he glanced back at the room's door to make sure it was closed and Derek couldn't see him. Then he shoved his wheeled chair away from the computer, dropped to one hairy knee, and thumped his fist lightly on the floor where he usually sat. A square of tile popped up no more than an eighth of an inch. It was just enough for Rod's fingertips to grip. He pulled and the tile lifted out of the floor. Rod dropped the disc inside, clearly believing that he was returning his own disc to his hiding place. After pressing the tile back into place with a foot he returned the room to darkness and left.

Time shifted into a glacial pace while Hannibal forced himself to breathe and strained to hear whatever sound leaked through the walls from the living room. He heard Rod brush off questions from Derek and say something about unfinished business upstairs. He heard the locks clicked into place. He heard the random tones of the security system being armed. He heard Derek's frantic movements around the room, like a half-grown puppy bouncing around its master.

Just as his knees began to ache, Hannibal heard the two sets of footsteps moving up the staircase. Doors opened and closed upstairs. Still he waited. Would Rod think to visit Mariah? Had he noted Smoke's absence, or was he too fixed on what he was doing with Missy? After two more minutes with no detectable activity above, Hannibal slipped his shoes back on and left the closet. He planned to turn the computer on but when he touched the mouse the monitor lit. Apparently Rod never turned the machine off. Good. By the monitor's eerie light Hannibal opened the floor's trap door and reached inside. He had half expected to find a hardcover notebook there, but now realized that Rod must have destroyed it. If it contained the handwritten notes that generated Cooper's anti-addiction formula, it would be gibberish to Rod but a danger to him if it fell into the hands of a chemist.

By touch Hannibal identified his fake disc by an "X" scratched into the back of the case. He located the only other item in the small space, another CD-ROM case. Having seized his prize he closed the trap door, leaving his imitation disc behind.

Hannibal pulled the chair back into its usual place and squinted into the screen for the next step. He grinned as he did the little bit of typing that would all but guarantee that Rod wouldn't retain a copy of Vernon Cooper's remarkable discovery. Hannibal was still surprised and a little frightened by how few keystrokes were required to reformat a hard drive. Just as Rod would destroy the hard copy of the formula, he didn't strike Hannibal as the type to make a copy of a disc, but he may have copied the data into his computer. If he did, it no longer mattered.

All that remained was for Hannibal to leave with his prize. The alarm would sound again, but he would easily reach his car before Rod or Derek even made it to the door. The contents of the computer disc would make Anita's life much more pleasant, and perhaps of equal importance, they would restore her father's legacy. Maybe later he would make an anonymous call to the police about the drugs in the house, just for fun.

Hannibal again released the front door locks but as his fingers touched the cold brass knob a resounding slap snapped his head toward the stairs. He froze in place as a second slap reverberated through the house.

"Wake up, bitch," Rod snarled above. Mariah, Hannibal thought. The brute must have at least reasoned as far as the identity of his thief and now he was trying to get confirmation from Mariah.

"You were in on it, weren't you?" Rod said. It was a course bellow that betrayed no disappointment, only anger. "You brought him in here to try to rip me off."

Well, it wasn't Hannibal's concern. He had what he had come for. Rod had been hitting women for a long time, and would continue to do so after Hannibal was long gone from his miserable life. Besides, Mariah wasn't like Anita or Marquita. She was a volunteer. She actually liked this stuff.

But did she like this stuff when she was half unconscious? And hadn't Marquita and even Anita initially volunteered for, and even asked for, Rod's destructive attention? They enjoyed being told what to do, and maybe even the humiliation until the party got rough.

Could he just walk out?

Even while he was considering his options, Hannibal was tearing a small hole in the cloth beneath the sofa. When the hole was big enough, he slipped the disc into it for safekeeping. Only then did he realize that he had made a decision.

At the top of the stairs he heard yet another vicious slap. The bedroom door stood ajar. Hannibal pushed it with one finger, easing the door open just far enough for his body to pass through. Facing Rod's broad back, thickly matted with hair, Hannibal knew he could take him. He could call him, face off, take a couple of good shots and then kick this vicious animal's ass. Derek was in another room, probably deep into the action with Sheryl. By the time he appeared, it would be over. Hannibal set himself, raised his fists and settled into a comfortable fighting stance.

Then it all changed. Rod pulled Mariah up by her hair, shouted, "You lying bitch," and slammed a fist into her face.

-21-

As Mariah floated backward toward the bed, time down-shifted to a sluggish pace and Hannibal found himself in one of those defining moments that we see in slow motion with high definition clarity. He saw Mariah's eyes, clouded yet aware, set in a face expressing more confusion than pain. Then his focus shifted to the enormity of Rod's fist extended from his body like a weapon wholly separate from Rod's body. Thoughts of a fight faded in the face of blind rage.

"You bastard," Hannibal said through clenched teeth. His own right fist launched forward as if of its own will. His body began to pivot, his hips and back and stomach driving that fist forward. He saw awareness pull Rod's face to the side. Rod began to turn to his own left. Rod's left arm was tensed but held too low as he spun toward Hannibal. No! This was not the way it was supposed to go.

But of course it was too late. Rod's hate filled visage turned toward Hannibal powered by the full might of his thick bull neck. Hannibal's right fist drove forward, a missile beyond guidance, and Rod's jaw moved directly into its path. The impact was jarring. Shock waves rode up Hannibal's arm and into his shoulder. Shock washed over Rod's face, chased by oblivion. As Hannibal withdrew his arm Rod began to drop toward the floor as if his soul had suddenly departed his body.

As the hulk crashed onto the floor life jumped back to full speed. Hannibal's knuckles pulsed with pain, reminding him why he usually worked in gloves. Now he had only seconds in which to choose a new path. A face-to-face battle with Rod would have been more satisfying, but he had learned long ago that the only direction to go in life was forward.

His shoulders feinted toward the door before his head yanked him back toward the bed. If Mariah was in sight when Rod awoke he might beat her to death. Leaving her behind could not be an option. He grabbed her wrist and saw a slight smile move her lips as he pulled her over his shoulders. Hooking an arm around one of her knees he hurried down the stairs. In the living room he lowered Mariah to the sofa, even as he watched seconds tick past in his head. Time mattered, but now sound mattered too. He didn't want Rod awake any sooner than necessary.

The basement held a storage area and a laundry room, but when Hannibal turned on the light his eyes scanned only the walls. He knew that home security systems were designed to defend from outside the walls, not from within. He found the small metal box he was looking for hanging beside the furnace. It was locked, and that would cost more seconds. He pulled a small Swiss Army knife from his pocket and opened the shorter blade. With it he defeated the lock in less than thirty seconds. Then he had only to flip two switches to shut down the alarm system.

Upstairs, silence and darkness continued to reign. Mariah leaked a soft moan. Hannibal hefted his human burden, not knowing how close to awareness she might be. With some effort he managed to sidestep out the front door and pull it closed behind them.

The air was thick and damp as he scampered down the street with Mariah across his shoulders like an ox's yoke. Hannibal dragged air deep into his lungs, wondering if the alarm company received a signal when the alarm was disabled from within. If they did, he hoped that they would send the police to the house right away.

Less than a minute after leaving Rod's house Hannibal was loading Mariah into his back seat. He felt naked and exposed under a white-hot full moon. Cars, trees and buildings hugged pools of blackness and when he closed the door and stood to his full height. Hannibal had the feeling that his shadow was taller than his soul. Still, he had more business to attend to. He pulled his backup piece, the Smith and Wesson Centennial Airweight, out of the glove compartment and ran back toward Rod's house.

In seconds he was crouching silently beneath a rear window, one that would lead into the computer room. He slipped the five shot thirty-eight caliber revolver into the back of his waistband. What had come to Hannibal when he was standing over Rod's unconscious body was a reconfiguration of values. The data disc containing Anita Cooper's legacy was one objective, but he couldn't abandon human needs for it. Even as he reached for Mariah he knew that he couldn't leave the other girls behind. Sheryl might escape danger since she clearly had nothing to do with the apparently unsuccessful attempted theft. Missy, on the other hand, was still an innocent in Hannibal's eyes. If he was going to stop to pull Mariah out of harm's way, he had to at least save Missy as well.

A car full of loud teenagers approached from the beach and rolled past, leaving Hannibal with only the sound of his heart, thumping in a world painted stark blue and white by the moon. Then the sound of crickets slowly swelled in the yard behind him. That sound grew until the racket was almost as painful as the alarm had been.

Hannibal stood, fingers locked into the edge of the windowsill. His stomach clenched in anticipation of the next effort. Sensing no movement inside, Hannibal raised the window. While he pulled himself slowly up and into the room, Hannibal wondered if Rod had regained consciousness. If he had, walking in through the front door would have been suicide.

Seconds later Hannibal was listening for the slightest hint of movement from his familiar hiding place inside the computer room closet. He waited a full five minutes before stepping out of the computer room. Gun in hand he stood briefly, sniffing the air for trouble before moving to the stairs.

He moved upward, one step at a time, sensitive to the slightest creaking.

The room at the top of the stairs stood open. Rod lay face down with his feet toward the door, unconscious or maybe just asleep. His hairy back rose and fell in a slow steady rhythm. A gentle snore rolled out of his mouth. Hannibal doubted his one punch could have done that much damage, but there was no way to know what effect drugs and alcohol would have added. All in all, it seemed that things were going his way this time.

At the second door he heard quiet conversation. Having been interrupted, Derek and Sheryl would be slowly getting back into the party mood. No danger from that quarter.

The door to the third room stood open by only a crack. Hannibal pressed it slowly open with his empty right hand, holding his gun close to his side. A muted lamp on one side table lent the room a ghostly glow. Missy looked up, her brown eyes round and wide. When Hannibal was growing up his mother had paintings of little black kids on the walls. Their eyes were bigger than any real person's ever could be. She found it cute, but as a child Hannibal found the pictures disturbing in some odd way. Missy's eyes almost reached that size now, and her pupils were stretched wide by the dark or maybe by drugs. Her face betrayed both surprise and relief. Her mouth moved but his finger pressed against his lips cautioned her to silence.

Only after taking in her beautiful brown face did Hannibal's appreciation of the scene broaden. Missy was kneeling on the bed, naked, with her arms stretched out in front of her, spread wide to display her petite breasts. She did not hold the pose out of respect. Her wrists were each handcuffed to the short posters at the foot of the bed.

"You don't have to take this," he whispered, stepping slowly toward her. Her wary eyes followed him as he approached her, and then turned to the cluttered dresser. The small silver key lay there in plain sight. He felt her eyes on his face as he unlocked one cuff, then the other, but could not guess what emotion hid behind them. She never pulled at the small chains to free herself any faster. She continued to kneel on the bed with her arms spread apart until Hannibal took one arm and gently pulled. She placed one foot on the floor, hesitated, then stood beside the bed.

Hannibal pulled the blanket off the bed and wrapped it round Missy's shoulders. When it began to slide off he pushed one edge into her hand.

"Hold this," he said. She did. Was she in shock, he wondered, or heavily doped up? Holding her free hand he guided her toward the door. She didn't resist, but she seemed in no hurry. They moved slowly through the darkness toward the stairs. They passed one room and were in front of the door to the other when Hannibal heard footfalls behind him.

"What the hell?"

Hannibal spun, leveling the gun in the direction of Derek's voice. "Just stay quiet and don't move," Hannibal whispered, "and you can live through this." Derek's breathing was quick and shallow. He was on the verge of making a move. Hannibal took a couple of slow steps backward toward the stairs. Derek moved forward, maintaining a constant distance from Hannibal who had no desire to fire his weapon. If questioned by police, could he convince them that he was in the right? Was he on a rescue mission, or was he guilty of an overprotective kidnapping? Could saving Missy from whatever she had agreed to do merit the use of lethal force?

A roar of rage from his left froze Hannibal for a couple of tenths. It was enough. Rod's bulk crashed into his side, a speeding freight train that numbed his gun hand even as its momentum smashed his right shoulder through the wall's plaster. He saw his pistol hit the carpet and tensed his stomach just in time to receive the bludgeon that was Rod's left fist. Rod's right smacked across his skull, birthing a flock of blue floaters before Hannibal's eyes.

"Raiding my stable, eh?" Rod said in a hateful snarl. "Well let's see what you got when you don't get to sucker punch me."

Hannibal managed to block Rod's next left hook, but his knees were already buckling. He had no space in which to move and his balance was thrown off. Rod had the momentum and just kept throwing punches until Hannibal slowly crumpled to the floor. Then kicks replaced the punches, flexing Hannibal's ribs in as they landed. He clenched his teeth and kept his elbows in. Each kick rocked his body and spread a burst of pain through him, but he knew the important truth. This kind of thing never lasted very long. A familiar gray gauze curtain slid up over his senses.

* * * * *

Hannibal mentally clawed the gauze aside. Somehow he knew time had passed. His ribs ached, but didn't drown the pain from rug burns on his knees. His view was narrow, like looking at close objects in a small room through a telescope. His other awakening senses tried hard to assemble a broader picture for him. An odd, hollow ringing in his ears blunted rhythmic grunting, above and too the left. The caustic smell of sex and sweat flared his nostrils. Salt in his mouth? No, that was blood.

Hannibal craned his neck upward, moving his narrow view until a small hand came into view. Missy's hand, again cuffed to the bed. So he was on the floor not far from the foot of the bed and she was back where he had found her. This time, her hand was clenched around the footboard it was chained to, holding her steady as she rocked forward and back.

He readjusted his view up and over to her face. Missy's long, straight hair flew forward and back lagging behind her head's movements. Her eyes were clenched and her lips pressed together in a straight line, stifling what would be squeals of pain if they got out. Hannibal felt his own eyes welling up.

Up and back from Missy's face he found Rod's. Focus was difficult. His whole body was pulling back and slamming forward. His eyes were vacant, and Hannibal wondered for a moment where he really was.

"Do her harder!" That came from the other side of the bed in a woman's voice. Hannibal managed to widen the circle of his view enough to find Sheryl. Her eyes blazed in a way he found at once frightening and sickening. Had she endured the same initiation? And now, was she joyous to see someone else having to take their turn? Beside her, Derek panted like a hungry dog.

Sheryl snapped, "Feed it to her," and shoved Derek to the foot of the bed. Missy looked up, eyes wide now. Derek lowered his zipper. Hannibal shut his eyes and turned away, tuning out not just Missy's shame but his own as well. *I'm so sorry* he thought. The world faded into a gray mist and slowly down into blackness.

* * * * *

Hannibal's eyes snapped open and the darkness came into sharp focus. A deep breath set off sparks around his rib cage. That was okay. The pain made his mind sharper.

He curled his lips in. The blood on them hadn't completely dried yet, so he hadn't been out for very long. The ringing in his ears had stopped. Rod must have given him a mild concussion, but the effects had faded. Now ragged snoring helped him pinpoint the bed. As his eyes became accustomed to the darkness he could make out two figures on the bed. The larger one, the source of the snore, lay on his back.

The smaller figure was almost lost in the darkness except for her eyes and small, brilliant teeth. Missy lay with her chin on her overlapped hands, staring into Hannibal's eyes. How long had she been watching him? While he stared back she mouthed the words, "I'm sorry."

What on earth had she to be sorry about? He was the one who had failed her. The image of her dramatic rape scene made his stomach lurch. He raised his right hand toward her but it moved only inches. He was still handcuffed, he saw, to a leg of the dresser. The dresser's legs were pedestals ending in wooden balls. No way to slip the cuff over it. At Hannibal's end, the steel bracelet was clamped tight on his wrist, cutting into the skin each time he moved.

What would Rod plan for him in the morning? Another beating? No, the most logical move would be to hold Hannibal until the deal for the formula was concluded, and then turn Hannibal over to the South American gang lords who made the purchase. Hannibal caught the stench of fear and realized that he smelled himself. South American gangs could be very accommodating to their friends.

Hannibal wasn't very good with locks and even if he could pick it, did he have enough time? Although he was still chained, he saw that Missy was free. Her restraints, he realized, had been part of the game, just there to enhance Rod's control fantasy. Maybe they enhanced her fantasies as well. Was the horrible rape he observed in fact consensual? Was she happy about all that had happened to her?

As if she was reading his mind, Missy shook her head in the negative. Then she swung her feet off the bed, moving only inches at a time stopping often to look at Rod. After it up, Hannibal could see her breathing rate increase. Watching Rod, Missy shifted her weight off the bed and onto her legs in tiny increments. The snoring never wavered. Once standing upright, Missy released a shuddering sigh.

Hannibal caught himself admiring her perfect form in rear view, and berated himself, turning his eyes away. He knelt there with his face turned aside until he sensed her kneeling in front of him. Then he heard the soft click of a tiny lock opening. He looked to Rod to make sure he hadn't moved. Then Hannibal moved his arm enough to be sure of his newfound freedom.

He rose silently to his full height and turned a thankful smile on Missy. She had pulled on white bra and panties that glowed in the darkness. She stood very close to Hannibal, leaning in to whisper into his ear.

"Take me with you."

Hannibal nodded. They moved toward the bedroom door, both watching the chest of the snoring Rod rise and fall. Hannibal quickly glanced around for his pistol but it was no place obvious.

Again Hannibal and Missy moved down the hall. She seemed much more alert this time. Whatever drugs she had been on must have washed through her system. Still, her movements were as awkward as his. Maybe she was sore as well, from rough use rather than a beating. And here she was, rescuing him.

At the living room door they paused again to listen.

"Wait here," Hannibal said. "One little thing to do." He crept across the floor to the sofa. The prize that had started all this was there, hidden in the material underneath. He knelt beside the couch, working his hand through the small hole he had made. Soon, the case would truly be over.

And then the world exploded in a sonic burst that froze the blood in Hannibal's veins. Missy held the doorknob as if it was all that supported her. Hannibal could see two inches of blackness between the edge of the door and the wall. Rod must have turned the alarm back on in the basement and then reset it while Hannibal was unconscious. By opening the door, Missy had changed them from escapees to prey.

"Time to move," Hannibal said, leaping through the door, dragging Missy by her wrist. Adrenalin drove him down the street toward his car faster than the girl was prepared to run. She stumbled behind him, only just remaining upright.

The night air burned Hannibal's lungs as his free hand dug into his pocket for his keys. The moon was a spotlight singling them out as the only things moving on the street that night. Missy's white underclothes glowed like fluorescent targets for anyone who might want to sight in on her. Hannibal prayed that Rod, once awakened, would first call the alarm company to prevent a police visit.

Ten feet from his car, Hannibal pushed the button on his key fob that unlocked the doors. He had not looked back but once in the driver's seat he was pleased to see that no one followed them. He was staring a Rod's house because he was parked facing it. The street was too narrow for a three-point turn around. Hannibal heard the throaty roar of his engine and glanced at Missy. She was staring in surprise at Mariah, still asleep in the back seat. His nose told him that she had vomited back there, probably without ever waking up.

"She breathing?"

"Yes," Missy said. "But she's a mess."

"We'll deal with that later. Right now, crouch down. We're driving past the house."

Hannibal slapped the Volvo into first gear and popped the clutch. After the briefest squeal of tires the car jumped forward. Rod's front door opened as they approached. Hannibal looked over Missy's ducked head and locked eyes with Rod as he raced past. Even in that brief contact he could see the naked hatred behind those dark eyes.

Seconds later Hannibal was driving down a narrow street with only occasional streetlights. In the yards just behind the lights he could see vegetation growing wild. On each block he spotted a pile of trash near the curb. This was not, he thought, the best neighborhood in Virginia Beach. In fact, the area he was in reminded him of his own neighborhood in Washington. He turned to Missy again, but she was bent over the seat leaning into the back.

"What are you doing?" he asked.

"Strapping her in."

"Good idea," Hannibal said, stopping at an unmarked corner. "Any idea where we are?"

Missy settled back into her seat. "Got a pretty good idea. Go left I think. That should take us to the beach again."

Hannibal nodded and made the turn. He thought he saw the lights of another vehicle in his rearview mirror, but it would be pure paranoia to think it could be Rod. He considered how he would explain his evening to the police, and which of these young women would back his story. Missy had already been unexpectedly helpful. His next day might have been very unpleasant if not for her having both the courage and the caring to free him.

"You look so unhappy."

Missy's comment caught Hannibal off guard. "I was thinking of what I woke up to back in the house. I'm really sorry I let that happen to you."

"Not your fault," Missy said. Here eyes drifted right, away from Hannibal. "I asked for it, really. And it wouldn't have been so rough except, that, well, Rod wanted to take me as a virgin."

Hannibal glanced right, swallowed, and then focused straight ahead. "You were a virgin?"

"Well, in that hole anyway."

"Oh."

"The drugs made it easier. I'm still a little numb all over."

It seemed clear to Hannibal that she was a lot more comfortable with this conversation than he was. His rearview mirror was still clear, but he made a couple of aimless, spontaneous turns just to be safe. He could imagine someone seeing the White Tornado's radiance in the moonlight. He tried to focus on driving but after a minute the silence seemed too heavy to carry.

"So why'd you do it?" Hannibal asked.

Missy stared out her window into the deep darkness. "A man like you could never understand. Giving up control of your own life is so liberating. That's what being a subbie is all about, after all."

"No." Hannibal shook his head. "I mean, why did you help me? It seemed pretty clear that you were under Rod's spell."

"Oh that." Missy looked at Hannibal and he saw a coquettish manner that had escaped him until then. "He only whipped up on you because you tried to help me. It was my fault you got stomped. I didn't need that guilt."

It was cool enough in the car, but the air was still and stuffy, prompting Hannibal to turn on the air conditioner. "Okay, so you let Rod dominate you, but you decided to do this against his obvious wishes. That kind of tells me that you're too strong a girl to be someone's submissive slave."

"Oh no, I'm definitely a subbie by nature," Missy said with a smile. "I like being told what to do by a strong man. I like being devoted to pleasing someone else. I like having rules I must obey."

"But you left."

She watched the moon for a moment. "You know how people take orders in the Army? It's kind of like that. They choose to follow, but only if the leader can lead. For me to sub to a man, he's got to be a Dom I can trust and respect. Rod is a strong man, but what he did to you just wasn't right."

Hannibal nodded in the darkness as they rolled to a stop at another corner. "This goes into a dead end," he said to himself.

"Hang a left here," Missy said. "You know, when I met you I thought you were in the life. Now that I know you're not, I'm kind of confused about why you got involved with Rod."

"Long story," he said, making the turn. The rambling beach houses had given way to smaller structures, each still with its deep front porch, but the houses themselves were shoved too close together for comfort. Older oaks and ashes arching over narrow sidewalks made the streets look even more claustrophobic.

"I guess you were just destined to meet," Missy said, as if it were a random thought.

"Is that the kind of defeatist crap you pick up on the streets these days?"

Missy's laugh was light, like a southern belle in one of those old movies Hannibal's mother used to watch. "Actually it's straight out of philosophy class."

"Some community college bullshit?"

"Actually I'm a sophomore at Wesleyan," Missy said. "Physics, with a minor in chemistry."

"Sorry. I just never imagined you for a co-ed."

"It's okay," Missy said. "You've probably just never seen one in her underwear." She laughed then, to Hannibal's surprise, and he smiled along with her. He thought he saw the beach in the distance and sped up just a little.

Hannibal didn't know why, but for a second he could smell Rod on her. "Rod talked about having a destiny. You don't believe all that destiny crap, do you?"

"No, not really. I do believe in karma."

"Karma? You mean like, if you do bad things, bad things will happen to you?"

"Something like that."

"Yeah, well I don't think it happens by itself," Hannibal said. The water glistened in the distance, but he didn't see the taller buildings that crowded the shoreline. "In fact, Rod's been a bad guy for a long time but he seems to be made of Teflon. Nothing sticks to him. He just goes along hurting people, but nothing bad has happened to him yet."

"Sure it has. You."

"Huh?" The road curved, and the water veered to his right. Hannibal turned the next corner to again face the silver he saw shining under the moon.

"You are the bad thing that's happened to him. I think maybe you are an agent of the cosmos, sent here to right the balance."

"Okay, you're higher than I thought." A loud cough from the back seat cut across his mind, shorting out any other ideas. Mariah coughed again, louder, and Hannibal pulled to the curb.

"I think she's choking," Missy said, twisted around in her seat. Hannibal slipped the shifter out of gear and yanked the emergency brake, jumped out of his car, ran around to the passenger side and yanked the back door open. Mariah appeared to still be only half conscious, gagging on her own vomit. Hannibal grabbed her under her arms and slid her out onto the narrow strip of grass at the edge of the sidewalk. Her breathing deepened as he wiped her mouth. Sitting up seemed to be all she needed so he propped her against a tree. The cool, wet grass dampened his knees. Her pulse was a little slow, her breathing irregular, and her pupils dilated under the streetlight, but all that could be caused by any number of drugs. If he knew where a clinic was, he'd drive her to it.

A feeling of relief washed over him when he heard an engine approaching. It was one of those four-wheel drive monsters from the sound of it. It was probably a local resident on his way home from a late party. Who else would be out on the streets at this hour? Surely the driver would know where the nearest hospital was.

"Hey Missy! Flag that guy down."

Missy rolled her window down. "What, in my underwear?"

Hannibal stood. "Good point." He walked to the middle of the street. Bathed in the headlight beams he waved his arms overhead. The vehicle stopped just past the corner and turned to the right so that it blocked the street. Without the lights shining into his eyes he could see the vehicle more clearly. It was a Jeep.

A red Jeep.

Derek's Jeep.

"Damn." Hannibal yanked his car door open. He had one leg in the car when a gunshot split the night silence and he felt the slug punch into his car door. Missy's scream drowned out the slam of him pulling the door shut. He yanked the shifter into first gear, cranked the wheel and spun his tires whipping the Volvo in the opposite direction from the Jeep. He heard another shot, but couldn't tell if it had hit his car or not.

Now the welcoming narrow residential streets were far less hospitable. Instead they were too small for maneuver. The Jeep's lights burned his eyes in the rearview mirror. At the second corner he pulled his car into a sharp right turn. The Jeep followed.

"Are we in trouble?" Missy asked.

"Not if we can find a cop car."

Missy jumped at the sound of another gunshot. "Don't you have a gun?"

"Sure," Hannibal said. "My Sig Sauer is strapped under the glove compartment. You want it?"

"I can't shoot a gun."

"Well I try not to either, when I'm driving."

As Hannibal approached the next corner another car was racing toward them. The other driver slammed to a halt at the intersection. Maybe the driver was waiting for Hannibal's car to pass. His elbow stuck out the window. The engine thrummed so confidently Hannibal could hear it over his own humming engine's sound. It was a big car. The top was down and its white interior glowed ghost-like inside a fiery red shell.

"Jesus," Hannibal mumbled through clenched teeth. It was half curse, half prayer. Rod leaned forward behind the steering wheel as Hannibal cranked hard to get around the corner to his right. A high-pitched crack slammed his ears followed by the dull thud of a bullet punching through his rear quarter panel. Missy screamed again and fumbled with her seat belt, trying to crouch lower.

Hannibal drove as quickly as he dared through the residential streets with Rod's hybrid muscle car on his tail. In his mind's eye he imagined Derek in the Jeep coming around from his right at the next intersection. They would be herding him away from the beach, toward ever more isolated streets until they could corner him or run him off the road and Rod could exact his revenge on Hannibal for deceiving him and taking his women. He might never know what this was all about and that, to Hannibal, was unacceptable.

The corner yard on his right was wide enough for Hannibal to see the approaching Jeep halfway up the block. They moved closer and closer to one another, apparently on a ninety-degree collision course. Missy sat frozen, staring out her window at the incoming open vehicle. She knew these men better than Hannibal did, but he suspected that this was not a situation that fell within her understanding. She knew violence as play but he wondered if she had missed the rage underlying it.

In the second before Hannibal cranked his wheel hard to the left he was not quite close enough to see Derek's eyes, but he could clearly see the oversized revolver in his right hand. Rod had given the boy a .44 and probably carried one himself. Listening to his tires squealing as he whipped around the corner, Hannibal wanted to ask Missy if the boys were compensating for something, but didn't think she'd find this line of conversation humorous right then.

Another gunshot sounded, this one a wild shot that never came close to his car. Those boys were more dangerous to the locals than to him. If this kept up much longer some innocent would be hurt or killed. Where the hell were the police? Hannibal had heard that Virginia Beach had more cops per capita than any community in the nation except Las Vegas. Surely someone had reported these maniacs shooting up a quiet suburban neighborhood in the wee hours of the morning. How could they get away with it so close to the beach? And that was when he realized that the water he was working toward had no beach in front of it.

"What the hell is this?"

"It's one of the lakes," Missy said, sounding short of breath. "I think. Maybe Lake Holly. It's spread all over this area with little inlets and stuff where vacationers can keep their boats."

"Great." Hannibal's hand slipped on the gearshift lever, wet with perspiration. Now he had no idea where the ocean was. Breathing was getting harder. He pretended it was the humidity and powered down his window. A swampy odor wafted in. Lakes always smelled nasty to him.

A narrow bridge loomed ahead. He would have to slow down a little to cross it. Rod's Corvorado filled Hannibal's mirror, its engine so loud it drowned out his pounding heartbeat. On the grid in his head Hannibal could see Derek circling around in the Jeep to get to the first corner on the other side of the bridge. Hannibal couldn't afford to slow down very much.

"Come on, old friend," he muttered under his breath. "Get me over this one obstacle fast enough and I think we'll be home free."

The bridge was wooden, arched high like a medieval monastery gateway. The water on either side of it was thick with reeds, lily pads and flotsam he couldn't identify in the colorless moonlight. It must be lovely to stroll past on a warm summer day. Then it would be picturesque, charming, maybe even calming. This night, the bridge was simply an obstacle.

Hannibal slammed the accelerator to the floor just as his front tires touched the first slats of the bridge. He figured that Rod's rear-wheel drive car couldn't possibly hit the bridge this hard. Rod would lose ground and he would gain just enough to race past the Jeep at the intersection, dodging them both. All he had to do was to keep a tight grip on the wheel and allow the Volvo to go airborne past the crest of the bridge.

No! Hannibal's eyes stretched wide as he reached the midpoint and saw the headlights of the little Toyota. What kind of idiot was driving around at this time of night? And hadn't he heard the Volvo racing toward him? Why was he driving toward the bridge? In truth, they might have been able to pass each other if Hannibal was driving at a reasonable speed. But his speed was nowhere near normal and he would crush the other car in a second unless he did something radical.

In this case, radical meant yanking the steering wheel hard to the right just before the front tires left the ground. As the car pushed through the flimsy guardrail and began to spiral right, Hannibal mentally apologized to his old metal friend and asked it to protect him and his charge.

-22-

The steady tone in his head was the noise a telephone makes when it has been left off the hook. The pressure across his chest, he reasoned, came from the shoulder harness. His left arm was numb, but that was probably from his own weight being on it. Despite the darkness, he knew that pain and noise meant he was alive.

Hannibal touched his face, expecting wetness. Instead he felt a very raw abrasion on his right cheek. He opened his eyes a crack and saw the source. His airbag, now deflated, had popped out to hold him in place at the moment of impact. It had also scraped across his face at high speed like a cheese grater, and left him covered with a fine powder.

Turning his head he saw Missy, suspended above him like the woman in some magician's stunt gone wrong. Her arms hung limp, and her breathing was labored. A merciful fate had allowed her to lapse into unconsciousness while Hannibal experienced the entire horrible crash: the jarring impact as the Volvo hit the ground just past the waterline and rolled, and rolled again. The vicious blow from the air bag was followed by the sound of twisting metal. His stomach had flipped with the movement, and when he finally came to rest, the clanging sound in his ears overrode everything else.

But even though Missy had been spared the worst of the experience, he could not leave her hanging from her seat belt and shoulder harness for long. The gasoline smell that was making him nauseous was also a warning signal of possible danger. He knew what to do, but also knew that it would not be easy.

"Oh, well," Hannibal said aloud. "There's nothing for it."

After releasing his seat belt, Hannibal slowly and carefully pulled himself upright. In a moment he was standing with the steering wheel against his shins, his feet on the ground through the driver's side window. A shower of windshield safety glass cascaded out of his hair and off his shoulders. The full moon cast him in a spotlight in the narrow confines of the car resting on its side.

Hannibal was startled by the rush of silence when the horn stopped. The sudden silence prompted him to focus. Missy's head pressed against his chest as he unbuckled her seat belt. The shoulder harness was less cooperative, but by turning her body into a vertical position he easily slipped her out of it. He supported her, leaning against the back of the seats, but only for a few seconds. He felt her head shiver against his chest before she spoke.

"What happened? Where are we? Smoke?"

"It's me, only call me Hannibal," he said, easing her downward so that she could rest on the center console. "We crashed and rolled. We're in a small field near the edge of Lake Holly I think. You can now do commercials for Volvo's safety record. Now sit tight for a minute and try not to throw up."

Placing one foot on the console beside Missy's hips, Hannibal boosted himself up and out of the passenger window. As he turned to sit on the closed door he rocked gently to test whether the vehicle would be tempted to drop onto its roof or its tires. When neither seemed likely he reached down.

"Give me your hands, Missy."

"How come I'm not scared?"

"You're in shock," Hannibal said. "Give me your hands." Missy reached up with both arms. Hannibal grasped her wrists and pulled up until he could wrap his legs around her waist to hold her steady.

"Not feeling very good," Missy said.

"Just hold on for a few seconds." Hannibal wrapped both hands around her waist and pulled her up. Without being told, she curled her legs to clear the roof. He lowered her to her feet on the grass. She dropped to her knees and then fell forward onto her hands.

"Oh God! Can I throw up now?"

"Go for it," Hannibal said, hopping down from the car. He sat on the grass with his back to the roof of his car and fished in his pockets for his phone. He was surprised that Rod hadn't taken it from him, but figured he shouldn't have been. This guy never thought things through and Hannibal was at a loss to explain how a man who never considered consequences could be so dangerous.

Gazing into the calm lake waters, Hannibal slapped at a growing cloud of flying insects and listened to Missy begin to heave. Absently he reached over to hold her long hair back while she vomited into the grass. She had only been unconscious for a few seconds but he knew this to be one common reaction to being knocked out. When she was finished he leaned her back against the white roof beside him and pushed a button on his phone.

"Police?" Missy asked.

"They're next." In fact, he wondered why no police cars had found them already. Their landing was noisy and the nearest homes stood no more than fifty yards away. Besides, hadn't the driver of the little Toyota stopped to watch the crash? Surely he would have called an ambulance. Unless of course he was too drunk to think and didn't want the authorities to know he was behind the wheel in that condition. Or, he may have been sneaking home from someone else's wife's bed at four-thirty in the morning. Or, maybe he and the nearby residents were just in the habit of minding their own business. In any case, he would get the local police to come by and pick them up, tell his story and point out the bullet holes in his car. With police assistance he would return to Rod's house in daylight with Missy telling tales of rampant drug use and showing handcuff marks.

251

Hannibal's blood in the hall carpet, and more in the master bedroom, would hold their attention. While Rod answered questions he would retrieve the disc he left behind in the sofa.

In the meantime, they sat alone being eaten alive by the lakeside insects. But before he called for help he wanted to check in. There were people who might be worried about him.

He expected to hear a series of rings but Cindy's voice burst through after only one. "Hannibal! Oh thank God."

"Hey, baby…"

"Did Sarge find you?"

The question froze his planned words in his throat. He didn't know why, but the question started a chill up his spine, and fresh perspiration painted his forehead.

"I told Sarge I didn't need backup on this. I left him to guard Marquita."

"Hannibal, she disappeared," Cindy said. "Right after she made that one telephone call for you. We were all at Sarge's place and then she was just gone."

That was so many hours ago. So much had happened since then. Hannibal stood up, pacing with the telephone. "Where would she go? She knew she was safe with Sarge."

"He thinks she went to see Rod in person."

"She wouldn't even know where to go," Hannibal said, staring into the lake as if clarity lay there. "I only gave Rod's address to you, for safety's sake. Oh, Cindy. You didn't tell her, did you?"

"Of course not," Cindy said, indignation in her voice. "I'm not an idiot."

"Thank God." Hannibal breathed relief, slowing his pacing around the car.

"But Sarge thought she might already know. He took off after her."

Relief vanished in an instant, and Hannibal felt an invisible hand squeezing his chest. "You gave the address to Sarge," he said with grim certainty.

"I didn't think it could hurt. He was starting to act a little crazy. If he was going to be a loose cannon it seemed best for him to be with you." Hannibal closed his eyes and quickly did the math. Enough hours had passed. Sarge would be driving like a bat out of hell, with blood in his eyes. His search for Marquita would have quickly changed to a mad charge to get at the source of her suffering. What if Rod and Derek, both armed, returned to that house after running Hannibal off the road and found Sarge on the porch, spoiling for a fight? Hannibal had wanted to return to Rod's house in the daytime, but waiting for daylight could mean Sarge's life.

"Don't worry, babe," he said into the phone in calm, even tones. "I'll find Sarge and bring him home safe. Got to run now."

With his thumb Hannibal cut his connection to his support system. He panned slowly, his eyes scanning the houses across the nearest street. "So, where the hell is Rod's house from here?" he asked himself aloud.

Behind him, Missy said, "It's that way."

Hannibal looked down just in time to see Missy's arm drop.

"What makes you think it's that way?"

"I have a good sense of direction," she said. "But you don't want to be there. He'll kill you. Wait for the police."

"Can't," Hannibal replied, hopping up to grab the edge of the car's skyward window. He reached into the car, clawing for the clips under the dashboard.

"They have guns," Missy said, in an expressionless voice.

"Me too," he said, dropping back to the ground. After flashing his Sig Sauer to her he slid it into the back of his waistband. "How far do you think?"

She shrugged. "A mile. Maybe a little more."

"Okay." Hannibal looked down at Missy, chocolate skin highlighted by very plain white bra and panties, and considered how simple packages sometimes hold very complex contents. "You were experimenting, weren't you?"

"Yes." Somehow, she knew exactly what he was talking about.

"Well, was the experiment a success?"

She smiled up at him. "Well, I learned something about myself. Guess that would be a yes."

Hannibal nodded. "I don't see any injuries, but that doesn't mean you're not hurt."

"The shock thing."

"Exactly," Hannibal said. "Pick up that phone and call 911 and get an ambulance out here. When the police arrive, send them over to Rod's house."

"You could wait for them."

"No," Hannibal said, already walking toward the road. "A friend may be in danger. My fault. I have to put it right. And I need to finish this business with Rod." He turned to being jogging toward the street. He could just hear Missy's words behind him on the wind.

"Spoken like a true agent of the cosmos."

Darkness closed around him as Hannibal jogged toward the bridge he had driven off minutes earlier. Before he reached it he had settled into a good running pace and his breathing deepened. As always, he shifted his focus from his aching lungs to the rhythmic sound of his footfalls. Then, as always, his mind wandered to unrelated matters. When asphalt changed to wooden slats under his feet he was asking himself some hard questions.

He certainly didn't expect Rod to back off in a confrontation. Did the fact that the man tried to kill him justify using deadly force in return? There was also the matter of stealing from Hannibal's client. Bad, even evil, but not a capital offense. What about kidnapping? Hannibal had found Missy handcuffed to a bed. But it was clear that she had volunteered for that treatment. She might not even call her sexual encounter with Rod rape. And even if he killed Sarge, Rod would be able to make a case for self-defense.

Hannibal's mouth was dry and he tasted the dried blood in his mouth. Somehow that taste made a mental connection for him to Anita lying in her hospital bed. Then he pictured Marquita the first time he saw her, used up and well on her way to the bottom of a spiral from which few return. Ultimately, anything he did to Rod would be in their names.

Seven minutes later Hannibal stood across the street from Rod's house, breathing more deeply than he liked and smelling his own sweat. He had recognized enough landmarks to get straight to his objective, and he was sure it had in fact been little more than a mile. He owed Missy a big thank you. She had pointed him well. Too bad she couldn't tell him what to do now.

He stood with his hands on his thighs, feeling the weight of his P-226 at the small of his back. He was ready to charge the house and stage a rescue, guns blazing if necessary. He just wasn't sure if a rescue was needed. The blinds at the big front window were drawn tight, allowing only tiny drops of light to leak out. Was Sarge inside, or was he still en route? Or, was he in hiding someplace observing the house as Hannibal was? He might not even be headed this way. How was Hannibal to know?

Behind Hannibal, a heavily accented Hispanic voice said, "Don't move. This thing would wake up the whole neighborhood if it went off."

-23-

The man who stepped in front of Hannibal wore a gray suit, white shirt and conservative tie. His hair was cut very short. His complexion was swarthy but not in the Mediterranean way. This was Central American skin, golden, thick and rough. When he smiled he displayed a gold tooth. Hannibal judged him at about five foot seven. His easy manner told Hannibal that a second man must have been standing out of Hannibal's sight.

"Tell me, what brings you out so late at night?"

"Jogging," Hannibal said. "Just stopped to catch my breath. I can move on."

"Jogging?" Gold Tooth rolled it around in his mouth as if trying it on for size. "You were expecting serious trouble in this neighborhood, eh?"

Hannibal felt his gun being lifted from his waistband. He stood erect, waiting for the next step.

"What you say, Ruiz?" Gold Tooth asked.

"Sig Sauer P229 in .40 caliber," the voice behind Hannibal replied. "Serious shit, Manny."

"Professional shit," Manny said.

"Can't be too careful," Hannibal said, wishing he had been a bit more careful. At that minute he felt careless and stupid, but why should he have expected guards to be posted across from Rod's house?

"Know what I think?" Manny asked. "I think you come looking for the big fellow we met earlier. He at least had the guts to walk right up and knock on the door. You are maybe a little less bold. No smarter though."

Well, now he had one answer anyway. Sarge had been here. Hannibal needed to know what had happened to him. These guys seemed professional, so he thought he'd try the direct approach.

"The big guy. What happened to him?"

"Well, he wasn't our problem, was he?" Manny said. "And we don't get paid to deal with other people's problems. So, we invited him inside. Why don't we go see him, eh? Follow me."

Manny turned and, knowing that at least one gun would be trained on his back, Hannibal followed him across the street and onto Rod's porch. A third man sat on one of the wicker chairs holding a Tec 9 submachine gun with a casual air that could make an observer miss his heightened level of alertness. Manny rapped a knuckle on the door twice, then once, then twice again. After this simple code he pushed the door open and ushered Hannibal in ahead of himself.

"Found this guy wandering around outside, jefe," Manny said. "Thought he might be another friend of your host here."

All eyes were on Hannibal and he used the moment of silent appraisal to scan the room. The atmosphere in the living room was more cordial than he unexpected. Rod, in his own big chair, showed an unexpected degree of cool, although his eyes betrayed both surprise and anger at seeing Hannibal in his living room. Derek and Sheryl just looked stunned on the sofa. Hannibal looked for Sheryl's eyes, but she quickly pulled them away from him.

The man in the chair Hannibal had occupied a couple of days ago could have been Manny's older brother, but everything about him said that he was the boss. His half-smile was noncommittal, as if he was waiting to learn more about Hannibal before deciding whether they should welcome him, eject him or kill him. He wore a Breitling watch on his left wrist, diamond cufflinks and a stickpin in his tie that was probably worth more than the house around them.

Anything else Hannibal needed to know about the man he derived from the quality of his help. The man behind him watched Hannibal. The man across the room watched Rod. Neither of them looked to their boss for guidance. They would know what to do if things went wrong.

The last person Hannibal looked at was Sarge, sitting in the far corner with his hands behind him. Cuffed together, Hannibal assumed, or taped. He wore a black sleeveless tee, shorts and running shoes. Hannibal guessed it was what he had on when he heard Marquita was gone. Sarge turned his face away, probably to hide injuries, but it also served the purpose of hiding any look of recognition.

"All right, Mr. Mantooth, do you know this one?" the stranger asked.

"This son of a bitch is called Smoke, Mr…" The stranger raised a finger and Rod stopped. He didn't want his name dropped in front of strangers. And suddenly, Hannibal knew who he was.

"You're the Colombian buyer," Hannibal said, taking a couple of steps forward and getting back into character. "Rod told me he had a big hot deal going down. Didn't think he was this well connected though."

The stranger waved another finger, and the bodyguard on the left stepped forward. He reached into his jacket but instead of a gun he produced a flattened roll of duct tape. Hannibal sighed, nodded, and put his hands behind his back. Once his wrists were secured, the guard led him to the end of the sofa where he was lowered to the floor.

"You are too free with your business, Mr. Mantooth," the stranger said.

Rod sat forward. "I never told this boy anything about you. But now I know he's a spy. Snuck in here to rip me off. Stole a couple of my girls."

"You should have shut his mouth permanently."

"I thought I did." Rod's voice became harder, and Hannibal could see his control slipping.

"I prefer to do business with careful people."

"You'll deal with me," Rod said, standing, "because I got this." He waved the computer disc in front of himself like bait to attract a shark. This was an opportunity that Hannibal could not pass up. He locked eyes with Rod, rose to his knees, pushed out his chest and forced a big grin.

"You a joke man. Your dreams are bigger than you are. You ain't no gangsta, at least, not on a level where you can deal with this guy. Look at him. He's money."

"Shut the fuck up!" Rod was in front of Hannibal in two long strides with an arm raised to backhand him. Hannibal shifted his gaze to the stranger.

"You really want to work with this asshole?"

Rod spun to stare at his guest. The stranger's face was passive, showing the slightest hint of annoyance.

"Sorry, Smoke is it? Sorry but this man has something I very much want and I will work with him this one time. After which, I fear he will dispose of you."

"So you really want this formula he's got?" Hannibal asked. "You want people to be able to get off their habits?"

Rage and surprise fought for dominance on Rod's face. The stranger betrayed only amusement.

"You are smarter than these others," the stranger said, pulling out a silver cigarette case. "Of course, I would like for some of my senior staff to be able to sample our product without fear of addiction. But also, consider how much product some wealthy customers might purchase if they also did not have addiction to fear."

"Yeah, I can see that, but is it really worth the pile of cash I know this slug is demanding?" Hannibal asked. While he spoke he twisted his wrists, feeling the tape pull hairs from his arm.

The stranger tapped the tip of his cigarette on the case before putting it into his mouth. His nearer bodyguard jumped to give him a light. He took a casual drag on what used to be called a regular length cigarette and spoke through the smoke.

"Like my product, the formula's value is set by the demands of the marketplace. More importantly, I must control this formula in order to keep it out of the hands of those who might share it injudiciously, which could ruin my market. For this, I will pay this man a large sum indeed."

Hannibal took in the briefcase on the stranger's right, probably full of cash. A smaller black case sat at his left. Then an unexpected backhand slap from Rod rocked Hannibal's entire body.

"Didn't I tell you nobody can stop me?" Rod said, his lips curled back into a snarl. "I got me a date with destiny."

Hannibal tilted to his left, teetered on one knee, but managed to right himself without falling. "Yeah," he said, spitting blood onto the carpet before looking up again. "But it's a blind date. When your destiny does show up, you won't recognize it. And it might just be uglier than you expect."

The stranger barked one short laugh, and his bodyguard also grinned.

"If you continue to play with this one, he will eat you like a barracuda," the stranger said in his oddly accented yet cultivated voice. "Besides, I have a plane to catch. Let us complete our business."

That was the cue for the bodyguard on Hannibal's side of the room to cross to his boss and pick up the larger briefcase. He sat it on the coffee table and opened it, revealing the stacks of cash Hannibal expected. Derek sucked in a breath. The bodyguard looked to Rod. Rod nodded and handed him the disc.

Hannibal considered the rescue options to be slim. Sarge was bound and wedged into a corner where he would be slow getting into the action even if he somehow freed himself. Hannibal saw no possible allies he could turn in the room. The Colombian had what he had come for and would now leave Hannibal and Sarge to Rod's limited mercy. Hannibal though the police would be there by then if Missy had sent them. Perhaps she had decided to distance herself from the crash site before calling for help. After all, she believed Hannibal to be an underworld character. She might have decided not to have any more to do with him or Rod. Out of respect for Hannibal's undercover status, Cindy would wait hours before raising a general alarm.

With rescue hours away, Hannibal realized how thin his hand was. He had only one card, and the time had come to play it.

"He's ripping you off, you know. The formula you're paying for isn't on that disc."

Rod's face contorted into something akin to deep concentration. The stranger released another short, barking laugh.

"He's lying," Rod shouted.

"That would be a foolish lie."

"It ain't," Hannibal said. "It's a scam. This cracker's just trying to trick you out of your cheddar."

"That would be a foolish trick," the stranger said, tapping his cigarette ash onto the floor. "We will know, very soon, which of you is the more foolish."

The first bodyguard sat the smaller case on the coffee table beside the first. When he pulled a laptop computer out of it, Hannibal realized that his outburst had been unnecessary. He fought to maintain a straight face as the guard opened the computer, booted it up, and placed the disc into the CD-Rom drive.

Hannibal closed his eyes for a moment, sending a silent apology to Cindy. There was no way around what would come next. The Colombian would have to make a statement. Rod would resist. There would surely be a firefight. Barring exceptional luck, he and Sarge would die in the crossfire.

Unless he could bargain his way out of it. He still knew the location of the formula.

The bodyguard crouching at the computer tapped keys in silence. The smoke of a custom blend cigarette flared Hannibal's nostrils. Then the computer user's eyes flared as well.

"Boss, there's only one thing on this disc, but it's not a data file."

"That's crazy," Rod said. "You don't know what you're doing." Despite his hubris, Rod was easing back toward his chair. The stranger raised a finger to his chin,

"Well, what is it?"

"It appears to be an audio file," the guard said.

The stranger flashed a sly smile, glanced at Hannibal and said, "Well, play it."

The guard tapped keys and what sounded like a hip-hop beat came out of the laptop. Derek's hand slid toward the space between the cushions. The move was subtle, but Hannibal was sure the guard behind him would have noticed it. He sat very still, trying hard to look harmless.

The audio track evolved into a rap performance. Sarge finally looked at Hannibal when the lyrics started: "She was a fast machine, she kept her motor clean…"

The stranger's eyes hooked to Hannibal.

Sarge said, "Damn."

Hannibal reached for the stranger's attention. "Look this doesn't have to end ugly. You still want the formula, right? I might be able to…"

Rod screamed, "You son of a bitch!" His hand thrust under his chair. "I'll fucking kill you!"

The stranger stayed still, composed. The man at the computer performed some sort of sleight of hand magic trick and a pistol appeared in his right fist, pointed toward Rod. Derek pulled a gun out of the sofa. Sheryl dived for the floor. A hand landed on Hannibal's shoulder, he guessed to hold him still as a shield. He heard a safety catch click off near his ear.

And then Hannibal went blind.

-24-

A heavy revolver roared and the eye-scorching blast jarred Hannibal into action. He dived hard to his right, away from the couch, one hand already working into his pocket as two more shots were fired. He had no time to wonder why the lights had gone out. He just knew that survival depended on taking advantage of miracles when they came along.

Hannibal had a pretty good mental picture of where each of the players would go for cover. Listening to the rustling of bodies scrambling for safety between at least half a dozen more gunshots, Hannibal rolled to the wall beside the door, the last place he expected any of them to go. A gunshot on his right brought a scream of fear from Sheryl. Her pitiful sobbing came from somewhere near the middle of the room. Hannibal managed to free his pocketknife and begin work on the tape holding his wrists in place.

Someone was creeping along the wall to his right. Someone else was crawling behind the sofa. Then he heard a heavier thump at the base of the stairs. It had to be Rod. He was moving up the stairs. There was no way to know what kind of arsenal he might have there. Hannibal imagined Rod at the top of the stairs with a machine gun hosing down the room. He couldn't reach him without crossing the no man's land of the center of the room. But, could he get one of the others to bring Rod down?

His hands free, Hannibal eased up into a crouch. While adjusting his balance he bumped his head against the blinds.

The soft rattle shot fear down his spine. He snapped back to the floor, waiting for a bullet to find him. No one fired. Maybe the others were also focused on the stairs. And he had just bumped into the possible solution.

Focusing his attention on the denser darkness at the center of the room, Hannibal slowly raised his left hand, gripped the cord hanging behind it, and yanked hard.

With a loud whirr the blinds raced toward the ceiling. The pale blue moonlight revealed a frozen tableau of desperation faced with inevitability. Derek stood in the center of the floor straddling his weeping girlfriend. With his teeth clenched like Dirty Harry he held the big .44 Magnum thrust forward aiming at a space on the wall halfway between the two bodyguards. Before Derek could even decide whether to swing left or right, two automatics spoke at once. The Magnum revolver fired into the ceiling and Derek flew backward as if yanked by wires. Sheryl screamed again. The gunmen's eyes turned to Hannibal.

The stranger rose from behind his chair and walked calmly toward the door. When he was inches away from Hannibal he stopped and nodded once. Then his eyes went to the stairs. Rod must have already reached the second floor. The stranger looked again at Hannibal.

"Will we meet again?"

"No," Hannibal said. "Other priorities."

The stranger offered a half smile and then said, "Let's go" in a clear voice and opened the door. His men moved to follow him. Hannibal stood and bolted toward the stairs. Halfway across the room he bent long enough to scoop up the revolver Derek had dropped. With the muzzle pointed toward the ceiling he raced up the stairs, praying that he would meet Rod at the top. Instead, he found the hallway empty. It was the hall where Rod had kicked and beaten him. The second floor of this house held only ugly memories.

Moonlight showed him that the first room, where Mariah was beaten, was equally vacant.

The second bedroom, where Derek and Sheryl had played before the boy was blown away trying to defend his mentor, was unoccupied.

He entered the final bedroom, where Hannibal had been chained and forced to watch Missy being brutally sodomized. This empty room greeted him with a fresh breeze. The window stood open. Rod had not come upstairs for weaponry. He had deserted his junior partner. Hannibal followed.

When his feet hit the ground he rolled twice and came up gun first. Only then, gazing across the pistol's front sight, did he realize that he was on the hunt. Deep footprints in the turf and broken brush showed Rod's path back toward the street. Hannibal really had no choice but to follow. This had to end that night.

The street was again empty when Hannibal returned to it, but he could hear Rod's heavy tread moving away to his right. He heard sirens approaching from the opposite direction. Maybe Missy did call the police after all. But the Colombians had already made themselves scarce and Rod would disappear into the landscape if Hannibal lost track of him.

Hannibal pushed the big revolver into his belt and started an easy jog in Rod's direction. Within half a block he had eased the throttle up to a respectable cross country pace and was closing on his quarry. Residences flew past him to be replaced by a growing number of businesses. His lungs burned as he dragged air deeper and deeper into them. His ribs ached from Rod's earlier kicks. His whole body ached from the miscellaneous traumas it took when Hannibal's beloved White Tornado speared into the ground and the car collapsed around him to keep him and his passenger alive. It didn't matter how far Rod ran. Hannibal would catch him and see to it that he never damaged another woman.

Devoid of traffic, Pacific Avenue was just another wide street. What mattered to Hannibal was that when he crossed it he was close enough to Rod to see that he was dragging. The man was strong, but he was no runner.

Atlantic Avenue was dark except for the security lights that every store and shop had shining over its door. A minute later they were racing across the boardwalk and down the wooden stairs to the cool sand. Did Rod intend to swim to safety? No, he turned right just short of the waterline and pushed himself onward.

They ran in wet sand now, the salt smell so strong it wrinkled Hannibal's nose. They passed folding chairs and the periodic lifeguard platforms, but on this night there was no one on or even near the beach but the two of them. They were running south, passing single digit streets on the other side of the boardwalk. Their numbers, he knew, were dropping quickly. He couldn't see the end ahead, but he knew it was there, just past Second Street. He was panting aloud now, watching his towering shadow chasing Rod's across the sand, which was smoothed by the receding tide. He was close enough to hear Rod's labored breathing now. His legs were beginning to burn. Would he be able to bring Rod down if he caught up to him?

The silliness of that question suddenly struck him. He slowed to a jog and drew the long .44 from his belt. He held the weapon in both hands, thrust forward like a divining rod that was unerringly drawn toward evil.

With the lyrics to "Stagger Lee" running through his head, Hannibal shouted, "That's far enough, Rod. Come on back here and we go talk to the police. Keep running and I blow off a leg."

Rod slowed, then stopped but did not turn. His huge frame rose and fell in the effort to breathe. He was still dressed for a party. Barefoot, in shorts and a Hawaiian shirt, he seemed to belong on the beach. His head was down, turning first left, then right the way people sometimes do when they're trying to figure something out.

"Can't be," Rod said to the tidal breeze. "This is my time."

"Has to be," Hannibal said. "You can't just keep shitting on people forever. Eventually that shit blows back to land on you."

"Bullshit. Fate sent that asshole pharmacist to my cell for a reason. I didn't listen to his crap, pump him for info, and shoot that air bubble into him for nothing."

"Air bubble," Hannibal said under his breath. "A home made heart attack."

Rod turned ninety degrees to face the ocean. Moonlight danced seductively on the waves. Despite the splashing surf Hannibal heard the telltale click of a revolver hammer being drawn back. So this was it, Hannibal thought. The final clash between Rod's vision and Hannibal's, between Rod's destiny and his karma.

"It don't have to be this way," Hannibal called.

"Yeah it does."

Rod raised his right fist toward Hannibal but it was weary, sluggish, and too slow to matter. Hannibal had time to aim for Rod's right thigh and gently squeeze the .44 Magnum's trigger.

Click!

Hannibal's mouth opened an inch. The hammer had fallen on an empty cylinder. Derek had fired it dry in the house and Hannibal had not taken the time to check. He had been in too much of a hurry to catch up to Rod. *What a stupid reason to die*, he thought.

Rod took a step toward Hannibal with his right foot and stood still, his back to the ocean, his right arm projected straight forward. A small automatic filled his right fist. His back was to the moon, casting his face in shadow except for his hateful eyes. They burned through the darkness. Hannibal saw his death in them.

"Didn't I tell you? I can't be stopped."

Hannibal braced for the blast of gunfire but the next sound he heard was even more frightening. It was an unearthly sound, like the attack roar of some extraterrestrial predator. The sound seemed to freeze Rod for a full second. At first Hannibal thought it was made by a hairless black pit bull racing across the beach from inland. Just before it reached Rod, Hannibal realized that it was Sarge screaming his rage and charging Rod like the world's most vicious lineman intent on sacking a hated quarterback.

The impact seemed to shake the entire beach. Sarge's bulk lifted Rod off his feet, and jarred his gun free of his hand. It flew into the sea, just as the two men did. Hannibal inched forward, watching the wild splashing.

Waiting for them to surface, Hannibal had time to consider how long he and Rod had stood on the beach. Sarge must have freed himself pretty quickly and followed them,. He would have cut a block or two farther south, anticipating where they might end up. Hannibal imagined Sarge pushing on, his heart close to bursting, since he was so more built for speed than Rod was. But Rod and Hannibal had faced off just long enough for Sarge to catch up and save Hannibal's life.

Both men were underwater for long seconds, churning the waves like a washing machine agitator. Then Sarge flew backward, propelled by one of Rod's legs. Soon both men regained their feet in knee-deep water. They began to trade punches like a pair of heavyweights in the last round when points no longer mattered and only a knockout would have any meaning. They were about the same size and shape, with the same huge fists, deep chests and massive shoulders.

That was where the similarity ended. Rod fought with the arrogance of a man who had never been beaten and didn't believe he could. He was the bully who knew he just had to wait for the other boy to lose faith and crumble. Sarge's fists were driven by righteous rage. He slammed Rod's face and body not like a boy fighting a bully, but a man working to kill a rat that had brought disease into his home.

Rod landed several solid punches, but Sarge hardly seemed to notice. The pivotal moment came when Rod launched a right cross with his entire body behind it and Sarge somehow managed to block the punch with a forearm. Then Sarge drove his own right fist into Rod's solar plexus. Rod's legs turned to rubber and he dropped to his knees. Sarge opened his fists to wrap his fingers around Rod's throat and drove him back into the water.

Rod was invisible but Hannibal knew Sarge was straddling him. Hannibal couldn't see Sarge's arms much below his elbows either, but he knew they were holding Rod's head underwater. Sarge was panting like a man approaching orgasm. Rod's hands slapped at Sarge's arms, but the blows were weak, like those of a kitten with no claws.

Hannibal knew it couldn't end this way, but it took him the better part of a minute to force his body to obey the commands his mind was screaming. Then he took five long strides across the beach and dived forward. He hit Sarge's body hard enough to knock him off Rod. He landed on his back in the shallow water with Sarge on top of him, also facing upward. Sarge clambered to his knees, fighting the wet sand beneath him, but Hannibal whipped an arm around his neck and pulled hard. Sarge teetered backward. Hannibal could feel his friend's exhaustion after what had to have been the fight of his life.

"Come on, old friend," Hannibal said. "End of round one." Ignoring the fire in his own leg muscles, Hannibal dragged Sarge backward, up onto the beach. Both men were breathing hard and deeply, wiping salt water out of their eyes. Barely ten feet away, Rod got to his hands and knees. Choking coughs racked his body and he spit the water he had swallowed down into the ocean five or six inches from his face.

Keeping his eyes on Rod, Sarge said, "Fucking water's cold, man."

"Yeah," Hannibal said, grinning as he sat up on the sand, watching water run out of his shoes.

Sarge's voice became soft. "I had him, man. I could have…"

"I know," Hannibal said, slapping a hand on one of Sarge's shoulders. "But he ain't worth it, brother, and you're not a killer."

"Sure I am." Sarge turned to Hannibal, pride and sorrow mixed in his eyes. "That's what the Corps taught me."

"This ain't a war," Hannibal said. "And believe me, you don't want to turn that corner."

"Listen to your friend."

The new voice was a cold, harsh half-whisper. Hannibal looked up to find a man standing on the beach just past Rod. The newcomer seemed calm and relaxed, and his automatic was focused on Hannibal's face.

-25-

The moon was almost gone now. Only the stars and the distant lights some businesses left on for safety offered any illumination. This made the newcomer difficult to see, except for the movement where the breeze coming in from the ocean flapped his black suit jacket. He was a white man of medium build and average height. His hair and eyes looked black, but in the moonlight either could have been brown or even red.

One thing disturbed Hannibal, something that was plain to see. The man's face held no expression at all. It may as well have been a mask for all it revealed of the man's emotions.

"Okay, want to tell us who you are?" Hannibal asked.

"Not really."

"He's one of the Colombians, come to save this asshole," Sarge said.

Rod was regaining his breath. He looked at Hannibal and Sarge, and then raised a hand to the newcomer.

"Guess I owe ya thanks," Rod said.

"Not really," the newcomer said, answering both Rod and Sarge with a snap kick into Rod's midsection. Rod collapsed back into the surf. Stealthy. Smooth. Unpredictable. Very professional. Something about the man's movements tugged on a loose string in Hannibal's mind. He started to stand, but the newcomer waved him back down with his gun barrel.

"We've met, haven't we?"

"Not really," the newcomer said, stepping into the surf beside Rod.

"Sure, remember? Down in Grayson County. You wore running clothes, and you started jogging when I saw you, but you weren't sweating."

"You are everything I was told you were," the newcomer said, swinging his right foot in a snapping movement that bounced off Rod's temple. Rod dropped onto his left side. Hannibal suspected steel-toed shoes.

"How long have you been following me?" Hannibal asked.

"Since you accepted this assignment," the newcomer said. He stood straddling Rod, who struggled to rise until he was propped up on his elbows, still submerged except for his head and chest. He coughed hard, spitting up salt water and staring up at the man in the black suit.

"You're damn good," Hannibal said. "I felt I was being followed but still couldn't shake you. But why tail me?"

"The formula." He seemed to be speaking to Hannibal, Sarge and Rod at the same time. "I knew you would lead me to whoever had it. I was tasked to secure it."

"You ain't no gangster," Sarge said. "So you the feds, right?"

"Not really."

"I don't have it," Rod said. "Somehow, one of these niggers must have stole it from me. But what do the feds want with it? What happened to free enterprise?"

The man in the black suit looked down at Rod. Hannibal wondered if he suffered from some nerve damage that prevented expression from showing on his face. He decided the condition was more likely the result of training.

"We are at war, a war on drugs," the newcomer said, very seriously. "We must stop this illegal trade in our country. We believe that this formula, if put to use, would cause a runaway increase in drug use. Without the threat of consequences, meaning the possibility of addiction, there would be no disincentive for our youth to indulge in illegal drugs. I was sent to make sure the formula is never used."

"Well then let's deal," Rod said. "How do you know I didn't make a copy? I might have the formula hidden anywhere. And I don't give up."

"Yes, I know." With passive nonchalance the newcomer raised a foot and pressed it into Rod's chest. The big man was screaming "No!" as he fell backward, his face pushed under no more than two inches of water. Sarge leaped to his feet but the pistol centered on his chest kept him in place.

"Now, you and I, Mr. Jones, must come to an agreement."

"I don't know what I have to offer you," Hannibal said. He watched Rod's big hands slap against the leg holding him with no apparent effect. Despite Rod's struggling the man in black never looked down. He locked eyes with Hannibal.

"I'm standing on the last known holder of the formula. If the formula never surfaces again, my people will know that he never passed it on to anyone else. You understand?"

"Perfectly," Hannibal said, watching an enemy struggle in the surf and feeling as if he should be doing something. "I think you understand that the formula we're discussing doesn't belong to me."

Hannibal could not have explained why perspiration was bursting out all over his body. It happened when the cloud of bubbles burst to the surface just a couple of inches in front of the man with whom he was having a calm conversation.

"I've arranged for compensation for the owner," the man said, not reacting to the sudden stillness below him. "For my arrangements to be successful, you need to get back to Mantooth's house. The police have been delayed but it won't be long before they turn up there. You need to return quickly and get the girl before she becomes involved in all this."

"Girl?" Hannibal asked.

"Marquita," Sarge said. "She was headed there after all. I just beat her to it."

"You two had better get going," the man standing in the ocean said. "I'll clean up here." He crouched and pushed his left hand into the water.

Hannibal stood for a moment, staring at Rod Mantooth's hair waving in the surf. The hot breath of evening blew in from the horizon, and a random line drifted into his mind like flotsam on the ocean's surface.

"The heat smells like Eternity," he muttered under his breath.

"What?" Sarge asked.

"Maybe I could get poetry after all."

While he stood there the first sliver of sunlight peaked up over the end of the Atlantic. Its brilliance lanced into Hannibal's eyes. With his back to the sun, the newcomer's face was still hidden in shadow.

"Hang on. You'll need these." Hannibal turned as the man in black tossed something toward him. Hannibal caught it before he realized what he had. It was Rod's key ring. After slipping the keys into his pocket, Hannibal took Sarge's arm and pulled him toward the street.

* * * * *

Battling both physical and emotional exhaustion, Hannibal and Sarge covered the distance to Rod's house with far less speed than they had used to reach the beach. Each block seemed longer than the one before it. On their way they began to see people in motion and cars moving on the roads. At dawn on Monday, the world was beginning its day.

Sarge was dragging a little behind Hannibal but less than a block from Rod's rental he surged forward, passing his friend.

"Markie!" Sarge swept her up in his arms, holding her so tightly she gasped for breath. Hannibal didn't want to disturb the moment, but he had a sense that time mattered.

"Marquita what are you doing here? I know you started down here to find Rod, but I'm sure that after we left no one answered the door."

"He told me to get to safety," she said. "The man in the black suit. But when I told him I couldn't go without knowing what had happened to you and Archie, well then he told me to wait for you here."

"Well we're here now," Sarge said. "Hannibal, let's get the hell out of here, man."

"I've got one more errand to run," Hannibal said. "You guys wait here. I won't be a minute."

Hannibal climbed the steps to the porch half waiting for someone in uniform to stop him. A bullet hole in the door reminded him of just how long a night it had been. In his mind this was the scene of a vicious firefight, but as he stepped inside and pulled the door closed he felt as if he had stepped into a mausoleum. The air was too thick to breathe and the smell of death was almost overpowering. It seemed the cleanup man had been there too. The blinds were closed again, but now sunlight poured in through the thin spaces between them. The scene it revealed was not exactly what Hannibal had left behind.

Yes, Derek was exactly where Hannibal had seen him last, face up and spread eagled on the floor. Sheryl also lay where Hannibal expected. She must have been hit in the crossfire and, judging by the size of the red pool beneath her, she had bled out.

The others were a surprise. The Colombian boss was back in his chair. One of his bodyguards sat against the wall behind his boss' chair. His partner lay draped over the edge of the sofa. Hannibal got close enough to each of them to see that they had been killed very efficiently, execution style with a single bullet in the head. None of them had died in that room. Hannibal's memories aside, there was not nearly enough blood present.

Hannibal had no trouble imagining the chain of events. Someone had met them after they left the house, when they were feeling safe and secure and comfortable. That person, or team, had taken them out in rapid succession before they even knew they were under attack. Then the shooters had returned them to the house, perhaps to simplify things for the police who would soon arrive and would be inclined to ask few questions.

Because of his own federal government experience, Hannibal felt only a low level chill at the power the man on the beach was showing him. It wasn't just the death sharing the room with him, it was the casual way in which the local police had been diverted and delayed until he could finish his business there. He wasn't going to waste time being chilled by the people who would perform such executions to get their way. Later he would take a moment to remind himself how good it felt to no longer be connected to them in any way. Right now he had to kneel at the end of the couch and reach under the corpse on its arm. He locked his throat to keep his empty stomach from purging itself while he teased the cloth open to retrieve his prize. The disc, he realized, contained a great deal of power. No one should discover it by accident.

Hannibal didn't breathe again until he was past the door, past the porch, and leaning against the vehicle in the cement driveway. Squinting against the bright morning sun, he waved to Sarge and Marquita to join him there. Sarge walked in front of Marquita to within ten feet of Hannibal.

"Why'd you call us back here?" Sarge asked. "Markie, she don't want to get no closer to this house. What's here for us anyway?"

Hannibal waved the set of keys with one hand and patted the bright red paint of the Corvorado with the other. "Our getaway car."

Hannibal walked around to the driver's side and opened the door. He was about to comment to Sarge about the case on the passenger seat but he was too surprised to see Sarge waving Marquita back as he stepped closer to the car. Hannibal waited to hear what had to be said outside of Marquita's hearing. Sarge moved close to his friend and looked down at his hands with an expression of disbelief.

"I really was going to kill him, Hannibal."

"I know," Hannibal said. "But it didn't go that way."

"No. You stopped me, and then he gets killed anyway."

"Well, I guess it was going to happen, one way or another," Hannibal said with a nod.

"So maybe he did have a destiny after all." Sarge smiled, and Hannibal didn't think he was smiling at a man's death. No, he was sure that smile was for the odd sense of humor the universe sometimes has.

"Damn, I must be tired."

-26-

The sun blazed so brightly that Hannibal could feel it, even through his Oakleys. He slipped the shifter up into third, eased down on this new gas pedal and slipped past a Lexus whose driver wasn't paying attention to the flow on the beltway. It hardly seemed possible that only hours, not days, had passed since he watched Rod's hair floating in the water at land's edge. The pleasing thrum of his turbocharged five-cylinder engine gave him another opportunity to consider how quickly things can happen in this world when a person with real money calls for action. That lesson started almost as soon as he had driven away from Rod's last home.

Knowing how conspicuous Rod's car was, Hannibal drove directly to Huge's studio. The crew had been up all night working on a new track, but they welcomed Hannibal and his friends. Huge was there in minutes, offering aid. Hannibal recalled that when Huge saw that fire engine red Corvorado he declared it the shiznit (whatever that was) and demanded to know whose it was. Hannibal was quite certain that the owner would not come looking for it, and was happy to trade it for a ride home. Huge assigned a member of his posse to that task right away.

Hannibal managed to make the two necessary telephone calls from the passenger seat of a black Cadillac Escalade before his eyes drooped. Sarge and Marquita collapsed together in the back seat and all three of them slept solidly for the three hours it took to reach Hannibal's building.

Sarge and Marquita hurried up to his apartment, while Hannibal went to his own for a quick shower and a change into his regular black working suit. He chose one of his shirts with French cuffs, the silver cuff links and a textured silk tie. After checking himself in the mirror he scooped up the diamond ring that held his future and slipped it into his pocket. The case was over. This would be the day.

Hannibal had invited Huge's man in, but he waited outside in the Escalade until Hannibal returned. The driver dropped Hannibal at the Volvo dealer on Wisconsin Avenue. When he had given Ben Blair his report of the previous twenty-four hours, Blair never commented on the deaths, the apparent conspiracy or Hannibal's injuries. He simply stated that Hannibal needed a car. He insisted that Hannibal tell him what he wanted to replace his destroyed Volvo 850 GLT with. Hannibal's answer had surprised him. Still he told Hannibal to go straight to the dealer in question and he would find what he wanted ready and waiting.

Despite his skepticism, Hannibal had walked into the dealership as directed. The general manager recognized him somehow, and showed him to his new Volvo S60, a sleek, black, sporty four-door sedan loaded with every available option, and a couple he didn't think were normally available. Much less boxy than his previous car, the S60 reminded Hannibal of a stalking jungle cat with its nose down, ready to pounce.

After his recent experience, Hannibal was naturally concerned with safety features. This car's seats would rock back in a crash to absorb whiplash and even had overhead airbags in case he decided to roll another car over. He was sold. Except that the car was already paid for, and registered in his name.

Hannibal christened his new ride with a drive-through lunch and a short but nimble hop down the beltway to Blair's house. He wasn't sure how many Bang and Olufsen speakers were thumping Aerosmith from the satellite radio, but he was childishly pleased to be able to turn it down without moving his hands from the steering wheel.

From the number of vehicles gathered outside of Blair's townhouse, everyone he asked for had come to meet him. The face he most wanted to see smiled at him from the front steps. She had waited outside for him.

Cindy met him at the car door and he wrapped her in a crushing grip. After the hug he pulled away and held her at arms length, just to look at her. Her beauty still hit him like a tsunami and he wanted so badly to end the suspense between them but he knew that business must come first.

"Let me get this case out of the car, baby, then we'll talk through it all together, close out this ragged case, and be able to get on with our lives."

Inside, an air of tension charged the atmosphere. Ben Blair's living room felt more like a conference room to Hannibal. This was partly because it was larger than any room in a townhouse had a right to be. Adding to the conference room feel, the group gathered there was arrayed around the room with him as its focus, as if they were awaiting a briefing. Everyone had taken a champagne glass from a tray near the door, drinks probably poured by Anita Cooper. Standing in front of the big screen television, he felt as if he should thank the Academy.

His eyes went across his audience, noticing how they had arranged themselves. Cindy sat on his right in one of the armchairs, her fingers tapping the handle of the briefcase Hannibal brought in with him. She beamed up at him, sending out waves of support for what she knew would be a difficult task. Sarge and Marquita shared the loveseat, with Sarge being the only other person present who knew what was coming. Benjamin Blair had the sofa to himself. He sat directly in front of Hannibal, smiling but seeming wary all the same. His elbows rested on his knees with his fingers loosely laced in front of him, but his right heel bounced on the carpet.

Anita occupied the chair on Hannibal's left, with Henry standing beside her. Her right hand crossed her body to hold Henry's hand on her left armrest. She appeared ready for whatever came, as long as it meant an end to this business once and for all. That much, Hannibal knew he could promise. After a small sip, he raised his glass toward his host.

"Before I say anything else, I want to thank you, Ben, for being one of those rare clients who pays promptly. And also for the very nice bonus I drove up in." He paused a moment for Blair to nod but, he noticed, not blush. "I hope you don't regret it when I give you the rather disappointing news."

Blair didn't react at all, his poker face probably honed from years of business dealings. It was Anita who gasped, "I don't understand. Didn't you get it?"

Hannibal moved closer to her and looked into her brown eyes. He dropped his report quickly, wording it with great care, working to remain truthful, if incomplete.

"I'm afraid the formula is lost to you, Anita."

"Lost?" Blair asked. "Didn't this Rod Mantooth have it?"

"Yes he did," Hannibal said. "When I arrived he was about to sell it to a Colombian drug cartel. But there was a conflict, as you might imagine. That led to a gunfight. When it all ended, the Colombians were all dead, and so was Rod. Neither had the formula on them. It wasn't on Mantooth's computer either. Frankly, I can't say that it even exists anymore and I don't think it will ever surface."

Of that much Hannibal could be sure, since he erased, degaussed and reformatted the disc himself in Huge's studio. Someday, some kid would be listening to music on that once-valuable CD.

"So, you failed to return Ms. Cooper's legacy," Blair said in a cold voice. Everyone else was silent for a beat.

"But the monster who hurt Anita is gone," Henry said. There was no confusing his priorities.

"Yes, he is," Hannibal said. "Rod Mantooth died an ugly death. And, while Anita doesn't have the formula, she will still profit from it." Hannibal pushed the case toward Anita. "This is in fact the cash value of your father's formula, Anita. This case contains the money the cartel was prepared to pay Rod for the information he stole from you. I couldn't resist counting it. It's eight hundred thousand dollars in used, unmarked bills. And I can say with confidence that no one will ever come looking for this money. So, in my mind, this makes you whole. Along with finding Rod Mantooth and making sure he won't bother you or any other women again, I think this fulfills my contract."

While Hannibal spoke, Anita pulled the case onto her lap and opened it. Her mouth worked for a moment without letting out a sound, and she began to softly cry.

"I think she is satisfied," Henry said. Then to Anita, "Whatever will you do with all that money, my dear?"

"I'll need some help with that," Anita said. "Can you?"

"I'm prepared to offer whatever assistance you may require, Anita," Henry said, kneeling beside the chair, "for the rest of your life if I may."

"That sounded suspiciously like a proposal," Sarge said from across the room.

"Well if it was," Anita said, "It is certainly welcome." Henry's face reflected surprise as well as joy, and then their smiles merged into one. Blair stood up, his own smile beaming as well.

"It sounds to me as if we have a big and beautiful ceremony to plan."

Cindy and Marquita rushed across the floor to congratulate Anita, with Sarge bringing up the rear, shaking Henry's hand and slapping him on the back. Hannibal moved around the circle, waiting his turn. As he edged closer, Blair playfully slapped his arm to get his attention. When Hannibal looked up, Blair snapped his head to motion toward the kitchen. While the others celebrated, the two men slipped into the next room. Blair walked to the far end of the kitchen. Hannibal followed. When Blair opened his mouth with a question, Hannibal raised a hand to stop him.

"Let's cut to the chase," he said. "You wanted the formula for your own pharmaceutical concern."

"We could do a lot of good," Blair said.

"And make a lot of money, but the decision was taken out of your hands," Hannibal said in a cold voice. "You don't get it. No one does. It could mean Anita's life."

Blair nodded, maintaining his easy smile. "I trust you to have done the right thing. But at some point, do I get the whole story?"

Hannibal nodded. With all his other traits, he should have known Blair would be a graceful loser. "Not today but, yes, I owe you that. Leave it alone for now, and tomorrow in your office I'll give you chapter and verse." Hannibal offered a hand, and Blair took it in a firm handshake.

"Thank you. It isn't the outcome I hoped for, but my receiving the formula was never a condition of the case. You may not have returned Anita's property, but you saved her. I've never seen her looking so free."

"A few hundred thou will do that for some people," Hannibal said.

"No, knowing that her personal demon has been slain has done that for her," Blair said. "Getting the riches she could have expected for the mystery formula, well, that's a bonus."

"You really do care about her." At Hannibal's statement Blair shrugged and for the first time a little embarrassment showed on his boyish face.

When Hannibal left the kitchen he found Sarge and Marquita in the foyer locked in an embrace. After one false start he decided to just head for the door. Sarge broke from the kiss just as Hannibal was about to pass them.

"Hey buddy, I got to thank you for introducing me to this fine lady,"

"Well, you're welcome," Hannibal said, reaching for the doorknob.

"Anita's good fortune gave us a great idea," Marquita said. "But I think that Archie said we could never have a ceremony unless you agreed to be the best man."

Hannibal's jaw dropped. It was an epidemic. "Well, of course I'd be honored." Sarge grabbed his hand and almost crushed it in a powerful shake, then returned to Marquita for yet another kiss. Hannibal looked around, feeling a bit awkward.

"Cindy?"

"Outside," Sarge said.

Hannibal turned back to the door and pulled it open. As he stepped out he heard Sarge behind him say, "Only one shoe left to drop."

Cindy stood at the bottom of the steps, staring at his new car. Her hair was shaped that day so that it curled down to her shoulders like ram's horns. The skirt of her fawn suit almost reached her knees, and her matching pumps were just high enough to accent her shapely legs. He felt the hollow of his stomach begin to cave in. He reached into his pocket and gripped the ring for strength.

"Alone at last," he said, reaching her side. Cindy smiled at him, and then turned back to the Volvo. To his surprise he saw a look of confusion and maybe disappointment on Cindy's face.

"What?"

"Nothing, lover."

"No," he said, still smiling. "It's something. What?"

"The car," Cindy said. "We talked about you getting something different. I thought maybe you were ready for a change. You could have gotten anything, but here you are in another four door Volvo. Same same same."

Startled, Hannibal pointed to the car with both hands, as if trying to get her to see what was so obvious to him. "Cindy. It's BLACK."

"Whatever," she replied. Then her smile returned full force. God, he loved her when she smiled like that. He tried to dive into the empty moment, but they both spoke at once.

"I've got something I've got to..." It was a romantic comedy moment they both recognized, and they collapsed into laughter.

"What?" Cindy asked, gasping for breath.

"No no, you first."

"Really?"

"Yeah, go ahead," Hannibal said.

Cindy balled her hands into fists and she suddenly seemed to be vibrating in anticipation. It all spilled out at once, in a voice of pure joy.

"Oh, God Hannibal, I didn't want to steal your thunder in there, but I have had the most amazing forty-eight hours. The IPO offering has gone through the roof! So much better than anyone could have ever expected! We actually exceeded the twenty-five million we needed to raise by a solid margin. I am now the star of the firm."

"That's wonderful baby," Hannibal said, wondering in silence how his proposal would compare to this success.

"And that's not all!" Cindy grabbed both of Hannibal's hands, shaking him and actually bouncing up and down like a kid at Christmas time. Her eyes flew wide and her hair bounced on her shoulders. "My stock options just went crazy! Hannibal, as of today at noon I was actually worth something like seven million dollars! Oh my God it's like a drug. I swear, money is like a drug and I am as high as they get. Do you get it? I can have anything I want, baby. Whatever I think of, I can get it with a snap of my fingers."

Hannibal kept the smile frozen on his face, but thanked the Lord for the dark glasses shielding his eyes. She was right. She could get anything she could think of, all by herself. That being true, what could she possibly need him for?

Cindy must have noticed his reserve, because her breathing slowed a bit, her smile backing down just a notch.

"I'm sorry. That was kind of selfish, or at least self-oriented, wasn't it?"

"But well deserved," Hannibal said. "I'm so proud of you, baby. You really are the best. So far above…" he left that sentence unfinished.

"So, what was your news? What did you want to tell me?"

Hannibal looked into Cindy's eyes, but he thought about Anita and how her butler boyfriend did not react to a briefcase full of money. Of course, it contained just a sliver of Cindy's new fortune, and they had started almost even. Anita needed Henry to help her understand how her life would change now. She needed his guidance, his knowledge of how to handle her windfall. They would chart their new course together.

He thought of Sarge, now forming a relationship with a woman of independent means. But Marquita had a long way to go to find her former self. She needed him emotionally and, well, didn't everyone need to be needed?

He tried to imagine life with a wealthy, star attorney. He tried to picture himself taking her to a restaurant, or to a show, or driving her to an important social event. He tried to visualize their lives, in the evening, in her new home that she would pick out and have professionally decorated. The heiress and the detective. Nick and Nora Charles, he supposed, but it looked different from the inside.

He pulled his hand out of his pocket. Empty.

"Nothing, baby. It was nothing."

Author's Bio

Austin S. Camacho is a public affairs specialist for the Department of Defense. America's military people overseas know him because for more than a decade his radio and television news reports were transmitted to them daily on the American Forces Network.

He was born in New York City but grew up in Saratoga Springs, New York. He majored in psychology at Union College in Schenectady, New York. Dwindling finances and escalating costs brought his college days to an end after three years. He enlisted in the Army as a weapons repairman but soon moved into a more appropriate field. The Army trained him to be a broadcast journalist. Disc jockey time alternated with news writing, video camera and editing work, public affairs assignments and news anchor duties.

During his years as a soldier, Austin lived in Missouri, California, Maryland, Georgia and Belgium. While enlisted he finished his Bachelor's Degree at night and started his Master's, and rose to the rank of Sergeant First Class. In his spare time, he began writing adventure and mystery novels set in some of the exotic places he'd visited.

After leaving the Army he continued to write military news for the Defense Department as a civilian. Today he handles media relations and writes articles for the DoD's Deployment Health Support Directorate. He has settled in northern Virginia with his wife Denise.

Austin is a voracious reader of just about any kind of nonfiction, plus mysteries, adventures and thrillers. When he isn't working or reading, he's writing.

Website: www.ascamacho.com
Email: ascamacho@hotmail.com

Other Hannibal Jones Mysteries by Austin S. Camacho

Blood and Bone

An eighteen-year-old boy lies dying of leukemia. Kyle's only hope is a bone marrow transplant, but no one in his family can supply it. His last chance lies in finding his father, who disappeared before he was born. Kyle's family has nowhere to turn until they learn of a certain troubleshooter - that self-styled knight errant in dark glasses, Hannibal Jones. But his search for the missing man turns up much more: A woman who might be Kyle's illegitimate sister, the woman who could be her mother, and a man who may have killed Kyle's father. Hannibal follows a twisting path of deception, conspiracy and greed, from Washington to Mexico, but with each step the danger grows.

Collateral Damage

Bea Collins is certain her fiancee wouldn't just leave without telling her. Troubleshooter Hannibal Jones is skeptical until the missing fiancee turns up dazed, confused and holding a knife over a dead body. To find this killer Hannibal will travel to Germany, Vegas and through Dean's past, which includes the murder of Dean's father, his first childhood crush and brings Hannibal face to face with Dean's convicted mother.

The Troubleshooter

A Washington attorney buys an apartment building in the heart of the city, but then he finds the building occupied by squatters: drug dealers, winos, and professional criminals intent on staying. Police are unable to empty the building for use by paying residents. No one seems willing or able to take on this challenge until the lawyer meets an intense young man named Hannibal Jones. He calls himself a troubleshooter, but he finds more trouble in Southeast Washington than he expected. The people holding crack pipes are backed up by people holding guns, and Hannibal soon finds himself up against a local crime boss and his powerful, mob connected father.

Also by Austin S. Camacho
The NEW
Stark and O'Brien Action/Adventure series

MEET MORGAN STARK and FELICITY O'BRIEN

Morgan Stark, a black mercenary soldier, is stranded in the Central American nation of Belize after a raid goes wrong.

Felicity O'Brian, an Irish jewel thief, is stranded in the jungle south of Mexico after doing a job for an American client.

When these two meet, they learn they've been double-crossed by the same man: Adrian Seagrave, a ruthless businessman maintaining his respectability by having others do his dirty work.

Morgan and Felicity become friends and partners while following their common enemy's trail. They become even closer when they find they share a peculiar psychic link, allowing them to sense danger approaching themselves, or each other.

But their extrasensory abilities and fighting skills are tested to their limits against Seagrave's soldiers-for-hire and Monk, his giant simian bodyguard. A series of battles from California to New York lead to a final confrontation with Seagrave's army of hired killers in a skyscraper engulfed by flames.

Printed in the United States
122136LV00011B/3/A